Reading Blue Devils

A Novel

Jon Bennett

Published by Open Books

Copyright © 2018 by Jon Bennett

ISBN-13: 978-0692644614

For my wife, Nicole—my greatest inspiration and support
And for my daughter, Charlotte—my greatest distraction.

Then war broke out in heaven. Michael and his angels fought against the dragon, and the dragon and his angels fought back. But he was not strong enough, and they lost their place in heaven.

Revelation 12:7—8

Chapter 1

THE FIRST DAY back from summer break was the day Dieter
Vogel's shits returned—the ones that tied his stomach in knots
and kept him up at night; the ones that played loud rap music
and obsessed about sex; the ones that refused to read or write and
disregarded any direction that Dieter gave in class; the ones that
were putting his career in the toilet through their misbehavior and
poor performance.

Oh, those little shits, Dieter thought as he closed the beat-up
sliding door to his mom's mini-van, his means of transportation to
and from work until he could afford a bike.

Of course, nobody really wanted to be at school: the drudgery
of sunny days left unfulfilled saddled the students and staff alike
as they arrived on those warm August mornings. There were, of
course, the exceptions. The previous year's student body president,
Maria Lopez, came poised for another year of building her college
resume. She showed up at school thirty minutes before the first
wave of school buses, campaign button clipped neatly onto her
school-appropriate blouse. The sophomore biology teacher, Mrs.
Stewart, who vomited sunshine and excreted rainbows, was merrily
adjusting colorful posters that flaunted motivational clichés, the
scientific method, and pictures of famous scientists. Even the school

secretary was undertaking joyful last-minute preparations, removing her candy jar from her desk and replacing it with a stack of tardy slips—the sweet building blocks of detentions and suspensions.

For the students, rigid routines, early mornings, and a prolonged focus on something other than video games would burden them for ten months. On top of that, their teachers, who had little under-standing of their students' life circumstances, would lecture them on the importance of abstract concepts that would not put food on their families' plates for years to come, if algebraic functions could ever do that.

The faculty, who used the summer-break to sip away the frus-trations of the past year in oversized margarita glasses and spiked lemonade pitchers, faced eight straight hours of immaturity, poor decisions, and petty drama. For one hundred eighty days, they had to somehow seem more interesting than the students' phones and gossip. They had to teach nuanced reasoning and critical thinking. They had to offset years of bad habits and poor education. And they had to stake their educational worth on a pre-made curriculum and the bubbles of a scantron.

High stakes testing, an already disheartening facet of the Ameri-can educational system, would be especially ponderous this year. It would decide the school's fate and, by default, the teachers' jobs. On top of that, Principal Walter Sanders was pushing an extra initiative to build up the staff's educational efficiency. While many teachers accepted the motion, they soon discovered that it meant additional time, energy and focus, three things already in short supply.

And then they had to confront the school's physical structure.

Inside the building, brown-tinged windows filtered nature's bril-liant luminosity, blending it with glaring florescent light. Every inch of floor was perpetually dusty. And the colors of the walls alternated from dirty pastel green to putrid yellow.

Outside, dreary concrete walls, plain and prison-like, did almost nothing to insulate the classrooms from weather extremes. In those final days of summer, the building sweltered under the hot sun, unaided by faltering air-conditioning units and windows that only opened six inches. The rooms were saunas saturated with the sweaty stink of adolescence. During winter, the bitter cold enclosed certain classrooms in its frigid embrace. In classrooms with heaters, the same sweltering humidity from summer returned since the radiators did not turn off for hours at a time.

Beyond maintaining a reasonable temperature, the building required minor fixes as well as major projects. As a failing public school with a dying tax-base, repairs and improvements were always wanting. One glaring project was the flat, tar-and-gravel roof, which was especially problematic even after minimal precipitation.

The students all knew that their school was old and not as functional as the public and private schools in the upper-middle class, white neighborhoods that surrounded them. They also knew that their text books were outdated. They knew that the technology at their school was confined to a computer lab with only three reliable computers. They knew there were better educational opportunities elsewhere. But what choice did they have? This was their community, and this was their school.

The teachers, all veterans of three years or more, knew they would face complaints by the students that they could not fix. They knew that the hot air would cause drowsiness. They knew that their curriculum would be dissected based on standards constructed by politicians with few, if any, years inside a classroom. They knew that it would take nothing short of a miracle to turn the school around.

Yes, despite it being the end of summer, the first day back at Reading High School was a cold day for many.

Especially for Dieter Vogel.

Every time he stepped out of his mom's car in front of the school, a rush of acid surged in his stomach. Eleven years ago, it was because it was his first day of high school. Three years ago, it was because it was his first year of teaching. Now, it was because he knew he was one of the teachers being watched.

He was not teaching the students in accordance to government testing standards, and he wasn't enhancing himself as a professional. In truth, he was not cut out for teaching at-risk, minority youth.

They needed warmth, strength and innovation from their teachers; all they got from Dieter was a smug-wet blanket.

Returning to high school pushed Dieter in front of the mirror in which his many flaws and insecurities would be reflected daily. High school, Dieter found, was not just a turbulent place for high-hormoned adolescents, but for under-achieving adults as well.

Though a teacher, Dieter faced the same trials of many teens. He struggled with a negative body image, mostly because of his excessive junk-food binges. He had an infatuation for a woman who barely acknowledged him. He depended on his mom for transportation since he couldn't afford a car. He had a propensity for fast food over home-cooked meals. He couldn't keep meaningful social connections with people his age. He wasn't to be trusted to keep a pet alive for more than a week. And there was even a bully on staff that tormented him. At least he had lost his braces.

Dieter stumbled over the second of two concrete steps that led from the drop-off driveway to the extended sidewalk that led to the entrance. A "Welcome Back" banner, which was unfurled after summer, winter, and spring breaks, hung on the wall above the school's four double-doors. Even in the overcast light of morning, Dieter saw the banner as an artificial beam of cheerfulness that did little to alleviate the bitter fog that followed him.

His eyes drifted up to the banner as he reached the doors. The sign, upon closer examination, had been vandalized with a large black permanent marker.

on you're

Welcome ^Back!

"I hate adolescents," Dieter muttered to his shadow.

With a lowered shoulder, he pushed into the wooden doors, flopping into the maroon-carpeted main entrance, which smelled of a vacuum's burnt motor mixed with a cocktail of chemicals. Where the circle of classes began, freshly waxed linoleum tiles shimmered and stank of a stale coating wax. A congregation of students lifted dreary eyes in acknowledgement of an adult in their presence before they resumed grunting their frustrations to the other teens around them.

On the surface of this twenty-five year-old English teacher, there was little deviousness besides his slightly deviating belly. He had two lonely lives: one as a failing English teacher; the other was as a hopelessly thick-headed voyeur. Handicapped by his awkward social disposition, flabbier composition, and lower-middle class position, Dieter's own life was too boring to live in day by day, so he found himself examining every environment he managed to plop into.

This less than dynamic dual existence of fiction and reality gave Dieter just enough confidence to carry himself through the halls of Reading as a teacher, yet left him vulnerable enough to need to hide behind his books and his sarcasm.

And his place among the staff was akin to a bit of irritated skin. Professionally, his absent-mindedness often led to a recounting of school initiatives, delaying the end of a meeting that had already run longer than necessary. Personally, teachers couldn't even begin to know Dieter. His apparent lack of passion drove conversations that Dieter had with other staff members right off a rhetorical cliff. It also didn't help that his humor was as dry as his love life. And the way that he sometimes looked at certain members of the staff made them feel like he was visually strip-searching them for faults to be balanced and accounted for at some later time.

Dieter's awkward demeanor led the five other teachers in the English Department to *forget* to send him invitations to department meetings. If Dieter hadn't been so graceless, the others in the department would have readily embraced him, for he had a sincere love of literature that would have been infectious to both the studied aficionado and teenage novice alike. That was why he'd gone into teaching, after all. But Dieter's sarcastic comments and flightiness pushed his piers away.

The Department Chair, Mr. Canon, a man with a coffee addiction and a pack-a-day smoking habit, found Dieter too noxious for inter-action, and he abandoned all attempts at mentorship or professional development. When Dieter was put on probation, which was the first step toward getting a teacher fired, Mr. Canon saw it as a sign to further disengage from the runt of the English department. As a result of the absence of mentorship and non-existent feedback, Dieter's proficiency in the classroom steadily deteriorated. If there was a case study for poor classroom management, Dieter was it.

The students, when not lulled to sleep by painfully monotonous lectures, freely chatted with each other during lessons. Fights broke out with such consistency during one period that the disciplinarian at the school, Mr. Wilson, would only walk the isolated hall where Dieter's classroom was located. If the common-sense proposals to track teacher effectiveness and to give autonomy to school principals were ratified a few years ago, then Dieter would have been fired within his first months of teaching; however, the teacher's union had intervened, citing test numbers, student feedback, disciplinary data, parent complaints, and job reviews as inaccurate indicators of performance. Therefore, Dieter was indefinitely allowed to cul-tivate a learning environment that was composed of ineffective methodology and rampant misbehavior.

Fortunately for Dieter, this year's first period Junior English class provided him with an almost comatose audience. Since students who were sleepwalking through class were less likely to act out, Dieter dove into his introduction unhindered.

Most teachers spent a week setting classroom rules and pro-cedures, slowly re-acclimating students to school life, much like astronauts being reintroduced to gravity. Dieter, however, pressed right into complicated texts and boring lessons without any outline of classroom expectations, either great or common. And without a syllabus to prepare students, they would have to be surprised by the books on their desks and the grades on their assignments.

"Our first book this year will be *Great Expectations* by Charles Dickens. Make sure you put your name inside the cover," Dieter said to the ten sleeping students, three doodlers, four texters, five daydreamers and two remaining pairs of eyes focused on Dieter's premature double-chin. There was no room to write their names in the book. The inside cover had been filled by over twenty years of names, and by the various drawings that accompanied them.

Students greeted the Victorian novel with snarls and groans. One student let his forehead crash onto his desk after counting the number of pages. *Great Expectations* was not a book that was on the reading level of his Junior class, which averaged a seventh grade level. Certainly, the themes of poverty, abandonment, and criminal temptation could resonate with some of the students if taught well, but Dieter planned to plow through the book in three weeks with a summative test and paper at the end.

Today's lesson would serve as a brief introduction to Charles Dickens, one of Dieter's favorite canonical writers. It was a lecture meant to guide the students to an appreciation of the author. Instead, within five minutes, Dieter's vehicle for transporting his knowledge ushered the students into a state of indifference.

The silence of boredom radiated from the twenty-four students. Between the slightly cracking voice of Dieter and the clicking of fingers on cell phone keys, a metallic clang wore on the consciousness of the students unfortunate enough to be awake. Last year, when the roof leak had started, it took most of the class a few weeks to get acclimated to the pounding of water on metal. Rumor had it that the nervous breakdown of one particularly frail student was partially due to "the drip."

The psychosis could also have been caused by the bare white walls. Where most classrooms had colorful posters to comfort the senses of the students, Dieter's room produced a heightened anxiety, as well as optical strain, due to unchecked, synthetic brightness that beat relentlessly upon them. Sleeping and talking and doodling became defense mechanisms against mental turmoil.

A melody produced by the plodding lecture, the texting teenagers, and the leaking roof droned on until Dieter finally paused. He'd become distracted from the point he was trying to make, so he moved from the podium to sift through a stack of papers on his desk. In the mix of the papers he found a Dunkin Donuts napkin on which he'd scribbled bullet points that morning.

After perusing the notes, he strode back to the podium to resume his lecture. Dieter hadn't even provided a PowerPoint to guide students ambitious enough to take notes. Such a presentation would have equally benefited the unprepared educator. With an empty glance at his students, he resumed his soliloquy.

"Charles Dickens was—"

"Mr. Vogel, sir!"

A voice pulled Dieter's eyes from the napkin.

"Yes, Miguel," Dieter sighed as the sleepers perked up, the doodlers put down their pencils, the daydreamers' clouds lifted, and the texting students closed their phones. All eyes were on Miguel Saguaro, class clown and record holder for most detentions without being expelled. His learning disability and the absence of a truly egregious crime saved him from expulsion, leaving him to terrorize the school indefinitely.

"Didn't this guy create a drink? It's like a spicy apple thing. I think it's, like, spider or slider…"

"Cider," Dieter interrupted.

"Yeah! That's it. Dickens Cider!"

Giggles came from the back of class. Seeing no negative reaction from Dieter, who was slow to pick up the joke, Miguel sat higher in his seat and continued. He truly was a bright kid, even with a third-grade reading level and a propensity to butcher simple words. His awareness and use of sexual innuendo rivaled that of Shakespeare.

"Yeah, every guy who sees a good-looking girl wants his Dicken—"

The clatter of a dropped cell phone halted the advance of the bawdy joke. Miguel spun toward the source of the commotion. The rest of the teens stirred, awakened from their trance, disappointed in the distraction. Dieter, also jolted out of the conversation and still unaware where Miguel was going, turned his attention to the class president, who had dove onto the floor to snatch up her fallen device.

"Miss Lopez, you know the policy for cell phones in class…"

Maria sheepishly glanced at Dieter from her place on the floor. Avoiding drops of roof drainage, she trudged up to Dieter's desk and handed him the phone. As she walked past the texters on the way to her desk, they lifted their eyes in sympathy before turning back toward glowing crotches.

"Let's continue..."

Disappointed groans accompanied Dieter as he plodded forward on the life of Charles Dickens. Another minute into the lecture, at about the time they'd usually disengage, the students found themselves too aroused to drift back into their various retreats. The sleepers couldn't fall back to sleep, and the daydreamers stirred in restless sobriety. The doodlers tapped their desks, and the texters shifted in their seats.

"Charles Dickens was—"

"*Cider...*"

Dieter's eyes shot toward Miguel's face; however, no signs of movement existed nor was there any sign of a diabolical smirk. Miguel was drawing a large, hairy penis in his notebook with a black permanent marker. Dieter could see it clearly since Miguel sat in the first row of class per legal mandate in his Individualized Education Plan, which after being reviewed each year, tended to add more and more accommodations for the teachers to implement. When Dieter and other teachers would inevitably fail to adjust their lessons according to the IEP's requests, Miguel's attention and behavior altered as well. Drawing phalluses was the least detrimental behavior he could exhibit besides sleeping.

Feeling his teacher's gaze, Miguel looked up and locked eyes with Dieter. Testing Miguel's boldness, Dieter continued to speak. When he would say 'Dickens,' he made sure that he was looking directly at Miguel.

"...born in 1812. He was paid by the word, which is why the novel is so long. It will be long...hard...and difficult to manage." Miguel's face screwed in agony, which confused Dieter since he hadn't gotten to the test.

"Now Dickens—"

"Cider..."

Miguel's eyes dropped to his notebook: he knew not to test a teacher looking right at him. It was hard to deny wrong doing, but it also signified an absolute defiance that even Miguel did not want to portray. Besides, Miguel preferred to use the brushes of subtlety and surreptitious intent for his masterpieces of misbehavior.

The entire class held their hands to their mouths in attempt to stifle the laughter that was curtailed within their stomachs. To avoid guilt, they stared at notebooks, at the backs of heads, at book covers, at the leaking spot on the paneled roof, or at the only poster, an image of Dieter in a high school play, which hung behind his desk—anything but the rapidly reddening adult in front of them.

Dieter could not identify the culprit since it wasn't Miguel, his only suspect. The whisper seemed to be coming from the wall behind his desk. Of course there was no one there, and echoes plagued the room.

"Dickens," Dieter began as he panned the room.

"Cider!"

The class gasped in horror this time. Dieter's cheeks trembled violently.

"Who in God's name—"

A knock on the classroom door cut his diatribe short. Esther Bishop, a special education teacher who worked with Miguel and with other Juniors, peered inside the room. Dieter motioned for her to enter.

"Yes, Miss B. How can I be of service?" Dieter asked, eyes softening.

As the youngest faculty member besides Dieter, Esther was automatically attractive to most of the male students and staff. She had played volleyball at Reading in high school and had continued the sport throughout college, which gave her frame a toned core and a firmly rotund backside. She further enhanced her figure with tight pants and tucked-in tops. From the toes to the shoulder, she was as close to a model as one could find in Reading, Ohio, even with her prominent, pointed nose.

Esther rarely looked at Dieter. He was just another man who visually undressed her. He'd done that since they'd attended Reading as students almost eleven years ago. And he never spoke to her except for circumstances which required professional interaction, like this one. Instead of responding, she panned the classroom searching for a familiar impish face.

"Miguel," she said with an annoyed growl in her voice, "Principal Sanders wants to see you about the 'Welcome Back' sign."

Miguel stood up, turned to his friends in the back, and bowed triumphantly; he had finished his opening act.

"First period on the first day: a record."

He slipped his marker to a random student, pranced past Dieter, curtseyed in front of the class, and headed out the door, escorted by Esther, whose nose jutted toward the back of his head like a gun.

"No problem about the interruption," Dieter called out, weak, lustful, and continuing to stare at her butt until she disappeared. Some students exchanged perceptive glances with each other and shook their heads in disgust. Though he normally retreated to a fantasy world filled with fantasy women, Dieter was prone to sleazy thoughts about Esther. One surged through him now. And it was at that moment an epiphany popped into his mind.

Yanking open his drawer, Dieter slammed a detention slip onto the desk and wrote Miguel's name on the sheet.

"Dick-in-side-her," he snarled. The students snickered openly.

For the remaining thirty minutes, he referred to the author as Charles. It was a taboo for a literature aficionado, no doubt, but the sacrilege was reconciled in the desperate mind of a faltering English teacher faced with the immaturity of adolescence.

––––––––––––

Second period was a planning period for Dieter, which meant he could preview the menu for the week and pick up the scraps from breakfast like a pudgy hyena prowling the vacant lunch room. His copy of *Paradise Lost* accompanied him to the cafeteria, which was located at the opposite end of the circle-shaped school, almost directly under the entrance.

The school's lunchroom felt more like a bunker than a place where nourishment was taken. There were no windows. The smell of processed meat, accumulated dust, and years of mildew clouded the air, polluting the poorly ventilated space. The foldable table-bench seats stood like soldiers at attention, waiting for the janitor to clean the perpetually dirty floor with harsh smelling cleaners that puddled on the uneven tiles.

After scrounging the remaining ten pieces of bacon that the chef had saved for himself and the janitor, Dieter plopped onto a couch in the adjacent teachers' lounge and became lost in his book. The art teacher extended a cheerful good morning to Dieter, which ended up bouncing off the cover. That's when Coach Paul Manley walked in with an inflated chest and a fresh summer glow emanating from his skin.

Manley's muscular physique was complimented by his light orange-brown tan and made more impressive by the fact that he was approaching fifty years of age. Though he had molded himself into a hyper-masculine caricature over the years, he prided himself on being able to defy the stereotype of the basketball coach/P.E. teacher by also being one of the school's Spanish teachers. Two years living in Costa Rica formed the only knowledge he had of Spanish, so his success as a basketball coach was reason for his job security.

"*Hola, burro*," Manley chirped. Though normally baritone, his voice mimicked the high-pitched derision and sophomoric crudity of an adolescent bully every time he spoke to Dieter.

Because Dieter was twenty-five, pimply, unkempt, five-foot nine, and a flabby two-hundred pounds, he stood as Manley's opposite. Manley enjoyed football, basketball, women, and good scotch. Dieter enjoyed sci-fi movies, reading, fantasizing about women, and Mountain Dew. Unsatisfied with Dieter's silence, Manley tried to agitate further.

"Esther and I are going to see that new romantic comedy. You have any suggestions for a restaurant? I know how much you like stuffing your face." Manley chuckled in an attempt to convey good-natured ribbing.

Dieter's eyes peeled from the pages and onto Manley's gelled hair and slicked back grin. He had been annoyed with Dieter since the day Dieter had first arrived to teach, twenty pounds lighter yet still overweight. When Dieter bumbled through a lame attempt at asking Esther for a date last year (an attempt so bad that Esther didn't even realize Dieter's intention), Dieter moved from mild-annoyance to an affront to Manley's place in the school, which at that time included his romantic feelings for Esther. Even when Manley successfully courted Esther that Spring, Dieter had become the primary object of Manley's abuse.

Dieter's heart sank at the thought of Esther and Manley together. But he would not show weakness. He had been picked on enough during high school and college to know that any reaction beyond apathy would intensify the aggression.

"No suggestions? Well, if you can think of anything besides fast-food or pizza, let me know."

Pathologically, Dieter was ripe to go on a murder spree catalyzed by harassment from Manley, ostracism by the staff, and rejection from Esther; however, Dieter was too lethargic to act on his own and too captivated by fiction to obsess about reality. Manley's taunts fell like hollow shells around Dieter's disillusioned social standing. Dieter hummed automatically as he returned to the book.

Manley was gearing up for a more intense insult when Principal Sanders popped into the room, temporarily retarding the epithets.

Sanders, though not as burly, was cut from the same cloth as Manley, physically and developmentally: he was tall and lean, with a runner's build, which came from the marathon training Sanders constantly endured. If not for the outline of blonde hair around the sides of his crown, one would think he shaved his head regularly for the sake of aerodynamics. He prided himself in beating men half his age and took even greater pleasure in post-race boasting. After the medal ceremony, a hunger formed for more victory, more power, more augmentation to his own self-worth on the backs of weaker opponents. And while professionalism kept him from verbally denigrating Dieter, he allowed Manley free reign to do the work he was barred from doing, as long as it wasn't done in front of him, of course.

"Hello, Paul! How's the team looking this year?" Sanders asked while pouring coffee into his stainless-steel mug.

"Good, Walt," Manley responded, upset that he was interrupted during prime self-esteem lowering time.

"That Andre kid looks like he's going to jump through the roof one of these days!"

"Yeah, hopefully he'll stay uninjured this year for the playoffs."

"Hopefully!"

Sanders moved closer to Manley and his voice shifted from congeniality into urgency. "Paul, I know Spanish isn't on the test, but I need you to keep our teachers focused this year. I just got off the phone with the Superintendent. She's threatening to give us up. We *need* to show progress. We *need* that money."

Money was scarce at Reading High School. The school had lost much of its state funding during the past five years due to abysmal test scores and the resulting budgetary cuts that had resulted. In fact, Reading ranked last in English and in Math out of twenty high schools across the region. Since Sanders had been principal at Reading for seven years, he was so pressed to find something that would transform the scores that he had turned to unconventional motivation guides and management websites to form his new initiative. One of them suggested that physical fitness could enhance energy and focus. This came from a self-help website which was more dedicated to battling depression than improving pedagogy.

But Sanders disregarded the isolated audience for whom this information was intended. Surely if it worked for one person, it could work for an entire staff. Because he loved working out, and since he lacked any real pedagogical knowledge, he bought fully into the unintended advice.

He used three of the August professional development sessions to lecture on physical fitness routines, demonstrate various weight-based activities, and do a run through of cardiovascular exercises. The best practices around classroom management and instructional design took a backseat to staff aerobics. The new books and technology that were sorely needed to make learning relevant and engaging were backlogged by additional dumbbells and treadmills for the weight room.

Such unorthodoxy was further fortified by rumors that the district might close the school if test results for the current school year did not improve. This left three possibilities: one, the school would reopen as a "turn-around school" run by an imposed administration that would fire the entire staff then rehire each teacher at their discretion; two, close the school, redistribute the students to three different high schools throughout the district, and then sell the building; and three, the final option, which was a combination of the first two, close as a public school and re-open as a public charter school, which would allow the school to still receive a portion of district funding, but would also make them eligible to receive private funding and also be privately run. Rumor had it that the Archdiocese was licking its chops to open the school using public funds, which in this Catholic community was not as controversial as it might have been in other parts of the country. Regardless, all options put Sanders' control in jeopardy unless option four happened, which was that test results turned around on their own.

"Some teachers will be tougher than others," Manley replied, glaring at Dieter, who was oblivious to the conversation. It was when silence ensued for a full minute that Dieter deduced his involvement in some negative conversation, and it was not difficult to pick up why. His students had actually regressed on the end-of-year test last semester, while most other teachers' classes remained stagnant or improved minimally.

Sanders had tried to motivate Dieter during his first year of teaching. He'd sit in Dieter's classroom behind a glowing laptop screen with judgment written all over his tight-skinned face. He'd send summative emails from the observation with ten different deficiencies that Dieter needed to address. He'd then do follow-up surprise visits with follow-up condemnatory communication. When he put Dieter on probation, which would usually be accompanied by a list of deficiencies that the teacher should address to keep his or her job, Sanders merely wrote: *You are not fit for teaching at this school.*

When this produced little improvement, Sanders then tried other means of motivation. Last year, in lieu of a gift for Secret Santa, he had given Dieter a letter of recommendation for a job in a different school district.

Manley used more overt tactics. At the end of the previous year, he'd left Dieter a card on his desk that displayed a picture of a corpulent donkey sniffing a pile of poop. The inside read: "*Come mierda, burro.*" The union threw out Dieter's grievance since they could not prove Manley had written the card. And Sanders had commended Coach Manley for promoting healthy living through peer encouragement (even if one teacher was encouraging the other to "eat shit"). "*Burro*" stuck as a nickname.

The third-period bell bit the air with its shrill ringing. Dieter arrived three minutes late, exhausted and annoyed to find the class already a madhouse. Paper balls cackled against the walls, desks shifted from play-fighting bodies, and outbursts of laughter blasted the room.

"Antonio, sit down…please. Darnell, quit throwing things…please. KeAndre, stop touching Sharon…please! Alicia, stop dancing on the desks…now!" It took twenty minutes just to get the class seated.

Dieter's third period students, many of whom he'd taught as sophomores last year, passed around a graphic representation of a "beast with two backs." It was an impressive show of comprehension considering last year the same group of students had failed to grasp the translation of "thy" to "your" for an entire period. The sexual-saturation of the adolescent brain still surprised Dieter in its manifestations, triumphs, and shortcomings. Because of the outburst during first period, he stuck with "Charles" when introducing *Great Expectations*.

To top off the morning, Dieter had to substitute long-term in Mrs. Snider's Senior Film Studies elective. He thought the class would enjoy the opening scene of *Saving Private Ryan* with an accompanied reflection on the horrors of war and the resilience of man in the face of inhumanity. Though he was not a proponent of progressive, student-centered education, Dieter allowed the students to choose what topic they wished to discuss in hopes that they would be awe-struck by the graphic footage; or maybe feel a bit of disgust; hell, even a "dude, that was cool," would have sufficed.

Instead, the male students debated the weapon choice they would have used on the beach, citing their experience in video games as support. They came to an agreement that they would "snipe" the machine gunners in the bunkers, though one student adamantly asserted the Spartan Laser would be most effective.

Dieter was so exhausted that he didn't attempt to walk to the cafeteria to eat lunch. Instead, he pulled out a bag of chips and beef jerky, which he kept in the bottom drawer of his desk. Teachers normally kept supplies, exam keys, confiscated phones, and other teacher knick-knacks in their desk; for Dieter, the desk was his pantry, the food inside it, his therapy. By the time the bell rang for lunch break to end, his desk was speckled with yellow, oily crumbs and smudges of grease, which he fastidiously cleaned. Desktop orderliness preserved a semblance of control in an otherwise muddled existence.

Dieter ended the day with fifth and sixth period Freshman English. A group of ten freshmen moved slowly down the hallway, schedules inches away from their noses.

"Annex .01? Where's Annex .01?" Panic surged through skin and bones.

Reading High School was shaped like a big donut, except for the main entrance at the northern curve, the connected annex on the southern curve, and the gymnasium that was in a separate building. Classrooms with numbers in the one hundreds were on the first floor. Two hundreds were on the second level. The basement had the cafeteria and the theater. Since the annex was a break from the school itself, adding decimals rattled the first-year students' already shaky confidence.

Dieter gave a loud, throat-clearing cough.

"Freshman English?"

The students dropped the paper blinders, relieved to hear an adult's voice.

"Yes!"

Dieter nodded and beckoned them with a wave of his hand. However, only those ten freshmen filled the room when the bell rang. Dieter's roster had thirty students. So, they waited. The ten students in the class sat obediently for the first few minutes, but when four more students walked in tardy, then, two others, adolescence took over.

Seeing graffiti scrawled on the desks, a non-imposing adult at the front of the class, and a lack of structure all around, the students began to make their own fun. It started with simple talking. Students shared lore from their middle-school days, which led to boisterous laughing, which led to ribbing between students, which led to hurt feelings, which led to a girl calling another girl a name that Dieter had never heard before, which led to Dieter standing between two girls who were yanking each other's hair, which led to students taking out their phones to record, which led to Esther, who was escorting five students to Dieter's room, calling Mr. Wilson, which led to those two students being removed by the disciplinarian, which led to a renewed anger in the disciplinarian, who was already having to come to Dieter's room to remove students for fighting, which had been a weekly occurrence last year.

By the time the class had settled and all the students were in their seats—except, of course, the two fighters—only five minutes remained in the fifty-five-minute period. Dieter handed out the syllabus, a requirement for teachers of Freshmen, and mumbled the rules and expectations for his class, which had already been broken a hundred times in a span of fifty minutes and were being broken still.

Sixth period was equally draining, though it didn't have the noticeable diversion of a fight. Instead, the students talked cease-lessly with each other about the previous period's confrontation while Dieter weakly attempted to redirect the conversations back to the syllabus.

He spent the final period of the day sprawled on his chair while ignoring the lesson plan that he desperately needed to finalize. Summer had atrophied his body, leaving it easily battered by the rigors of teaching. His legs pulsated around the knees. His throat prickled. His back ached from the burden of standing for fifty-five minutes at a time. With his body in rebellion, the looming after-school workout session that Dieter was pressured to attend with Jose, the exhaustingly cheerful art teacher, weighed on him even more.

Chapter 2

DIETER HAD LITTLE choice about working out with Jose. Any morning that Dieter arrived early, Jose appeared in Dieter's room as he sat down to eat his fast-food breakfast. Any lunch period they shared, he watched Dieter's face as Dieter shoved forkfuls of food into his mouth. And any night that they left together, Jose extended an invitation to exercise with him in the school's workout facilities. On the final day of professional development, when Dieter had seen Esther walking hand in hand with Manley, Jose popped out of nowhere and again invited Dieter to work out. With one more pained look at Esther, Dieter accepted Jose's invitation.

During the course of the first workout, Jose spotted Dieter's squats, moaned during stretching, and suggested various hamstring and groin stretches that could only be done with a partner. Two members of the Science Department, huddled near the aerobic machines, giggled and whispered in amusement.

"Push it, DiVo! One more! Feeeeeel it!" Jose yelled in a half-masculine grunt, half-effeminate whisper. His hands supported Dieter's side as he dipped for a squat.

Tired, sore and defeated, Dieter trudged around the circle to his classroom. It was five o'clock, and the pangs of hunger gnawed at his stomach. He salivated over visions of various fast food options available along the ride home. His culinary dreaming abruptly vanished as he turned the hallway toward the annex, where he saw a tan, oily figure slide from his room and out the exit doors.

Manley...

Dieter walked quickly to his room and peaked inside. The room appeared to be in the same decrepit order in which it was left before his work out. The dirty green sewage stain still smothered the ceiling tile two feet from his desk; the slow drip still splashed into the spare trash can on the floor. The closed projector screen still leaned twenty degrees to the left. Paper balls and broken pens still littered the floor.

Yet, the vital component of the room remained intact. The laminated life-size poster of Dieter, frozen mid-performance during his acting days at Reading High School, hung unblemished except for the permanent marker graffiti that had been there for two years. The poster originally said, "Falstaff, 2005"; however, a student (or a malcontent basketball coach) had decided to cross the "1" and scratch the second "0," leaving it to read, "Fatstaff, 2015."

Dieter crouched to the ground outside the door, checking the floor for the unmistakable gleam of buttering. In any other school, the sight of a teacher getting eye level with the ground would have been out of the ordinary, but as Dieter's room had already been slicked three times, his scrutiny was justified.

Nothing there.

Dieter moved cautiously toward the cabinets. He snapped open a drawer, expecting a booby trap. Nothing appeared out of the ordinary. Satisfied, he made a quick scan of the students' desks, which retained the same appearance and alignment as before: rows of doodled genitalia, carved swastikas, inked gang symbols and initials, all enshrined on the wooden surfaces. Miguel's desk had various sayings in Spanish, often about a "maestro" who was quite "gordo" and "feo." There were also some comments about "su mama." When he finally turned to his own desk, he found the one difference in the room—a solitary Twinkie, preserved in its original packaging and resting upon a white napkin that read: "Sorry about Esther. Stuff yourself, burro."

"Manley," Dieter wheezed.

Words, written and spoken, composed all of Manley's insults up to this point, and they were easily brushed aside. But this symbolic object, a physical representation accompanied by innuendo, became a first for Manley vs. Vogel: a gesture that, for most people, would be benign but after a disastrous first day became a needling jab that caught Dieter right in the temple.

It was clear that Sanders would do nothing about this obvious violation of staff conduct. Plopping onto his wooden desk chair, Dieter pulled out his cell phone to lodge a complaint with the District's HR representative. Frustrated that he was neglected by his Principal and by the department, angered by Manley's amplified attacks, and cautious about Jose's persistent concern for his well-being, Dieter programmed the number for HR as his second speed dial. His mom was number three. Rosa's Pizza was number one.

As he dialed the number, a ruffling sound and a muted thump arose from the center of the desk. Dieter stared at the Twinkie as he held the phone to his ear. A couple of seconds passed with no further disturbance and his attention shifted back to the call. The voicemail began its recording as another crinkling sound came from the package. Dieter ended the call to focus his attention on what he only assumed would be an additional grievance.

He guessed that the movement was due to a string that would drag the Twinkie along the ground in the hope that he would chase it, so he slowly picked up the treat and examined the packaging, rotating it and maneuvering it back and forth. Nothing was evident. Dieter shrugged and decided to stash the treat inside his bag to enjoy during the ride home.

But in the process of ferrying the Twinkie from the top of his desk to his bag, Dieter felt an unexplained heat on his hand. Faint at first, it quickly approached a level of discomfort. Upon inspection, he found an orange-red aura glowing within the cracks of his fingers. Stunned, he tossed the Twinkie back onto the desk.

The package bucked about on the wood surface, rocking back and forth for a few seconds until the packaging suddenly burst open, leaving the Twinkie intact and exposed on a bed of clear plastic packaging.

Too bewildered to react, Dieter continue to stare as an imaginary knife cut an upwardly curving crease across the length of the pastry, exposing the soft white cream underneath. When the line had finished forming, Dieter leaned over to examine the slit when a murmur slipped from the lacerated Twinkie.

"Check, check-check. Check one-two."

Dieter gasped.

"Fa, la, la, La, La, LA, LA." the Twinkie continued, progressively louder.

"What in God's name?"

"Can you hear me?" the Twinkie asked.

"Yes, I can."

The lights suddenly dimmed and the Twinkie began to glow. A puff of smoke rose from the sponge-cake as an ominous voice commanded, "Prepare yourself, mortal, for the Prince of Darkness, Commander of the Fallen Angels, Ruler of Demons, King of Babylon and Chancellor of Duke University..." It paused a moment to allow the glow to intensify. "Behold, Luciferrrrrr!" the Twinkie shouted, spewing its white filling all over the desk and onto Dieter's pants. Another puff of smoke emanated from under the pastry, more reminiscent of flatulence than infernal fury. The Twinkie huffed and waited for a reaction.

Looking from the Twinkie to his crotch, Dieter complained, "You creamed all over me!"

Why was he screaming at a magically verbal snack? He didn't know, or even bother to wonder how the confection had come to life, because Dieter had inserted himself into so many fantasies throughout his teen years, and continuing into adult years, that this surreal occurrence did not immediately spark incredulity. Besides, he sometimes hallucinated after long nights of video games and anime. A few years before, he'd dreamed that his Yoda figurine had convinced him to order late-night pizza in the same raspy, backwards manner that it did in the movies. Another time, he'd dreamed that a cute anime character was in bed with him (this time it was not a consciously-willed fantasy). The most recent time, he'd lucidly dreamed that Colonel Sanders and Toucan Sam were readying his bedroom for his subsequent torture and murder. The tub in his bathroom would serve as the deep fryer after Colonel Sanders had plucked Dieter hair by hair.

The Twinkie spoke again: "Aren't you scared?"

Dieter glanced at the door before fixing his eyes on the conversing convenience store snack. "You're a Twinkie. I could eat you in a second," Dieter mumbled.

"A *Twinkie*? I was a snake. I was a monster. I was a red-faced demon with horns. I could scare the be-jeezus out of anyone. Now, I'm a Twinkie. Humiliating!"

"Are you saying that you're the Devil?" Dieter proposed. "I always wondered why these things were so damn addicting." He chuckled at his own joke, surprised at how cool he felt in the presence of a Satan-possessed piece of junk-food. "To tell you the truth, I'm seconds away from feeding you to Jose. I bet he likes cream filling." Dieter shook his head at his gratuitous insult, not sure where it came from.

Content in Dieter's moral slip, the deviled delight continued: "Sorry about your pants, but I'm here because we each need something from the other."

What could a Twinkie give him other than a moment of delicious indulgence?

"I don't think—"

"Listen, I wasn't anticipating this form. It's not—"

Would the Devil notice if he slowly inched his hand forward to pick up the finger cake and take just one little…

"Put your hand down!"

Dieter quickly obliged.

"As I was saying before you so rudely decided to ingest me, I naturally appear as something a person needs or wants. Apparently, you like snack food."

"So, you are trying to seduce me. What do you want?"

Dieter's boldness surprised the snack-food Satan, who sighed before elucidating: "Here's the situation: you and I are both low on recognition—"

"But Father Manny says you are behind all evil. Murder, infidelity, other things…"

"Ah, your priest… Catholics still pay me some attention, but everyone else has forgotten about the Prince of Darkness. These modern-day churches just hump Christian brotherhood and to the point of nausea. You mortal men—"

"—and women," Dieter blurted. The Twinkie's lips pursed, a remarkable feat considering the lack of muscle. Of course, this wasn't a normal Twinkie.

"—you mortal men *and women* forget who led you all to moments of greatness, like cheating on your spouses, selling out your business partners, becoming a filthy rich televangelist, or inciting fear of minorities to become President…"

Dieter shrugged again.

The Devil continued: "People are arrogant, Dieter. They will do my bidding but won't give me credit. Fear and recognition; that's what I want! When people need hope, or when they do good, who do they credit? God. Or His bastard son, Jesus!" The Devil's voice spiraled into a whine. "When something bad happens, people point to twisted psychology, lousy parenting, violent video games, but they won't recognize that I caused those things. I corrupt their souls. It's me! And I want my name back in the mouths of humanity!" A sob of jealousy snuck into the Devil's voice. "People are so quick to invoke God's name, but no one talks about me anymore."

"So, you want me to kill Manley? I accept," Dieter said, surprisingly less sarcastic than he'd anticipated.

"Something more sinister," the Devil growled.

Dieter tightened, preparing himself for unadulterated evil. His heart, which hardly knew a workout, jumped to life. Would he poison the lunch food? Create a tragic "accident" for Miguel? Steal from the library? Have premarital sex with Esther?

"I want you," the chair creaked as Dieter leaned forward, "to destroy Gretel!" the Devil cried triumphantly.

Dieter fell back against his chair, deflated, perplexed, and silent.

"Too much, too soon?" the Devil asked.

"No…"

"Then what's wrong?"

"You want me to destroy *Gretel?*"

Gretel the Pretzel was Reading's mascot. When Reading High School was called Penrod Helfenstine High School, the mascot was a Conquistador, a vaguely European-appearing man with a helmet. Due to consolidation with the neighboring minority communities in the '70s, Penrod Helfenstine High School relinquished its glorious name and became Reading High School. Because there was a developing consciousness against racial insensitivity, the Conquistador had become an object of contention between the all-white school leadership and the diversifying community. Eventually, the Superintendent had put pressure on the school to change.

In hopes that they could keep the mascot, the school's leadership proposed a community vote. On the ballot, they put the Conquistador and the pretzel, a laughably unthreatening mascot. It was a passive-aggressive response, for sure. The school's principal at the time was Sanders' mentor: a large, mustached man with an affinity for dark beer and subtle racism that was strong enough to be noticed but too weak to be discerned. If those "liberal pansies" forced his hand, he'd rig the process to showcase the ridiculousness of their oversensitivity. He'd give them an option that only a bed-wetting fool would choose.

From his love of bar food, he crafted *Gretel, the pretzel.* He assumed no one would vote for her: she was a cartoon pretzel with a yellow bow. She wasn't even acceptable as a children's book character, let alone a mascot. But with an overwhelming majority in support, Gretel replaced the culturally insensitive Conquistador.

"Yes, Dieter! Destroy Gretel, and in her ashes, enshrine *me,*" Satan responded, giddy.

"Why me?" Dieter asked.

The Twinkie pivoted on the ends of its tubular body. "I want you to do it because you are the silent pushover—you've spent your whole life being trampled by others. Only you can incite the students and no one will suspect you," Satan said.

"Sanders has treated me like garbage, it's true, but the school runs well enough," Dieter said before the projector flashed on, cutting him off. He turned toward the wall where a video played against the white board. In the scene, a younger Dieter sat in a corner of the library, his eyes glued to the pages of a book. A girl walked past him. She was tall, thin, with tan skin and a beautiful, sharp nose.

Adult Dieter glanced at the Twinkie then turned back to the memory just in time to see his teenage-self glance up from the book when Esther embraced her football-player boyfriend, who scowled at Dieter while engaged in the hug. High school Dieter sighed into the pages, love struck and heartbroken.

The projector flickered. In a rapid series of clips, Satan pulled moments from Dieter's three years of teaching. Unseen moments of gossip between Sanders, Manley, and various teachers, all snippets of jokes and snide comments at Dieter's expense.

In one, Sanders called Dieter a "worthless waste of space" to a grinning Manley. In another, Manley whispered to hungry staff members that Dieter cried every day after class and had peed himself out of distress on multiple occasions. Manley even mimicked Dieter's shrug and voice, saying "Hmm, I peed myself. Hmm…" Other clips merely portrayed teachers, including Sanders and Manley, expressing their disdain for Dieter.

Dieter's anger surged. Why was Satan showing him these incidents?

"I get it. I'll be able to take my revenge. But what does this have to do with Gretel? She's just a mascot."

"After you corrupt the school, I want the community to worship me in the chaos. I want people to forget who they are and praise me instead. Imagine the cheerleaders on the sidelines: 'Give me a 'D'; give me an 'E'; give me a 'V-I-L'… What's that spell? Devil! Devil! Devil!'" The Twinkie shivered in excitement. "It will be the beginning of my reclamation! And in return, you will have vengeance against those who have mocked you and neglected you."

Skepticism still played on Dieter's brow. Satan had clearly chosen Dieter for this mission. Why else would he reveal such candid moments? But Satan's reward seemed trivial.

"I don't understand: there are plenty of schools with you as mascot."

"Yes, but why stop there? I've got the white communities locked up, so why not a black and Hispanic school?"

Dieter shook his head. If that's all he wanted, so be it. But how could he change things, even with the help of Satan?

"How am I going to convince Sanders, who loves his German heritage, to abandon dear Gretel? The man loves Gretel. He's defeated five different movements to create a new mascot."

"We don't need to convince Sanders: we need to take him out."

Discomfort raced through Dieter. "I'm not a murderer!"

"Who said anything about murder? I'm talking about getting him fired, or pushing him to resign. I don't think you realize how much he relies on this job to feed his ego."

Dieter relaxed a bit.

"Look, all we need is a coup to push him to the edge. What do you think is the greatest threat to the community of Reading?"

"Economic decay, a crumbling infrastructure, climate change..."

The Twinkie sighed.

"Think, Dieter! What's the most visible conflict in this community today?"

After some moments of pondering, he said, "Our community is losing manufacturing jobs and its tax base. Some people blame crime on black people and immigrants. But the minorities claim discrimination—"

An epiphany had Dieter in its grasp.

"Play the race card, Dieter. Play it hard, play it fast, play it often."

Race. There was tension in the air at Reading. The staff was ninety percent white, with the exceptions being Jose, Father Manny, who was hired as a guidance counselor and was Mexican-American, Mr. Wilson, who was the disciplinarian and was black, and Esther, whose mother was black. Even so, those teachers had assimilated themselves within the white culture of Reading, Ohio, having grown up during a time when they were a very real minority, alienated if they did not blend into the dominant culture. Rarely, if ever, did they speak about the struggles of people of color in school, community, and country. With few faces pigmented like themselves, students felt disconnected with the adults in the building.

Gretel's image represented the hesitancy to accept diversity. Each class that went through the building, with its white teachers and white curriculum and white culture, came out with a vague anger that came from a vague awareness that there was a vague hostility directed toward minorities. None of the teachers were contentious enough to direct this resentment, but that damned smiling pretzel...

Her crooked smirk was the façade of a school that claimed to be concerned with educating all students, though disproportionate rates of minorities were suspended or expelled, though buses wouldn't go into the most impoverished areas of Reading, though students of color with special needs were routinely denied services.

"Even if I accept," Dieter hesitated, "I still don't see how I can destroy Gretel. The statue is solid steel, and Sanders has been principal for seven years. He's practically tenured. Plus, most teachers like him enough to support him. I don't think you realize how hard it will be to change things here."

Again, the projector.

This time, the video appeared to be taken from someone's point of view. The camera walked down the hall. Students extended their hands for high-fives and fist bumps. The person from whose vantage this video was taken returned the affirmation before turning to Sanders' office and pushing through the door.

Waiting inside was a solemn faced Manley, who watched as the cameraman sat behind Sanders' desk.

"Look, I'm sorry," Manley sputtered.

The man responded in a very familiar voice: "Too late. You're fired."

Manley fell to his knees.

"Please, I need this job."

The man behind the camera responded, coldly, "But this job doesn't need you. Get out before I call security."

Manley wiped his eyes, hesitated by the door, and then left the room. Before the door closed, Esther burst in and guided it shut, turning the lock in the process. She eyed the camera with a hot blush on her cheeks and a mischievous glint in her eyes.

"I've wanted to have you alone all morning. I'm glad you finally got that loser out of here."

Esther walked to the desk while her hands crept to the top of her blouse. She slowly guided the top button from its slit.

"Now, Dieter, let's get down to business," she whispered, climbing onto the desk. Her bra peeked from her blouse as she crawled over the wood toward the camera. Right as she neared the screen, the projection vanished.

"I'll guide you," the Devil purred. Dieter's lips quivered as he adjusted his pants. The Devil continued: "I can handle all of this. You just follow my direction and think about the future. You will be principal while Manley and Sanders are trampled by your army of students. You, sitting in the office, Esther catering to your every need. You can slam the books of justice on all the delinquents who dare to defy you. You can be Java the Hut!"

The Twinkie stifled a snicker.

Although Dieter was slightly annoyed at the patronizing (and incorrect) allusion, he drank in the Devil's vision of power and possession, not wondering for a moment if it was just an illusion.

"You can make this happen?"

Dieter crossed his legs and sat forward, replaying everything Satan had shown him. All the disappointments, all the insults, and all the tantalizing possibilities! This was the first time he'd felt a sense of optimism since coming to Reading High School.

"I can punish those punks who kept whispering 'cider' today," Dieter smirked.

"Exactly," the Twinkie smirked.

"Do I need to sign a contract? Or do you just take my soul?" Dieter asked.

"Nothing to sign; and I don't *technically* take souls."

Content with the answer (and somewhat guilty since this question was apparently a sore subject for Satan), Dieter picked up the Twinkie and brought it to eye level.

"You can make me principal? You can get me Esther?"

The Twinkie rolled forward and backward as an apparent nod.

"As long as I become the mascot. But one other thing…"

Dieter frowned. It seemed too good to be true. What was the Devil going to throw in right as Dieter was agreeing to the mission? What unspeakable expectation? What soul-sucking requirement? What evil would be required of him?

"What?" Dieter replied.

"There's also the possibility that the Archdiocese will take over the school after this year. I need someone to help me block that move. With the students on your side, and with you as principal, we can stop those Jesus-freaks."

Dieter shrugged in response. He was technically Catholic. He was also technically pre-diabetic. These were just labels, distant and inconsequential.

Satan had given Dieter a mission more innocuous than immoral. One that did not ask for violence or criminal behavior. In return, Dieter would gain retribution against a staff that had ignored him and ridiculed him behind his back. And he would have Esther!

Dieter leaned forward. "Okay. Where do we start?"

Dieter and Satan spent the next hour hashing out a plan for the year's curriculum, which was supposed to have been completed in July. The pale light was creeping toward darkness when Dieter finally called his mom for a ride.

The plan was simple enough. Incite the students to hate the German roots of the school, further stoke their disgust at having a pretzel as a mascot and Sanders as their principal, manipulate them to put pressure on the administration, hold an election with the Devil on the ballot, eliminate or repress anyone who stands in the way, including Manley and Sanders. During Sanders' inevitable battle to maintain his grasp on the school, Dieter would seize opportunities to undermine his authority.

For Junior English, Dieter would usually spend the entire first semester on British literature, leaving only the second semester for African literature, Asian literature, Middle-East literature, the Holocaust, Colonialism, Post-Colonialism, *The Metamorphosis*, *Don Quixote*, and a required play by Shakespeare. But, as the Devil pointed out, Dieter needed to fan racial fires. What better way to attack the proud pre-twentieth century German culture that formed the school's identity than by baselessly generalizing all Germans as Nazis? Thus, Dieter scrapped his original plans for the Devil's design.

The first unit would focus on racial identity and the opening chapter of *Invisible Man*, "one of the most troubling racial stories" an online synopsis claimed. He would then teach the entirety of *Julius Caesar*, abandoning *Great Expectations* in order to spark the idea of revolution. After that, Elie Wiesel's *Night* and German (Nazi) oppression. Dieter's GOAL: make any vaguely German person, name, ritual, or symbol become inescapably tied to mass genocide of the Jews and other races. European and German imagery would be seen as a racial challenge to the minority population. After that, he would find texts that spoke to oppression and justice.

For his freshman class, he would corrupt the soft minds and fickle morals to create a mob of ruthless little demons. To do this, he'd start with *Peter Pan* (to develop a distrust of adults), then *To Kill a Mockingbird* (to stoke racial tensions), and *Animal Farm* (a how-to guide to get what they wanted). Eventually, Dieter would teach *Lord of the Flies* (to prove the power of mob rule).

With the film studies class he inherited, he would have to figure something out. In the meantime, he decided he'd finish *Saving Private Ryan* before continuing to *Schindler's List* to coincide with the anti-German theme.

To snare Esther, Satan tactfully insisted that Dieter continue exercising.

"Lose those rolls, if you want Esther for dinner," the Twinkie snickered.

Dieter nodded. "Do I have to keep working out with Jose?"

"Who?"

"Jose, the art teacher."

"It will keep you honest to work out with someone else. By Thanksgiving, you'll be a new man!"

Dieter felt a surge of enthusiasm as he walked out the front door. The rustle of canvas drew Dieter's attention to the right side of the entrance, where the "Welcome Back" sign was in the process of being taken down by the security guard and the janitor.

"Animals. Another year in a zoo. A fu—"

Dieter hurried past, expecting the janitor to displace his anger. Once a safe distance away, he shook his head with a smirk. The kids were terrors, but they would be his to wield as he saw fit. He'd simply use books and lessons to champion an army. Dieter had the perfect texts and the Prince of Darkness as his guide. Now, he needed to do something that had escaped him for three years.

Dieter needed to become a good teacher.

Chapter 3

TO MAKE HIS classroom more conducive to learning, Dieter needed to find decorations in addition to the poster of him that was mounted at the head of the classroom. He had read that the students should see positive models of people like themselves, so Dieter purchased posters of Civil Rights activists and famous authors. He also found motivational posters with inspiring quotes.

Then, the Friday before Labor Day Weekend, he took a sick day. While this was a request that would normally be denied by administrators, Sanders and Manley both hoped that this was a sign that Dieter was looking for a job elsewhere—or maybe that he was heading for a mental breakdown.

Instead, Dieter pulled together as many teacher's guides as he could find and studied them like a law student about to take the Bar exam. Classroom management techniques, lesson planning, theories of learning: he poured over each and recorded his notes in a notebook so he could refer to them later. He had four days to recount and internalize all the theories of teaching that he'd ignored in college and neglected in practice. At home (and with the help of Satan, who had now taken the more conversable form of Julius Caesar on the cover of Dieter's book), Dieter meticulously crafted lesson plans: something he was supposed to have done during the summer but had neglected in favor of super-hero movie marathons and junk food binges.

On his kitchen table, he spread out the texts for his two literature courses. Both *Julius Caesar* and *Night* lay open with small slips of paper poking out from the pages. The opening chapter of *Invisible Man* was copied and made into a packet. *Animal Farm* was cracked with a legal pad of notes next to it. *Peter Pan* was highlighted wherever the Lost Boys made appearances. And Dieter had stolen a copy of *Lord of the Flies* from the library.

He was taking a break when his mother called.

"Dieter?"

"No one else lives here."

"Is Dieter home?"

"Ma, you called me. You should know your own son's voice."

"Sorry, I thought it might have been my grandson that answered," his mom replied.

"Ma, you don't have—" Dieter cringed. He'd taken the bait.

"And I never will if you don't *shape* up."

Dieter sighed. "What do you want?"

"Did you buy that gym membership?"

"No, Ma."

"What about the juice cleanse?"

"No, Ma."

"Did you ask Mrs. Lichtenstein about her daughter?"

"No, Ma."

"Does your tummy still hurt?"

"No—" Dieter sensed her voice softening. He was, after all, her only child, and his stomach was revolting against the new diet that the Devil had demanded. "Yes, Ma."

Mrs. Vogel now became the nurturer that she could occasionally be after her barbs had wounded Dieter into submission. "I'll be over in five minutes with soup."

"But—"

Dieter's pants were down and smut was churning on his

computer. He hobbled to the bathroom for a quick shower.

———————

When he got out, his mom was already sitting at the table with two bowls of steaming bean soup. "You were in there for a while," his mom said, eyes focused on crumbling crackers into Dieter's bowl.

"Yeah, I worked out before you called," Dieter said as he slid his arm into his shirt.

"More like after I called," his mom said just audibly enough for Dieter to hear, but soft enough that Dieter doubted what he heard. She stood up and walked toward the refrigerator, stopping by the pile of pizza boxes near the kitchen sink. "Don't you think your stomach issues are the result of eating all that unhealthy food?"

Dieter said nothing of his new eating plan, choosing instead to blow on the spoonful of soup. His mother continued to talk as she cracked the top box open. Seeing an uneaten slice, she pulled it from the cardboard container. "Eating junk food will give you a heart attack or a stroke or diabetes. They'll have to amputate your foot, Dieter. How will you find a wife with one foot?"

Dieter gave her an incredulous look before she shifted to self-pity.

"Maybe it's partly my fault…"

And it *was* her fault, partly. Being a single mother, she was afraid of losing Dieter the same way she lost her husband. Every time Dieter would cry or demand treats, she would give in, not wanting another man to abandon her.

"…I should have made more home-cooked meals. If only I wasn't working two jobs to give you everything you needed—"

One job was working as a Mary Kay saleswoman. The other was as president of the PTA, which only met once a month. Her alimony and child support payments had been sufficient for a middleclass lifestyle.

"If only I could have kept your father from leaving…" she paused dramatically (it was no wonder Dieter went into acting in high school and college) "…then I could have been a better mother and provided healthy meals every night, and you wouldn't be eating fast food every day, and you'd be married with three beautiful children, and they would call me Oma—"

She stopped and nibbled at the corner of the pizza, staring with a heavy sigh and sad, dreamy eyes while Dieter slurped the soup. Sensing his mother was slipping into a coma of depression, Dieter attempted to cheer her up.

"I'm going to start exercising after school."

"That's good," his mother responded weakly, still staring beyond the empty pizza boxes on the countertop. Dieter jumped up and gave his mother a kiss on her forehead before shuffling off with the bowl.

"Thanks for the soup. I'm going to finish lesson plans."

His mother turned her head, sending her fading brown hair across her face. "Since when do you plan lessons?"

———————

Dieter arrived at school on Tuesday with a cautious confidence and a plan for the day. He took his turn at the copy machine, double-checking his notes as copies were made. After collecting the papers, he binder-clipped them by class and walked to his room, bypassing the cafeteria on the way. The first two days would be centered on students' perceptions of injustice and their feelings about Reading. Then, he'd drop the bomb that was...*Invisible Man*.

Before he could flick the lights to his classroom, they flashed on and Satan's voice cackled from the PA system. "You've ordered two hamburgers, one portion of fries, and a super-size milkshake? Pull forward and pay at the window."

"Funny," Dieter said as he placed the copies on his desk.

"What's the plan for today?"

"Introduce Julius Caesar and the history of his rule. Give the freshmen an article about the bystander effect. You know, when people stand by as innocent people are attacked."

"I know what it is. I invented it."

Dieter belittled the Devil: "You're so bad; you're just a bad-ass Twinkie."

"Listen, why not give the bystander article to the juniors, too? After all, Brutus *had no choice* but to assassinate Julius Caesar..."

A light went on in Dieter's head. If he could make the students see the dangers of inactivity, then he could present a violent, but "justified" response.

"By the way, your mom is piece of work," said Satan.

"Yeah, I know. I thought that you had possessed her."

"She doesn't need me. Besides, I was in your computer screen."

"Wait. You were in my...and I was looking at...and I was starting to...?"

The PA system remained silent. The stand-off ended by the clanging of the annex doors. "Well, have a good day!" said the devil.

The PA system clicked off.

———————

Dieter stood outside his classroom as the opening bell rang. He wanted to greet the students as they walked into the classroom to establish rapport with them. Many of the books he'd read over the long weekend had stressed the need for a connection between teachers and their students as a means of minimizing misbehavior and encouraging learning. To Dieter, this idea was a revelation. To competent teachers, it's a common-sense concept uncommonly implemented.

So, there he stood, waiting. From inside Jose's classroom, the only other one in the annex, acoustic, guitar-heavy music radiated into the hallway. Dieter could see Jose bouncing around the room as he set up easels and arranged flower-filled vases. Jose's energy baffled Dieter. The man hadn't stopped moving during the entire ten minutes that Dieter had stood in the doorway. When the shrill, five-minute warning bell for first period sounded, Jose's door finally burst open, sending a flood of light and sound into the corridor.

"Morning, Divo!" Jose chirped. "Fancy seeing you out here!"

Dieter forced a smile as he nodded. The sound of squeaking

sneakers echoing through the hallway halted his response. A wall of teens converged on the dimly-lit annex. Some students trudged around the corner with drooping eyes and sagging book bags. Others pushed and slapped each other, not sure how else to show genuine affection.

As the students neared Dieter's class, their eyes widened in anticipation. Any change in a teacher's routine was cause for concern. Was there a quiz? Was Mr. Wilson waiting in class to dole out discipline? Was there a guest speaker setting up a presentation about *their changing bodies*?

Sensing confusion, Dieter pasted a wider smile onto his face and extended his hands to the nearest student, star basketball player Andre Williams. "Good morning, Andre."

Andre's eyes never rose from the floor, and he fumbled with Dieter's handshake. Normally, Dieter would have command Andre to lift his eyes and respond with an appropriate greeting and a firm handshake, but he had read that eye-dropping was actually an unintentional sign of respect, so he gave him a soft pat on the shoulder and ushered him into the classroom. Andre peeked inside, and seeing no other adult inside the room, he called out, "It's okay!"

The students exhaled and resumed their approach, each being greeted in turn by Dieter.

"When is your first soccer game, Tony? Great, I'll be there. Maria, are you ready for another run for class president? Awesome..."

Dieter even welcomed Miguel, who was usually the target of a teacher's ill-favor. He was well-accustomed to their short and cold words, their body language habitually conveying both annoyance and suspicion. In response, Miguel played the role projected upon him: class clown, special needs burden, potential criminal.

"Miguel, it's great to see you today," said Dieter.

The words contained no sarcasm or deadpan with them, which left Miguel uncharacteristically speechless. When the bell cut through the odd silence, both Dieter and Miguel entered the classroom together.

With everyone in their seats, Dieter flashed the prompt on the board: *Write about your biggest frustrations with this school.*

"You will write for three minutes, non-stop," said Dieter.

To the students this felt like a trap. Why would a teacher compromise authority? And why would a teacher acknowledge the possibility that something was wrong with the school? Why would he let the students vent? What was his game? If they honestly shared their opinions, would they receive a detention?

Dieter sensed the hesitancy and softened his voice.

"None of what you write will be shared with *anyone* outside this classroom. I promise, you will not get in trouble for anything you write…" Dieter paused, seeing Miguel perk up, "…as long as it isn't sexual, or threatening, or doesn't mention people by name."

Miguel slumped back onto his seat. Everyone else conveyed various signs of agreement.

"Let's do this, then. Three minutes to write."

The students nodded.

"Time starts now."

Students' heads lowered to a few inches above their desks. Their pens and pencils scratched rapidly across their packets. The sounds of scratched paper and deep breathing harmonized into a symphony of student participation. Dieter had never seen one hundred percent engagement in his class, and he certainly had never seen himself in absolute control. He also had never seen Andre or Miguel comply with an assignment. Miguel's lime green crayon looped wildly on his sheet, and Andre only paused his writing once to turn the sound off on his phone.

The three minutes went quickly, and when Dieter told the students to stop writing, he was met with protest. He extended the writing period for another three minutes before opening the floor for discussion.

"Alright, who wants to share what they have written?"

Arms popped out of sockets. Hands waved aggressively. Butts lifted off their seats as if the extra inches would elevate the chance of being acknowledged.

Dieter knew that the first person he called would set the tone of the discussion, so it was critical to establish the difference between silliness and productivity.

"Maria, you're the acting president: what did you write?"

Maria, though she was effusive in her zeal to share, became meek in the class spotlight. She was, after all, the students' diplomat. Even at sixteen, she realized the responsibility of such designation, as symbolic as it was in actuality. She also realized the hope that was held for her future, hinged upon her performance in high school.

Her parents were born from immigrants. They remembered crossing the border with Maria's grandparents: the running, the hiding, the utter desperation, and then the temporary relief when they made it to Texas and then to Reading. Since then, her parents stressed an appreciation for American culture alongside their Mexican heritage.

Throughout her childhood, her parents would sit her in front of *Sesame Street* and other PBS children's shows. They would enthusiastically celebrate Memorial Day, the Fourth of July and Flag Day (much to the confusion of their neighbors who didn't realize Flag Day was a real holiday). But on the weekends, her family would watch *Sábado Gigante*. They would cook tamales in the late autumn, and make champurrado in the winter. And though they were barred from Heaven's Gates Cemetery after the groundskeeper witnessed them throwing a picnic on a grave, they found ways to celebrate Dia de Los Muertos at home. Her identity changed with the seasons, but at its core, educational success was the foundation for all her hopes of thriving in America. Every activity carried the urgency of this dream.

"Well, I, um, think that we aren't respected..."

Some students hummed in agreement. Others snapped their fingers, a tactic taught to them by their beatnik sophomore English teacher used to show agreement or appreciation. Gaining confidence, she continued, "I mean, the school lunches don't serve food we like. We don't recognize African American history or Latino history. We are treated like prisoners, with no time to talk to each other and no chance to choose classes or change things around here…" The students became more vocal in their support. Maria's passion snowballed into a final tumultuous boulder aimed at the administration. "…and, I mean, we have a *pretzel* as a mascot. Why can't we have a new one, a *different* one?"

The class erupted in a chorus of outrage. Students mumbled their own opinions while restating Maria's sentiments. Dieter simply stood there, smiling. *This might be easy after all*, he thought to himself.

Most of the period was spent sharing their reflections. Because of the tone set by Maria, students took their gripes seriously. When sharing was over, Dieter defined 'tyranny' and reviewed the system of government the Romans had instituted, emphasizing and slightly manipulating the levels of democracy that existed. As the students exited, grumbles of oppression were heard at Reading High School.

Dieter Vogel had just turned wisps of injustice into a visible condensation. Now, he needed to conjure up a tempest.

On Wednesday, he featured an article from the early 1800s. It talked about the great opportunity that a newly founded land held. There was a letter from Reading's founder that suggested that abolitionists were meddling cowards who weren't ambitious or industrious enough to run their own businesses. The founder had also suggested that God had willed the Whiteman to settle the wilderness in place of "those not civilized enough to contribute to society in any other fashion." There was also the frequent use of the word nigger.

Through Dieter's guiding questions, the students could parcel the implications of the documents and could articulate them with great certainty. But there wasn't the same fire that the previous day's lesson had produced. A few students were angered, but most hovered between apathy and annoyance. Only the four white students felt a shade of real discomfort, but their parents had already explained away the history of Reading, pointing out that their families were no richer than the minority families anyway, which is why they couldn't afford the private school up the road like those insufferable show-offs in Hilltop with their fancy SUVs and excessively large houses and smug self-importance.

Dieter pulled Andre to the side and asked him what he felt about the founder of Reading and his opinions.

"Man, it's past history. That was like a thousand years ago."

"History can be relevant in the present," Dieter said, checking his urge to correct Andre's redundancy, but Andre had already begun sketching a basketball on his packet. Dieter's class phone rang.

"You're losing them," Satan hissed at Dieter.

"I know, but I don't know what to do."

The buzz in the class began to pick up—a sign that misbehavior was soon to follow.

"Turn on the projector."

"What?"

"Just do it!"

Dieter clicked on the projector. When the screen finally booted, there was a copy of the original document that Dieter had taught. The language, though outdated in a Shakespearean sense, was clear. "Reading is God's given land, founded by our proud German ancestors, and worked by the godless slave, to be tamed and built upon for generations to come." Signed, Penrod Helfenstine.

But the image under the letter, the visual that Dieter needed, quickly grabbed the class's attention. The crest had a white man and woman with hands joined. Between them, a setting sun in the distance. Over their shoulders was a forest. And at the bottom of the crest, bowed in submission, were the dark outlines of three figures with slash marks across their naked backs. Dieter made sure that the class saw these figures, especially the smallest one that most surely represented a child. For the last ten minutes, they talked about the meaning of the picture.

On Thursday and Friday, Dieter used the opening of *Invisible Man*, a barbaric vision of racism, to provide further visuals to the scourge of inequality. When they left for the long weekend, the words "Founders Day" were accompanied with sharp hisses, disgusted grumbles, and even spit by some students. Even the white minority in the school felt the sharp sting of shame at their ancestors' language and hypocrisy.

Dieter was quite satisfied as his mom pulled up in the dented mini-van. She had taken his request to drive behind the building so that under the privacy of the unpopulated service entrance, Dieter could plop triumphantly into his carriage.

In only one week, Dieter had finally experienced the interaction he'd wished for as a teacher. Hope radiated inside him. Maybe he'd finally be successful. Maybe he'd finally be in control. Maybe he'd finally be accepted within the walls of Reading High School.

Chapter 4

IN READING, THE celebration of Founder's Day followed Labor Day Weekend. It was the time to celebrate the brave white settlers who expelled a peaceful tribe of Native Americans and built the community of Reading on the backs of African slaves. And as the community had returned to its original state, where minorities far outnumbered their white counterparts and had significantly less wealth, this bicentennial celebration was truly historic.

As with any holiday, a parade was in order. The half-mile stretch of Reading Road, which had the school on the south side and City Hall on the north side, would be lined with most of the five thousand residents, who would watch the other residents march down a street because they had enough free time to sign-up for a club or political office.

Because the school was at the base of the parade route, it housed the fifteen-member marching band, the town's fire truck, the current mayor's convertible, this year's political candidates' sedans, and the various other floats.

Dieter's mom dropped him off at 7:30, a full hour before he needed to be there because Reading Road was going to be closed at 8:00 am, and the new coffee shop was bound to be crowded before the parade, and she'd heard that they had a great Frapalatte. "Give me a call when you want to be picked up," she told him.

Dieter nodded before sliding out of the front seat. Figuring that he could get inside the building to plan lessons for an hour, he slipped through the annex doors, whose locks had stopped functioning years ago, and right into his classroom.

Sharp beams of morning sunlight illuminated the desks and dusty linoleum floors. Incandescence swirled around Dieter's body as he walked from the dark hallway. A warmth from some unnamable element enveloped him—it was the hug of an unseen companion that he had sometimes felt by his side but had never named. Before he could bask any longer, the furthest blind was snapped down, and the others followed like dominos.

Taking the hint, Dieter fixed himself onto his formerly cushioned rolling chair and pulled out his computer to complete an engaging lesson on six stages of moral development. Dieter had read that the theory had little real credence in the scientific community, but his students wouldn't know that. And even if they did, they wouldn't care. Dieter didn't care either. It fit his purpose.

The task was to make stages one through four (the first stage being fear of punishment and the latter stage marked by an adherence to authority and laws) seem so childish that the students would naturally resent any suggestion that they operate within that range of behavior, which was what Sanders and the staff demanded each day, of course. While stages five and six, in theory, suggested that the person's morals be shaped by justice and some undefined universal good, Dieter wanted to emphasize the idea of law-making and law-breaking as traits of truly superior citizens.

Dieter had never before felt such a singular focus. Nothing entered his thoughts but the lesson. He built each activity to perfectly satisfy both the stated objective of the lesson and the subversive plan hidden within his heart. By the time he finished his lesson plan, forty-five minutes had crept from the bottom right corner of his computer screen. Dieter gave a satisfied stretch against the back of his chair when a new screen popped up. Concerned that the previous night's carnal research had inserted a virus,

Dieter moved to shut down the computer.

A familiar voice came from the computer's speakers.

"Hey, wait! I wanted to play you some tunes."

"I need to pack up. Parade meeting in fifteen minutes."

"Put the desks in groups, like you were planning, and I'll play you some music."

"Why are you so worried about—"

"Just do it!"

Dieter raised his hands in resignation. Truth be told, he was curious as to the Devil's selection of music. Inevitably, Dieter decided, it would be Top 40 or modern country. But surprisingly, the smoky voice of a singer-songwriter created a fog of vocals that hovered throughout the room. Dieter had heard the woman's voice before in the local coffee shop: she sang songs about failed relationships and waxed seductive tracks that dared her lover to leave his partner. Dieter found the songs aesthetically pleasing enough, so he worked along with the melody.

He had pushed the last desk in place when he sensed a change in the room's pressure. Had the door opened? He glanced behind him and discovered the unmistakable frame of Esther outlined on the door. Surprise spread across her face.

"I never would have pegged you as someone who would listen to Adeline." Ester shifted on her feet and brushed aside a strand of her straightened hair.

Dieter's chest fluttered. "What music did you imagine me listening to?"

Esther froze in embarrassment. "I guess I don't really know you like that."

They stood silent for a moment, eyes searching the floor for some natural transition to another talking point. Esther found something first.

"Going with groups? That's a tough set-up to manage."

Dieter nodded again. "I think it might help our struggling students, especially the ones with disabilities, like Miguel and Angie."

Esther's eyes widened. "You're one of the first teachers at this school who is actually trying to accommodate our students with IEPs. I would never have expected you—" A blush saturated her cheeks.

"That's two things you didn't expect from me," Dieter interjected through a smile. Celestial comfort crept into Dieter's body, but the loud clang of the doors to the annex snapped them out of their reverie.

"Uh, I better get going," Esther began.

"Yeah, me too."

Esther's straight brown hair fell from her loose ponytail before she hastily tied it back into place. When she turned toward the annex doors, Dieter couldn't help but take a long drag from the view of her backside, holding it in for later. A small pocket of guilt ballooned within him.

As he stood alone, encased within warmth and heat, Adeline continued to sing: "You've got a hold on me, Dieter. You're so smooth. Like a job transfer, you make me move."

Dieter shook his head violently.

"That was terrible."

The Devil's voice replaced Adeline's.

"Yeah, but you were great!"

Dieter smiled. It was the most significant exchange he'd ever had with Esther during the course of their eleven-year history. And the Devil had laid the foundation. Dieter noted this truth, and counted it as vindication for the path he had chosen. As he moved toward the doors, he whistled one of Adeline's signature tracks, ready for any annoyance the day would inevitably bring.

———

A sea of Boy Scouts, Miss Reading contestants, and decorated flatbeds filled the parking lot. The town's firetruck tested its lights and sirens while the Scouts jumped and hooted in appreciation. All the pageant contests surrounded the lone float that they would stand upon, eyeing their spot on the tiered, sky blue papier-mâché cake. Nearby, a collection of fez-wearing men sat in tiny race cars, ogling the dolled-up, younger women. One especially fired up old man revved his engine and grinned with appreciation.

Even amongst the many distractions, Dieter located Reading High School's float. As art teacher, Jose had been drafted to head the project. During their recent workouts, he had talked excitedly about the design: a model of the school, four feet high. Out of the circle a papier – mâché sculpture of Gretel would stand proudly, her signature goofy smile bared to the audience. She would have her arms extended with a banner that read: "Reading High School: 80 years of servicing your kids." Dieter didn't have the heart to tell Jose the difference between "servicing" and "serving" since by the time Jose divulged the plan, he had intonated that he was already finished lettering the sign.

So, there was Gretel, hovering over the crowd, with inadvertent innuendo raised for all to see. Besides that, however, the float was impressive, especially since Jose had had only two weeks' notice and nobody else to help him.

The three schools in Reading alternated participation in the parade each year. Since the elementary school had marched in the previous year's parade, it was the task of the middle school to plan this year's float. However, the organizers had told the high school administrators that the middle school had backed out at the last minute, and Sanders was incredibly eager to take over. In fact, he seemed to have anticipated the opportunity.

As Dieter approached the float, he realized that all the teachers wore red t-shirts with a large white box on the front and the slogan that read "Sanders for Mayor" emblazed in bright blue. Underneath the box, the words "Purity, Promise, Pride" were cast in a threatening block font.

Though Sanders assumed the job of principal full-time, the Mayoral position in Reading was technically a part-time position. Per the village charter, the Mayor needed to log at least ten hours a week in office, in addition to running board meetings twice a month. Since school let out at 2:30, Sanders could theoretically carry both jobs. It remained to be determined if he could adequately perform both. In his mind, though, this presented him another opportunity to assume ascendency over other people. And the additional salary was equally enticing.

Before Dieter could catch it, a large red campaign shirt hit him in the face. Pulling it away, he looked for the culprit. In front of him stood Manley with his teeth exposed in savage pleasure. Esther hid behind him.

"Miguel's family had to pick an entire field of cotton for that shirt. Don't lose it."

Dieter couldn't quite tell, but he thought (reflecting later that night as he prepared for bed) that he had seen Esther turn her eyes downward in shame.

───────────

When the parade began, the teachers formed a circle around the float. Dieter hoped to walk with Esther since he now had three things he could talk to her about besides their shared years at Reading. He could talk about Adeline, about students with IEP's, or about his burning love for her. However, she walked next to Manley, and Dieter was stuck parading with Jose, who recounted the facts of the float: how he created the frame of the building, the struggles of capturing a cartoon pretzel with only paper and glue, the amount of water he'd consumed while working on it, and the help he'd received from his father. Dieter nodded and mumbled, but his eyes remained focused on the hand-holding couple walking at the front of the pack.

Initially the teachers ambled along Reading Road as Sanders zig-zagged the sidewalks, shaking hands and courting potential voters with his crooked smile. The Boy Scouts tossed candy by the fistful, creating a rocky trail of Tootsie Rolls and Jolly Ranchers. Children darted into the street to grab loose pieces of candy while parents double-checked their phone calendars for their next dentist appointment.

Young families sat at the beginning of the route since it was there that the kids could collect the most candy. The older folks and teens gathered at the end of the route, where the parade would reach the festival grounds near City Hall. As they neared the parade's midpoint Dieter noticed the crowd growing curiously hostile.

It started with a small click. Then sporadic splatters resounded on the pavement. Dieter realized that rather than candy being thrown toward the audience, members of the audience threw candy toward them, and the candy falling around the teachers was directed at the pretzel directly to his left. In a unified movement, he stopped walking and pulled Jose back with him. Jose looked at Dieter's right hand clenched around his arm and grinned.

"Divo, what a grip you have!"

After Jose's quip, they stopped and watched the barrage against Gretel at a safe distance from the float. Other teachers were not as fortunate. Hard candies caught them in the temple, against the chin, or on the nose. They turned, bewildered, like injured animals searching for predators. Eventually, they herded in front of the float or behind it. This opened a clear path to Gretel, which pushed more members of the parade audience to assail the pretzel.

Former and current students took aim at the pretzel with zeal. Jeers of "bitch" and "gringa" rained over the papier-mâché. A rainbow of wrapped candies rained against Gretel in rhythmic droves, pattering like hail. It wasn't until they reached the stretch of elderly citizens that the teachers could safely continue their march.

As the parade crept to its endpoint, a few teachers had welts on their heads and hands. They commiserated with each other on their poor luck, finding solace in mutual pain as they waited for their leader so they could leverage their wounds into appreciation for their sacrifice.

But Sanders was unscathed and unaware. From the first half-mile onward, he was ever more distant from the Reading High School contingency. Ignorant and blissful, he had submerged himself within the crowd of white, elderly citizens, schmoozing until the very last float had passed.

Dieter and Jose followed the convoy to the entrance of Mueller Park, which was adjacent to City Hall, where like a bridal procession they split off from the grinning pastry and onto a field covered by white and red-striped tents. The festival's activities would not start for another two hours, but since the Reading High School staff had also volunteered to work at various stations, they had to finish setting up. Dieter hoped he'd be paired with Esther at the dunking booth, but again the situation had been rigged to pair her with Manley. Dieter was assigned the deep fryer with Jose.

"What do we need to do to get set-up?" Dieter asked. Manley had picked up the hose to fill up the dunk tank and playfully sprayed a little on Esther. Esther shrieked in flirtatious feigned fury. When she went to wrestle the hose away, Manley pulled her into a tight embrace and prolonged kiss.

Jose's hand clasped Dieter on the shoulder and wielded him toward the cart. "We need to get the frozen food from City Hall, carry it to the freezer in the cart, load up the condiments, set up the utensils, get change, preferably in one dollar and five dollar increments, and heat up the oil. I'll start wiping down the counters."

Two hours of prep went by quickly, which Dieter appreciated since it took his mind off the object of his infatuation. Jose test-cooked a funnel cake before the fair officially opened, so Dieter sat with him in the doorway and ate the sugar-coated treat.

"You know, Dieter, they aren't going to work out in the long run."

Dieter had just shoved a large piece of cake into his mouth. His puffy cheeks and bulging eyes were the only response he could produce. Because it would take a solid minute of chewing before he could respond, Jose continued unabated.

"She's looking for commitment and validation. It's hard to be a twenty-something, educated woman in Reading. And him—he's trying to deny his age. Eventually they'll figure out that they are in different places with different purposes."

Dieter's jaw ached from frenzied chewing. He wanted to protest. How did Jose know that Dieter was pining for Esther? Was it that obvious?

"Dieter, if you simply wait and just continue to be yourself around her, you'll find that she'll be available soon enough, and it'll give you time to figure yourself out, too, so you can be available for her."

Only a few more moments of agonized masticating until Dieter could defend himself, but Jose gave Dieter a quick pat on the shoulder and walked back into the trailer. As soon as he entered the mobile kitchen, he poked his head back out.

"I'm going to start working out in the mornings. You should join me."

Though Dieter had been chewing for some time, the funnel cake seemed to be the same consistency as when he'd started. His head nodded in an attempt to push the food down his throat. If only he could say no...

"Great! See you Monday morning. Why don't you work the fryer, and I'll man the front."

Dieter coughed powdered sugar.

"Okay."

––––––––––

For four hours Dieter dipped flour-caked treats into the boiling oil. Each time he grabbed the basket handle, golden droplets scorched his wrists. And in the already humid afternoon, the added heat from the fryer left his shirt clinging to his skin. He didn't know where the funnel cakes came from, but Jose brought him a new batch as soon as those in the fryer were finished cooking.

They cooked so many extras that Jose packed a bagful of funnel cakes for himself. With a whistle and a smile, he said to Dieter, "Let nothing be wasted. Help me give these to the less fortunate?"

Dieter wanted nothing more than to take a cold shower and wallow in air conditioning until school began on Monday morning, so he declined Jose's invitation before he stumbled into the blinding sun.

The drink tent was next to the fryer. A Chemistry teacher with neutral feelings toward Dieter managed the booth, so Dieter decided to slip into the back and take a bottle of water. But when he bathed his arm in the cooler for too long, a frown formed on his peer's face. Dieter slowly withdrew his arm, along with his concern: she would become yet another teacher under his control once the Devil had worked his plan.

Motivated by the vision of his air-conditioned room, he weaved through the crowd, giving awkward nods of acknowledgment to students who were suddenly acknowledging him. While the beating sun and unfamiliar social spotlight made him uncomfortable, he found a growing happiness rising within him. It lasted until a voice barked at him from behind a chain-link cage.

"Burro! Burrrrrrrrrooo!" A loud braying followed the catcalling.

Manley sat perched on a bench above a full tub of water. A metal pole with a red bulls-eye stretched out like an arm. Esther stood in the foreground with softballs in her hands.

"Show us what you're made of, Dieter. I'll bet you can't hit the target." Manley's eyes squinted in an attempt to draw Dieter near.

A few teens looked on as Dieter froze.

"C'mon, don't be chicken. The money goes to our school, remember?" Manley called out. Dieter rubbed his head as he glanced at the ground.

"Uh…I got to go."

"C'mon, burro! It's all good fun."

Esther smiled at Dieter, but her smile vanished when Manley began to rattle the cage and resumed braying and snorting. Soon a crowd formed around the spectacle. Esther's voice temporarily cut through the noise.

"Dieter, you can have two free throws, if you'd like."

Dieter turned to Esther, whose eyes scoured the ground at Dieter's feet as Manley's barnyard noises intensified. In the periphery, Dieter could see Miguel laughing and pointing at him.

"I'm not much of an athlete," Dieter alibied.

Esther leaned toward him. "If you lob one, I'll stand near the target and push it anyway. He needs to cool off."

Dieter and Esther locked eyes as they chuckled. Manley leaned back and took a labored breath before growling. "What's wrong Vogel? Not used to big balls?"

Esther's head shot round to her middle-aged boyfriend, who

was taunting a fellow teacher with the language of a teenage boy. Since the beginning of summer, when they had started dating, she had never seen him act in such an immature manner.

Miguel was openly guffawing, too. A couple of the other teens licked their lips at the taste of the barbarism. But most of the spectators simply eyed the situation in confusion. Some were older citizens who had known Dieter since he was a little boy. Others were parents of students who vaguely recognized his face from various school functions and report card pick-ups. Some fellow teachers also watched; they alternated between curiosity at how Dieter would respond and vague discomfort at the intensity of Manley's goading.

"C'mon, Burro! I'll bet you a case of Twinkies that you can't get anywhere near that target."

Dieter took a half-step toward the table, but stopped. He was beyond uncomfortable now: the heat outside and the anger inside made his stomach churn. Manley wasn't wrong. It would take a miracle to hit the metal circle, which now stood like a demonic eye, hypnotizing him with its mocking red pupil. Esther hissed "stop it" to Manley, who shrugged.

"It's for the kids. Don't you support the kids, Burro? Burrrrrooooooooo!"

He rolled his r's with the mocking force of a tank barreling over the ground below it. A buzz tickled Dieter's pocket. He thought he had turned his phone off, but the phone continued to vibrate forcefully.

"Eee-ah! Eeeeeee-aahhhhhhhh!" Manley again rattled the cage.

Dieter looked at his pulsing phone. He did not recognize the number, but the message calmed him almost instantly. After reading it, he coolly slid the phone back into his pocket and stepped to the table.

"You sure you want to do this?" Esther whispered.

Dieter nodded resolutely.

"Good! Now we can finally see what a donkey throwing a softball looks like!"

Esther turned to Manley as he spoke. Meanwhile, Dieter shifted the ball from his left hand to his right and then back to his left.

He couldn't remember which hand was his throwing hand, but through a ball-handling activity of a different kind, he figured it was probably his right hand, so he grabbed it again with his right.

He took a long look at the bullseye. The crowd looked on, and Manley sucked in his gut to prepare for another round of abuse.

"You couldn't hit your mother's fat—"

Dieter had no idea how he put so much velocity on the ball. The whizz of the throw ended with a sharp metal clang as the soft-ball crashed into the fence directly in front of Manley's face. The surprise of the throw and the momentary forgetfulness that there was a protective barrier in front of him jerked Manley's body as he attempted to duck the flying object zooming toward his head. Due to the slipperiness and narrowness of the bench, he tumbled forward. The futile attempt to slow his downward fall only added to the comedy of his face smacking against the metal links while his body plopped into the cool water. Esther and Dieter smiled savagely at the wet, wounded man.

Not wanting to give Manley time to resume the insults, Dieter quickly moved into the crowd past stunned staff members. As he strode past a series of congratulations from random students and adults, he pulled out his phone to text a thank-you to the person with a 776 area-code for helping him give Manley exactly what he deserved. Judging by the previous week's events, he knew exactly to whom the message was going.

———

Fireworks exploded in the distance. Dieter strolled out of his bathroom, smacking his lips after a long yawn. The taste of toothpaste remained on his tongue. The moment he resolved to get a glass of beer to counteract the taste of fluoride, a glass of water appeared on his nightstand.

"Drink from the water I give you and you won't thirst," a tiny voice said from somewhere in Dieter's collection of figurines.

He didn't turn around though the sound was deeper than Satan's typically nasal voice. Dieter figured it was due to whatever manifestation Satan had assumed that night. Surprisingly, he was indifferent to Satan's presence in his life, if not grateful, and he even found himself comfortable during the Devil's visits and various appearances. It had become a guiding light in his life, even if it pushed him to change stubborn habits. His teaching had greatly improved. His body felt more energized. His relationship with Esther had blossomed. He had saved an extra two hundred dollars by not eating out. And today, for the first time ever, he had defeated Manley.

Dieter drank the water.

After Dieter set the alarm for 7:30, he considered that perhaps the Devil had been given a bad rap all these years. Satan certainly wasn't asking for anything dastardly from him; if anything, he was enriching Dieter, not undermining him. Besides, God hadn't interceded in his life up to this point, and He certainly hadn't intervened during these past couple of weeks, so it seemed to Dieter as if Satan were the only being, mortal or divine, to take an interest in his lowly, pathetic life.

His head flopped onto the pillow as distant explosions died away, and his mind melted into the fantasy world of unrestrained power, and of Esther's unbridled love.

Chapter 5

IT SEEMED HE had only begun his courtship of Esther in Willy Wonka's candy-filled world when the loud blare from his alarm pierced the soft-rush of the chocolate waterfall and the approaching marriage vows, over which the now friendly Toucan Sam presided (the vile Colonel Sanders was nowhere to be seen). Dieter's fingers walked along the faux-wood top, wandering for the snooze button until he realized his alarm clock was no longer there.

Groaning, he sat up on his elbow and looked around the room. Using his hearing like a bat, he surmised the alarm was hidden six feet away on his bookshelf behind anthologies of Shakespearean dramas and comedies. Those books were flanked by figurines, old comics, a handful of graphic novels, and a model of the Death Star. Walking over to the bookshelf and removing those texts and collectibles just to hit snooze was too complicated. He shook his head and lay down again. He didn't care that he had resolved to work out in the mornings. His bed was comfortable and his body content.

"Gooooooood morning, Diet-nam!"

"Damn you," Dieter grumbled as he shifted his body to face away from his bookshelf.

"Dieter—Dieter—Dieter—Dieter," the Devil's voice mimicked the alarm.

Dieter pulled the pillow over his ears.

In response, the Devil-controlled radio flipped to an accordion-accompanied Spanish song. The jumble of unfamiliar words and festive instrumentation annoyed Dieter enough to shoot up and scream. "Damnit, I'm awake!" He rubbed the 'sleepers' from his eyes and grumbled. "What time is it?"

"Itttttt's time to work out, fatty!" Satan responded in the voice of a popular morning DJ.

"Ass," Dieter whispered as he pushed himself out of bed.

He took two groggy steps toward the bathroom when his feet tripped over a bulky gym bag. Dieter stumbled a few more steps before he grabbed the wall for support.

"Gym bag is on the floor, packed for the day with work clothes and lunch," the Devil exclaimed with the perky voice of the radio station's weather girl.

"Thanks, Mom," Dieter mumbled.

"Hey," the Devil replied as Dieter slammed the bathroom door to pee, "I'm not *that* evil."

Ten years ago, before the opening of Seven Summits, the private school just five miles down Reading Road, a significant victory in the polls had given Reading an influx of money. Bolstered by passionate parental advocacy and the enthusiastic support by a popular national news figure who'd grown up in Reading, the taxpayers voted to approve Reading High School: Levy 13, which allocated five million dollars for new "facilities" and ten-thousand dollars for new science textbooks. The new science books replaced the ones that had been in use since the 70's, since the time the school had become the flagship for desegregation.

It was desegregation, ironically, that caused the current rift between the minority and white communities.

The predominately German community of Reading had built strong schools, from kindergarten to high school, which contained the best resources, drew the best teachers, and infused itself with a community of like-minded conservative families willing to do whatever it took to support education.

In Lincoln Heights, the community next to Reading, the all-black schools were similarly successful but with inferior facilities and resources. Their educational success was also built on community. Brilliant minds born and cultivated in the community staffed the schools. The administration stood as steadfast examples of success for the youth to admire. Staff members were mentors that could relate to every bump in the road the students would face. And the teachers still lived in the community.

But all that changed with desegregation. Black families soon found that "integration" did nothing to fix inequality: in fact, it created deeper injustice and widened the achievement gap. Desegregation would only work if the two sides built a school at the intersection of geography, history, and culture. But the process favored the white families in Reading.

The formerly all-black schools were closed, and the families had to find transportation to Reading. At first, the system appeared to be successful, but as the years passed, the black students had more misunderstandings with faculty as they were cast with lower expectations while being forced to travel to a community that was not their own. The honors classes were predominately white, and the teachers were of the same hue. The black students began to act out in frustration, grades dropped, and a cycle of educational disparity ensued.

White families blamed black families for making their kids' education suffer even though students all across the country were becoming lethargic and distracted. When rezoning merged the two communities, the white families began to blame the black families for pushing out jobs and bringing in crime, though it had been globalization that had moved the engine plant and its jobs to Mexico, not indigenous black families.

To further the tension, Latino families were moving to the outskirts of Reading, adding to the school's population as well as the racial tension. Most of the white families retreated up the hill, where favored zoning filtered their kids into the tax-rich, almost all-white Hilltop High School.

Except for the temporary resurgence of pride in the community, which allowed for a new gym and new science textbooks, insensitivity and ignorance plagued the culture and climate of Reading High Scholl.

But at least the gym had a nice weight room.

———

Dieter's hand groped the dark concrete wall as he walked cautiously down the steps to the entrance. A series of grunts, which would have seemed to be sexual in any other context, echoed off the walls. The rattling sound of the weights clattered through the cracked windows. Had Dieter never met the Devil, then he would have imagined that he was descending into Satan's bedroom, but as a result of his experience so far, Dieter couldn't imagine the Devil as anything other than a whiny teenage virgin.

At the bottom of the stairwell, a sign welcomed Dieter to the gym: *Leave excuses at the door.* He pulled open the door and a rush of humid, sweaty air smacked him in the face. Jose's overly enthusiastic voice added in the pre-dawn assault.

———

"Hey, Divo! You made it!"

"I thought I'd take you up on your offer," Dieter responded unenthusiastically.

"Super! Get warmed up and I'll meet you at the bench press." Dieter forced a smile as he pulled off his sweatshirt.

He looked over at the pull-up bars, where Manley fluidly lifted himself from the ground to the bar, and then back down again. He did fifteen pull-ups effortlessly and grunted his way through another ten. With a graceful dismount, Manley bent over and grabbed his gallon jug of water. His arms poked out from a sleeveless, gray sweatshirt.

Tiny blue athletic shorts fell limply against his ridge-lined thighs. His molded calves rose into a tight ball when he turned and walked toward the free weights. In the mirror, he saw Dieter watching him.

"What are you looking at, creep?" he snarled at the reflection.

The aggressiveness didn't surprise Dieter. Manley had, after all, just been embarrassed by the staff pariah.

Dieter responded with an apathetic shrug. He pulled his sweatpants back up, though, in unconscious intimidation. At the opposite end of the gym, Jose danced along the bench press, sliding the weights after each rock of his hips.

"Spot me, Divo?" Jose asked as he slid onto the padded bench.

Dieter walked to the apparatus and watched as Jose pushed the bar off the supports. Jose lifted his legs horizontally off the ground and pumped out fourteen rapid successions. For as tiny as the man was, his strength and agility were remarkable. He was like an ant lifting ten times his body weight. And as he jumped off the bench to spot Dieter, he darted like a hummingbird.

"Your turn…"

Dieter looked apprehensively at the weight.

"You can do it! I'm here for you."

Dieter slumped under the weight of uncertainty and Jose's perky supervision. His hands crept along the bar. Finding the grooves in the metal, he jutted his chest up to lift the weight off the stand. The bar collapsed onto his chest, forcing him to push it off with a groan.

Again, the bar dropped, and again he pushed it up. He did this two more times with the shaded face of Jose hovering over him and whispering, "You got it, Divo!"

After his final rep, they switched positions.

"How's the school year going for you, Divo?" Jose asked.

Dieter paused before responding, choosing to watch Jose pump out twelve more repetitions. "Fine, I guess."

"Your kids seem really excited about your classes," Jose said as he bounced from the machine.

"That's good," Dieter responded. Jose coaxed him back onto the bench.

"Yeah, they're all charged up after your class. They've become quite aware of their racial identities. I was wondering why there was such hostility during the parade."

Jose lifted the bar so that Dieter had to support the weight on his own. Dieter's arms shook violently from the load of the bar and the fear that he might be foiled before his plan gained more momentum.

"Well, whatever the reason, it's time that the students took an interest in their school, even if misdirected at a harmless mascot."

The burden was now unbearable. Dieter lay hopeless with the bar on his chest as Jose continued his analysis. "But I wonder if the students might try a more civilized approach to changing things. Perhaps a petition drafted by student government. I understand that they're covering the Declaration of Independence in Mr. Lee's class this week…"

"Humph," Dieter gasped.

"Sorry, Divo!"

With one quick pull, the weight was lifted.

"Okay, let's do some squats!"

———————

Dieter's first period juniors quivered with suppressed energy.

"What do you do if someone mistreats you?"

Hands shot up, forming a dancing field of tan and brown stalks. Dieter decided to point to students quickly for rapid-fire answers.

"Fight."

"Let my hands fly."

"Knuckle-up."

"Write passive-aggressive posts on social media in the hope that they will feel guilty for what they are doing!"

This elicited laughter from the students.

"White kids," Andre mumbled as he shook his head laughing.

Dieter, suppressing a smile, began his walk around the room. His head rotated with each step, touching each student with his vision.

"Fighting is, of course, our natural-instinct. It is the ultimate response, especially in the face of injustice. Truly level 6."

The students grinned in pride. Level 6. The top of morality.

"But!" Dieter paused for dramatic emphasis, letting his transition tantalize for a second, "fighting without thinking first is animalistic behavior."

The students were hushed.

"You see, our Founding Fathers fought—"

"The Romans!"

"Close, Miguel, close."

Miguel eased back into his seat, slightly ashamed but still engaged.

"They fought the British. But before they fought, they crafted one of the most powerful documents in the history of civilization..."

"The emasturbation proclamation?" Miguel asked.

Dieter shook his head.

"No? It must have been the Prostitution, then," Miguel proposed.

"...The Declaration of Independence..."

The students nodded.

"You see, before the war, it was important to explain why they were fighting, because it showed that they had good reasons to fight. It told the British that what they were doing was wrong, and if they wouldn't fix it, then they would have no other choice but to fight."

The students again nodded their heads.

"If you, as students, find that something is wrong, then you need to craft a document that is signed by all and states your grievance."

"And what if they don't listen to us?" Maria interjected.

Dieter smiled and winked. "Then you do what our Founding Fathers did."

"Buy slaves?" Miguel baited as the others laughed.

Dieter held up his hand and the students quieted on cue. "You start a revolution."

The document, crafted during the next student council meeting was a perfect imitation of the Declaration itself. Jose, the moderator of student government, was sanding a table he had been restoring after school. His detached adult presence in the room allowed for a flow of untapped creativity and collaboration among the five-person council.

Maria and her friend Angie led the process. They grabbed extra copies of the Declaration of Independence from History class, and, with the help of the other members, found moments to substitute their own ideals and grievances. While the English teachers would have given the document a zero, citing clear, unabashed plagiarism, the critical thinking that went into the select changes was exemplary.

On Friday, Maria printed the finished copy in the lab and circulated during breakfast and lunch. Students had to sign a fifth sheet of paper for their signatures to be included. Before the final bell rang, they taped the finished document, with the signatures alongside it, to the wooden doors at the front entrance (a touch, Dieter later learned, Maria picked up from last year's World History lesson on Martin Luther).

The administration had no idea that the declaration existed until a crowd of students formed around the doors. Sanders, visibly exhausted by the various election meetings and candidate photo-ops he'd been prioritizing over running the school, stomped out from his office.

"What's going on? Why are you loitering?" Sanders barked.

The students parted a path for him to approach the bold proclamation.

"What is this?" he growled.

The document was titled, *Declaration of Student Independence.*

Sanders began to read aloud: "It becomes necessary for one student body to solve the problems that divide them...we hold these truths to be self-evident...students are endowed by the District with certain Rights...That whenever the form of a School becomes destructive, it is the Right of the Student to challenge it, and to choose a new mascot that best represents the student body."

Having read enough to spike his blood pressure, Sanders pawed at the door. After an emphatic turn to the crowd, he theatrically balled up the documents and stormed back to his office with the disregarded student grievances in his hand. The only physical vestiges of the Declaration were the taped corners that remained on the door. The students silently turned toward each other, and with unified resolve pulled out their phones to inform the rest of the students via social media about what had transpired, about how the administration had disregarded the students' opinions, about the opening salvo fired by the adults in the building.

Friday marked the symbolic beginning of the revolution. The actual battles would commence on Monday.

————————

Dieter, at the suggestion of the Devil, convinced Maria to make a copy of the original student Declaration before she posted it. Over the weekend, Dieter printed out dozens of copies at a commercial copy center. Esther was also there.

"Lesson plans?" Esther said as she walked from across the store to Dieter's copier.

"Something like that," Dieter said, shifting himself slightly to hide the flow of rebellion being printed behind him. "You?"

"Color-coded accommodation guides to give to teachers with students on my case-load. Plus, I have to print all the reports from previous years that I had to pry from the district. And I have to print out Miguel's new behavior plan. That kid keeps me busy."

"He's a handful."

The two teachers stood in silence. Esther brushed aside her hair and lifted her hand in a wave. "See you tomorrow?"

"Sure…"

Esther backed away, but stopped when a sudden urge compelled her to speak: "Dieter, I'm sorry about the way that Paul treats you." Dieter smiled in acknowledgement. "I'm trying to change it."

With that, she waved and went back to her task.

————————

On Monday morning Dieter skipped his workout with Jose to

post the fliers in the various bathrooms throughout the school, and when he was sure there were no witnesses, on walls and lockers throughout the building. Dieter did not hang the document right outside Sanders' office or in the gym because those were the only places that had security cameras.

When the first students arrived at school a full thirty minutes before Sanders or Manley, they found the posted Declaration, which reminded them of the events they had temporarily forgotten during the weekend. They talked excitedly in whispers. Plans were made and resolutions passed. The insurgence sprang into action.

The battle for Reading High School began with bathroom graffiti. In the handicapped stall of the bathroom by the annex, which provided the largest canvas for delinquent da Vincis, couplets and comics sullied the faded brown walls. The vandalism varied in profanity and complexity, but the subject was unanimous: Gretel.

"*Not to be rude, not to be boorish, but Gretel the Pretzel is salty and whorish*" was written right below a large penis sketch, which had adorned the stall since Miguel's first year. His anatomical renditions had been quite rudimentary at that time; his phallic portraits had since evolved.

On the opposite wall, someone had written a poem exhibiting a more base humor involving Gretel being covered by somebody's "musturd." An image of Gretel being sodomized by a personified popcorn ball hovered right above the toilet paper dispenser. And these were just in the men's bathroom by the annex. Dieter imagined that more drawings and slogans adorned the stalls and the walls in the five other men's restrooms throughout the building.

Desks lost their place as posting-boards for self-promotion. Instead, they became signs of the resistance. Various attacks against Sanders were carved into the wooden desks or permanently marked onto the plastic ones. Teachers who dared to favor Gretel were also targeted in the verbal vitriol, which continued well into October.

In their classrooms, snarky comments about the school preceded discussions on content. Misbehavior became more prevalent. Icy insubordination soon followed.

If the teachers had simply listened to the students when they expressed dissatisfaction, then the defiance would have dissipated within a matter of weeks. Instead, most of the teachers antagonized the students with contemptuous denunciations of the students' opinions. Supercilious speeches about selfish, scatter-brained Millennials replaced fruitful class discussions.

Disdain from the adults pushed the students to further rebellion. During Homecoming Week (the time of the year when schools express their de facto prioritization of a single sport) the students refused to don Reading High School spirit-wear. The football players even "forgot" to wear their uniforms to class on that Friday. When asked, they simply said, "We don't rep a pretzel."

While Gretel was still the primary focus of student activism, Dieter's lessons on race catalyzed a growing consciousness of racial history, however misguided it was. A poster in Mr. Lee's class was found torn into pieces in the middle of the lunch room. Its crime was that it innocuously juxtaposed the Confederate flag next to a map of the various battles of the Civil War.

In a science class, the students disrupted so frequently that the teacher had to drop the lesson completely. The content, which in previous years had been successful in piquing student interest, was "black holes." The class repeatedly asked, "Why do they have to be black?" Miguel even withheld a joke about being more partial to brown holes.

The disruptions and subversive vandalism kept Gretel in the mouths of the students, though her contested existence floated outside the concern of the administration. On the last Thursday in October, the student council officially voted to remove Gretel from her place as the school mascot: a mostly meaningless gesture since the student council was merely a mock government that would be ultimately overruled by the administration. More significant, however, the council printed out ballots that would be given out on Election

Day, the day on which Sanders had been singularly focused for the entire first quarter—the reason the students' desecration of the school had gone unaddressed—the reason the students' movement had gained traction for almost two months—the reason the students' fires of insurrection would be nearly impossible to extinguish.

Chapter 6

"SIR, HE WAS killed by his *friends*. How great could he have been?" Val asked.

Dieter had spent the first half of the hour proclaiming the greatness of Shakespeare's play, *Julius Caesar*. But for the pesky questioning by this future Ivy-league student, he felt he had nearly stirred the emotions of everyone in the class to the point that they might rush out the room and, short of conquering Germanic barbarians, rally behind any cause set before them. In reality, Dieter had motivated a heavier student to stir when he'd accidently said, "Caesar salad." It was a rare dud of a lesson that was engaging in theory but ineffective in practice, and Val had only made it worse.

She was a renowned momentum killer. Novice teachers love to exclaim, "Ask any question: there are no stupid questions." With lofty notions of student agency and its place in the classroom, the tenderhearted teacher would spend a semester answering every question Val posed, relevant or not. However, at the start of the second semester, those very same teachers would make it clear that questions should be tabled until the end of the lesson or written on slips of paper to be addressed the next day.

Today, whenever the students did begin to show interest in the forced similarities between Reading and the fall of Caesar, Val's concerns would certainly dilute the moment. Dieter had to find a way to quell her mutinous participation.

"Yes, he was killed by a friend. But does that betrayal fall on him? Doesn't deceit and back-stabbing happen every day?" Dieter asked.

Val's hand shot up in response, but Dieter looked beyond the orange-haired know-it-all. In the corner, he found what he was looking for: Andre, the student with the highest cultural capital at Reading, was sitting up and looking moderately engaged.

"Andre, you look like you want to say something" Dieter invited.

Andre fidgeted in his seat as he prepared to speak in class for only the third time this year. "People back-stab each other all the time. Like LeBron left Cleveland. And then he shit on Miami. And, when KD left OKC, he shit on Westbrook. People look out for number one, know what I mean?"

Val displayed her disbelief at Andre's language choice with a high pitched "Huh!" Dieter ignored her dog-like yip and Andre's "shit." Miguel had perked up at the use of profanity. Other students turned to the basketball star.

"And were those betrayals egregious?" Dieter probed.

Andre pursed his lips in confusion and turned his head sideways like a flustered puppy.

"Why was *The Barn* leaving Cleveland bad?" Dieter tried again. The students hated when teachers patronized them. But Andre was too involved in the conversation to care.

"I don't know if it was bad. I mean, LeBron just trying to get as many championships as MJ. No reason to hate on that. He came back anyway, know what I mean?"

"Yes, I do know what you mean," Dieter replied. Normally he would have shot a sarcastic comment about the use of "know what I mean," but Dieter had a sinister purpose, one that did not find reason to nip at Andre's oration, one that prioritized student engagement and learning over petty criticism.

"Andre, do you ever want to *crap on someone?*"

Andre, annoyed at Dieter's terrible attempts at cultural connection, glared at his teacher before Dieter realized his mistake.

"Sorry… What I mean is, do you ever want to switch teams or betray something or someone?"

Andre, content that Dieter had learned his lesson, responded, "We have a lame-ass pretzel as a mascot. How embarrassing is that?" Andre was becoming more passionate. "Our uniforms have the word Pretzel on them! Why would anyone want my high school jersey after I go pro?"

Dieter's stomach somersaulted in joy, as more students tracked Andre's words.

"Teachers got all these stupid rules. After this year, I finna leave this place and go to a real school for my senior year," Andre asserted.

The rest of the class murmured in agreement.

"See me after class," Dieter replied. "I have an extra credit assignment for you."

The students had stirred with interest, but only minutes later returned to a semi-comatose state, except for Val, who stewed at the mention of an extra credit assignment in which she was not included. She returned to writing in her notebook, stopping occasionally to highlight random words and phrases, even though Dieter wasn't speaking.

"What in the world are you taking notes about?" Dieter asked.

Val looked up in confusion, so Dieter went back to his lecture, and Andre went back to sleep.

———————

"Andre, what up?"

Dieter's choice in uncharacteristic slang temporarily took Andre by surprise.

"Um…nothing…"

"So I saw you got interested in what I was sayin'. Yo, I feel ya!" Andre grimaced.

Dieter, remembering what happened moments earlier, turned back from the affected persona. "We can fix this problem. You might not need to transfer." Dieter said, "You carry some weight at this school."

Andre jumped back and stammered, "I don't know whatchu mean! I don't do nothing like that here. I only got a small bag, and that's for re-creational purposes."

"Small bag? What? Never mind, look, you are the most popular student at this school," Dieter said.

Andre exhaled, relieved that Dieter didn't seem to care about his accidental confession.

"You are the star player. Coach Manley would do anything to keep you happy," Dieter observed.

"Like the time he changed my grade in Miss B's—"

"I don't need specifics," Dieter cut in. The thought of Esther being tarnished by the vile undertakings of Manley made his already growling stomach moan in angst.

"Listen, if you are unhappy with something at this school, change it. You are Brutus! You can take out the thing that is oppressing you."

The passion of Dieter's comments moved Andre.

"I can be Brutal all over this place," he exclaimed. "That pretzel's gotta go. I'm on this."

Andre extended his fist to Dieter. Unsure of what to do, Dieter high-fived the balled-up hand. Andre gave a nod before he strode from the classroom without a remembrance of Dieter's promise of some vague assignment with extra credit attached.

Dieter sat down within a euphoric bubble. Satisfaction swirled inside him. *This is what it must feel like to be a decent teacher,* he thought. He was impacting the lives of his students, and he was igniting passion and critical thinking within malleable minds. What he wanted from this profession had started to come to fruition, and he was doing it without as much guidance from—

"Well done."

The familiar devious voice slid from the copy of *Julius Caesar* on his desk. Dieter looked down, and, sure enough, the picture of Caesar on the front cover was talking to him.

"Our plans are going well," the Devil said.

"Thanks," Dieter said.

"Now you need to keep the momentum going. Today's lesson

wasn't great, and you keep getting—"

"Interrupted… I know, Val."

The possessed dictator sighed as he brought his hand from within the toga to his forehead. "Yes, Val. *She* is the interrupter. She's also quite the diversion. We need to silence her."

"I can't kill her."

"Let me finish!" Caesar scowled at Dieter. "There are other ways to silence her. She's a strong student, right? So, give her something to do. An *independent* project…"

"Perhaps something related to our *proud* German history," Dieter said, rolling his eyes.

Caesar nodded vigorously.

"German oppression in the twentieth century will be a great introduction to *Night*," the Devil added. After a nod of concordance from Dieter, the Roman leader returned to his frozen state.

All this scheming had made Dieter hungry. With a plop, he fell onto his seat and opened his desk drawer to scarf down his double cheeseburger and fries. Instead, a simple zip-lock bag filled with green grapes and edamame sat where his fast-food bag should have been.

"Your body is a temple," a muffled-voice called from inside the desk.

Dieter sighed and glared at the area from which the sound had emanated. He pulled apart the plastic and started tossing the sweet green grapes into his mouth, too distracted to be disappointed.

"Mr. Vogel, you wanted to see me?"

Dieter looked up as Val's freckled cheeks elevated into a forced smile. "Yes, Val," Dieter began as he rose from his seat. "I've noticed that you are visiting colleges already and—"

"Oh, yes, Mr. Vogel! I'm hoping to get into an Ivy League school. I've asked about GPA, test scores, essays, letters of recommendation, extracurricular activities, family history—"

For teachers, there is a great deal of frustration in dealing with students whose apathy is only matched by their affinity to problematic media like profane songs and violent video games. But there's an equally annoying student type, and Val epitomized that student.

Some of the teachers call these students "vacuums." Any morsel of extra credit, any sliver of meat for a resume, any crumb of a percentage point meant to help students on the cusp of failure, the vacuum would gobble it up before it left the hand of the teacher or administrator offering the opportunity. And even though the vacuum was already full, he or she would still suck-up without remorse.

Dieter held up his hand to stop Val's chatter.

"—and I know that colleges love letters of recommendation."

Dieter lied. He suspected the fluff that administration officers call "letters of recommendation" ranked about fifth on the list behind test scores, GPA, extracurricular activities, and class rank. Maybe even behind race and socio-economic status.

"I think I can write you an exceptional letter, and I'm willing to give you a leadership opportunity in my class that colleges would love to hear about."

Val squealed and grabbed her notebook.

"We have a unit coming up on the memoir, *Night*. What I would like you to do, Val, is to teach the class about Hitler and about the horrible things the Germans did in the concentration camps. You are, after all, a minority here, a *white* minority, so it would be powerful coming from you."

"Can I use slides?"

"Yes."

"How much time will I have?"

"It's up to you."

"Do I get extra credit?"

"Yes."

"How much?"

"Um—"

"A perfect test grade?"

"Sure."

"But that only will get me to a 98%"

"Fine."

"If only I could get more points on the group assignment I did with Miguel…"

"Fine!"

Dieter paused. Looking at Val's wide eyes, he softened his voice and began again.

"If you include plenty of pictures, I will replace that presentation."

Val shrieked in approval and bound toward the door.

"Val!"

"Yes, Mr. Vogel?"

"It'll be due a week from Monday. You have this weekend and next weekend to prepare."

"Thank you, Mr. Vogel!" She bounced into the hallway.

"One more thing, Val…"

She turned again.

"Make sure you include what Hitler did to gain power. You know, silencing and arresting the opposition. And include lots of pictures."

Val gave a compliant nod, grabbed a pen from her pocket, and wrote down the last bit of information.

Dieter's bliss from his various moving pieces carried into his afternoon workout. Jose suggested that they jog around the soccer field since they had been lifting weights in the morning. "After all, we are in the death of the fall."

Dieter agreed, noting Jose's imperfect grasp of English, which was probably due to his Mexican-American upbringing. Of course, this was speculation since Jose had never told anyone about where his family had originated. His face carried no betrayal of race or ethnicity, though his skin was dark enough to be Hispanic.

The ground crunched as they ran over divots and rocky patches of dirt that the boys' soccer team had created during a grueling season, one in which Miguel had revealed himself as a soccer stand-out. After four laps in silence, Jose spoke.

"Hey, Divo, are you going to vote next Tuesday?"

"I don't know."

Dieter could taste iron in his throat. They had been jogging for fifteen minutes, fourteen minutes longer than any run Dieter had done since high school. Repressed memories of gym class humiliation and failure, some of which had taken place on this very field, coursed through his memory. Throughout the jog, Jose stayed stride for stride with Dieter, and after half a lap, Jose continued.

"It's going to be hard to work with Sanders when he's both Principal and Mayor. I hope it doesn't affect our school."

Dieter shot Jose a glance.

"Oh, it's not a sure thing, of course. But there are still many people who are afraid of what Sanders' opponents represent. Just like what will happen with the student vote, it will be a day that doesn't truly represent the needs and wants of the people."

Dieter nodded.

"Speaking of which, would you take over student government for me? They only meet once every two weeks. I want to build some chairs for my table."

Dieter nodded again. Normally, he'd shirk any responsibility that included additional time spent at school, but since Maria was the president, he figured he could affect additional manipulating during that time.

"Perfect! Let's do five more laps, Divo!"

Just as Jose had predicted, the Reading mayoral race was a mockery of democracy. In the week before the vote, a national organization took great interest in the community of five thousand people, using their influence to thoroughly vet the candidates. An anonymous citizen created a petition which demanded a copy of the birth certificate belonging to Sanders' main opponent, Pedro Iglesias, who was a mere three percentage points behind Sanders in an October poll. The national organization, which claimed to be non-partisan, found that the candidate had questionable markings on his birth certificate, which would suggest "forgery or deliberate manipulations that would compromise the integrity of the document."

Taking these findings to court, the authenticity of the document was found to be compromised and an original proof of birth needed to be verified at the hospital in which Iglesias was born. The candidate would be withheld from the ballot until his natural citizenship could be proved. Of course, this would take months. Thus, through racism and the outdated by-laws of Reading, he became ineligible to run for office.

The only other candidate was a nineteen-year-old college freshman, who had gotten the cursory five hundred signatures from recent Reading alumni in his quest to defeat his former principal. His platform included comprehensive reform on the laws surrounding marijuana and the drinking age. And while his knowledge of infrastructure, political systems, tax codes, municipal ordinances, business development, and overall professionalism was quite limited, his social media presence garnered two hundred 'likes' on his research surrounding "The Medicinal Benefits of Primo-Ganja."

Such an outpouring of support turned him into a threat in the eyes of Principal Sanders, who shuddered at the thought of being bested by a punk kid that he had suspended twice. And while many didn't figure the nineteen-year-old to be a legitimate contender, someone called in a bomb threat to Reading's community center shortly after noon on election day, well after the time that all the senior citizens had voted, and well before the time the twenty-somethings could rouse themselves out of their hangovers, college classes, and part-time employment to vote for the charismatic candidate who promised pot and freedom from underage drinking citations.

After the dust had settled and the opposing candidate had forgotten to file a challenge to the results, Principal Sanders became

Principal/Mayor Sanders. The elderly rejoiced, the hardworking parents shook their heads, and the young adults promised to be ready for the next election before they passed out next to large, empty pizza boxes and overpriced college textbooks.

When the results were finalized that Thursday after the election, Principal Sanders sailed above the linoleum floors. The school's secretary had made a large congratulation sign above the entrance to his office and cheered enthusiastically when he entered the building. Most of the staff gave a requisite head nod and congratulations. Since most teachers lived outside of Reading, his election carried no significance to their lives as long as his new position didn't distract from his leadership at school.

The students, who now lived under Sanders' governance inside *and* outside of school, avoided looking at him. They had held their vote for mascot, but heard no word about any progress on the transition. They temporarily forgot about the movement as they awaited any sign of change. Only a few students showed a remaining desire to protest, but they were isolated.

With student behavior back to a relative norm, nothing could dampen Sanders' jubilation. Nothing, save for a frustrated Manley, who stumbled into the teachers' lounge second period.

"I don't know what the hell has gotten into Andre," he grumbled.

Sanders looked up from the newspaper article that recounted his glorious coronation. Hearing nothing, Manley continued.

"All of a sudden he thinks he doesn't have to practice. Every day it's a new thing: has to take care of his mom, has to run errands, has a *previous engagement*." He made quotations marks with his fingers as he spoke.

Sanders gave a sympathetic nod before attempting to raise the newspaper once more. But Manley didn't take the hint that the Mayor was basking in the people's mandate.

"And when I talked to him, he said he didn't need to practice since he was the best player. He had the nerve to say that maybe if there was a better team around him, we'd win more games. The punk—"

Sanders casually cut Manley off.

"Why don't you just kick him off the team?"

"He *is* the team!"

Sanders shrugged as he folded the newspaper and stood up to leave. Manley moved in front of the principal. Desperation clung to his words.

"Walt, you know he's the whole team. You even said to do whatever possible to—"

Sanders lifted his hand in acknowledgement. Jose and Father Manny had opened the door to grab their morning decaf. It was true that Sanders had said that Manley should do whatever was necessary to keep Andre happy and eligible. But now that he was Mayor, all other padding of his inadequacies became insignificant. He felt a tinge of pity for Manley. Placing all his hopes on a single, not-to-be-trusted teen... And there was chatter circulating indicating that he was becoming increasingly short with students *and* staff, including that tasty morsel that he was dating. As Principal *and* Mayor, it was now up to Sanders to be the voice of authority and reason.

"Listen, Paul, he'll come around."

Manley shook his head. Sanders knew a lost cause when he saw one, so he put on a decisive tone to mark his exit from the conversation.

"First game isn't for another three weeks. Basketball is like crack to him."

Sanders hadn't noticed Father Manny shaking his head in disgust, or the smirk on Jose's face, but Manley nodded in agreement with Sanders' consolation. Feeling like he'd appeased his first constituent, Sanders retreated to his office.

But as the door swung shut, it immediately burst open again. Esther rushed in with her eyes clenched around her prominent nose. Her hair fell from the loose bun formed on the back of her head.

"Paul," she exclaimed through tightened lips. Manley looked up. Still brooding over Andre, he didn't pick up on his girlfriend's anger. "Where were you this morning?"

Manley stared for a second, mind moving in futile fervor. "Home?"

"Wrong answer!"

As Esther turned and stormed through the door, and as Father Manny hurried his eyes into his Bible to avoid Manley's confused gaze, Jose quietly stood up. "Were you supposed to pick her up?" he asked.

The wheels in Manley's head jammed to a sharp halt, and his face flushed with guilt.

"Dieter lives down the street and saw her walking to school," Jose said, unable to contain the grin forming on his face. "She was grateful for the ride this chilly morning, though I'm sure she wasn't thrilled to be driven to school by his mom."

Manley's hands trembled around the coffee mug he was holding.

"What the hell is happening?" he whispered to no one in particular.

"So Divo, I continue to hear splendid things about your class."

Dieter could only respond with a quick "hmm" from his sweat coated lips. The treadmills whirled and their feet rhythmically pounded. Jose, who had already done pull-ups, sit-ups, and thirty minutes of running, spoke with the same clarity and energy that he carried when at rest. Furthermore, his skin was immaculate. Not a drop of sweat. Dieter, meanwhile, had sullied his light shirt with dark-gray splotches.

"Yeah, all the kids are abuzz with how much they are learning. I've never seen them recount Shakespeare with such fervor."

Dieter couldn't respond as his mouth held the acrid taste of iron and a congestive pain in his chest blocked his words.

"And they're suddenly aware of the systemic racism that surrounds them. I've heard that Val gave a stirring account of Germany and the rise of Nazism and that the freshmen are calling you Mr. Finch."

Dieter grunted. It was true that Val's extra-curricular presentation had been quite effective. Graphic pictures of Holocaust victims, along with a sweeping analysis of Nazism and Germany in the 1930s and 1940s, engendered an appropriate revulsion to Fascism, and an irrational hatred of German people on whole. Dieter made no effort to correct this over-generalization, nor did he protest being equated with Atticus Finch.

"While I don't condone some of the bathroom writing and swastikas I've seen around the school, they really have found their voices. I thought they had given up, but instead they seem to be cultivating activism. And I hear that Andre' has taken a leadership role? He's waking up to his potential. It's just too bad there's been no word on the mascot…"

Does he know something, Dieter wondered? Jose continued his workout, talking without any hint of exhaustion.

"I only wish the students could push Principal—excuse me, *Mayor*—Sanders into action. He should count it as a blessing that they don't hear some of the things he says. Just this morning he called Miguel a—"

Dieter's mind now ran at a feverish pace, mirroring Jose's verbal marathon. If only he could catch Sanders. He would gain complete control. But how?

"—and speaking of Miguel, that lovable little miscreant, I wish I could record the things he says. He's such a firecracker of wit—"

Of course… Tape-recording. But who would do it?

"—I know one student who has a small tape recorder for class. Can't remember who, but I think she's a junior. Maybe she has a 'best-of-Miguel' tape—"

The student's face and name popped like a firecracker.

"—if not, you could provoke Miguel to say some of the most wonderfully problematic things and catch them then. He makes me laugh—"

A plan materialized in Dieter's mind.

"Hey, Jose, I forgot that I had to make some copies before school starts. Gotta run."

Jose gave an understanding nod before hopping off the machine and launching into lunges. Dieter toweled his face, wiping off a wide grin in the process. He now knew how to take the revolution to a whole new level. And he knew just the person to help him do it.

—————

Angie Castillo was dyslexic.

Like the other students with Individualized Education Plans, her personhood at Reading was reduced to a ten-page report, laying bare to all her teachers and administrators her flaws and her struggles. Mandated accommodations bled through the different sections, pumping forced changes into teachers' pre-planned curricula. Test scores, psychologist evaluations, teacher comments, her years of schooling interconnected to form one simple identity contained within two words: First name, Learning; last name, Disabled.

Angie Castillo was beautiful.

She had smooth cinnamon-brown skin with a burst of blush on her checks that outlined her dimples when she smiled. Her wavy, jet-black hair and bright green eyes were exotic.

Angie Castillo was a chameleon.

Her mom was black and her dad was Puerto Rican. To the students, she was a "Mexican," but because of her disability, she struggled with reading, and she nearly flunked first-year Spanish.

Her hoop earrings, sharp confidence, and ability to code-switch from formal English to adolescent slang to informal Spanish, helped her gain an unspoken acceptance with all the students. The more confident guys would flirt with her and ask to follow her on social-media, but she rejected them with a sly, self-assured realness that left them intrigued and without hostility. The girls aspired to exude her self-assuredness, and because Angie avoided petty drama, she held the respect of most female students, whether they were white or black.

And, of course, she was readily accepted within the Latino contingency. Her fluency in Spanish allowed her to access hidden gossip and conversations. She earned approval when, in a moment of extreme frustration during sophomore year, she said *"pinche tonto"* directly to a teacher, who did not know he had just been called an idiot. He merely thought Angie was a fan of Westerns.

Her friendship with the well-respected, two-time Student Body President, Maria Lopez, further elevated her social standing and proved to be a very resourceful partnership in her educational affairs as well.

Angie Castillo was resilient.

Like many of the other students, she knew poverty. Her parents had the family stay with cousins until their low paying jobs secured them rent from a landlord who was neglectful enough to let the Castillo's mind their own lives and the decrepit property he was leasing. But the Castillo's were happy and focused on the one thing that could secure their family's future: education.

Therefore, Angie Castillo was motivated.

She arrived early to school prepared for the day. Color-coded binders for each class were well-organized with color-coded labels. Her homework sat in her binder like a crisp, obedient servant waiting to be summoned. Sharpened #2 pencils and multi-colored pens always lay neatly in the groove at the top of the desk, awaiting the random utensil preference that varied by content and teacher with little rationale. Math almost always required pencil. For Spanish, Manley required red and black pens depending on the exercise. In U.S. History, Mr. Lee hated black pens and only wanted to see red or blue ink on his white paper. And in Biology, Ms. Stewart required green pens since *green was the color of life.*

Angie's most resourceful tool, her digital recorder, was tucked inside the binder. When she came to Reading High School, she found that the teachers would no longer plan their lessons with engaging kinesthetic activities or creative projects as they had in elementary and middle school. Lessons were drilled into students from period long lectures guided by word saturated PowerPoints and double-sided handouts. Students were expected to be sponges that could discriminate between useful and useless information without training, and then disseminate those nuggets into their notes.

These unaccommodating classes, already daunting to unhindered students, were even more oppressive to students like Angie, who took longer to read and would get stuck reviewing slides and handouts when the teacher had since moved on. Though Angie advocated for help from the Special Education Department, teachers dragged their feet at the prospect of having to do more work modifying tests and notes every week.

Angie confided her struggles to her friend Maria, who, after doing as thorough research as one could do on Google, found that she could threaten the administration with a lawsuit if they did not provide for her friend. Even though she was lost on how to begin the process of suing for accommodations, the mere mention of legal recourse pushed the school to quickly find a solution that would assuage the two persistent girls but still require minimal work on their part. They assigned Esther, a first-year teacher at the time, to work with Angie personally.

With Esther working for Angie, the administration settled on a digital recorder, which would meet Angie's "special" needs and put the onus on her to review and transcribe the lectures. Angie was satisfied, and Maria backed off her threats.

Dieter walked into the lunchroom huffing since he hadn't cooled down from the gym. He had already decided how to pull Angie into his plan. He'd tell her that student activities throughout the school were waning. Challenges to authority were also declining, and since this seemed to ease tension between teachers and students, Dieter feared that the movement might die. He needed a bomb to set the students off again. And to affect Angie, he needed to show urgency.

He also needed to act natural.

"Angie, hey, how's it going? Co-mo hay-stack?"

She looked up from her math handout to see Dieter standing there soaked in sweat, still clad in his workout clothes. The long white chord of Dieter's headphones slid from his pocket. One bud was buried in his ear while the other dangled over his chest.

"Um, hey, Mr. Vogel. I'm good."

"Boo-wheno, Boo-wheno!" Dieter extended his leg to stretch his hips, causing his body to lunge and thrust. To Angie, the visual was disconcerting, as were his attempts at *Espanish*.

"I gotta go, Mr. V."

"Wait! Sorry," Dieter stiffened up, "I have a question for you." Angie stopped packing.

"How did the votes end up?"

Angie shook her head.

"Wildcats won. We gave it to the principal but we haven't heard back. It sucks. Why won't he hear us out?"

Dieter nodded in sympathy.

"It's frustrating when your voice isn't heard. If only there was a way to make him listen…"

Angie returned the nod, adding a sad drop of her eyes that revealed the resignation of her circumstance. Dieter saw his chance.

"Have you ever used that recorder for anything other than notes?"

"Like, outside of class?" she responded.

"Yeah, you know, like to interview someone, or—"

A voice in his right ear chimed in.

"*Correct someone.*"

"—correct someone?"

"Correct someone?"

"*I was just thinking…*"

Dieter scratched his chin.

"I was just thinking…"

"*you could use that recorder,*"

"…you could use that recorder,"

"*to fight back.*"

"…to fight back."

"What do you mean?" Angie responded.

"*If you can show him the errors of his ways, and then give him the grace to change—*"

Dieter pulled out the earbud.

"I saw a movie the other night where a worker caught his boss talking about cheating the company out of millions of dollars. He had a hidden video camera and used it to get the guy fired. I just wondered if you'd ever done something like that."

Angie's mouth slowly opened.

"Anyway, random thought. I just figured that I'd ask, since we'll be watching some documentaries this week." Dieter winked. Angie nodded in understanding. Before Dieter walked away, her voice turned him around.

"Oh, Mr. V, I found this in the hallway."

A gold necklace with a simple cross dangling on a chain hung from her hand. Dieter cradled it in his hand and thanked Angie for her integrity before heading to his room.

———————

As Dieter turned the annex corner, he could see Miguel talking to Esther.

"Honestly, I just wanted to ask Mr. V about homework!"

When Esther turned to Dieter's room, expecting to find Dieter sitting at his desk, an avalanche of paper cascaded from Miguel's arms onto the floor beside her. With the quick compassion of a teacher, she bent over to pick up the pile, not realizing that the papers were dropped strategically by the wall so that she would have to turn toward Miguel when she bent over.

Dieter initially felt the drop of disappointment that she had turned away from him, but then quickly realized why that was the case. And when he saw Miguel's eyes popping, Dieter stormed down the hallway.

Miguel's preoccupation hid the noise of Dieter's advance; however, the rumble from his approach drew Esther's eyes to Dieter, who was looking at Miguel with righteous anger, which caused Esther to look back at Miguel, who was now looking at her with pure lust. Before Esther could utter a single word of indignation, Dieter had already barked at Miguel.

Miguel's smile evaporated and his lip quivered as Dieter stepped between them.

"You have a lot of nerve, Miguel, especially since she's help-ing to pick up your papers," Dieter said. He didn't know how to frame the accusation of misconduct, so he hoped Miguel wouldn't fight back with denial. Fortunately, and surprisingly, Miguel's eyes dropped to the floor in guilt.

"Miss B has worked hard for you. She cares about you, and this is how you treat her?"

Miguel rocked onto his heals.

"Mr. V, it wasn't like that—"

"Miguel, whether you meant it or not, I imagine Miss B feels... disrespected."

Miguel nodded and Dieter stepped aside. With a long, deep sigh, Miguel apologized. "Miss B, I'm sorry. I didn't mean to disrespect you. I won't look at you like that again."

Esther gave an appreciative nod. Miguel turned to Dieter.

"Mr. V, I wanted to show you my paper. I worked on it for three hours last night."

"But Miguel, it's not due until next week."

"I know. I just wanted you to look at it."

Dieter lifted his hand to Miguel's shoulder. "Why don't you go into my classroom, and I'll take a look at it."

Miguel nodded. He gave Esther a remorseful wave before he walked into Dieter's room. As the door clicked shut, Dieter turned to Esther. He was about to apologize again when she stopped his words with a very unexpected hug.

"Thank you. Miguel can be a pain," Esther sighed.

Dieter felt ashamed for harboring the same thoughts that he'd reprimanded Miguel for acting upon, however he also felt relief that he had been there for Esther at such an awkward moment.

She disengaged the hug and smiled at him. At that moment, Dieter wanted to say something meaningful, but the swirling con-flict of his many desires made him divert to the mundane. "Do you know whose necklace this is?" he asked her.

Dieter held out the gold chain with the cross dangling from his hand. The fluorescent light hit the gold so that it glistened against his palms. Upon seeing the necklace, Esther exhaled. A halo of joy radiated from her face. For the second time Esther hugged him—this one lasting considerably longer than the first one.

"I can't believe you found my necklace. Thank you."

Later, after Dieter had looked over Miguel's impressive paper, he deferred to happy visions of Esther, visions unlike any that he'd had before. He wanted to become the source of her joy and comfort. He wanted to be her advocate and her friend. He wanted to connect with her meaningfully and more frequently than they had in the past.

The blue bird on his screen turned to him. With the Devil's voice, it asked: "What are you smiling at?"

"Thanks for the necklace."

The bird shook its cartoon head in confusion. "What are you talking about?"

Chapter 7

IN HIS OFFICE, Principal Sanders re-watched his victory speech. The blue, red, and white semi-circles wrapped around the walls beneath the school's stage, and the large cartoon portrait of a waving Gretel hung behind him like a loyal running mate. Mayor Sanders gave an impassioned speech about the necessity of preserving the community's roots; about how the community had grown thick and hearty with tradition; about how the branches were the voters; about how there was a growing infestation of weeds that threatened to strangle the life from this wondrous tree. The ten citizens in attendance clapped dutifully.

It was truly his finest hour.

It was also his only reprieve from the chaos that had developed within the school seemingly out of nowhere. What had started as immature heckling during the parade had turned into a treatise which had, in turn, digressed into delinquency. The vote had assuaged the students for a couple of weeks, but they were growing restless again. Students were consistently calling out in class to ask why Gretel had to be their mascot. Every day, broken eggs were found splattered against the building. Unrelated, but nevertheless concerning, freshmen were mixing up his name. While he certainly shared the leadership of the man, 'Sanders' was a far pronunciation from *Napoleon*. Perhaps they were confusing him with one of their middle school's principals? He also heard the name *Julius* whispered frequently in the hallways around him.

He clicked "play again" on the computer screen.

His scripted words soothed him once more until an email from Ms. Stewart expressed concern at the growing rebellion. She said there were gloves and goggles missing from the lab. She also said that other members of the staff had expressed concern at the state of student culture, worrying that the grumblings of the students would lead to more serious infractions if not addressed.

And they had good reason to be concerned. The students needed complete focus for the final tests. Their pre-test scores were the worst of area high schools. When a middle-school in a district across town failed, all the staff members were fired and forced to reapply for their positions. If Reading High School should fail, it was almost certain that the same fate would follow from precedence set forth. This would include leadership.

Adding to this, something was fundamentally wrong with Manley, and it affected the mulatto he was dating. She had grown quite bold in her demands for the slower students. "All they really need is a good kick in the butt, not stress balls or chairs with bike peddles attached," he grumbled after reading Esther's most recent email.

Sanders eyes wandered from the screen to last year's city championship trophy near the entrance to his office. Manley was his most loyal teacher; he had a way of keeping student and staff in check through his standing as a basketball coach—no, *successful* basketball coach. If Manley lost his touch, who knew what might happen?

He clicked 'play' again, but a knock interrupted his therapy.

"Come in," he responded with an angry click of the mouse.

The door cracked open, sending the black waves of Angie Castillo rippling into the room.

"Principal Sanders? Can I talk to you for a moment?"

"Of course," he said.

His annoyance was not lost on Angie, who paused for a moment before slipping into the room and closing the door behind her.

"I was expecting you after school for your disability meeting, Miss Castillo."

"Sorry, sir. I'm meeting with Mr. Vogel for help this morning, so I thought I would see if we could—"

"—but since you are here, I may as well discuss with you another pressing matter. Take a seat."

Sanders stood up and walked to his water cooler. Dramatically, he went silent as the blub-blub-blub from the air bubbles burst in the plastic container followed by a metallic trickle into his mug. He took a loud sip before returning to his seat.

Even though she never had problems with authority, Angie knew the non-verbal signs of disapproval. She'd frequently observed teachers about to pounce on a disruptive student, and she'd sat in on the meetings with Maria and the student council as they talked about the administration's attempts to suppress their voices.

Detrea, star linebacker and an honor roll student, told them that the security guard had searched his locker on an "anonymous tip" that he had drugs. Kelly Donnelly, the passionate ally of minorities and advocate for women's rights, complained that she wasn't permitted to post fliers for Breast Cancer Awareness Month due to her "subversive activities." And Maria told student council members about Sanders' direct threat to send negative letters to colleges and scholarship committees if she didn't speak out against the surging movement to overthrow Gretel. Maria always spoke about injustice with passion, and Angie wanted to prove she was just as committed.

"Miss Castillo, do you know that what you are doing is punishable by death?"

Angie's eyebrows gripped her nose in confusion. "What?"

"What-you-are-doing-is-punishable-by-death."

"What am I doing?"

"Treason, Ms. Castillo. Treason!" Sanders shouted with a smack on his desk for emphasis.

Angie's mouth was agape.

"What are you talking about?" Angie heard her voice edge, but she did not care.

"I know of your plot, moo hair," Sanders snarled.

"Mujer?"

"It started with the document you and that rabble-rousing president created. And now, there's madness, and you're causing it!"

"Sir, we just want a new mascot."

"And you won't get it! Gretel is a fixture at Reading. She is the proud symbol of our community. You can't come into this school after three years and think you can tear down over two hundred years of history. She *is* Reading."

Sanders' face flushed. The red spread through the dome of his head making him look like a turnip. It wasn't actually about Gretel; it was about his failing school, his dying white base, his new responsibilities, his insubordinate students: all things that were increasingly oppressive as the euphoria from his victory wore off.

Angie softened her voice. "Mr. Sanders...sir...the students are asking—"

"Principal Sanders or Mayor Sanders—"

"What?"

"It's either Principal Sanders or Mayor Sanders. I earned those titles, so you will respect them."

Angie took a deep breath.

"Okay, *Principal* Sanders. I am representing the students. We want a new mascot. We want something that represents Reading as it is today. It's diverse—"

Sanders shot up. "What about the proud German immigrants building a community with their blood, sweat, and fears!"

"You mean 'tears?'" Angie smiled at his mistake.

"I meant what I mean!" He smacked the desk again.

Angie continued to smile as Sanders' lips began to tremble. Sitting before him was what he hated most: a disrespectful outsider with no regard for *his* people's history and *his* beloved school and all that they represented to him. She was an agitator, an insurgent. A cancer!

Angie would not allow herself to be pushed around by this man who represented all the shopkeepers who looked at her with distrust, the bosses at her parents' jobs who demanded more hours and unrealistic physical exertion, the negligent landlord, the countless contemptuous stares she received when she walked with her infant brother.

"But sir," she began. She fancied herself as the man in those documentaries that Mr. V had shown last week—the guy who went to evil corporations and charged them with abuse and corruption. "The community *is* mostly African-American and Latino."

"What would you have us replace Gretel with? Teresa the Taco? Freddy Fried-Chicken? Wally Watermelon? Not on my watch, *chica*! Our heritage will not be taken from us by thugs," Sanders growled as he lifted a finger and pointed it squarely in Angie's face.

The boiling, racially charged language that spewed from his mouth left residual spittle at the corners of his quivering lips. His chest rose and fell, and his eyes searched Angie for a reaction.

Angie shook her head with the condescending sadness of someone beyond her years. And as she stood up, a soft pop clicked from her pockets.

"What was that?"

Angie gave Sanders the most confident and sinister and satisfied grin he had seen in three decades of education. Angie brushed off her jeans and walked toward the door.

"Miss Castillo, I will not repeat myself," Sanders said, lip still trembling. "What *was* that?"

Angie turned toward him as she grabbed the door handle. She continued to smirk.

"What was that noise?"

The door creaked opened to the sound of passing students. Before she stepped out of the office, Angie produced a small tape recorder. She held it out with a smile that stretched further than her arms—further than the hour-long drive her mom made to get to work—further than the lengths she was forced to go to get the accommodations she needed and deserved.

Sanders' jaw popped as his bottom lip fell.

Angie put the recorder back into her pocket, swept the smile from her face, and produced a folded piece of notebook paper from her pocket.

"Three weeks ago, student council voted to overturn Gretel as mascot. Two weeks ago, the students voted for a replacement. Here is the list the student body has created for potential mascots," she said as she unfolded the paper and put it on the table by the door. "You will put the mascot up for an official vote before Christmas Break...or else," she patted her pocket, "the students and the citizens of Reading will hear your words."

Angie walked off to Dieter's class, hoping he would know what to do with the recording. With that, Gretel the Pretzel and the newly elected Mayor were thrust headlong into the oven of democracy in which they would either rise or burn.

———

During first period, Andre was writing intently in front of Dieter. A clip of a fictional dictator played on the projector screen as Dieter paced around the room. He was reading over Andre's shoulder when Andre paused at an apparent roadblock in his thoughts. Dieter saw why he was struggling.

"Remember, class, with connotation what is actually said could have a different meaning that is either implied or can be *inferred*. Remember, the audience can also interpret the words differently. It's all about what lies *underneath* the words. For instance, if someone says that they want to keep tradition, you can say that they are trying to suppress other cultures. Or if someone says there are threats to freedom, we could connect them to some tyrannical, historical government like—"

"White people!" Miguel exclaimed.

Before Dieter could point out that "white people" isn't necessarily a government, the students had already begun to make their own connections.

"Teachers," a handful of students blurted out.

"Nazis," a host of students said in unison.

"Slave masters," Andre murmured under his breath.

Dieter turned toward his desk and grinned. Never had slippery slopes slid so well.

He thought he saw the poster of himself in high school wink, but his joy didn't allow him to worry about the Devil's approval. He was an effective teacher now. And the kids were eating up the breadcrumbs that Dieter was leaving them. There was no disrespect. There were no interruptions. There was no lip-smacking or eye-rolling when Dieter began a lesson or assigned a reading. Everything had real purpose to the students: an immediacy that Dieter could never have imparted before. And when it came time to deconstruct the text, every PowerPoint, every lesson, every word that came from his mouth held their eyes and ears captive.

Such power was truly intoxicating.

A buzz tickled his thigh as he sat on his chair. Dieter pulled it out to see who was messaging him during school. Fittingly, the assignment that night had students writing their own fallacious arguments about why a cell-phone prohibition in school was unfair.

My office. Need ur help.

Dieter scoffed at the abbreviated "your" and the desperation embedded in the text. It would be the first time he had felt so confident strolling to the Principal's office.

———

"Dieter, take a seat. Can I get you some water? A power bar?"

"I'm fine, thank you." Dieter smiled politely.

Sanders adjusted his tie and paced to the window that overlooked the lawn outside the school entrance. He stood pretending a pensive stare. His bald head, dark circles, and increasingly frailer body undermined his attempts at poise.

The trophies from various championships over various years glimmered in faint, bronze glory from three bookshelves that were void of books. Behind his desk was a quote about grit, with a picture of a mountain climber standing at the peak of a snow-capped ridge.

Sanders walked from the window and adjusted a framed decree that he drew up for himself; it was his first act as Mayor, and it declared that he was, in fact, *the Mayor*. Slowly, he turned to Dieter. "We have a crisis on our hands."

"We do, sir?" Dieter replied with the feigned seriousness of a parent given a grave prognosis by a child while playing doctor.

"The enemy is turning our students against us. They are turning into savages, Dieter, and they will not listen to anyone. Even Manley has no rapport with these—" he paused and shook his head, "—these beasts."

Dieter shook his head in incredulity. Where was Angie?

"I know, Dieter, I know. I'm disappointed too. The only person toward whom they are gravitating is you. They do not appreciate our strength, so, naturally, your weakness allows for them to feel respected, and this is good for us, Dieter. You are our secret weapon; our silent assassin."

Sanders' patronizing comments made Dieter's face flush. Agitation blocked his filter. In an instant, he leaned forward to bite back. But as he opened his mouth, he noticed the basketball trophy on Sanders' desk move. The male statue, petrified in perpetual dribbling, turned to look to Dieter and shook its head. Dieter understood. He forced his eyes to the carpet so that he would not betray his anger.

Sanders began again.

"Dieter, I need your advice. These *animals* are vandalizing the school. They are terrorizing the teachers, making irrational demands. They are—" Sanders paused, "—accusing me of being a Nazi! Ms. Castillo also has some *doctored* audio of me." Sanders voice softened. "We need your help, Dieter. I will drop your 'Probationary' status if you can fix this."

Dieter sat back and put on his best attempt to look equally troubled and even grateful. Then, with a start, he sat up as if he'd had an epiphany, though the plan had already been laid out for him. "Let's put it to a vote."

"A vote? Dieter, that's precisely what these brutes want."

"Sir, listen..."

Sanders quieted in the face of his subordinate's boldness.

"We ask the students to give us mascot ideas. Then we give them three options, so we look generous. One of the options is Gretel. Another is something crazy, like balloons or Banana Slugs or chickens. The third is something so egregious that no one in his right mind would choose it: something like the Redskins or the Devils. I mean, how ridiculous would we be if we were the Reading Redskins? Or the Reading Devils? In *this* community? We practically have a church every thousand feet. Parents wouldn't tolerate their kids voting for such a mascot."

Sanders eyebrows relaxed as he ran his hands over his bald head. A smile cracked from the corner of his lips. He was blissfully ignorant of how easily history is forgotten and repeated. While Sanders' own mentor was vanquished in a similar plot, Sanders embraced Dieter's plan.

"Reading is a Christian community. No way would our students choose the Devil," he assured himself. "They wouldn't dare."

Dieter again shook his head.

"Dieter, I'll think about it, but I need one thing before I allow this to happen."

"What's that?"

"I need that tape."

"I'll see what I can do."

Dieter had the recorder. Angie had given it to him during first period. After listening to Sanders' reprehensible remarks, Dieter downloaded the recording and created an anonymous email account. That night he planned to send the Superintendent an email with the explosive recording attached.

"Dieter, I want to form a committee, you and another teacher or two, to meet with these *hoodlums*."

Dieter smiled, but returned to seriousness when he responded.

"I could use a female presence, you know, to reach Maria and the girls. But our female staff are older, and white, so I don't know how effective—"

Sanders cut in: "Esther! She's half-something!"

Dieter nodded his head, pretending like he'd just recognized Sanders' brilliance. Then, with a cool grin that he'd seen a detective flash on TV, Dieter gave his approval: *"That would work..."*

"Good, we'll discuss this after Thanksgiving. In the meantime, I need to find some way to stop all this nonsense."

"Trust me, it will work."

Dieter looked at the document on his computer. The wording was too similar. Sanders would question it. Manley, as dense as he was, would research it. It was too bold.

"This is almost exactly like the original copy."

The Devil floated in the form of a cartoon paper clip at the bottom left margin of the word processing document. The paper-clip bent over slightly.

"I helped him write it."

"That's not surprising."

"Listen, I like you, Dieter. You and I have a mutually beneficial thing going here—"

"You make it sound like we are having sex or something."

The Devil sighed.

"Sorry," Dieter said to fill a sudden gap. "But isn't *Mein Kampf* a dangerous text to reference? Maybe something a little more subtle?"

"I've manipulated millions throughout history. Don't you think I can push this through? You doubt my abilities, Dieter?"

The cartoon's eyes glowed dull red. Though they approached a slightly menacing effect, Satan's incarnation was about as imposing as a baby animal.

"Fine. I'll print it and put it on his desk," Dieter said. He was about to hit print when a pathetic series of barks came from the hallway.

Intrigued, Dieter walked out his door to find a tiny, black and brown spotted puppy peering into the building from the partially opened annex doors. Dieter crouched down to pick up the pot-bellied ball of fluff and carry it back to his room. Stroking its fur, he sat down at his desk. He didn't know what to do with such a precious thing. First, he supposed, he'd look up what a dog needed in order to live. Holding the puppy in his right hand, he typed in the search bar with his left. The screen suddenly spasmed, and for a second, it went blank. When an image appeared, a picture of a lost dog poster showed up with a video chat application opened next to it just as a voice chimed by the door.

"Are you returning lost puppies now?"

Dieter jerked, leaving his heart two feet lower and trying to climb back into his chest. Esther stood in the doorway. Her arms were crossed casually, and her body leaned against the door frame, right hip and shoulder bracing her. Dieter could feel his eyes linger too long on the spot where her hip touched the frame, but he was too entranced to care. An email notification caused the puppy to wriggle in his hands, snapping him out of his lustful trance. His search popped up on the screen.

"Yeah, I found this poor guy outside. Couldn't leave him home alone, so I brought him here for the day. I..." Dieter glanced at his computer, "gave him one cup of puppy food with omega-3 fatty acids and essential vitamins for healthy digestion and shiny fur." Dieter looked back at Esther. "I was lucky to see the flyer when I was jogging through the neighborhood."

Esther moved her hand to her heart, made a pout with her lips, and whimpered her approval.

"Well, I won't keep you from returning him. I just wanted to thank you again for finding my necklace *and* correcting Miguel a couple of days ago. The necklace," Esther's eyes dropped and her voice choked up, "was from someone special to me."

Dieter nodded sympathetically. He was rewarded by a full glance of Esther as she turned to leave the room after waving to him. Back on Dieter's computer screen, the paper clip faced away from Dieter, apparently holding conversation with someone, or something, inside the laptop. Dieter waited for a few seconds, but the dispute wasn't going to abate anytime soon.

"I'll print it over the weekend," Dieter said before clicking the computer shut, not caring if Satan heard him or not. As if it were a projection from the computer, the puppy disappeared from Dieter's hand, leaving him cradling emptiness instead of living dog-flesh. A small whimper slid from Dieter's mouth. Quickly replacing his disappointment, however, was the realization that he probably wasn't ready to take care of an animal, especially while in the middle of an intensive, mildly-sinister uprising. The puppy had served its purpose anyway.

As he moved through the halls and out to his mom's car, he whistled an old song while twirling his room keys. Even the students waiting hopelessly for their tardy rides in the bitter, autumn air could feel the radiant warmth from the love-struck English teacher. When he slid into the car, his mom heard the tune.

"Someone's in a good mood," she commented.

Dieter nodded as she shifted the van into drive. She turned to him as they lurched forward. "You know, you were conceived to that song."

———

A typed letter materialized on Sanders' desk Monday morning. It did not say who it was from but simply read: "Thought we could send this out to parents. Get them on board as we head into Thanksgiving break."

The Devil truly was insidious:

Dear Parents,

I want to make you aware that a handful of students have chosen to vandalize our school and corrupt the student body into rebellious behavior. This cannot stand.

When one student is bent on spreading malicious rumors and hostile theology, they can push your young men and women to terrible actions. In the primitive simplicity of their minds they more readily fall victim to the big lie.

The students who want anarchy reject the fundamental principle of Nature and replace the eternal wisdom of power and strength with the ignorance of misled youth and inexperience. Thus, they deny the value of years of education, contesting the significance of history, and take from this school the reason for its existence: its culture. As a foundation of this school, this disorder will bring about the end of any order created by our founders. And as, in this greatest of all organizations, the American school, the result will only be chaos, since on it will only be destruction for the inhabitants of this institution. If the student is victorious over the administration, his crown will be the funeral wreath of education and this school will move to become dismantled and turned into a charter school.

Therefore, parents, today I believe that I am acting in accordance with the will of the Almighty: by defending myself against the instigation of students, I am fighting for the work of Superintendent Ward. Any student caught instigating other students to protest, or captured vandalizing school property, will be immediately suspended for ten days and put up for possible expulsion, depending on the action. The administration appreciates your communication with your young adult(s). We wish to stop this vandalism and blatant disrespect before student learning is compromised, and we hope you will help us message the need for compliance. Please sign below and have your student return the signed copy.

Thank you in advance for your cooperation.

Sincerely,
Principal Sanders, Mayor of Reading.

After Angie bottled his voice and racism on an electronic tape, Sanders was desperate for a solution. Without proofing the letter, and without informing anyone on staff, he signed under his name and ran to the copy machine. He enlisted the secretary for the entire day to print addresses and stuff envelopes.

By Tuesday, the last day before Thanksgiving break, seven hundred copies had been mailed to homes in Reading.

Chapter 8

IN YEARS PAST, the first day back from any break was filled with pent-up energy. After a week of isolation from their peers, and nights under the stricter statutes of their parents, the teens would almost instantly regress in the presence of their fellow teenagers. The rowdy classrooms would sizzle with teens play-fighting and barking obscenities. The blackboard would be covered with various signatures, epithets, and social media handles.

Today, Dieter's junior class was silent when he entered the room. The rows were perfectly aligned, the students upright and still, and the blackboard clear of graffiti. This should have pleased Dieter, except the students seemed depressed and defeated.

"What's going on?" Dieter asked.

Angie answered first. "My mom took my phone."

A couple of other students chimed in: "Mine too!"

"So?" Dieter asked. In response, arms raised and faces twisted in angst.

"The school sent a letter saying we been tearing stuff up. And since my mom got the letter, she been tweakin," Andre said as he slammed his book down on his desk.

Dieter's expression pushed Maria to break it down further. "She punished him for stuff he didn't do," she clarified.

More students spoke out. Miguel shifted in his seat and gently rubbed his left butt cheek, grimacing and shaking his head.

Another student spoke up: "We're trying to fix things but nothing is happening and we're just getting punished."

This time, the chorus was loud. Dieter nervously stroked his chin. Why had the Devil insisted he print the letter if this was the result? The students continued talking to each other, commiserating on their bad luck. Dieter noticed a poster in the back of the room move slightly.

It was a poster of Martin Luther King Jr. The quote that accompanied the photo was moving. Dieter searched the class to see if anyone else had seen the movement, but the students were still holding conference with each other.

"*Look up Niemoller quote*"

Dieter strode to his computer and typed "Niemoller quote." He instantly recognized the poem, and while it was ironic that the Devil would want him to use it, the situation begged for a reading.

"Listen, class. *Listen!*"

Dieter hit the projector's power button. As it warmed up, he resumed his dramatic strut around the classroom. "Every movement has struggle. If there's no struggle, there's no victory."

Doubt dangled upon the students' eyebrows.

"Look," Dieter pointed to the Martin Luther King Jr. poster, which had resumed its original form. "The Civil Rights movement was full of beatings and death, yet you all would still be slaves if it weren't for people like Dr. King." Dieter knew he was stretching, but his audience (at least 75% of them) wouldn't realize it or care. "Dr. King was happy to suffer. He spent time in jail for the cause. He *died* for the cause."

Dieter turned to Angie.

"I know it must have been hard for you to go without your phone over the break." Dieter forced himself to be sincere. "It's a small price. Especially when you are so close—*so close*—to getting what you want. This is the only thing they can do. But you students haven't even unleashed your potential!"

Heads were nodding. Dieter's confidence rose again.

"Look at the quote projected on the board. It's from a German holocaust survivor. Maria, will you read it?"

Maria squinted her eyes and then began to read. "First, they came for the Jews, and I did not speak out—Because I was not a Jew. Then they came for the Asians, and I did not speak out—Because I was not an Asian—" Dieter did a double-take, but let Maria continue. "—then they came for the Black people, and I did not speak out—Because I was not Black. Then they came for me—and there was no one left to speak for me."

A shudder went through the room after the last words were read. He had the students. For the next ten minutes, they wrote about what they thought the poem meant and what it might mean for them today.

"Your homework over break was to annotate the excerpt of German propaganda looking for rhetorical devices and misinform—"

Val's hand shot up.

"You never taught rhetorical devices."

"—I know, and I realized that."

Dieter didn't, but he needed to save face. With all the excitement and conniving the week and a half before break, his lesson planning had dropped off.

"So how were we supposed to—"

Dieter glared at Val. "—so instead of doing that..."

He was stalling, hoping that he could pull an activity out of the air. Martin Luther King, Jr. again came to his rescue.

"Look in your desk drawer"

Dieter side-stepped to the desk and noticed a packet of papers—the excerpt from *Mein Kampf* that had inspired Sanders' letter, complete with comprehension questions that would guide student reading. With only five minutes left in class, Dieter would give it to them for homework.

"...you all will instead read this small text that was written by Hitler."

The students groaned at the mention of homework. Even though they were invested, it was still the first day back.

"Hey, hey, hey! You *might* find something interesting after you read this…something that *could* solve your problems." Of course, Dieter did not tell the students that it was he who had drafted the letter for the administration.

———

The next day, Miguel was the first to state the connection. The class had been discussing the comprehension questions in pairs when Miguel pulled out the school's letter.

"Mr. V, this is bogus as hell! I mean, they basically took Hitler's words, you know? And the Germans, they were about to—" His face glowed with a sudden, dark realization. Andre perked up in anticipation of Miguel's comment. "Ay, Dios mío! They trying to extra terminate us."

The class buzzed. Other students had copies of the letter and were holding it side by side in comparison.

"This is crap!" exclaimed the avid fifteen-year-old Pokemon collector.

"Pura mierda!" spat the seventeen-year old aspiring lawyer.

"Bullshit!" shouted the nineteen-year-old with a court mandated ankle bracelet.

Maria stood up and faced the class.

"Fellow classmates, listen!" She turned to face Dieter and he gave a quick nod of approval before raising the projector screen.

"The administration has become a tyrannical aristocracy bent on forced assimilation, cultural imperialism, and dogmatic conservatism. They've forced us to abandon our identities and ascribe to their racist ideologies. If we don't, we will be punished or we will be—" she paused dramatically "—silenced."

Miguel's eyes nearly clenched shut from confusion. "What the fu—?"

"They are making us be German. And while they are not letting us protest for a new mascot, soon they will silence us completely and make us wear uniforms and maybe some of us will start disappearing. They want to take away our identities."

"Those pretzel-loving mother—" Andre moved to stand-up.

"We've got to do something!" Val exclaimed.

Dieter felt a surge of excitement rush through him. Val's comment was a perfect transition. And in his hand was the answer.

"Even though MLK Day isn't for another two months, I thought I would give you one of his famous writings, 'Letter from a Birmingham Jail.' In the document, King lists the steps one must take to fight injustice."

The students eagerly read the excerpt. With ten minutes left in class, Dieter checked for comprehension.

"What's the first step?"

"Collection of facts."

"Do you have evidence that there is injustice?"

The students sat quietly, eyes searching the article to find clues. Surprisingly, it was Miguel who spoke first.

"I heard Miss B talking about IEPs—"

Dieter interjected, "Let's leave out teacher's names for now. But go on."

"Okay, a *teacher*, talking about IEPs and how the school don't actually acorn-or-days our needs."

Dieter smirked.

"For the students in here, Miguel, explain what an IEP is."

Miguel stood up unnecessarily, but since he was experienced in the IEP process, he wanted to take advantage of this rare moment of superior knowledge. Liking the effect it had, Dieter made note to have students stand when answering in the future.

"EIP stands for Individjerized Education Plan. People with learning problems get one. And it tells teachers that they have to do special stuff for the slower students. Like I get more time on tests and I get notes printed out and stuff. Plus, I got ED."

Andre laughed uncontrollably.

"Like, you need Viagra and shit?"

Maria turned, stern faced, toward Andre. "It's something different. Miguel, go on."

Andre gave into Maria's defense and went silent. He was listening intently to Miguel since he also had an IEP. Miguel gave Maria a nod before walking to the front of the class to continue his lecture. He didn't realize that he had outed himself as also having an emotional disability, but as most students assumed that there was something different about him, he wouldn't have cared anyway. He clenched the podium and resumed speaking.

"Right, well, these teachers don't do nothin'. Coach tells me I don't get more time for being slow. Mr. Lee tells me that notes are too much work and I should just get them from someone else. Mr. Canon said I should just read more. Ms. Stewart says I just need to stop pretending like I'm dumb. I told them it's on my PIE. These teachers are retarded."

"So," Dieter picked up, "this could be one fact. I would be interested to know what the racial numbers are for people living in Reading. I would also find information about test scores, suspensions and expulsions by race on the State's website…"

The fires of insurrection, which had been but smoldering ash during the five-day break, were slowly being coaxed back to a visible flame. Now, Dieter just had to hope that something over the next three weeks would fan it into a destructive blaze.

By Thursday, a renewed charge pulsed through the halls of Reading High School. Unlike most student movements, which would be championed by one class and perhaps moderately engaged by another, this one spread across all four grades, catalyzed by the students from Dieter Vogel's class and their immediate circle of friends. They were armed with discrepancies in test scores and discipline data, and shielded with the racial make-up of Reading. A banner of injustice was colored by stories of teachers refusing to practice cultural sensitivity, failing to meet the varied learning needs of their classes, favoring select individuals while neglecting the majority.

Miguel's passion for "come-and-dating" students' needs was

infectious. Dieter's freshmen finished *Of Mice and Men* right as the school's treatment of students with disabilities was being scrutinized. Vexed by the end of the story, freshmen began accusing various teachers of being 'Georges.' Ms. Stewart, thinking the students had called her beautiful, blushed and thanked the students for the compliment, which further outraged the teens. Unknown to Dieter, Esther, with Maria as a translator, was meeting with parents of students with disabilities to inform them of their children's rights.

Besides students with IEPs being denied services, it was discovered that there were other infractions occurring at Reading High School. Students found that more black students were being suspended than white students, that black and Latino students scored lower than the white students, and that the white staff members held more positions of power than the staff members of color. This was mostly due to the fact that there were only four minority staff members, but that in itself was further proof of racial inequities.

To keep from alienating their white peers, Maria and Angie also pointed out the discrepancy between the test scores of whites in Reading and the test scores of whites in Hilltop. They invited and welcomed white students into conversations about the school. They even went out of their way to broker integration at the various tables throughout the lunch room.

At the student council meeting, which Dieter had taken over as moderator, the students made a list of the data and included anecdotes and testimonies purporting discrimination. Thirty minutes into the meeting, the tall, muscular body of Andre Williams slid into the room.

"Andre, what brings you here? Don't you have basketball?" Dieter called out with surprise.

Andre nodded, flinching when the door closed behind him.

"I, uh, know I'm not on student government, but I, uh, wanted to see if I could, you know, do stuff to help the school."

All faces beamed with approval. Dieter shrugged his shoulders.

"If the student government will allow it, we can appoint you Secretary of Student Activism."

"Nah, man, I don't think I can be a secretary..."

Maria tried to explain that a governmental secretary was different than an administrative secretary, but Dieter held up his hand.

"Okay, President of Student Activism."

Andre grinned.

"I'll be like Obama in this mother—"

With decorum from his new position acting as a censor, Andre stopped himself from finishing the profanity. Dieter smiled and pulled out a chair for Andre, who took the seat with smug satisfaction on his face.

Maria made a laminated poster with boxes representing each step from King's letter. A picture of King represented the students. Throughout the meeting, which lasted an hour longer than the allotted time, the student leaders decided that they had already tried the second step: negotiation; and since Sanders had rejected their attempts at mediation multiple times, they moved the civil rights icon's head to the next step: self-purification.

"What is that?" Maria asked Dieter.

Dieter truthfully didn't know, so in conjecture he said, "It means to make you sure that you are doing this for good reasons and that you keep yourselves pure."

Andre grimaced.

"So, like, no sex or anything?"

Dieter shook his head vigorously, hoping to alleviate Andre's concern.

"More like, make sure you don't do stuff that hurts your cause."

The students looked confused, so Dieter tried again.

"Keep your grades up, and don't fight with each other. Channel your anger toward fighting the school. That's what it means."

Andre whipped out his phone.

"What are you doing?"

"Posting a status update. To get the message out."

"What are you saying?" Dieter whispered, nervous that a quote connecting him to the rebellion would be readily available.

"We need to squash the beef and go after the pretzel."

Maria jumped up.

"Andre! I think we just found a slogan!"

Andre, temporarily confused, looked at what he'd written. Then it made sense.

"Yo! I just went full Obama."

The session ended with everyone posting the status. The resolution to resume actions against the administration became lost in the social media rush. Dieter had to ask the council while they were leaving, "So, what step are you on?"

Maria turned quickly, stone-faced: "Forgive my language, Mr. V, but it's time we mess stuff up."

Andre laughed and said, "You mean, 'time we fuck shit up.'"

Maria laughed with him: "I just wanted Obama to say it for me."

The students, 3 Latino, 2 white, and Andre, walked out smiling and talking excitedly with each other. They even decided to grab dessert at Don's Creamy Whip to celebrate the appointment of 'Andre Obama' to student government. The following night, parents arrived in droves to the PTA meeting to demand an explanation for why the school's letter home was inspired by Adolf Hitler. Three different sets of questions also revolved around the administration's persistent refusal to let the students choose a new mascot. Pretending to be sick, Sanders bowed out of the meeting early, leaving a flustered school secretary in his place.

With formal complaints lodged with the district, Sanders' position at the school teetered precariously close to a steep downward fall. Fortunate for him, the union had already taken steps to explain away the letter. The union also beat back the Superintendent's anger after a recording of Sanders' insensitive remarks had somehow reached her desk. The union unanimously recommended Principal Sanders for multiculturalism training over the break and placed him on 'Probationary' status. For the time being, Sanders' words were buried in the district's digital file having only been heard by Dieter, Angie, and the superintendent.

Sanders had weathered the first storm, but these incidents had shaken him.

———————

Motivated by Dieter's propaganda, and subliminally driven to hate the school's mascot, the students amplified their displeasure of the school's longest lasting relic: Gretel, the Pretzel. Even those remaining students whose families loosely identified with German heritage were speaking out against the mascot and the administration. And while the parents' anger was subsequently felt by Principal Sanders, the parents continued to respect the authority of the school and did not push any further beyond emailed consternation.

The students, on the other hand, directed their ire by altering Sanders' picture, which hung in the hallway just out the security camera's range. Permanent marker had given him the recognizable Hitler mustache, and across the expanse of his forehead, a tattooed swastika hovered as if it were an emblem on a flag.

The movement gained traction. The white students, the school's minority, purchased buttons that read '#YouSalty', which the students knew promoted the upheaval of Gretel. It took until the third quarter for the adults to realize what was being said.

Other students wore t-shirts with a picture of Gretel on the front with "R.I.P." stenciled on the back. The juniors, led by Maria, brought in banners, which they paraded through the lunchroom during lunch or study hall periods. The remaining students filtered into the three groups as they were able. It was the first time the student body had come together since the Chicken Nugget Revolt of '99.

Other acts of rebellion showcased the courage and unity of the diverse student body. When two black students were disciplined for talking in class, a white student also involved in the disruption but not given a punishment spoke out and demanded that he be given a detention as well. Students who excelled in various subjects made time to tutor their fellow students who were struggling. Maria even begged Dieter to use his room twice a week to house tutoring sessions during lunch hour. Dieter almost cried with pride.

And amid the surge of support, the student leadership kept their focus on deconstructing the inequalities perpetuated by staff members. Teachers still wavered on implementing the recommended support to students with disabilities. Defensiveness and further disciplinary actions plagued each moment where students righteously advocated for themselves or their peers. As a retort to the attack against their authority, teachers dug in deeper. Homework doubled. Papers were hypercritically dissected. Tests were given on uncovered material. And office hours were cancelled indefinitely. Far from demoralizing the students, these actions worked to cement the students' resolve in such a manner that even when the movement would wane, it could be rebuilt on the foundation that had been laid. Fed up that they were not being taken seriously, Angie and Maria penned an ultimatum for Principal Sanders.

Vote before break or else.

———————

On the following Wednesday, as Dieter began to pack his belongings, a red-faced Sanders blew into his room.

"Principal Sanders—"

"Mayor," Sanders shot back.

"Forgive me," Dieter said with a slight bow, "Mayor Sanders."

"As you know, a letter I sent out over break has been misinterpreted as Nazi propaganda."

Dieter gave an apologetic nod.

"I fault myself, sir, for assigning the excerpt from the textbook. Maybe they wouldn't have discovered it."

The textbook did not have any excerpt from *Mein Kampf*, but Sanders wouldn't know this: he had as much familiarity with the curriculum as he did with cultural sensitivity.

"It's okay, Dieter. I was able to fix that issue. But now we have another situation. The punks have gone too far!" Sanders declared.

Dieter noticed that Sanders lip had a pronounced twitch. His right eye was also squinting in sharp contrast to his very open left eye. Sanders' honeymoon with dual-leadership roles had worn off.

"Have you *seen* the statue?" Sanders asked.

Dieter shook his head in frustration. Perhaps it was the demonic promise of becoming principal, or maybe it was the sincere regard for the students' well-being, but Dieter had become cognizant of and sensitive to the administration's negligence. Why wasn't Sanders mentioning the outbursts that were affecting student learning in class? Why wasn't he talking about the legitimate instances of injustice in his school? Why was he allowing for such tone-deaf responses by the staff to continue? Sanders mistook Dieter's silence for ignorance.

"Come with me."

Together, they blew through the double doors outside Dieter's classroom and marched down the concrete sidewalk toward the gym. When they were twenty feet away, Dieter could make out the statue of Gretel, which was positioned outside the gym's main entrance. He already knew what he would see, but he let Sanders move him closer for the revelation. Fashioned out of weather resistant steel twenty years before Dieter began teaching, the statue was a dull gray with occasional splotches of white decoration from defecating birds. The typical pretzel loop was inverted, with the large loops at the bottom of the mascot and legs and arms protruding outside the accepted pretzel form. The loose strands of pretzel at the top were shaped to look like a bow. In the center of the pretzel, Gretel's cartoon face exhibited a cheesy grin.

Various parts of Gretel's pretzel body had been spray painted with red horizontal lines that Dieter immediately identified as mock stab wounds. It was clear they had been done a while ago since they were faded. A clearer, black-painted Hitler mustache floated over Gretel's cartoon smile like a tiny black cloud, thus moving the allusion from Caesar to Nazi Germany. Sanders shook his head as Dieter stifled a smile.

"This is unacceptable," Sanders said with sadness in his voice.

"Yeah," Dieter responded, "first a picture of you, and now this?"

Sanders jerked his body violently toward Dieter. "My portrait?" Dieter responded with a tilt of his head. "You haven't seen—"

But Sanders had already taken off in a sprint towards the school building.

———————

On Friday, just two weeks before Christmas break, Principal Sanders called an emergency meeting of the entire staff. He stood underneath a cartoon cutout of a sombrero-clad Chihuahua holding a sign teaching the preterit tense. His hands gripped the podium, which was actually a music stand. Teachers shuffled in, annoyed that an ad hoc meeting delayed their weekend relief. Most assumed that it would be yet another self-congratulatory speech from Sanders, thinly veiled as a request that they inform the Principal-Mayor of issues in the community. After two such meetings, the staff had gossiped about the uselessness of this invitation since the Mayor seemed decidedly unable to address the issues in his own school.

"Ladies and gentlemen, we are at code black. Students are attempting to overthrow *our* school," Sanders said with disgust. The room hushed as Sanders scanned the room with an air of suspicion. "One of you is provoking this."

Sanders' eyes skipped over the white teachers and didn't even attempt to look at Dieter. Instead, his eyes alternated between Mr. Wilson, Father Manny, and Jose. The racial implication of this deliberate stare-down was only noticed by those teachers, Esther, and Dieter, who was fascinated by the effects of his work.

"While we have little proof of an instigator on staff, we all know *these* students do not have the capacity to care about anything other than rap-hop, video games, and flaming-hot chips. But now they suddenly care about their education. And they are speaking out—"

"—for democracy," interjected Father Manny.

"I don't care if it's democratic or not! They have no right to—"

"—speak their minds? Take ownership in their school? Choose an identity for themselves?" Father Manny's voice became more impassioned. "Why can't they change the face of the school? It's part of who they are. We should build the body of the academics. You and the rest of the administration should keep the physiology running smoothly. But the kids? They are the bones of the school. They *are* our image. You are so intent on holding onto a silly mascot that you cannot see the ridiculousness of that character in this time and place. We need to let our students become more involved; if we don't, then they will become indifferent to the injustices of this world."

A rumble began among those staff sitting against the walls behind Father Manny. Jose, too, was nodding. Teachers were whispering. Dieter was smiling. And Principal Sanders' face grew flushed.

Father Manny's words had caught Sanders right on the left temple, where a vein now visibly elevated. Subverted and emasculated, he reverted to the only defense he could find.

"How dare you play the race card?"

Father Manny opened his mouth to retort but was cut short.

"I will be forming a committee for student relations, and I need volunteers. Volunteers that will *not* further instigate the students," he said, staring directly at Father Manny. "Dieter and Esther have already agreed to help."

Esther looked at Dieter in confusion. Dieter shrugged and mouthed the words 'I guess we volunteered.' Esther smiled in return.

The staff rolled their eyes. There were already eight different committees: the school character committee, the discipline committee, the committee for standardized testing, the curriculum implementation committee, the committee for school culture, the committee for healthy living, the data committee, and the committee to form committees based on other committees' recommendations.

Silence greeted Sanders' proposal. Teachers dropped their eyes or looked around to avoid being selected. Many wondered how this committee was different from the discipline, school character, and school culture committees.

Esther locked eyes with Manley and nodded her head as if to push him to action. Manley shrugged.

"Anyone else?" Sanders said as he drifted from the podium to the front of the room. His button-down shirt ruffled out from his pants, falling short of covering the small coffee stain by his left pocket.

A hand waved enthusiastically in the back over a toothy, unrestrained smile.

Sanders sighed. "Cordero?"

Jose chirped in excitement. The rest of the staff exhaled.

"I want the three of you to meet with me on Monday to draft plans for suppressing this...this—*insurgency*."

With that, Principal Sanders turned quickly from the room, stopping by the door when he saw an old "Maria y Angie 4 Student Council" flyer. With a loud snatch, he tore down the paper, setting off the motion-sensor cartoon cactus that sang "Feliz Navidad." Upon hearing the song, Sanders turned to the cactus and smacked it from the ledge.

"We still have two weeks until Christmas Break, Manley," he growled, leaving the still-singing cactus to flop on the floor. Manley looked on, stunned. It was the first time Sanders had raised his voice to him. It was also the moment his nerves quickened their rapid, irreversible unraveling—a spiral that would expose his vulnerable masculinity.

Due to his mayoral duties, the after-school meeting of the Student-Staff Relations Committee was delayed until the Wednesday before the break. By that time, tension in the school swirled like icy air.

Students were open in their disengagement. Even the front runners for valedictorian in each grade spent class time on phones or in conversation with their peers. Teachers were short with the students, which pushed the teens to lash out. When teachers requested that the students listen, the students, trained by Maria, retorted, "Why should we listen when you won't listen to us?" Most teachers responded with a lecture on the importance of education, but when students mocked them, some teachers tried threats of disciplinary action. Mr. Canon gave out detentions, but when he found a rubber rat inside his desk, he quickly became subdued. Manley also tried to give detentions, but the students who received them complained to the new President of Student Activism, who in turn confronted Manley. No one was present for the conversation, but it was obvious that Andre threatened to withhold services towards Manley's ego if he didn't cool it with the discipline. Manley had to retract the already given detentions.

As a last resort, teachers tried calling homes, but the calls had no effect. Word had spread about the inequalities at the high school, and while the parents weren't fully convinced that Nazism ran rampant, the growing number of hyperbolized tales wove a blanket of distrust that covered the mostly white staff.

When Wednesday afternoon crept up, Sanders' face clearly conveyed the code level that would exist if the school were on the military or fire safety systems.

"Desperate times call for desperate measures—"

Jose and Esther cringed in anticipation of more bad ideas. Dieter sensed a dark trajectory, so he quickly intervened.

"Yes, which is why I have thought of some initiatives we could implement after break."

Sanders shifted in his seat from pent-up pressure in his bowels and in his positions of authority, but allowed Dieter to continue.

"If student-staff relationships are at a breaking point, we need to find a way to unify them."

Sanders, who had begun by listening intently, suddenly gazed out the window.

"I was thinking we could have the school day shortened by thirty minutes for extracurricular activities. To build a healthy connection between the adults and the students, the staff could share a passion or hobby of their own—you know, like art or dance."

Dieter nodded toward Esther at the last suggestion. She smiled approvingly. Jose also grinned broadly at Dieter's suggestions. But Sanders appeared to have missed everything that Dieter had said.

"Yes, yes, good idea," he trailed off. Jose entered the idea into the meeting minutes. "But what if—" Sanders stood up suddenly,

"—what if we take down the rebellious individualism by instituting something that will *uni*-fy them?"

When Sanders placed the emphasis on the first part of unity, he gave a sales pitch grin to each teacher. Dieter sighed. He knew what would follow would be a terrible idea.

"If students want to change the face of the school, we can start with *uni*-forms."

Dieter and Esther glanced at each other, each one wishing that the other would intercede. But Sanders had already begun ranting about the possible benefits of the proposal. Jose continued to sit attentively, allowing Sanders' flow to go unchecked, and by the time Esther and Dieter could mount a protest, Sanders had stated his intention to send a letter to homes announcing the decision.

"But what about Dieter's idea?" Esther weakly called out

"Yeah, okay. But we'll make teachers stay after school. We can't shorten the day. High stakes testing this year."

With that, Sanders ran from the room to craft the new school policy, leaving Dieter and Esther dumbfounded. Jose rose from his chair. "Well, *that* was certainly productive," he laughed.

Dieter and Esther did not share the joke. To them, it was apparent that the situation was going to get worse, not better, after the break. Dieter could feel pessimism clotting his hopes.

Though chaos and upheaval had been his goals, he genuinely wanted the students to prosper. As he and Esther walked to the parking lot together, Dieter realized that becoming principal was not an urgent pursuit anymore. If he could affect teens in the classroom, what need did he have to direct adults from the office?

That sentiment lasted from Esther's "good night" to when Sanders decided to announce during the homeroom period—two days before break—that the school would mandate uniforms.

———

At a school already simmering with distrust, another instance of disenfranchisement sent a flash of anger through the halls. Immediately after the dress code was announced, students mounted a chorus of jeers followed by the violent screeching of dislodged chairs and desks. When the bell sounded, teachers were thrust into the hallways, carried by the wave of disgust. Dieter rode the surge as it swelled toward Sanders' office.

Previous years' adverse announcements and ill-conceived initiatives had led students to grumble their disapproval through sarcastic jabs and snide comments, but this year's students, inspired by stories of activism, violence, and unity in Dieter's classes, all marched to the source of their discontent. Before the second period bell rang, the entrance vestibule of the school was a clogged artery of multiracial teenagers, enraged by the adult authorities that had already refused to listen to their pleas for an identity change—adults who now declared a dress-code homogeneity that would choke the individuality teenagers crave.

Black students and white students, who previously sat in different corners of the lunch room, spoke enthusiastically with each other about the ridiculousness of the latest decision. Poor students and middle-class students equally scoffed at the idea of wearing khakis and polos.

A potent force accumulated outside Sanders' door. After a minute, the speakers cackled: "Second period has started. Students late for class will be given a detention. Teachers must mark tardy students so they can be held accountable."

The mob roared in frustration and incredulity. A chant rose above the noise from Miguel and his friends.

"Havoc! Havoc! Havoc!"

"Students need to go to class—"

"Havoc! Havoc!" The juniors from Dieter's class began to chime in.

"—we will be moving to suspensions—"

"Havoc! Havoc! Havoc!" Other students, not quite knowing what the word meant, but feeling pulled by the urgency and vitriol with which the word was being chanted, joined the chorus. Rhythmic pounding pulsed against office doors. The students' cries were insistent.

"Havoc! Havoc! Havoc!"

Dieter felt a vibration in his pocket. The text message was to him, Esther, and Jose.

wat do we do?

"Havoc! Havoc! Havoc!"

He smirked. A vision of Sanders holed up in his office like a trapped animal formed in his mind. Dieter paused, wondering if this was the moment that Sanders would be destroyed. Could this be it? Could the students displace Sanders? Could this be the beginning of his rise to principal? A message from Jose cut the dream short.

Get Maria. Hear her out. Say you'll rethink it.

"Havoc! Havoc! Havoc!"

Within ten seconds the loudspeaker boomed.

"Maria Lopez to speak to Mr. Sanders in his office—"

"Havoc! Havoc! Havoc!"

An audible sigh followed his words.

"—and we will talk about addressing this issue."

A cheer welcomed this sign of potential defeat. The student body sizzled with excitement. An aisle cut through the heart of the group as a stern-faced Maria strode to the office door.

The students' voices tapered off, allowing Maria's deliberate knock (for the sake of decorum) to be answered. A muffled response led to Maria cracking open the door and peeking her head into the room. With one leg in the office and one in the vestibule, she poked her head back out to the students, her razor-sharp brow assuring them that she would not waver. With a nod, she disappeared behind the closed door.

———

In a meeting that lasted ten minutes, Sanders proved his mettle as a politician while simultaneously showcasing his failure as a role model. Maria burst from the room and announced the results to the waiting students.

"Mr. Sanders—"

A cough shot from behind her.

"Principal Sanders—" Maria began again, but was quickly interrupted by another cough.

"Principal-*Mayor* Sanders has agreed to reconsider uniforms if we stop writing graffiti."

Maria paused as the students absorbed the first bit of information.

"He also said that we will vote on the mascot when we get back from break…" The students rumbled. They did not believe the ambiguity of this arrangement. Maria realized her error. "… the Tuesday after MLK Day break."

This information, a date set in stone, symbolic in its timing, assuaged most of the concern.

"Finally," her voice rose for a rapturous announcement, "he has cancelled classes for the rest of the day!"

A whoop of excitement shot into the air. High fives and pumped fists streamed above the joyful faces. Students forgot about "the cause." They also ignored the "because" behind Sanders' benevolence. While the students thought it was the culmination of their activist fervor, an unexpected ice storm was rapidly approaching. Forecasters on the local stations frantically advised all businesses and schools to shut down immediately.

Most schools had already shortened the school day. In fact, Sanders had already sent out a call to the parents that the students would be dismissed early. He had also included the new uniform policy, on which he had no intention of reneging. By the time the students realized that they had been duped, they were already home.

Only a light, powdery snow fell, and the streets were cleared by midnight. Still, Sanders made a surprise call to cancel the last day of school before break. Confined to their homes, the students began to forget the previous semester and everything that they had fought for up to that moment.

By Monday, as students slept into early afternoon, parents had ironed their children's khaki pants and polo shirts, Andre had returned as a full-participant to practice, and Dieter stirred from restlessness.

Chapter 9

THAT CHRISTMAS, DIETER found himself in the same living room he had spent his past twenty-five Christmases, sitting in the same lumpy chair, eating the same apple strudel recipe, with the same lone birthday candle wedged in the same red-dyed frosting, with the same solitary woman standing next to him singing "Happy Birthday" followed by "Silent Night". His mom put extra emphasis on 'Round yon virgin' every year after Dieter's twenty-first birthday. This year she practically shouted it.

By noon, she was napping under a blanket of spiked eggnog, which conveniently bailed Dieter out from having to go to Mass. So, he celebrated Christ's birthday and his own by consorting with Satan, who assumed the form of a two-foot-tall Santa statue. The rosy cheeks illuminated as Satan spoke.

"I enjoyed your mom's rendition of that terrible song."

"The part where she sang 'you look like a monkey, and you smell like one too?'"

"I meant 'Silent Night', but yes, that was also good."

Dieter wasn't as fond.

Sensing Dieter's sensitivity, Santa-Satan merrily quipped, "Well, your nights won't be so silent once Esther breaks up with Manley."

Dieter took a swig of eggnog and gave a weak nod.

"Seriously, Dieter. You've lost weight, you're killing it each time you talk to her, Sanders is losing it, the school—"

"—is on break," Dieter cut in, "and the students will forget everything. We were *so close*."

He held his fingers a half-inch apart, but stopped, not knowing if the Santa statue could see him or not.

"Dieter, Dieter, Dieter. Oh ye of little faith! Don't you think we can pick up right where we left off?"

"It's not that easy. You don't know these—"

"—human beings? It's not like I have been around for thousands of years corrupting Adam and Eve, politicians, pop-stars, and pimple-faced pubescents or anything."

Dieter sighed, "That's not what I meant."

"Listen, Dieter—"

Santa shifted a little so it could better face Dieter, but the movement pulled on the extension cord, which in turn shut off the indoor lights and the Christmas music playing on the stereo.

Dieter's mom shot up with a snort.

"Thief!"

"Ma, I just tripped the cord. Go back to sleep."

Dieter's mom looked at him through squinting eyes.

"Okay, wake me up in time for Mass."

She plopped back down on the couch, snoring immediately. Dieter turned back to Santa.

"The kids deserve to be heard. I know Sanders is going to squash any resistance."

Santa did not respond. Annoyed, Dieter got up to plug in the singing statue, thinking somehow Satan's magic was predicated on electricity. When Santa lit up, there was no intonation of life.

Instead, a deep, crooning voice from the record player sang, "Just my nuts roasting over an open fire, Jack Frost picking up some hoeeeees."

Dieter sighed. The crooning voice responded to his exasperation. "Lighten up, Dieter! Trust me, I have plans for second semester. Take time this week and relax. I'll catch up to you on Friday. I've got to go get some more pundits to scream about the War on Christmas."

"Doesn't that work against you?" Dieter asked the record player.

"You might think so, but believe me, it doesn't. Happy Holidays, Dieter. And Happy Birthday."

The Perkolate Coffee Shop, like Reading, was a relic of the past, slowly slipping into the nostalgia of a time when the community patronized small businesses. The café loitered like a scraggly teenage boy between the pristine exteriors of Huld Law Firm and Dr. W.C. Williams, Pediatrics. The owners of other businesses waited to pounce on Perkolate's prime location once it closed in failure, which had become inevitable when a corporate coffee shop opened a half mile down the road. The new shop was shiny, hip, and tasty. Perkolate was dim, empty, and chalky. But, like a malfunctioning car window, it stubbornly remained open.

Its seventies decor, guaranteed isolation, and its basic menu was sentimental enough for Reading's gray-haired citizens, who hobbled in every morning for routine social interaction. It was also kitschy enough for the edgy, suburban teens from neighboring communities. On Saturday mornings, the elderly trudged out around eight, leaving tattered arm chairs and creaky wooden tables begging for use until the teens' arrival in the early afternoon.

Dieter happily patronized the shop. There were no distractions and no pretensions. He could sit in his corner booth by the window for three hours uninterrupted and alternate between lesson plans and people watching on Reading Road. He was especially alone that Friday since New Year's Eve fell on a Saturday that year and many people had taken the long holiday weekend to travel to see family in exotic locales like Pittsburgh or Cleveland or Buffalo.

It came, therefore, as a surprise when the splintered brown door chimed, sending a rustle of snow and wind around the shop. A thin woman stepped from the light outside into the dim interior. A scarf bundled her face and a puffy winter jacket covered her torso.

Under the coat, tight black leggings betrayed youth and physique, creating a tenuous image in Dieter's mind as to who this person might be. And as the mysterious patron shed her outer garments, Dieter's eyes widened in confirmation.

Esther's gaunt face hung underneath a bright red, crocheted hat. Faded make-up caked on her cheeks. Mascara congealed on her lashes. And even in the poor lighting, Dieter could see the black-stained remnants of tear streams flowing from the corners of her eyes. But she did not see him. She never veered from the chalkboard menu behind the register as she shuffled forward.

Her voice was quiet and defeated, as if coming to this place was rock-bottom.

"Just a small cup. Cream, please."

She reached for her purse in the side pocket of her coat. Trembling hands jingled the coins inside until she had pulled out the dollar twenty-five needed for caffeinated comfort. With the vision of a broken Esther in front of him, Dieter's normally hungry eyes mellowed into compassion. There was a terrible darkness that Esther was encased in—one with which Dieter had grappled for most of his teens and early adult life—one that had only been lifted since he'd met the Devil, since he had become an effective teacher, and since he had begun to make human connections that held sincere, reciprocal affection.

Esther gasped when she saw Dieter staring at her with a mixture of empathy and confusion. She turned her eyes toward the floor to guide her quick exit, but Dieter pre-empted her escape with a tender invitation.

"Esther, come sit with me."

She nodded weakly and crept to the table. Dieter used his foot to move a chair to a position across from him. It was a simple gesture, really, but Esther needed to know that someone—anyone— wanted her around. That she wasn't simply an object for abuse. That she had at least one friend in this pathetic town.

"Hey, Dieter," Esther said bashfully.

Dieter smiled. "Everything okay?"

"Not sure if you can tell, but…" Agitation hung on her words. Dieter had already pulled his lips in. Her pain was obvious.

"It's been a rough break. Paul hasn't been—"

Dieter held up his hand, partly to save Esther from having to recount her troubles, but also because he didn't like hearing Manley's first name. It betrayed an intimacy he wished he had with Esther.

"The break is almost over," Dieter smirked, "and there will be a new beginning that you can look forward to once school starts."

Esther shook her head.

"I've moved in with my mom."

"Well, home cooked meals aren't the worst thing…"

"When they're served with a side of guilt for not being married?" Esther's voice trailed off.

"Ah, yes. That sounds familiar. My mom thinks I should have had two grandchildren for her by now. It's like I'm responsible for filling the void left by my dad." He flinched. Why had he shared such an embarrassing and seemingly irrelevant detail about his life?

Esther's eyes widened, pushing up her brows. "I didn't know your parents were—I mean—how old were you when it happened?" She unwittingly shifted in her chair and leaned toward Dieter, who now realized he had an obligation to answer her questions that stemmed from his confession.

"I was ten…classic story of dad leaving without a note or even a goodbye."

Dieter hadn't talked to anyone about the divorce since it happened fifteen years ago. At the time, his mom seemed to have known it was coming and had already prepared her "we're better without him" speech when Dieter eventually asked about his father's whereabouts. Beyond that one talk, she hushed Dieter's questions about his father. It was during those years that Dieter coped with the emptiness through food and fantasy, escaping his fatherless world into one that would reward him with consolation through imagined heroism.

Esther's short laugh startled Dieter.

"Sorry, I'm not laughing at you. It's just that my dad did the exact same thing when I was twelve."

Dieter nodded.

"We're practically the same," Esther said. She paused, noting Dieter's sullen eyes, and started again. "So, you also spent your childhood looking for ways to replace him…" Dieter nodded. Esther continued: "For me, it was a string of meaningless relationships during high school and college. And apparently today…"

Dieter nodded, thinking it was his turn to console. But she resumed talking. "I don't know if Manley and I are going to work out—" Dieter's heart palpitated. "—he's older, has different priorities, looks at the world differently—"

"And he has another relationship," Dieter cut in more sharply than intended.

Esther smiled.

"Sanders?" she laughed.

"I'm sure it's hard having to share Manley. Does he alternate nights with you and Sanders?" Dieter cringed as he spoke the words. He had let his fears come through in his comments, laying bare his recurring vision of Esther's familiarity with Manley. But still she smiled.

"Wouldn't surprise me," she chuckled before her face turned a beautiful shade of crimson and her voice again slipped into a quiet confession, "and we stopped doing—" She ran her fingers around the top of the coffee cup before finding the right word, "—*stuff* a few weeks ago."

Dieter's face froze. He couldn't believe she was confiding such details to him.

"I want to know that a guy can love me as a person first. I mean, I didn't care about that before. I guess that's why I've been prone to fall into bad relationships all these years."

Dieter forced himself to soften his face and nod in agreement.

"And maybe it's from talking with Father Manny so much, but I started going to church again and I feel so much happier. You know, Dieter, you should come with me—"

A burst of steam hissed into the air behind the counter. The one espresso machine—the glue that kept the younger clientele coming to the shop—bellowed streams of hot air, sending the owner into a frenzy. He danced frantically around the machine, twisting nobs and pulling levers, urgently trying to do something to keep the over-heated contraption from spiraling into the complete disrepair that would hasten the coffee shop's bankruptcy.

Esther and Dieter both watched the spectacle, and by the time the machine was unplugged, Esther had forgotten her train of thought. With conversational static hovering between them, she shifted her seat, leading Dieter to jump to conclusions.

"Yeah, I've got to go too."

"Oh, I wasn't…but, yeah, me too."

"It was—" Dieter couldn't finish his sentence before Esther cut in again.

"Yeah, it was." She smiled, genuinely. Dieter breathed in her warmth and affection, a connection they both sought.

"Dieter?"

He inhaled in anticipation. "Yes?"

"I feel like you are one of the few teachers who really cares about our students," she flipped her scarf over her shoulder, "and about, well, me. I just want you to know that I really appreciate everything you've been doing. I hope we can continue to get to know each other."

Dieter nodded in agreement as Esther grabbed her purse and gave a hasty wave before turning to the door.

When Dieter got home that night, he found a long email from Sanders with an important new requirement listed along with an abundance of superfluous information. As per decree, all teachers were to be involved in some form of tutoring or after-school activities. Since Dieter was already involved in student council, he went to delete the email without response when a voice popped up from the energy bar on Dieter's desk. The climber in the middle of the packaging released his hold on the mountain and dangled comically.

"You should sign up for something else."

Dieter shook his head.

"Student council and lesson planning take up almost all my free time. I'm spent."

The climber swayed side to side, gesticulating wildly with his hands.

"You are so close! Look, do something else. It will bring you closer to the students."

"I'm already close."

"But this will give you more one-on-one time."

"I'm tired."

"Dieter! Dieter! Listen to me—ah, damn it!"

The Devil-possessed climber had rocked himself too violently. With a forceful, pendular motion, his head smashed against the rock façade. A series of epithets swirled from the packaging until the climber composed himself once more.

"Look, just do something easy," the climber said as he rubbed his head, "something you like to do…something you are knowledgeable about."

Dieter racked his brain for enriching activities he had once participated in since he no longer had time for hobbies, and his dream of acting had been deferred indefinitely. In fact, drama and theater had become repulsive to Dieter. His life's plot was developing rapidly, and it carried with it more satisfying characters anyway.

As for his areas of expertise, his mind was consumed by Esther, teaching literature, and because of the conversation today, once again his father's abandonment. Dating Club, Future Teachers Club, and Children of Single Moms Club weren't ideal extracurricular activities. His dalliances with Satan could produce an interesting club, but Dieter supposed Satanism in a school would only be permitted in California.

So Dieter spent two minutes struggling to identify anything to turn into an activity until he saw an icon twitch on his computer screen—an apparent suggestion by his divine accomplice.

"Chess Club?"

The climber nodded in approval.

"And Sanders will allow it since it seems academically enriching."

Satan again nodded vigorously before he added his own insight:

"It's a good metaphor for what we are doing, too! You can use chess to corrupt them—an extended metaphor for the movement!" The climber waved his hands excitedly as he spoke, but the movements caused the hook holding the rope to separate from the rock. Dieter had only blinked when he lost sight of the climber, who had dropped from the image on the package. With an unconcerned shrug, he turned his attention to the computer and fired off a quick email.

He received a response at 11:00 o'clock on New Year's Eve. In the email, Sanders begged Dieter to take over Ms. Snider's film studies class. His request had an embedded trail of contempt for the new mom. From what Dieter could insinuate, Sanders was disgusted that a woman could feel such an attachment and concern for her child that she'd ask for part-time hours. Dieter gladly accepted the new class and saved the email for possible use toward Sanders' downfall.

Around his apartment complex, muffled screams welcomed the New Year. When he slipped his feet underneath the covers, he thought he saw a "Happy New Year" message from Esther. But when he opened his phone, there was nothing. Dieter sighed into his pillow and clicked off the lamp on his nightstand. He mumbled a muffled request to whatever divine power was listening that this would truly be a great new year.

Chapter 10

ON THAT FIRST day back from Christmas break, the school filled with groaning khaki-clad zombies. They shuffled down the hallways, tugging at tight pants and scratching at itchy cotton shirts. Their glazed eyes stared forward in empty agony.

Dieter's classes, as he feared, sleep-walked through the day without a murmur of the excitement that had existed only two weeks prior. Andre, who had become aware of his own exploitation by Manley and Sanders in December, sketched plays that the team practiced over break in preparation for that night's game. Miguel sat with his head on his desk, arms tucked inside his shirt like a withdrawn turtle.

Further discouraging, Dieter's freshmen seemed to have forgotten every expectation in his class. It took Dieter five minutes of correcting behavior just to get the class to a relative calm while they shared answers.

For better or for worse, uniforms truly affected the students' dispositions. It would remain to be seen who or what they would benefit long term.

Dieter hadn't felt such frustration since the first day of school, and he carried the tension to his after-school activity, unsure if anyone would even show up to Chess Club.

Maria was the first person to arrive, soon followed by two freshmen boys that could have walked into any fifth grade class and passed as students. Dieter had figured that numbers would be low, so he closed the door to keep the students from being exposed to the janitor's racist grumblings pouring from the bathroom. Every day over break, he soaked the walls with chemicals to combat the persistent permanent-marker graffiti. There were so many tainted surfaces within the school that he wasn't able to address the annex until that first day back.

Dieter walked to his computer with the intention of shutting it down for the night when he noticed an email with no subject from Esther. He moved his mouse to click the message, but the cursor on the screen jumped in the opposite direction. Dieter again tried to pull it toward the bold font that indicated "unread email" but the cursor seemed to pull back.

"*Satan*," Dieter growled.

The cursor fought with Dieter until, finally, it jumped toward the 'x' on the top right of the screen, closing out the web browser.

"Alright, I guess we will get started."

The door creaked open, and the unexpected, untamed mane of Miguel popped into the room.

"Hey, I was wondering if I could, uh, play chest?"

Dieter softened his lip when he realized that Miguel was not deliberately making sexual innuendo. Still, his presence in the extracurricular with the lowest social-capital (and with the highest thinking and patience demanded) perplexed Dieter. Was he there to sabotage this group? Was he there to torment Dieter through his ignorance? Or...

Miguel's eyes bounced from Dieter to the rapidly blushing face of Maria. Two sets of eyes fluttered when they met before dropping in adolescent flirtation. Miguel shifted back and forth like a boy fighting the urge to pee. Maria coyly brushed a cluster of hair from her face, tucking it behind her ears.

"It's *chessss*. But, yeah, come on in. Why don't you and Maria partner up."

Perhaps this mutual crush could act as a sedative for the hyperactive Miguel, who shuffled to the desk next to Maria's, furtively glancing at her as Dieter passed out the chess sets. While the co-ed pair stole glimpses at each other, the freshman boys stared at their hands, at the poster of Dieter, at the water stain, at the graffiti on the desks—anything that would fight back the creeping, awkward sexuality that was decidedly heterosexual but extremely fragile.

Dieter noticed the peculiarity, so he hastened the beginning of the game.

"Okay, go ahead and open your boards!"

Dieter's voice burst with enthusiasm as if the hinged plastic boards would reveal a treasure greater than the plastic pieces contained inside it. Maria confidently plucked the light tan figures, bending across the joined desks to snatch up the queen and some pawns from Miguel's side. Miguel, in return, grabbed peeks of her breasts that squeezed together with each lean forward. Though the school mandated polos and khakis, the polos came in different styles with different numbers of buttons that trailed down at different lengths, letting the girls test the school's dress code and the potency of their femininity.

A smile crept across Miguel's lips. His gaze lingered in lust, similar to the way he had looked at Esther. But Dieter also noticed Miguel's sincere interest in Maria from his gentle voice and bashful countenance in the moments her chest was covered. Feeling like an over-protective father, Dieter vowed to keep tabs on where this relationship was going.

After a minute, one of the freshmen raised his hand.

"Mr. Vogel, sir?"

"Yes?"

"Is this like checkers?"

Dieter's head dropped reflexively. The day's various disappointments had tested his patience. Despite his progress in shaking bad habits, he jumped into the instinctual response of repeating the question.

"Is this like checkers?" Dieter responded.

The kid looked at the other boy, then back at Dieter.

"Yeah, that's what I...yeah?"

Dieter stepped next to the freshman's partner.

"Is *this*," Dieter grabbed the king from their pile, "like checkers?"

The boy dropped his eyes as a sign of surrender. Dieter noted the boy's act of resignation, an act of respect that soothed Dieter's irritation, which dammed what would have been a prolonged verbal assault. For it was often the case in Dieter's first years of teaching that when he lashed out, the student would make a series of increasingly aggressive comments, culminating in Dieter calling security or stomping off in frustration. During one such encounter, a three-time junior had called Dieter a "piece of shit" after Dieter had berated him for coming into class ten minutes late (the junior, in his defense, had just spent fifteen grueling minutes expelling a particularly pernicious portion of undercooked breakfast sausage). But Dieter had noticed over the past four months that interactions with students were softer, and the teens were more likely to acquiesce, and the lessons were permitted to continue smoothly. This encounter with a student he had met only minutes before evinced the rapport Dieter now carried.

Seeing that they were clearly lost, and seeing that Maria was already tutoring Miguel, Dieter set up a series of different exercises. In each one, the student had to use a specific piece, whose abilities Dieter had just taught, to capture the King. By the end of the hour, the boys could confidently show the movement capabilities of each piece, though the "caballo" needed to be reviewed for the next meeting.

Maria had also taught Miguel enough so that he knew what a pawn was and what it did. He also knew that the "queen was a bigger boss than the bitch-ass king."

The four teens moved toward the door, but paused before leaving.

"Yo, Mr. V. You going to the game?"

Dieter smiled.

"Yeah, got to close-up shop, but I'll be there. Starts in twenty minutes, right?"

They nodded.

As Maria and Miguel walked out, Maria gave Dieter a bright, genuine smile and mouthed "thank you" before sliding her hand into Miguel's. Dieter felt a blush of joy from her gratitude compounded by the wonder of witnessing adolescent infatuation. The day's disappointments vanished.

He truly enjoyed the kids. In fact, he recognized how deeply he had missed interacting with them during the break. And, Dieter thought, chess club might prove to be a welcome augmentation to his classroom interactions, in the way that coaching basketball brought a varied sense of purpose to Manley.

Despite himself, Dieter began humming the old tune his mom used to sing when he was a kid—back when his dad was still a face and a name. After straightening up his desks and wiping the board, Dieter sat down to finalize lesson plans. As he went to open one of his documents, a box popped up on his screen: "Reminder: Email Esther about coffee."

Since Dieter never used the calendar feature on his computer, he could only assume some irreverent, omnipotent being was to blame. While staring at the screen, the arrow crept across the background, settling on the upper left envelope that represented his email. The computer burst with a new window, where the mouse again moved purposefully, this time toward the "New Email" option.

Dieter had watched everything up to this point without surprise. He mused how disconcerting this would be if he hadn't known the Devil was active in his life. Probably would have suspected a hacker, though who in his right mind would want to enter into the life of a lowly high school English teacher?

The various interactions with Esther this year had happened by chance. Now, in the form of an email, he was being asked to initiate contact on his own. Hesitancy filled the place where words should have formed. After a minute, words sprouted next to the flashing vertical line in the body of the blank email:

What are you doing?

Dieter was perplexed by the question. Hadn't the Devil just

commandeered his computer for a clear purpose?

Earth to Dieter...

Dieter leaned forward.

Trying to ask out Esther.

What are you going to say, Romeo?

Why don't you type it? I don't know what to say.

There was a pause before more words popped up.

I can't...

Why not? Dieter typed.

I JUST CANT.

Dieter stared at the screen—a shiver slithered up his spine. Caps lock really was an abrasive way to write. After ten seconds, the Devil typed again.

☺ *Sorry. I just think you should do it. It won't sound real coming from me.*

Dieter typed furiously: *I thought you were the expert on the human condition?*

I am. You need to do this for your sake.

Dieter sighed and leaned back. His stubble itched and the familiar buzz of frustration and defeat swarmed his brain. Normally, this would be the moment he'd close down. But the Devil was on his side—or rather—on his screen.

Start with something casual, something about wanting to see her...

Dieter put his fingers to the keys and began: *Hello Esther. How are you? I am great, thank you.*

Quickly Dieter's words were highlighted and deleted.

Are you trying to ruin your chances? I mean, you want to sleep with her, right?

Dieter frowned.

Try to be causal. Don't sound desperate.

Dieter mentally replayed all the seduction scenes and coy, clever dialogue that he'd seen in the movies. Unwittingly, he felt his lips purse in suave confidence before he leaned in for his second try.

I hear Perkolate has a new dark roast. Want to swing by after work to try it?

Dieter paused, and then closed with:

Coffee tastes better with company LOL. Sincerely, Dieter.

A burst of all-caps flew under his email.

WHAT THE HELL MAN?

Dieter paused, confused. He typed back:

What? I thought it was good?

It was fine 'til the LOL crap

Dieter admitted it was a bit juvenile. Satan continued typing furiously.

I thought we were on the same team. Count me out of this...

What are you talking about?

LOL, 'like our lord' you think your code is so tough to read, but I picked it up.

Dieter shouted at his screen: "Shut up! Shut up! Shut up! LOL means 'laugh out loud.' Seriously, you say you are all-knowing?"

The screen quickly deleted everything but the message. A sentence hastily popped up.

I didnt say I was all-knowing. I just know human behavior.

For being the King of the Underworld, the Devil was truly pathetic at times. Nevertheless, Dieter deleted the LOL. With one click, the email was sent and a surge of pride swept through him.

Another email popped up.

Feels good, huh? LOLoudly!

Dieter responded by shutting off the laptop and stuffing it into its carrier bag before heading to the gym. He had forgotten to open Esther's email.

With four games left before the rivalry game versus Hilltop High School, students and staff suddenly took interest in their 9-0 Pretzels. The normally apathetic students were showing up in clusters of three or four, waddling through the parking lot like scared flocks of geese peering around cars for potential predators. They moved slowly toward the student entrance, which was relegated to the shady side of the building since it led straight to the baseline bleachers. Sitting by the double-door entrance was an obviously flustered Jose, who was trying to check ID's before admitting the students into the gym.

"Divo! Hey, I could sure use a hand!"

Dieter walked over to the open doors. The squeaks of sneakers and rhythmic bouncing of rubber on hardwood became more pronounced as Dieter followed the sidewalk past the students.

Jose hovered in the glow of the gym, encircled by light.

"Just check their ID then let them enter. Non-students need to go to the main entrance to pay the entrance fee."

Dieter nodded, catching a glimpse of Manley massaging Andre's shoulders while talking strategy with his superstar athlete, who responded with focused head nods. *So much for the rebellion,* Dieter thought as he turned back to the line. Even though Chess Club was a joyful moment in that dark first day back from break, he could not help his disappointment at the nonexistent activism, which had almost blown the top off the school two weeks prior.

The first student stepped forward bashfully, handing off the school ID. Methodically, Dieter glanced down at the plastic card, back to the student's face, then, without bothering to say a word, he allowed admittance. Jose, however, was more joyful in the process.

"Here you go, Ms. Johnson! Enjoy the contest! Ah, Mr. Vazquez, math superstar! Come inside and find a seat!"

It was well-known among the staff that Jose knew every student by name and by strength. He had the uncanny ability to recognize other students' abilities, even those he didn't personally teach. It was creepy, really, to the adults in the building. It was also convicting since most teachers didn't bother to get to know the students that well, even the ones they taught. For the students, Jose's presence created a profound affirmation that buoyed them in whatever tempests they were facing in their lives.

After five minutes, the line dwindled and a warning buzzer resounded inside the gym. While the players made their way to their respective benches, Jose turned to Dieter.

"Can you check these last few? I'm going to check on concessions in case there is a food shortage."

Dieter didn't have time to answer since Jose had already turned the corner. Pangs of hunger clenched his stomach and a wandering thought entered his mind: what could Jose do if there was a food shortage?

"Okay, Mr. Cordero," Dieter called out before resuming his duties.

When Dieter turned back to the line, an overpowering stench of marijuana punched his nose. A pair of sheepish, gangly white kids stood in front of him. Their boat shoes and pastel colored polos aroused suspicion.

"IDs?"

"Oh, um, yeah, we, uh, left them in, uh, homeroom."

"Who's your teacher?"

"Oh, uh, Mr. Corduroy"

"Cordero?"

"That's what I said."

Dieter paused. He prepared to ask their names so he could simultaneously get them in trouble for the heavy weed smell and check with Jose about the validity of their claims. But then the intoxicating scent of Esther altered his intentions.

"Oh, hey Miss B!" Dieter said with a burst of eagerness.

After a pained smile and wave, she pushed past Dieter, staring at the court. Her angry lean made it seem as if she was going to charge the bench, but she turned toward the bleachers instead.

After she took a seat next to Father Manny, Dieter turned back to the line of kids. The two weed-scented teenagers had vanished. Dieter shrugged and motioned the rest of the students inside with a sweep of his arm. The doors clicked shut, and the opening whistle summoned the players to the center of the court.

Evendale was a predominately white community that bordered

Reading. Where Hilltop was affluent, Evendale's residents were newly minted white-collar workers, who came from blue collar parents that had realized the importance of college for their children. The families were conservative, humble, and held a reverence for Catholicism (at least when Easter and Christmas rolled around). The progeny of these first-generation college graduates assumed much of their parents' identity. They worked hard in school and excelled academically. However, they seemed to lack tenacity or an acuity for athletics.

Through teamwork and a dogged adherence to a painfully boring basketball strategy, they had held the Pretzels to a slim five-point lead after the first quarter. The slow pace of play had thwarted much of Reading's offense, and the fans stirred with anxiety as the buzzer sounded for the second quarter.

Then Andre took over.

Dieter, viewing the six-foot, seven-inch junior for the first time on the basketball court, was amazed at the quickness and ease with which Andre dribbled, ran, shot, and defended. Where every other player seemed to simply play the game, Andre made it an art. He sliced through the defense in a heartbeat, dancing around the area Dieter had mistakenly called 'the taint' before an old man with an oxygen mask corrected him. His steps would then stomp the ground violently, his body thrown with frantic force. After he had thrust into the air, he gracefully cradled the ball off the clear glass and into the basket while the defense looked on helplessly.

Down court, Evendale would then take a long shot, sinking it about one third of the time. Then Reading would sprint back upcourt, give the ball to Andre, who would then easily weave through the defense, culminating in either a basket or a pass to one of his teammates for a score.

After Andre made a long shot from beyond the three-point line, Evendale took a time-out. With fifteen seconds left in the half, they were down by twenty points. The Evendale players stood calmly while their coach drew up a play. On the opposing side, Andre never stopped moving. He was like a caged lion, waiting to be unleashed.

Manley's words were tiny morsels that only made Andre hungrier for the freedom to roam.

The whistle blew and play resumed. Evendale moved the ball with quick passes, avoiding dribbles that went for longer than a step or two. It was clear to most of the fans that they were delaying for the final shot. But while they were moving through their pre-set play, Andre broke between two offensive players and pounced on their pass.

As Andre snatched the ball full stride, five-hundred butts lifted from their seats while five-hundred sets of lungs inhaled.

5-4-

He sprinted across half-court, the ball bouncing back and forth as if it were a yo-yo.

3-

His stride slowed as he reached the free-throw line.

2-

Even Dieter, a grown man clueless to most aspects of the game, could feel his heart quiver as Andre lifted from the ground, right arm cocked back, ball gripped in his palm.

1-

As soon as Andre threw the ball through the hoop, a roar blasted against the walls of the gym, dulling the drone of the buzzer. Even the Evendale fans who had the seats next to the basket cheered, much to the chagrin of their players.

Reading's fans whooped in delirious joy as both teams left for their respective locker rooms. The Evendale players slogged off the court, afflicted by their imminent defeat, while the Reading players charged jubilantly past their fans. Manley's arm never left Andre's shoulders, nor did the wide grin on both of their faces. Dieter felt a sting of jealousy in his stomach.

With nothing to watch for twenty minutes, the fans headed toward the concession stands and restrooms. Some of the teachers, now anxious about the collection of teens drifting out of sight, moved from the bleachers and strategically surrounded the herd like Border Collies.

Within the group of spectators that had remained in the stands, Dieter could see Esther, eyes still faintly bloodshot and turned down to her phone, which rested on her lap.

Dieter knew this was his chance. She was fragile, and he could drape her in friendliness. But every time he went to lift his foot, it only arched, his toes fixed firmly to the ground. Something pleaded with him to respect her vulnerability, while a different emotion encouraged him to take advantage of her defenseless situation. At the root of this conflict grew the crippling fear of rejection that Dieter had carried since adolescence.

He stood on the hardwood floor, shifting from side to side, until a sharp 'ding' and the accompanied vibration came from his pocket.

Message: 666-6969

Dieter's eyes rolled in annoyance: Satan was as crass and pre-dictable as his adolescent students. He slid his finger across the phone and opened the message.

Talk to her. She's waiting to be taken

Dieter responded quickly, but out loud.

"I will! Relax."

A couple of straggling students shot Dieter perplexed glances, to which Dieter responded with his best 'teacher stare' (the one that says, "I know what I'm doing, don't question me," which is, in fact, different from the "you know what you did" stare).

Dieter's phone pinged again.

Type. Don't talk. L Out L

Sorry. What do I say?'

Talk about break. Ask how Nerdy Ears was

Nerdy ears?

News years! God dame autocorrect

Dieter closed the message and discovered his background had been changed. The three-star decal of a professional football team replaced the *Star Wars* wallpaper that Dieter had put there a year ago. Dieter recognized the logo since it was the only thing the men (and some women) were talking about. Something about the hated team making another playoff run.

Dieter reopened the message to Satan.

You know it's not Stealers, right?

I know. Still my favorite team.

Ok

I also like Bill Bella check

Dieter closed the phone. He knew the Steelers, but as for this Bill "Bella check", he was probably too vile to concern Dieter.

Scrolling through his messages, Dieter realized the more he conversed with the Prince of Darkness, the more he felt an intellectual authority, and perhaps even an ascendency to this *divine* being. These days, ideas for lessons flowed from him far more often than from Satan. The connections that Dieter had made with his students, and with Esther, had come without guidance from his mischievous mentor. After sending the email to Esther that day, he'd known that he no longer needed Satan's prompting. Dieter resolved to detach himself from his immoral mentor and took his first step toward the spot on the bleachers where Esther sat. Despite her obvious pain, she forced a smile. Could that one coffee-house encounter have changed everything? Esther's eyes glistened over her shy smile.

"How was your New Year celebration?" Dieter asked.

Esther slid over on the bleachers as an invitation for him to sit next to her. A small rush threatened to elevate his pants to an embarrassing, noticeable level, so Dieter sat quickly.

"I ended up staying home," she said. "How about you?"

"Pretty much the same. My mom has a crush on the silver-haired guy from CNN, so I hung out with her to make sure she wouldn't have a heart attack when he kissed his co-host at midnight."

A genuine smile spread over Esther's face. Dieter crossed his legs before continuing.

"Hey, I sent you an email, which I know is super tacky, and it's not meant romantically or anything, but you know, I enjoyed having coffee with you, since I feel like we never really got to know each other, and I, uh, thought if you wanted to meet up again, then I could use some help planning lessons for Miguel and the other kids."

Esther was still smiling. "I'd like that—" she began.

The head on Dieter's shoulders was now flush with blood, and he couldn't help but feel his eyes twitch with excitement. She hadn't rejected him! And he remembered seeing that she had sent him—

"—I actually sent you an email to see if you were free Saturday night to go to—"

But the loud siren from the scorer's table drowned out all conversation. Unlike the other times during the game when the buzzing was deliberate and lasted for two seconds, the siren kept blaring, causing the fans in the gym to wince from the prolonged blast. The score keepers hastily pressed buttons and flicked switches, but to no avail. Dieter grimaced and plugged his ears with his fingers. Esther also cringed.

Finally, someone from the bleachers walked over to the table and pulled the plug, silencing the two minutes of racket. Her decisive action was met with facetious cheering. Due to the lengthy siren blast, the players came back to the court prematurely, and the students began to return from the hallway. Dutifully, Esther and Dieter rose to reassert their silent presence to the students, whose mouths were stuffed with cheesy pretzels and sugary treats. Dieter forgot Esther's invitation.

When all was settled and the buzzer resounded (purposefully this time) to call the teams to the court, Dieter felt his phone buzz again. Esther smirked as Dieter pulled out his phone to check the message.

"Girlfriend?"

"No, just Satan." The words slipped from Dieter's mouth. His body convulsed in an effort to pull the words back in. Surely, that was a creepy answer, Dieter thought.

But the grin held on Esther's face as her hand playfully pushed Dieter's shoulder.

"Why would my mom be texting you already?"

Dieter could have passed out from light-headedness. Stunned, but smiling, he simply stared at her in response. Esther gave a girlish giggle before excusing herself to use the restroom.

Dieter's phone dinged.

Shes as good as yours. Smooth moves!

Dieter checked the message that preceded the Devil's praise. Another message from the 776 number.

You should sit in the bleachers by the basket

Dieter did not want to move from his place near Esther. Why would Satan suggest this, and why had he switched numbers? Before he could type a response, a whistle blew and sneakers resumed squeaking.

With Andre dominating the first half, the Evendale coach had decided to throw out the pre-scripted game plan in favor of a new plan to surround Andre at every chance. When Andre got the ball, two Evendale defenders would fly toward him, and if he somehow got past the first two, another defender flew in front of him to impede his progress.

Andre passed the ball most of the time, but as the third quarter waned, and when he was held scoreless, a pent-up agitation began to show. He plowed into the opposing players. He stopped passing the ball to teammates. And when he did get a chance for a lay-up, the biggest players on Evendale jumped fully into Andre, sending him skidding across the floor in front of the section of bleachers filled with Evendale's fans.

On one such occasion, the referee turned his back on Andre to announce the foul to the scorekeepers, and as Andre picked himself from the floor, he became incensed. Fury twisted his face. He scoured the pockets of spectators near him for some unknown target. The spectators, too, searched within their midst for the object of Andre's ire.

His teammates, sensing a volatile emotion swelling within Andre, moved to take him to the free-throw line. Like a frustrated child, he was dragged away from the scene, still looking back at the fans.

"Andre, get to the line! What's wrong with you?" Manley shouted across the court.

Andre glared at his coach before fixing himself behind the line.

After both teams had lined up, the referee blew his whistle and casually tossed the basketball to Andre, who took a deep breath and started his pre-free throw routine: a bend of the knees, a double bounce of the ball, another bend of the knees, and a lift of his body as he shot the basketball.

But as his body rose up in the subdued gym, a sharp scream came from the section of the bleachers where Andre had been fixated. He jerked as he released his shot, and the ball slid awkwardly from his fingers, falling with a thud after missing the basket completely.

Two teenagers with malicious grins laughed ecstatically in the otherwise quiet stands. A few of the spectators around them frowned and turned toward the teens. Dieter knew that he had encountered those two before.

Andre scowled before the ball was given back to him for another shot. He went through the same pre-shot ritual, but as he went to shoot, his movements went rigid. Once again, the boys shouted, and though Andre was not surprised, his free-throw clanged forcefully off the side of the rim. Due to the velocity of the miss, the ball ricocheted off the basket, taking an Evendale player by surprise. When the player knocked the ball skyward, a mad scramble for the rebound ensued.

Like kittens batting at a ball of yarn, the players swatted at the ball in feeble attempts to control it. Andre, seeking to amend his embarrassing miss, entered the scuffle. During the feverish battle, he was again tossed toward the baseline. And again, there were words shouted by the two boys in the stands, only this time, what they said sparked an explosive anger in Andre. As quickly as he fell to the ground, he jumped up and lunged into the bleachers. Swirling bodies pushed spectators aside as Andre and the two teens grappled and shoved.

By the time teammates, fans, and two referees had pulled Andre from the grasp of the instigators, a flurry of punches had been thrown. One referee pointed at Andre and then swiped his hand to the locker room, sentencing Andre to miss the rest of the game. Andre did not protest the call. Instead, he motioned to the stands with a single-finger uplifted as he mouthed a threat to the two boys. He stormed off the court followed by Manley and the school's lone security guard.

Before Andre left the fans' line of sight, Manley cut him off.

"What's gotten into you? You're acting like an animal," he barked.

Andre dropped four fingers again, and replied, "He called me a nigger. I don't let nobody call me that."

Manley shook his head and let the security guard escort the seething teen the rest of the way into the locker room. When Dieter turned back to the bleachers, he saw that the two boys had disappeared out the side door, presumably satisfied with the result of their antagonism.

Esther's eyes watered as she hugged Dieter. Without thinking, his left hand crept behind Esther's back to give reassuring pats between her shoulder blades. In response, she laid her head on his shoulder. Suddenly, she jerked from the embrace.

"I need to talk to him."

Dieter turned to her. "If you let him cool down, we can talk to him tomorrow. I can't imagine what it's like to be called that name."

"Yes, Andre too," Esther said as she dabbed her eyes with the back of her hand, "but I meant Manley."

Chapter 11

A NEEDLING GUILT followed Dieter after the game and throughout the next morning. During the time he'd known Esther, he had
seen her as an object to acquire rather than as a person to know. Part
of him still felt this crude infatuation, but through his encounters
with her he'd come to recognize a personality that actually captivated him. He wanted to draw closer to her, yet he was frightened
by his conflicting conscience. Lost in thought, he ran into a rushing
mass of untucked shirt and frizzled, greasy hair barreling down
the hallway.

"Watch it, Burro," Manley growled.

When Manley had rounded the corner, Dieter noticed a piece
of paper on the ground with the school district logo on it. Dieter
grabbed the paper and read it.

"To the parents of Andre Williams:"

A suspension notice: seven days away from school, including
school related activities. Dieter had already resolved to assemble a
packet of make-up work for Andre, including a letter of support,
when he ran into Esther, her face stained by running mascara.

"Esther, are you—?"

"I'm fine," she sniffed.

Dieter reached out his arm to give her a reassuring pat on

the shoulder; instead, he had opened himself for the full force of her body to curl into his. His left arm draped around Esther as his right arm hung awkwardly, his hand clutching the suspension notice. As she sobbed softly onto his right shoulder, Dieter again felt two battling currents of affection: one burning, the other soothing. Her vulnerability stimulated Dieter's compassion, but it also tempted the predatory drive that Satan had cultivated through his messages, and the vision that he had projected during their first meeting. Esther sighed deeply and pushed away from Dieter.

"Thanks for that. It's been a difficult morning."

Dieter smiled politely and nodded.

"I wanted to talk with you anyway: I need make-up work for—"

"—Andre," Dieter cut in.

They both frowned in frustration.

"I'll get it to you by lunchtime," Dieter replied.

Esther smiled. Dieter was one of the few teachers who gave her enough feedback so that she could write education plans and address particular disabilities. And Dieter was the only teacher whose class had students making gains. On the mid-year state assessment, the reading scores were the only ones that had grown.

Dieter smiled again and began to walk toward his class.

"Oh, Dieter…"

Dieter glanced back at her.

"I hate to trouble you, but could I get a ride to and from school for a week or so? My mom's car will be in the shop, and she'll be using mine."

Forgetting for the moment that his mom was driving him to school each day, he nodded.

"Thanks. I have rides this week, but I'll see you Monday morning around 7:00 o'clock."

"What about Saturday?" Dieter asked.

"What *about* Saturday?"

"Coffee? You and me?"

"Perkolate at ten?"

"It's a date."

———————

While she and Manley were not officially broken up, Esther never-theless kept her Saturday morning date with Dieter. She sent him a message on Friday night confirming their meeting.

Dieter proved to be a sympathetic ear, and they found mutual laughter in the awkward stories and comic characters of years past and present. After a particularly funny story about Miguel, Esther leaned across the table.

"Dieter, why do you come to this coffee shop?"

Dieter took a long sip of coffee that caught the back of his throat unaware.

"*Cough*...the delicious...*cough*...coffee...*cough*."

Esther giggled and gave Dieter's hand a playful pat.

"Seriously, everyone goes to the other shop, but you insist on coming here."

"I've been coming here since high school. It was always a place I could go to get away from other people. Now I guess I appreci-ate that, through everything, this beat-up, old shop is still here," Dieter said.

Esther smiled. "Just like Reading?"

"Just like Reading."

"Do you think you'd ever move away?"

Dieter began, "I've never thought about it." Esther nodded, and Dieter continued. "Part of me is sick of all the fear, all the hurt, all the poverty..." Dieter traced his finger on the rim of the coffee cup. "...but that's also why I want to stay. Our kids deserve..." Dieter's throat closed-up and his eyes grew teary. Embarrassment flushed his face from this unexpected emotion, but it also caused the sweetest sensation within him as Esther reached out her hand and grabbed his.

Her voice cooed in compassion. "Dieter, I love the way you've changed this year. You are everything our students need and I—"

Esther stopped talking. Her finger rubbed Dieter's knuckle in nervousness, "—well, I needed a friend like you. I'm glad we're getting to know each other."

Dieter smirked as he looked at the interlocked hands. "It only took us eleven years."

"Worth it," Esther said, giving his hand a squeeze.

For the next hour, they shared more laughter and stories amid confessions of various insecurities and frustrations. Esther admitted that she was going to break up with Manley soon. She even confided to Dieter that she had lied to Manley about her whereabouts this morning and that she had moved the rest of her things from his apartment.

After they said goodbye, Dieter wanted to continue with the divulging, so he shared with those that he could that he had met a woman for coffee on Saturday. Disappointingly for Dieter, he only had his mom, her cat, and Jose to entrust this news.

Dieter's mom plotted a timeline for marriage, and dreamt each night of squealing, pudgy cheeks. Whiskers seemed to lick her butt a little more vigorously. But Jose was concerned.

"That poor girl has dealt with such emotional abuse by Manley these past few months." Jose shook his head as he took a seat on the bench press. "This is only going to be trouble, Divo. You need to slow down and be friends first." Jose plopped his back down and began placing his hands on the bar.

Dieter stood above Jose but glanced around the gym for any sign of Manley, who had been absent from morning workouts for the past month, including the two weeks over Christmas break. While Jose went through his exercise, Dieter tried to defend himself.

"She seems fine to me. Besides, she's initiating stuff, too. It's not just me, you know?"

Jose puffed his chest out for one final push of the bar.

"I-I-I know," the bar collapsed onto the supports, "but she's still with Manley. There's something within her that wants commitment. She needs someone who is devoted to her and willing to dedicate time to building her up. Why do you think she ended up with an older man in the first place?"

Dieter crawled onto the bench and set his hands. He silently pushed through eight repetitions, eyes staring blankly into the strip of lights above him. The added weights rattled, but Dieter hardly took notice of his newly acquired strength.

"Are you ready for a *committed* relationship with her?" Jose asked as he leaned over Dieter.

Dieter stared up at Jose, whose face was now only a shadow with a fluorescent halo around it.

"Why do you ask?"

Jose sighed and they rotated positions.

"I know how it feels, Dieter. People come to you feeling vulnerable. It would be easy to exploit them, but you need to think about what you want from this."

"What *I* want from this?" Dieter shot back.

"Everyone knows you're infatuated with her." Jose pushed off the bar. "There will come a time when you will have to choose between pursuing her and something else you want. There will be tension."

Jose didn't know what he was talking about. He couldn't imagine ignoring her for another person. She had such a wonderful sense of humor, and she was so down to...

"Gah! Divo!"

Dieter snapped back to Jose, who had let the bar collapse upon his chest.

"Sorry," Dieter mumbled.

Jose sat up, rubbed his chest with one hand, and held the other one up to acknowledge his forgiveness. "Anyway," he coughed out, "it's a tense situation all around. Manley is due for a melt-down. He still has a small shred of confidence that is keeping him sane. If he loses that, who knows what will happen? Be Esther's friend until you both are ready, and start getting yourself right."

Dieter nodded.

"She's a good woman, and she wants a full commitment from a

good guy. If you can't give that, then just be her friend until you can."

———————

"We need to chat, Dieter."

Kenneth Branagh, playing the role of Iago, paced back and forth on Dieter's television set. Dieter had frozen the video while he responded to Esther's texts.

"Okay…" Dieter sat up on the couch.

The Devil possessed Branagh stopped his strutting and turned to Dieter. "I know you and Esther are getting along now, and that's great, but—"

"But?" Dieter snapped.

Dieter had just spent ten minutes messaging with a clearly distraught Esther, who had just had an ugly break-up with Manley. Though she wasn't his girlfriend, Dieter felt inclined to defend her. To have his nemesis berate her irked Dieter. So, with Satan pulling the "we need to talk" conversation starter, Dieter's irritation cracked like a whip at his supernatural partner.

Satan replied softly, "Look, Dieter, you are doing great."

Dieter's lip loosened.

"I'm afraid that you'll get distracted. That's all."

Dieter shook his head.

"Esther is part of my reward, right?"

Devil-Branagh nodded in agreement, holding up his hands to acknowledge Dieter's assertion.

"You are correct, but rewards come from jobs well done. Don't forget that, Dieter."

Dieter's lip tightened again.

"Is that a threat?"

Satan chuckled apologetically. "Not at all… I'm just saying that there's a time for everything. Remember that we vowed to make you Principal and to make my name glorified. We should not divert those goals, okay?"

Dieter nodded. "Is that all we need to talk about?"

Iago brushed the dirt in front of him with his right foot. "Well, there is one other thing…"

Dieter groaned. "What?"

"The goal is for me to be worshiped. So, if you could stop defending Jesus and his bible-humpers, that would be appreciated."

"You mean Bible-*thumpers*?"

"Just remember we're on the same team." Satan's voice sharpened. "We help each other, we focus on the mission, and we both get what we want. Agreed?"

"Okay, okay," Dieter mumbled as a message from Esther lit up his phone. "I really don't know where this is coming from."

But Branagh had resumed his position on the screen. Satan had left the conversation.

"Sir, why didn't he just kill him?" Val's face revealed her sincere concern, and while Dieter wasn't surprised that Val asked the question, he was taken aback by the bloodthirstiness in her tone.

"That's a good question, Val."

Dieter stumbled on that question himself. Needing to stall, he pulled a risky teacher tactic, one that could dissolve the classroom atmosphere into chaos, but Dieter was convinced that any off-task behavior would be minimal. "Talk to your neighbor, and then write down a possible answer. We'll share in three minutes."

While the students talked, Dieter poured over the story by Gabriel Garcia Marquez. The dentist had the Mayor, a corrupt, violent tyrant in his chair. He had him subdued as he pulled his tooth. He even said, as he inflicted pain through removing the tooth, that the pain was vengeance for the Mayor killing twenty of his men. So why didn't the dentist kill him?

Dieter still didn't have an answer when time was up and the students began to grow restless. He hoped that something from the students would spark a definitive answer as he called the class back to attention. Immediately, Miguel begged for an audience.

"Mr. V, Mr. V, choose me!"

With only ten minutes left in class, Miguel's comment, and the uproar it was bound to create, could carry the class to the bell, leaving Dieter twenty-three hours and fifteen minutes to figure out an answer.

"What you got, Miguel?"

Miguel stood up with his chest puffed. Before he spoke, he put his foot on his seat and crouched over it.

"The dentist didn't kill him because he made the Mater—"

"Mayor…"

"Right, the Me*jor*. He made the Me*jor* look like a little bitch, and the Me*jor* would have to live with that forever." As he talked, his eyes squinted and his finger jabbed the desk for emphasis. "It's like Shakespeare said: A cow dies a thousand times. The Me*jor* would die whenever he thought about it."

Students vigorously nodded and snapped in agreement, but they still turned to Dieter for affirmation. Dieter scratched his neck-stubble in thought, letting Miguel's words simmer. His pride in Miguel throbbed in his chest. It was a perfect, perceptive answer from the unlikeliest of sources. And he had made a non-sexual, albeit partially inaccurate, allusion to Shakespeare.

"Interesting idea, Miguel." Miguel smirked in satisfaction and mouthed "I'm interesting" to Maria, who was already beaming at him. "Sometimes death and complete destruction aren't enough. Sometimes taking away someone's power and humanity is more catastrophic."

Students nodded their heads in agreement. A poster of Shakespeare gave a thumbs up.

"Well, Miguel, we will have to end class on your brilliance. Let's pick this up next class."

––––––––––––

"It's cruel."

"It's necessary."

"It can't be. There are other ways, right?"

Dieter's eyes darted from the box of erectile dysfunction medicine to the Devil-possessed picture on his desk. It was an old photo of him from the summer when his dad had left. He was ten, and his mom had taken him to Disneyland. His thin arms jutted from the florescent green Mickey Mouse shirt like windshield wipers. Dieter's feathery brown hair and wide, euphoric smile peeked out from under the mouse-ear hat. At that time, Dieter's mom hadn't told him what divorce was and what it would hold for him (or rather, what it withheld). Dieter's innocence was still intact.

"This *is* the best way. Uncontrollable erections will be the straw that breaks his back. He needs to be broken—trust me. I feel like you aren't trusting me." Dieter's ten-year-old self eyed him through the glass pane, arms resting on his ten-year-old hips.

Dieter had thought about Satan often since the beginning of Christmas Break when his days were less occupied by teaching and planning. As much as Dieter hated to admit reliance, things were still progressing quite well while, even though he'd had his doubts during break, and even though he wanted to distance himself from the Devil.

Manley and Sanders were back on the defensive. Esther was tantalizingly close to being his. His body had slimmed down considerably. The students were eating from his hands. And his lessons were effective and engaging. Dieter had never thought that teaching was anything other than burdensome, but now he found it enjoyable. He was even relinquishing control during lessons by letting students guide and moderate discussions.

On weekends, he yearned for a return to work and the conversations he had with students. The way their faces illuminated during successful lessons. The way their eyes begged for more knowledge. The way they built each other up when one struggled. The way he could push their thinking to heights they'd never believed possible, and the way they, in turn, rewarded Dieter with unexpected brilliance, just as Miguel had done on Friday.

Though he loved working with all his students, he had his

favorites. Maria and Angie frequently sought him for guidance in English, school, life, and everything else in between, allowing Dieter to absorb a bit of their passions and problems.

Dieter also became a mentor to Andre, who had confided to Dieter that he wasn't a great reader, which was why he had been so apathetic in the past. During his suspension, Andre sent Dieter an email asking Dieter if he thought that he could score high enough to go to college "with or without basketball." Looking at Andre's mid-year score, Dieter had hope.

Even Miguel, the perennial pain-in-the-ass, was a joy. His sharp observations and wit complimented Dieter's lessons. Outside of class, Dieter found his humor to be goofy and endearing. And outside of the school structure, Miguel became a unifying topic between Dieter and Esther on their Saturday morning meetings.

Esther... The girl that Dieter had pined for since high school. The girl who represented the normal life he'd previously lived in shadows. The girl who now looked at him with eyes he'd only seen in movies. Dieter found her love for her students to be an enamoring quality that he'd never expected to stir admiration in him. Dieter concluded that Satan was at least partly responsible for getting the proverbial ball rolling.

"I trust you."

"Good. Now we just need to figure out how to get the medicine into him."

Dieter leaned back in his chair. He couldn't just hand them to him—he couldn't be connected to the medicine. Nor could he replace Manley's vitamins—the blue triangle pills would be instantly recognizable.

"I've got it!"

On the last weekend of Christmas break, he had been coerced into helping his mom give Whiskers the cat some medicine. Trying to hold the cat and squeeze the dropper of medicine into its mouth had failed and, furthermore, resulted in numerous scratches. Dieter had suggested that they infuse the cat's food with the solution, an idea taken when he overheard two grandparents reminiscing on how they had tricked their kids into eating vegetables by mixing them with smoothies or masking them in sandwiches. Their good parenting became fodder for this diabolical plot.

On Monday morning, Dieter would do as Manley had crassly done in the past: he'd leave a little treat, but spike it. The plan was perfect, but a hint of shame dulled Dieter's resolve.

"What's wrong?" the picture asked him.

"Nothing. I feel a little bad. He just broke up with Esther."

"Think of all the things he has done to you."

Painful memories rushed forth. Manley had insulted him and, as Satan had shown Dieter, Manley had mercilessly mocked Dieter in front of other staff. In addition, Manley had put Esther through months of emotional abuse. Dieter felt his guilt burn away like the fat in his body during workouts with Jose.

Standing in front of the bathroom mirror, he noticed he was looking more like the ten-year-old in the picture than his peak pudgy, self-loathing self in his high school yearbooks. His chest and arms had clearly defined ridges of muscle, and his stomach was no longer an obstruction to Dieter's line of sight when he peed. Confidence rippled, and should things with Esther progress...

"What are you doing?"

It took a moment for Dieter to find Satan's new incarnation. From the magazine sitting atop the toilet, a men's health cover model with a six-pack stomach and vein-topped biceps gazed curiously at Dieter. Dieter's left hand gripped the box of erectile dysfunction medicine, which he tried to hide behind his back.

"Just looking in the mirror," Dieter mumbled.

The model scowled in response. "Why are you trying to stash the pills? You don't seem to have *that* problem."

The implications of the comment caused a shiver to ooze down Dieter's back. "If you are watching me when I—"

"I don't!"

"I'm just keeping the extra pills in case I need them for—"

The fitness model gave a wink that sent another wave of revulsion through Dieter.

"I'm serious: stop watching! The moment you suspect I'm—"

"Okay, okay! I got it. Once the pants drop—"

"Stop! I'm not having this conversation with you."

The model held up his hands in understanding, leading to a conversational pause that lingered longer than was comfortable. Dieter moved to put the pills away into his medicine cabinet when the voice chimed in again.

"Delivery girl fantasy...not the worst!"

Dieter slammed the cabinet door and walked to the toilet. He dumped out the unused medicine, and then grabbed the magazine, rolled it up, and tossed it into the garbage. Finally, he bolted to the computer to clear its history.

Whether the Devil meant for it to happen or not, Dieter's appetite for pornography dissipated. The possibility of spiritual voyeurism, the distaste that came from the Devil's approval of such an act, the lingering conflict he faced between virtuous and vile desires—because of these things, Dieter, save for a few slip-ups, abstained from viewing pornography, starting that very day.

———

"Thanks for the ride!" Esther walked gingerly over the icy driveway outside her childhood home.

"Morning, dear," Dieter's mom's shrill voice bit the air. "Sorry about your car!"

Esther smiled graciously, appreciative that Dieter probably left out that another reason for the ride was because she had moved out from her ex-boyfriend's place.

"Dieter, where are your manners? Let her sit in the front."

Dieter pushed open his door.

"Have you even said 'hello' to her yet?"

"Hey," Dieter mumbled, eyes cast on Esther's boots.

"Morning!" she chirped in response. "Thanks for being *such* a gentleman!"

Dieter sensed the sarcasm in her voice, but it wasn't what he was used to. Sarcasm at the hands of others was usually bitter and sharp, souring even the most positive moments. But Esther's words fluffed around him, lifting his embarrassment and temporarily floating him above the cold ground.

Not knowing where he found the confidence, he pantomimed a valet, ushering her into the front seat of the mini-van with an overly humble bow that was topped off with "m'lady." Feeling a profound sense of self-assurance, Dieter softly closed the passenger door before turning to the sliding door.

The confidence he felt, though, was shattered when the sliding door refused to open, rocking the car with his failure. He tried twice more, but the handle gave a defiant click after he released it. He peered into the car for help, but his mom was already chatting with Esther. Again, Dieter pulled the handle and yanked, but the door again refused to open. He was forced to knock on the window.

"Ma, unlock the car!"

The door clicked, and Dieter pulled the handle. It didn't move. He shook his head and desperately continued tugging while his mom continued clicking 'unlock' and the car continued to rock. After five more pulls (and twenty clicks), Dieter glared at his mom.

"You don't need to keep hitting 'unlock': it's frozen."

Esther rolled down the window and smiled.

"It's okay. I'll slide in back."

In one motion, she managed to place her bag in the middle row, climb out of the front seat, and crawl over the arm rest. Dieter caught a glance of her sky-blue underwear, which peaked out during her maneuvering. The frigid weather outside became a sauna.

"Thanks," he muttered as he plopped into the car.

"I thought you'd been working out?" Dieter's mom shouted with sincere concern.

"I have," Dieter responded in agitation.

"Maybe run *and* lift from now on," his mom added as she lurched forward.

Minus the flirtatious moment outside the car with Esther, Dieter thought the morning had been a complete failure. Here he was in his mid-twenties, no car, riding with his mom, unable to open a sliding door to a minivan. He could feel the disappointment sitting heavily around his neck. But when he looked into the side mirror, he saw Esther's face looking back at him with a smile stretched across her beautiful olive skin.

———————

The chosen method for drugging Manley would have been impossible months before. Dieter hadn't seen Manley imbibe anything other than fruit, protein shakes, and sandwiches in the three years he had been teaching at the school. However, when the student revolt intensified after Thanksgiving, Dieter had caught Manley picking up donuts in the teachers' lounge. Dieter also heard whispers of Manley buying boxes of candy bars from students when they sold them for fundraisers. And from Esther, Dieter had also heard that Manley was pouring extra glasses of scotch at night.

Still, finding an organic reason for Manley to get a sugary treat, one that was sullied by Dieter but not tied to him, seemed improbable. Ten minutes before first period, he had formed the idea of buying the staff donuts anonymously and lacing all of them. Thankfully, the opportunity Dieter had been praying for presented itself in a tiara-clad Maria, who had on a shiny purple sash that read "Birthday Girl." Behind her stood a sheepish Miguel holding a platter of pink-frosted cupcakes.

"*Hoy es mi cumpleaños*, Mr. V! The cupcakes are for my friends, but I wanted you have one too."

Maria's gesture touched Dieter. His cheeks pulled wide in gratitude.

"What a great day! *Feliz cumpleaños!*" Dieter exclaimed, extending his arm out for a high-five.

Maria blushed and bashfully clapped her hand against his.

"This is truly a cause for celebration! Maybe I'll cancel the homework for tonight."

Maria's eyes dove hard to the floor, and her face turned a deep shade of amber.

"As long as you tell the class why," she giggled. Remembering something vital, she turned to Miguel, who took a second to grasp why Maria was glaring at him and the cupcakes.

"Oh, uh, Mr. V. You want one?" Miguel asked.

Dieter feigned apprehension.

"Oh, I don't know—the holidays have done a number on my waist."

Maria laughed, but Miguel interjected in exasperation. "Dude, Mr. V, you've lost, like, a hundred pounds. You can have *one*."

It was Dieter's turn to become flush. He hadn't weighed himself out of a self-conscious fear of failure. But Miguel's affirmation gave Dieter enough validation. The scale meant nothing compared to positive observations from brutally honest teenagers.

Miguel's hand hovered over the box like a claw. Finally, he snatched Dieter the largest cupcake.

For the first three periods, Dieter basked in the day's euphoria: the smile from Esther, the adolescents' admiration, the perfect vehicle for deviousness. When the lunch bell rang, Dieter was three feet above the dusty linoleum tiles ready to dive into his hellish scheme.

––––––––––

Since Manley had been running to fast food restaurants during basketball season, Dieter was certain that he could slip into Manley's room unnoticed and unobstructed. He pulled the baggie from his backpack, which contained three finely crushed pills, then delicately sprinkled the blue powder onto the cupcake, noticing with joy that the medicine looked like an acceptable garnish to the pastel pink frosting. Now was the tricky part: clandestine transportation.

Satan, speaking through an animated Marlon Brando, suggested that Dieter hide the cupcake in an empty packing box from a book order he had received a week ago. Dieter opened the container and slipped the cupcake inside. As he did so, he thought he saw the eyes on his cover of *The Great Gatsby* blink to life. But no words came from the book, and his delirious rush to carry out the plan didn't allow time for concern.

His haste also resulted in smeared icing on the inside of the box, although the level of concealment was adequate. And since a third of the school and staff were at lunch—the other two-thirds in class—not a single witness stalked the hallways.

Still, Dieter peeked cautiously down the curved stretches of lockers and doors before diving into Manley's room, where paper balls, broken pencils, and cluttered desks greeted him. Quickly, he walked to the front desk, pulled out the cupcake and set it down. Dieter froze in a temporary flash of guilt. The man was clearly becoming unhinged. Napkins and receipts and half-eaten sandwiches and ungraded papers from weeks before were strewn across the desk. If this plan succeeded, who knew what would happen?

"*Vamos! Rapido*!" the battery-operated jalapeno whispered behind him, snapping Dieter from his moral trance.

Panic sliced through him. He bolted from the desk and leapt from the room and into a scurrying Jose, sending a flurry of brushes and paint into the air. Jose's hands fell onto Dieter's shoulders.

"Divo! My apologies!"

"No, my bad," Dieter said as he broke the embrace to bend down and pick up the supplies.

"Oh, perfect!" Jose looked at the box in Dieter's hand.

Dieter smiled and nodded in recognition. They piled the paint brushes and tubes into the cardboard.

"What are you doing in Manley's room?" Jose asked innocently, a glimmer of light sparkling in his right eye.

"Oh, I, um—" Dieter stammered as he continued forcing brushes into the box.

"Were you trying to talk to him about Esther?"

"Yeah."

"Divo, I'm impressed! He's probably out for lunch. So, you'll have to catch him later. But it's great that you are being so mature."

Dieter nodded.

"Well, I've got to get these to class! Catch you later, master dater!" Jose said before bounding down the hallway

Dieter's head shook at the sign-off. He remained standing there, stewing in confusion, until the lunch bell sent him scampering off toward his classroom. As he jogged around the building, he felt renewed remorse at participating in such a dastardly act, especially if it worked. He had never dabbled in nefarious deeds before, and Jose's misplaced praise renewed his conviction. As his students filed into class, he sent an email to Manley warning him of laced cupcakes.

But Manley didn't get the email on time, if at all.

Dieter heard most of what had happened from various students gossiping in frantic, euphoric excitement. They spoke of how he didn't get up from behind his desk for the entire last period, and how he walked out of the building with a Spanish text book held over his crotch.

Since Manley called in sick Tuesday, Dieter knew the plan's intended effect had been achieved. The physical result of the laced cupcakes was captured on camera-phone images, which had circulated quickly from Monday night through Tuesday morning. Maria showed Dieter the most damning pictures.

In the first one, Manley stood at a music stand, which the school had provided for teachers to use as podiums. The photographer, a sophomore in Spanish 2, had been at Manley's one o'clock position. Manley was staring at his book on the podium. A faint outline bulged from his right thigh. The caption on the picture read: "*Our Espanol teacher gusta page 142.*" Maria showed Dieter the page, which had a picture of a woman dancing the tango in a tight evening dress.

Dieter admitted to himself that the picture might serve to arouse the right viewer, although he didn't find himself mentally salivating as he might have at the start of the year. He was amazed, however, by the potency of the drug. He also felt a slight discomfort at the size of Manley's member.

It was the second picture, though, that was even more

embarrassing. In the picture, Manley stood in the office, leaning against the secretary's partition, arms crossed on the top of the counter, but his body was bent, leaving his hips and legs two feet from the wall. The student, who was in the office waiting for an early dismissal, sat almost directly perpendicular to the scene.

Manley was talking to the secretary. Her thin hair, yellow teeth, and sagging cheeks were even more pronounced in the picture. Though her body was hidden, Dieter could imagine the curtains of loose skin hanging from her arms and back. But as the picture suggested, Manley was aroused by her figure. Clearer than the first picture, the angle of the image captured a fully alert Manley, who had a tent-like triangle in the front of his sweatpants.

"There's no caption for this picture," Maria laughed.

"It doesn't need one," Dieter muttered, before hastily changing the subject in a feeble attempt at professionalism.

By the weekend, the staff knew Esther and Manley were officially finished. Manley wouldn't return to school until Monday, not even showing up to coach the last of the two games for the week. A rumor circulated that someone had drugged Manley—a rumor that most people readily assumed to be true. Miguel's name was floated as the prime suspect since he'd helped Maria pass out cupcakes.

With Andre fired up after being suspended for seven days, he ran the basketball team in Manley's absence and renewed talk of foregoing the season if the school did not follow through with the vote on Tuesday.

———

While Manley was absent, Dieter continued pushing his anarchic agenda. In his freshman classes, the students continued delving into stories of mayhem. After *Narrative of the Life of Frederick Douglass*, Dieter would begin teaching *Macbeth*, where the students would learn how to carry out a plot and plant evidence. They would also learn how to emotionally dissociate themselves from their actions, unlike the weak-minded Macbeths.

Dieter's film class was finishing *The Godfather*. Next, he'd show *V for Vendetta* followed by *Breakfast Club, Idiocracy,* and *Fight Club*.

The various lessons were consistent with Dieter's themes for the year, but Dieter had no idea how they would manifest in the movement. All he could do was feed and groom for the time being until another fatal flaw revealed itself in the administration.

Dieter was so lost in his conniving that he hardly saw much of Esther beyond their morning commute. When he did encounter her in passing, he experienced a pressing desire to spend more time with her. On the last Thursday in January, she cornered him after sixth period.

"Dieter, I haven't seen you all week!" she chastised playfully.

Dieter looked up from his papers and returned the playful admonition. "That's because you've been hiding from me."

Esther's face turned chestnut under her fluttering eye lashes. "Well, I'm here now. And I'm free Saturday night."

Dieter's face turned pale and his blood rushed to his head.

"Pick me up in the man-van at seven?"

Dieter nodded with a dopey smile. Esther simply giggled and slid from the door frame.

Still wearing his goofy grin and work shirt and tie, Dieter stumbled into his afternoon workout. Jose immediately knew the situation.

"Oh, Divo! What puppy dog eyes! How love-struck are you?"

"Somewhere between a pick-up truck and a semi."

Jose chuckled and shook his head.

"Hey, Divo, I have to cut the workout short today. I found an old Gretel costume and need to mend it for the pep rally."

Dieter shook himself out of rapture. "She has a costume?" he sputtered.

"It's a silly old thing. But it'll be good for the students to personify the cartoon character. Maybe it will encourage more school spirit."

Dieter shook his head and murmured to himself, "It will encourage *something*."

———————

On the Tuesday after Martin Luther King, Jr. Day, the school failed to hold a vote during homeroom. On Wednesday, the administration explained that election was going to be held by "the board," a mysterious hidden entity of which even Dieter had no real information. On Thursday, the results were announced that "the board" had selected Gretel. At the end of the day, Sanders found in his mailbox half a soft pretzel covered in gooey nacho cheese and a scribbled note that simply read: *revenge is a dish best served cold*. On Friday, the day of the Reading versus Hilltop pep rally, the student body fully began its siege upon the heart and soul of Reading High School.

Chapter 12

THE SIGNS OF a deteriorating staff can be easily seen by those not wrapped up in the daily grind of teaching. To those in the school, it is an unseen, subtle suffocation. To those on the outside, whether it is a knowledgeable visitor, staff from a different school, or a successful teacher in the school (a position in which Dieter oddly found himself), all the symptoms of massive failure are obvious.

Even though the students were calmer in the weeks after Christmas break, the mutinous behavior before the break had left the staff strained by the knowledge that they truly did not have control of the environment. Schools, much like any organization, only thrive if the veil of authority is drawn over the subordinates—in this case, the eyes of students. When students discover the truth that teachers are, in fact, subject to the students and not the other way around, the teachers' power and confidence becomes constricted. All the students need to do is congest the flow of lessons with antagonistic questions or a strategic lack of participation.

At Reading, students squeezed their teachers' vessels of instruction. Students who had previously been ignorant or apathetic to the details of teaching now scrutinized punishments, classroom management techniques, lesson effectiveness, professionalism. With the prompting of Maria and coaching by Esther, students who had only been vaguely aware that they had a learning disability demanded the accommodations on their IEP's.

One class of juniors exclaimed that an uncharacteristically unkempt history teacher looked unfit to teach that day, and the students passed a full fifteen minute conjecturing about why the particular teacher was tired and slovenly looking (they settled on a long night of drinking, culminating with a crying session in the shower).

Freshmen openly lamented boring lectures and seemingly worthless lessons. They called out their Math teacher for not using more culturally relevant word problems. The seniors persistently questioned why teachers could wear jeans and leggings when the students had to dress in uniforms.

With the tension that now filled the halls and classrooms, the school's positive influence faced a shortness of breath. Ironically, the protest the students raised compromised the very learning for which they so passionately advocated.

Both students and staff knew that the end of year assessments were looming. Both students and staff had a stake in the test. But neither students nor staff could reconcile with the other side.

And so, the staff culture was in fibrillation, and because they felt their authority pulsing uncontrollably, the teachers sought to control everything else.

Copier disputes became full on battles. Print jobs went missing or were suspiciously cancelled when left unattended. Entire departments staked out the copier, forming human walls around the machine. Teachers took to hiding reams of paper that they snatched up whenever shipments would arrive.

Because teachers had to buy their own supplies, white board erase markers became prime commodities, enticing even the most level teacher to criminal behavior. Two teachers almost came to blows on the suspicion and accusation of marker theft. In actuality, those guilty were the teens in the school, who delighted in seeing adults exhibit the same behaviors for which they chastised their students.

Coffee makers also became territorial. At the beginning of the year, Math and Science shared the machine in the Math office because it made larger portions. Because Science drank more than any other department, Math started thinking that Science had no right to their primo-caffeinated goodness. After an impromptu department meeting, Math decided to put its foot down. With passive-aggressive signage and decoy brewing of decaf, Math and Science became entangled in a series of skirmishes that spiraled beyond coffee.

These juvenile actions spilled into injurious rhetoric. Rumors and criticisms about other faculty members filled the hallways and break rooms. Teachers gossiped about everything: a Math teacher's weekly breakdowns in the women's bathroom; the suspiciously flirty Bio teacher that always had female students around him; the obnoxiously perky Jose; the Manley-erection incident and the demise of his relationship with Esther; the Principal's faltering grip on sensibility. Teachers even accused the janitor of playing favorites in regard to classroom cleaning.

The only person impervious to the malicious whisperings was Dieter. Perhaps due to his isolation in the school, or maybe it was his transformation from sarcastic fat-ass to amiable, successful young man, but Dieter could simultaneously participate in these conversations as a listener and avoid guilt as a non-contributor. It also gave him fodder to continue provoking student rebellion. However, the students did not need much more instigation.

In the teachers' lounge, animosity erupted in a conflagration of spiteful language. With venom shooting through clenched teeth, the staff pronounced their desires for a variety of misfortunes to befall the students under their care. Even the most compassionate teachers openly entertained acts of revenge they could carry out on those *punks*. Grades became weapons of retaliation. Requests for help were denied. And since the teachers had come to fear what might happen if they engaged in discipline or taught mediocre lessons, they cancelled all-extracurricular activities except basketball.

Every aspect of school protocol had devolved from the pursuit of higher learning to barbarism and pettiness.

———————

"He kills himself? He was such a badass, though. He cut a dude's head off."

Miguel's incredulousness at the ending of *Things Fall Apart* worked perfectly into Dieter's discussion. The students had already established the themes around cultural imperialism, and while the issue of religion was prevalent in the book, Dieter skirted it in favor of race as many of the students were Christian, if only in name.

The few white students in class made it a point throughout the discussion to articulate how terrible the forced assimilation was in American history and in the story. The minority majority gave their nods of approval, appeasing their peers' white guilt. The only person who did not make any movement was Andre, who sat in a state of profound agitation.

One of his black peers connected the story to Andre. She said that Andre must feel a similar pressure when he sees that he has to sell-out to the school culture. She even implied that he was forced to carry on for the white administration and Manley as if he were a slave or a mime in a minstrel show. She concluded by asserting Okonkwo had had no choice but to "give himself up" to fight one last time.

Dieter cringed slightly: partially because her comment was con-troversial, but also because she struck a deep suspicion within him that he was doing the very thing of which she was accusing the administration. In a way, he too was exploiting the students' trust in him, mining their passion and talents so that he could extract it for his own objective. When they finally overthrew the leadership, Dieter would swoop in to assume power.

Dieter's jaw slackened as he contemplated the dynamics of his plot. Meanwhile, Andre's lip became tighter and tighter as the class continued. When he left the room after class was finished, Dieter could see Andre mouthing to Miguel: "I'm no one's nigger."

———————

Dieter's freshmen came into class with enthusiasm written all over their faces, and it wasn't because of the pep rally at the end of the day.

"What'd you think of last night's reading?"

Thirty different hands blasted into the air.

"Yo! Douglass is a beast."

"He beat the crap outta ol' dude."

"I can't believe he threw them fists."

"What a powerful section of the book. The way he fought his slave master, physically and mentally? Awesome!"

Dieter diverted the flow of participation after this flawless response. He pressed the student further. "Any particular quotes stand out?"

"I really loved the quote…" the student flipped through a few pages before jabbing his finger into the page. "…my long-crushed spirit rose, cowardice departed, bold defiance took its place; and I now resolved that, however long I might remain a slave in form, the day had passed forever when I could be a slave in fact."

Dieter pushed the student—Andre's little brother, who had taken to books the way Andre took to basketball—one final time. "In your own words, Jaylen, what does this mean to you today?"

Jaylen looked at Dieter, then at his classmates as he responded: "It means we are only slaves if we let them make us slaves. If we want to be our own people, we have to fight…by any means necessary."

———————

Reading versus Hilltop was a historic rivalry that, in the minds of both communities, transcended other rivalries. Against this annual game, Duke and North Carolina looked like a cordial shoot around. Ohio State and Michigan was merely a game of tag football between second cousins. USA and Canada hockey became a team figure skating event. Outside of this tiny corner of Southwest Ohio, nobody cared.

It had started during the 1940s as a match between two working class white communities divided by a railroad and "the hill." Reading sat at the base, Hilltop on high. Competitive high school basketball was relatively new then, but due to many fathers being overseas, the boys became representatives of homes and communities, and while cordiality was the expectation, the delineation of us versus them was implied. Fresh with war language, it was dubbed "The Civil War."

The growing economic and racial disparity between the two communities compounded with their proximity to one another. The rivalry's intensity snowballed at the turn of the millennium, becoming noticeably more aggressive, forming a dimension that should never exist in a high school arena. Scuffles and epithets plagued the games. And that was just among the dads and uncles in the stands. But it had become so interwoven in the identities of both communities, it continued, even as the hostility and racial bitterness persisted in debasing the rivalry.

This year, the Hilltop Highlanders were ranked ahead of the Reading Pretzels after a blazing 13-1 start. Reading's 11-2 record, both losses coming during Andre's suspension, placed them in second. The incident that had led to Andre's suspension added to the competitive fire.

The two students that antagonized Andre started for Hilltop, and word of what they had said spread. People from both communities lashed out at each other on internet message boards. Adult men, who had graduated decades ago, staked their emotional well-being to the outcome of this game.

The Friday pep-rally, then, was the administration's opportunity to push the students and student-athletes from their focus on rebellion to a frenzy of school spirit. They appointed Jose, the creative mind on staff, to plan the pep-rally with Manley, who was hopeful that the basketball team's success could somehow divert the flow of attention from below his waist.

With the students in the stands and the band playing "Final Countdown", the dancing figure of Gretel shimmied around the basketball court with a cartoonish smirk on her face. A girl from the junior class was supposed to be underneath her costume. Miguel, however, had slipped her twenty dollars and assumed the role unbeknownst to Manley or anyone else.

The original plan was to have Gretel be taken hostage by a student representing Hilltop's kilt-clad mascot. At that point, the basketball team would dunk around the two mascots, thereby suddenly and illogically causing the Highlander to tremble in fear. Andre would then run up for a monstrous dunk and drive the opponent from the gym while the students cheered. Manley and Andre would take the microphone and give a passionate speech about how much they were going to win by and how they needed the students to support the team, and after all of this, the students would leave forgetting about the board's decision.

But the rally did not go as expected and the students did not forget.

After the band played the school fight song, to which only a handful of students mumbled along, Manley walked to the circle that enveloped the school logo at mid-court. He produced a microphone from his back pocket. Gretel stared menacingly behind him.

"Good afternoon, Reading High School!"

The students grumbled a mixture of "good afternoon" and "shut up."

"I can't hear you!"

Dieter cringed: this wasn't the time to try to push the students toward civility. While there were a few students that responded, the dutifulness expressed by those teens was drowned under a chorus of boos. Some students dropped water bottles down their pants and turned so their friends and Manley could see the resulting bulge.

Manley leaned back, wide-eyed, before pushing himself back to the microphone.

"That's-um-better."

Students laughed in sardonic joy.

"Well, um, tomorrow is the big day. And Hilltop wants to come into our house and ruin our season—" he pointed to the visitors' tunnel.

Detrea, a senior in Dieter's film class, swaggered into the gym wearing a vaguely Anglo-Saxon kilt, which was in actuality a uniform skirt from an all-girls Catholic school. His body was painted forest green, and he hoisted a large, fake battle axe over his shoulder.

Manley, relieved that students were distracted, perked up again: "—but we have something to say about that. Here is your Varsity Basketball Team!"

A line of noodle-armed boys emerged from the right side of the bleachers. Bouncing rubber pounded the floor as the scrawny teens jogged in a line to midcourt. When Gretel was taken hostage, the student body began to laugh rather than boo. Students jeered: "Eat her!" And, "Dip her in cheese!" The players, those that could, dunked around the pretzel and the Highlander.

The three students that could dunk took two rotations each as most of the students cheered. For Miguel's part, he still pretended to be helpless as Detrea held Gretel hostage.

After the dunking was complete, the band struck up a tune that vaguely resembled a recent hit rap song. Some students danced and sang along. Upon hearing the music, the team stopped their movement and formed a line behind Detrea and Gretel, leaving a clear view for the audience. Both mascots looked to the far end of the gym, where Andre walked out from under the opposing bleachers, ball in hand. Andre stared for a moment at the other end of the court then suddenly began to run. Like a train careening toward a wall, he held straight at the Highlander and the pretzel, taking long strides that betrayed his desire to dunk on the two figures. However, when it was time for him to jump, he slowed down his run, stopped, and turned toward Detrea, who pushed Gretel to the ground. Miguel, playing a defenseless pretzel, flopped around, eliciting laughter from the crowd.

Miguel transitioned Gretel from feeble floundering to sexual undulations as Andre approached the faux Highlander and cocked back in a punching motion. But as his hand moved forward, he slowed it and met Detrea in a handshake and an embrace. The student body roared its approval. Manley's microphone dropped in stunned silence. Dieter grinned from his position in the stands.

Detrea and Andre turned toward the gyrating pretzel, who then turned toward them. In a moment of comedic acting, Miguel pantomimed fear, scooting backwards on the ground toward the basket with one hand extended in pitiful defense. When he was a few feet in front of the rim, Andre walked to the top of the three-point line. The students knew what was coming and the gym grew silent again. Miguel stood up, and the Highlander stood back, forming a clear path for Andre, who gave a quick lick of his lips. The basketball team bowed in approval. Manley shifted on his feet.

With five long strides and a forceful leap, Andre jumped over and into Miguel, throwing down a monstrous one-handed dunk. Students and staff alike convulsed.

Teens slapped hands and smiled and laughed. Andre was swallowed up by those sitting near the basket, and the rest of the team doubled over as Miguel ran around the gym doing cartwheels and hip-thrusts. Manley was left in the center of the court, head down and despondent.

The thrill of rebellion coursed throughout the bleachers as the chill of apprehension spread among the staff. It seemed as if the day would end with students charging triumphantly from the gym with the staff slinking around them until the unmistakable glean from Sanders' head glistened at half-court.

Manley met him with the microphone and then walked toward his team. He got halfway to the group before he realized that they didn't care if he was there or not. He knew that they would not listen to him. So, he settled at the top of the three-point arc, in purgatory between his team and his principal, who stood mute with microphone in hand.

It took ten seconds of being ignored to flush Sanders' face completely. Ten seconds to lift the veins in his neck to such prominence that Dieter could see them from the top row of bleachers. Ten seconds until his voice trembled with rage:

"Silence! Silence! You *will* listen!" he growled.

The students slowly turned toward him, their eyes ablaze.

"You-you-you-you don't even know what pride is!"

Sanders' free hand waved recklessly. His index finger pointed at the students first and then shot up to the ceiling.

"You think that this is a joke? You think that this is funny?"

The teens snickered at the flustered adult. It didn't help that Miguel stood behind Manley mimicking Sanders' gestures.

"This school wasn't founded so you could act like animals." Sanders turned to Andre: "I have a mind to suspend you," he turned back to the students, "and anyone else who thinks they can—"

As if in slow motion, a half-empty bottle of water was flung from the depths of the bleachers. Dieter noticed it almost instantly from his elevated vantage point. He could hear the small *whoosh* that trailed the plastic comet that headed directly toward center court. Sanders also saw it descending.

For most adults, the fluttering of the bottle would have betrayed its lack of mass, and thus its minimal threat of bodily harm. The reasonable course would have been to side-step it casually, stare down the students, and then command them to take their seats. This would have shown composure, righteous anger, and a reasonable response.

But Sanders' intense agitation blurred into an irrational fury. He imagined this as an assassination attempt. A bottle meant to pummel his body and undermine his authority.

The principal jumped back and the bottle landed at his feet, the cap exploding from the impact, leaving a puddle of water by the microphone stand. If Sanders hadn't been so keen to lay into the students, he may have found his footing; instead, as he leapt to the microphone to shout his rage, his foot accelerated off the slick ground, sending his body into a comical backward fall.

The boom of student laughter followed the pathetic thump of the water bottle and Sanders' flailing body. Students used their phones to video their principal lying on the gym floor. Sanders peeked up before allowing his head fall backward again. Playing dead seemed to be the best decision at the moment.

Meanwhile, Miguel resumed his dance. He pranced enthusiastically behind Manley, who was gazing forlornly at the bleachers. Not content with being ignored, Miguel began to sashay in circles around the increasingly upset basketball coach. After three rotations, Miguel stopped in front of Manley. Phones shifted to the spectacle.

"Hey, Coach, why you lookin' so salty?" Miguel shouted before turning toward the assembly.

Seeing the attention concentrated on him, Miguel waved at the students under the guise of Gretel, then bent the costume over and wiggled his butt at the scowling adult.

"*Bésame el culo*," Miguel shouted while peering back between his legs at Manley.

In a hasty action that would find permanence on the Internet, Manley crouched into a three-point stance and dove into Gretel as he stood up. Because most of the cameras were obstructed by flabbergasted students, the best video was taken from the top of the bleachers. It ended with Gretel pinned to the floor by Manley, who pulled the costume off to reveal a clearly stunned Miguel, who writhed under the coach's firm grasp.

While the pep rally was an absolute disaster for the staff and the administration's efforts to distract the students from the mascot issue, it did succeed in uniting the many student cliques into a confederation opposing school policies, and especially the silly cartoon-like representation, Gretel the Pretzel. It had served as the climax of the change of mascot movement from which the students resolve would no longer be diverted. Pride in their school and community became their rallying point and their standard—a banner on which Gretel and the current administration had no place. And Miguel's role in the rebellion, though already important, had just begun.

The hype for the game grew exponentially after school and into Saturday afternoon. Students arrived an hour early for the four o'clock tip-off so that when the game neared commencement, the gym tremored in enthusiasm.

Manley still coached the big rivalry game since the wave of outrage from the video would not boil over for another week. But he was only coach in title. Humiliated by ill-timed erections and an impulsive, physical attack against a student, Manley slunk behind the athletes, which allowed Andre to run the team. Any concern Dieter had that Andre might seek violent revenge against the two Hilltop players who had called him nigger evaporated as he watched Andre before the game.

He marched up and down the warm-up lines high-fiving and pumping up his teammates. He never even stole a glance at the other end of the court. When it was time for tip-off, he shook the hands of the two players with a stern force that conveyed his respect for the pleasantries of the game and his insatiable hunger for the right kind of payback.

Andre's in-game leadership was transcendent. He dribbled, drove, and defended with urgency while calling out plays and defensive schemes in the process. During timeouts, he rectified mistakes, strategized, and refocused his teenage teammates like a veteran coach. Dieter, though ignorant of the game of basketball, could see that Andre's guidance elevated everyone around him. As the team walked off the court, up by ten points at halftime, Dieter felt a sharp surge of emotion as he watched Andre take a struggling teammate under his arm, clearly pouring encouragement upon the young man.

A voice sidled in from next to him. "Can I confess something?"

Dieter almost had a Manley moment upon hearing Esther's whisper tickle his ear. He couldn't, however, prevent his upper body from a spasm.

"I'm enjoying this rebellion."

Dieter turned to Esther, who had a wide grin across her beautiful face. No longer was her hair straight. A dark fern of tight curls hung freely from the top of her head. Dieter smiled back at her.

"The students are so passionate now. They are discovering their voices and their purpose and their identities and their possibilities. I can't even describe how refreshing it is!" Her lips trembled as she spoke, and her eyes danced from Dieter to the students behind him.

"I know. I feel like their enthusiasm is infectious," Dieter whispered back, acting as if he too had just become a part of the conspiracy.

Reading students started a booming chant about being number one, so Esther leaned even closer to Dieter. The faint whiff of her coconut scented moisturizer curled into Dieter's nose. Already feverish, Dieter almost fainted.

"Maybe it's because I've seen the students take their lives into their own hands. Maybe it's because of everything that's happened since break. Maybe it's—" she paused and her eyes dropped bashfully, "—something else..." Her eyes locked with Dieter's. "I know you were going to pick me up later, but do you think we can slip out of here now?"

The next day, Dieter found out in an email from Maria that Reading had won the game decisively and that Sanders, drunk with victory, promised that they would hold an actual election before Spring Break. He even had asked Maria to give him a list of student suggestions on Monday. If the students got what they wanted, Dieter no longer cared about assuming Sanders' job.

He had awakened that Sunday morning with a blanket of happiness draped around him from the previous night, even though he'd slept on his couch because his mom was in his bed sniffling through most of the night and into the morning. Instead of eating breakfast, Dieter lay on the sofa and enjoyed the replay of his date with Esther.

When she had suggested that they leave early, Dieter received a message from Satan while Esther went to the restroom: *wait til game is over.* Dieter didn't give the message a second thought, nor did he respond. An intimate date with the clearly interested woman he had pined for took precedence over the Devil's reason for Dieter's continued attendance. So when Esther met Dieter in the lobby, all thoughts of Satan and his plans were put aside.

At Esther's suggestion, they bought a pizza and a bottle of wine and went to her house—rather, her childhood home. Dieter wouldn't have cared if Esther's mom was there, but she was out of town visiting her sister in Chicago, giving them the promise of an evening uninterrupted.

Dieter entered the front door with wonder. For most of high school, he had driven past her house, wishing he could go inside. Now, he was there…by invitation, nonetheless.

"How's living with your mom?" Dieter asked while offering Esther a slice of pizza.

"About as exciting as you might expect… But considering what happened with Manley, she's been terrific," Esther responded, popping the cork of the wine. "She and I have been through a few broken relationships."

Dieter could sense some sadness, so he changed topics.

"Hopefully this won't sound creepy, but whenever I rode past your house during high school, I wished I would see you looking out at me. I had such a crush on you."

Esther looked up. "You've liked me for that long? I was such a dork in high school."

Dieter chuckled, "Clearly you don't remember me in high school."

They both laughed.

"Glad we grew up since then."

Dieter nodded.

They chewed the pizza in silence, taking sips of wine in between bites. Dieter's phone buzzed intermittently with text messages that begged for an audience, but he did not notice the vibration in his pocket. Esther readjusted her sitting position.

"Dieter, why do you still teach at Reading?"

Dieter glanced at her quizzically.

"I mean, Manley's and Sanders' abuse would have pushed me out. And the other teachers are so cold to you."

Dieter seemed surprised that Esther knew of the various torments he had faced.

"I don't know. I thought maybe this would be my last year, but—" Dieter hesitated. He had never really thought about his place at the school besides the vision presented to him by Satan.

"But?" Esther asked as she poured Dieter a healthy glassful of wine

"—something clicked this year, I guess. I really, really like the students, and it's our old school, you know? Reading is a part of me, for better or for worse. It took me awhile to realize what the school means to me," Dieter said as he stared into his wine glass. "And, well, there's also this co-worker…" Dieter trailed off into a dramatic sip, flirtatiously avoiding Esther's eyes. Esther giggled.

"Oh, go on," she laughed.

"Well, I've started hanging out with her and…you know, I think there might be something."

Esther blushed and moved her chair closer to Dieter.

"I've also been thinking a lot about a coworker, you know."

Dieter blushed this time. His face started to feel flush. When Esther leaned her head on his shoulder, he almost spun to the floor.

"Dieter, if we are going somewhere, I want to know if you would be willing to consider something? It's become really important to me."

Dieter had moved his hand onto Esther's shoulder. Esther still leaned on him, with one hand cradling the wine glass and the other caressing the cross on her necklace. "What's tha—aaah!"

Dieter's phone seemed to be amplified five times its usual volume. The noise and the mere existence of the ring tone stunned Dieter since he'd remembered turning the sound off as he'd stepped inside the house. He fumbled to silence the phone but it refused to stop blaring.

Esther was unperturbed. "Go ahead and get that. I'll be right back," she said as she slid from his arm and bound towards the hallway.

Dieter blissfully watched her prance off and out of sight. All happiness slipped from him when he saw the caller ID.

"Ma, what do you want? I'm busy right—Ma, calm down. What about Whiskers? How do I know if she's gotten into—How would I know why her eyes are red—Sorry I'm not a vet!—So, what if she's walking up the walls—I don't know, they have claws, right?—I thought you hated that chandelier—How would the cat have gotten drugs—No, I didn't give it cocaine—She's not going to die—Okay. Okay! Give me a minute."

Esther stood in the entrance of the living room wearing pajama shorts and a tank top. A DVD of a recently released romantic comedy dangled in her hand. Seeing Dieter's mix of longing and despair, she gave a knowing nod.

"Mom emergency?"

Dieter's body tensed in frustration. He nodded his head before shaking it violently.

"For as much as that woman wants me to get married, she sure knows how to ruin—"

But Esther had already walked over to Dieter. Gently grabbing his shoulders, she cut Dieter off with a long, soft kiss on his forehead. The tension in Dieter slipped into euphoria.

"Don't worry about it. I'm not going anywhere." She smiled at Dieter, whose forehead tingled. "I'll catch up with you on Monday."

––––––––––

The words "I'm not going anywhere" had played ceaselessly in Dieter's brain as he drove to the emergency veterinarian clinic with his mom in the middle seat of the van steadying a rocking carrying case that confined her spastic cat. The memory of Esther's lips had caressed his consciousness as he sat for two hours waiting for the damn cat to be diagnosed and treated. The dream-like review of the night dulled the frustration when the vet came out with no answers, fresh scratch-wounds, and a heavily-sedated feline. And when his mom had refused to be dropped off at home, thinking that there might be chemicals or fumes that had caused the manic outburst from her cat, the promise of a second date guided Dieter through the storm of frustration that he felt.

That night, he drifted among images of times to come at Reading: a relationship with Esther adding even greater joy to the already fulfilling moments he was experiencing through interactions with his students. But darker plumes of the revenge and power promised to him persisted in clouding his more unadulterated thoughts. Finding a solid gray vapor to rest upon, he glided gracefully into sleep while his phone flashed twenty message notifications from 513-666-6969.

Chapter 13

DIETER AND ESTHER couldn't stop staring and smiling at each other through the side-view mirror in the mini-van. Dieter's mom drove in anxious silence on that Monday morning, oblivious to the amorous glances her son was exchanging with the girl behind him. Whiskers spent the weekend in her cage, being fed kibble and water through the holes in the gate and the breaks in her hysteria.

When Dieter and Esther arrived at school, they parted ways at the beginning of the school's circle, vowing to meet in Dieter's room for lunch. Dieter nearly skipped for joy to his classroom. Jose greeted him with a smile at the door.

"Divo! I missed you at workout this morning. Boy, you seem chipper today."

Dieter's cheeks were actually aching from smiling so frequently over the past thirty-six hours. "Sorry, Jose; I had to give Esther a ride—"

"Well, I hope it wasn't too hard on your mom. You know, since she's dealing with the episode from the weekend."

"How do you—"

"Anyway, Divo, I don't know if you saw Principal Sanders' email or not, but you are on the Mascot Selection Committee. You meet today at lunchtime."

"Mascot Selection Committee? What a stupid—"

Jose nodded in empathy.

Dieter checked what might have been a fury-filled rant against Sanders to race into his room and read the email himself. The message instantly deadened the weekend buzz. It appeared that his intention of releasing Gretel as mascot had abruptly changed during the span of twenty-four hours. He favored, instead, a ninth committee at the school, which put the entire decision-making process in the hands of adults rather than the students. And Sanders revealed two other disastrous decisions within the message to the ill-advised committee: the students would be informed about the committee during homeroom, and Dieter was to be joined by three ardent Gretel supporters—Ms. Stewart, the Biology teacher, Ms. Mueller, the school secretary, and, of course, Sanders himself.

The first meeting was scheduled that day during lunch hour, and meetings would continue for the rest of the week. Sanders' announcement that adults would still be making the mascot selection baffled Dieter and the other teachers. What could it possibly do to alleviate the teens' indignation? And what might the days and weeks ahead hold as a result of this new wound inflicted on the student body? And why had Sanders said "laughing loudly" in his email?

Irritation and disappointment stole the students' focus from Dieter's lesson during first period, so he scrapped his plans for the day and instead instituted a prolonged, therapeutic writing time for students to vent and share their increasingly violent thoughts, but only after he had assured them that he had asked to be on the committee so that he could voice their concerns. The students readily accepted his explanation before launching into their ink-stained tirades. They had no reason to distrust Dieter.

However, because Dieter did not teach all the students, the writing exercise's benefits were isolated. By Friday, the janitor had discovered dented lockers, spray painted walls, entire lunches strewn on the floors, and a Science teacher locked in a storage closet. Throughout the week, a barrage of emails flooded in from parents, staff, and even some constituents, who were hearing the clamor of the mascot battle in church and on message boards. They begged Sanders to exercise more wisdom, to which he, or rather his secretary, responded with an email assuring [insert name] that everything was under control and that the students were learning an invaluable lesson in life and that Principal-Mayor Sanders appreciated [insert name]'s support.

––––––––––

"So, sometimes you need to give up a piece to win?"

Miguel was ruminating on a move one of the freshmen had made—a move that led to Miguel overplaying his Queen, which left his King open for checkmate.

"It's a strategy that pulls the opponent out of place by taking advantage of their greed and overconfidence."

"Seems like a bitch move to me. I want to win with all my pieces."

Maria scoffed at Miguel's irrational, hyper-masculine comment.

The freshman shook his head: "Winning's the goal. It don't matter how many pieces you got. As long as you—"

"Chest-mate them," Miguel cut in.

"Yeah, but you have to make sure it's the right piece at the right time. You can't give up the Queen for nothing," the freshman added.

Miguel nodded. Content with the day's chess lesson, Dieter called the meeting to an end. While the other students walked out, Miguel stopped at the door.

"Mr. V. You ever notice that 'chest' is like life?"

Seeing a moment to self-deprecate and, thus, puff up his student, Dieter replied, "I guess I never really did. You're becoming quite the thinker, Miguel."

Proud and validated, Miguel gave Dieter a thumbs-up before chasing after Maria. Dieter was happy that at least something was salvaged on that Monday. Not only had he given up his lunch date with Esther, but the Mascot Selection Committee meeting had gone as terribly as he'd expected. The students' suggestions had been read with mock interest before being ripped up by Sanders. Instead of carefully considering student concerns, the meeting had focused on strategies to stamp out student activism.

Each subsequent lunchtime meeting that week was the same rehashing of ill-conceived authoritarian ideology. Forty minutes that could have been spent with Esther were instead forty minutes spent with three delusional adults.

In an act of solidarity with her leader, Ms. Stewart reworked her gradebook so that Andre was now failing her class. A single 'F' barred Andre from games until he brought his grade up to passing. This meant he would have to forgo student council and basketball practice if he wanted to play again this season. Sanders gave a maniacal laugh as they discussed the development. Really, it wasn't about the games themselves, but rather the fact that it stole Andre's power to protest. Andre knew it, and spent that week pouring over notes for the big exam that week. When he earned the only perfect score that Monday, he extended his hand to Ms. Stewart, who pretended not to see the gesture.

The secretary, for her part, began walking the halls to catch any student that was even a fraction of a second late to class. On a legal pad, she etched the names of every student she saw in the hallways after the bell had rung. She then dutifully logged all the tardy notices. Since twenty tardy infractions per quarter resulted in a one-day suspension, a host of students were missing throughout the coming weeks.

Parents, community members, even a handful of business leaders, who had ardently supported Sanders and his mayoral bid, sent emails to him inquiring about issues at the school. To them, the problem rested with the teachers, and they were concerned that Sanders, with his Mayoral duties and his role as leader of the school, was stretched too thin to adequately handle a deteriorating situation.

But those inside the building knew that Sanders' grip on reality was what was actually waning as his realm of influence dwindled from all of Reading to his tiny office and the small cohort meetings within it.

Since he had become principal seven years ago, the staff had come to recognize Sanders' authoritarianism. But that tendency had never manifested because he had never been challenged. The school, though faltering scholastically, ran smoothly in its daily routines. Now, as students assailed order and decorum, and as adults retreated into ineptitude, all the pressures of leadership besieged the befuddled principal. After months of negative public opinion, poor student performance, and absent school management, Principal Sanders descended into a bubble of paranoia and delusion.

By Thursday, Sanders had draped a large German flag on the wall behind his desk, covering his motivational posters and serene landscapes. A large coffee maker hummed on the shelf. Next to it a microwave sat under wholesale containers of instant noodles. A large purple-padded chair, something like a king's throne, replaced his ergonomic swivel seat. Where assuring an excellent adolescent education and fostering socio-emotional development should have been his focus, his sole enterprise became securing the cartoon persona of a time long since passed.

It came, therefore, as a surprise that on Friday Sanders told Dieter that the panel had settled on three options for mascots: Gretel, a chicken, and the Devil. Sanders thanked Dieter in person for suggesting the weak options to run against Gretel. Inevitably, Sanders disclosed, there would be enough disagreement within the students that no clear winner would be chosen. As a result of the uncertainty, Gretel would be declared the winner, regardless of the actual count, and the students would have no further grounds to protest.

During the last period, he announced that students would vote on Monday. A mass phone call was sent home informing parents of the three choices. Surely, the parents would talk some sense into their children.

Over the weekend, on phones and computers throughout Reading, two of the options were deconstructed by merit and reconstructed for various plausible scenarios (News headline: The Chickens, led by Andre Williams, were slaughtered last night. Next up on the five o'clock news: The Devils lose on the last possession). The third option, on the other hand, was merely turned into a meme to be laughed at and then dismissed.

With opinions being disseminated and digested every minute, the debate between "Chicken" and "Devil" had reached a quagmire until a user by the name '"Balla4lyfe" gave a concise but potent assessment: *We are already acting like devils terrorizing the school (laugh out loud). Why not make it official?*

A subsequent poll revealed overwhelming support for this sentiment. A picture of Andre with photo-shopped devil horns on his head circulated various social media pages. The original post came from a user by the name "sexiechica5." In the picture, Andre was dunking a basketball over a defender, who was replaced by Gretel. Andre loved it. He made it his new profile picture, and it was shared over a hundred times.

On that Monday morning, Sanders and Manley walked into school together expecting their façade of democracy to finally put the Gretel issue to rest. But their obliviousness was quickly exposed as the halls reverberated with the word "Devil." For the first time in over two decades, the school had full attendance in homeroom, and there was no time to stop the vote.

Teachers diligently passed out ballots. Students who were late or not involved in the Internet discussions over the weekend received text messages with the preselected choice.

As quickly as they were distributed, the ballots were back in the teachers' hands. Almost all said "Devil." A few said "Jesus." None said "Gretel."

One notoriously truant student didn't know the choices. Thinking they were voting for student government, an election that had been held back in October, the student scribbled his friend's name on the paper. Thus, there was one vote for Jesus Blanco.

Some of the more devout Christian students also wrote 'Jesus' in defiance, even while acknowledging that a Reading Jesus didn't carry the same aesthetic as a Reading Devil. Jesus carried twelve votes total.

After homeroom, the teachers had stacks of papers but no instructions on what to do with them. Like a neon sign, the uncollected ballots flaunted empty promises that grew more apparent as the day went on. The students went home that night with vision of their voices collecting dust on desks, ledges, and podiums.

When Sanders announced on Tuesday that Gretel had won the vote, the students howled in dismay. But they did not charge his office as they had done before Christmas Break. This new disappointment created a temporary paralysis among the students, who waited for their instigators to plot their next move.

The students' inactivity troubled Dieter. He left school Tuesday with the sting of defeat shooting through his back. It seemed to him that nothing was going to happen to the administration without a truly egregious event, one that maybe even threatened the students' lives. He began to wonder why he even cared about this frivolous quest to usurp a mascot when it was just bringing more distractions to his lessons, to his students, and to his relationship with Esther.

Due to an endless stream of meetings and after-school activities, Dieter and Esther rarely ran into each other beyond the car ride in the morning. Dieter moderated Chess Club and Student Government on Mondays and Tuesday; Esther led Dance on Tuesdays, Wednesdays, and Thursdays. Esther also had IEP meetings and various tasks to satisfy the varied and numerous legal demands connected to accommodating students with disabilities.

And due to their disjointed schedules, Esther had to bum rides home from students and other faculty members in the afternoon. Weekends were equally discordant.

For Esther, writing IEP's, grading, and attending church functions consumed her Saturdays and Sundays. Even when she had a free evening, situations at home shackled Dieter.

193

The problem was that Dieter's mom refused to go back to *her* home. At first, she claimed it was a chemical or gas leak that had ostensibly sparked Whiskers' outburst. Dieter used three hundred dollars from the money he had been saving for a car to hire an inspector to assess the house. The inspection report came back clean.

In addition, the cat still sporadically lost its mind inside Dieter's apartment. It seemed to happen especially at the time Dieter had a notion to make plans with Esther. Whenever the thought of a date popped into Dieter's head, the cat's eyes glowed and her behavior descended into madness.

Dieter spent his weekend pulling Whiskers from his walls, picking up feathers from his shredded pillows, and preemptively taking down everything breakable from shelves and ledges. In addition, he had to frequently spray the cat with water to keep it from humping his Princess Leia mannequin. It wasn't until Sunday evening that Dieter finally stuffed the bedeviled cat into its crate.

Busyness, exhaustion, and distance dulled the rush of emotion that Dieter and Esther had shared on that Saturday date. Esther gave Dieter wide, warm smiles during that first week, but after they failed to make plans on following weekends, Dieter noticed a cloudier countenance on her face when they crossed paths. Dieter, for his part, also felt a tinge of agitation toward her. He had sent her numerous text messages, but her responses had come back terse, non-revealing, and riddled with typos.

To make the situation worse, his mom's incessant complaining about her cat and her uninhabitable home turned the commute from a joyful ride into a ten-minute burden. The sullen atmosphere in the car, the gloomy days of winter all congealed with the stress of school and their varied schedules. Two weeks after their date, Esther began taking her own car to school. Her old Jeep became a means of transporting her *away* from Dieter.

———

Hoping to rekindle the amorous emotions only two weeks prior,

Dieter went online to order flowers with an accompanied teddy bear for Valentine's Day. He paid an extra five dollars to assure his romantic indication of interest would arrive at school before lunch. It was the second time he'd spent more than ten dollars on a gift for a woman other than his mother. The other time was for the secretary during last year's Secret Santa.

But at the end of that Valentine's Day, having spent most of the morning watching teenage girls carrying oversized teddy bears and dozens of roses into his classroom, a sting of disappointment throbbed in his chest. Esther hadn't indicated that she'd received the present, nor had she presented her own Valentine.

Dieter spent the afternoon beating back the implications of her silence, maintaining hope that he and Esther as a couple were still possible. But years of loneliness and rejection had primed Dieter to believe that Esther would be just another person who got to know him but ended up leaving.

A familiar voice, one that Dieter hadn't heard for a few weeks, slithered from the poster of himself by his desk.

"Hey, champ; what's got you down?"

Dieter didn't turn. "Nothing."

"Doesn't sound like *nothing*."

Dieter sighed. "Thought Esther liked me. Don't know why she's been avoiding me."

"I wish I could help, but love is not really my thing."

Dieter gave a defeated chuckle.

"Hey, buck-up. Esther's not the end goal."

"She's part of it," Dieter snapped.

His poster sighed in response.

"Sorry. You're right. But we aren't at the end yet, are we? If I may make an observation, Dieter, she has distracted you. What have you done recently to further the cause? The administration is dangling by a thread. They've made a critical mistake, and you haven't capitalized. You could have been principal by now."

"I don't care."

Dieter's high school 'self' quickly interjected, "I know it must be hard. I feel frustrated too. But we both can get the revenge we've wanted...together."

The computer replayed the clips from the first time they met. In his periphery, Dieter watched and listened to his disparagement at the hands of others. New scenes cut in: Manley yelling at Andre after he'd gotten into a fight; Sanders berating Maria for her activism. After these candid moments, a projection of Dieter in power played, but it stopped before Esther crawled upon the desk.

Dieter felt his eyes moisten in frustration. He had two equally daunting paths in front of him: Esther, his crush since freshman year of high school, whose feelings he now doubted, or this cause that he had pursued since August, which had seemed so obtainable but was now indefinitely paralyzed.

"Dieter, I know you are worried that you'll lose Esther, but her distance is telling you something?"

"She kissed me..." Dieter replied, voice cracking.

"On the forehead, yes. But she hasn't responded to your messages," high school Dieter quickly interjected. "She's busy. You're busy. Pushing a relationship on her will just push her away. You've seen what neediness has done for you in the past."

Dieter's eyes grew wet again. He thought about his dad, about how he'd begged him to take him to the park or to the movies or to the Creamy Whip before he left them. He thought about former friends through the years who all had drifted from him suddenly.

"Dieter, if you want her back, you'll have to wait. It's hard, but doing nothing will actually do more for your chances. It's what she wants."

Dieter had never been in this position—sure he'd been ignored by women many times, but not after they had shown interest. He had no history to advise him. The Devil, and the media he'd consumed throughout the years, became his guides.

"It's the best you can do," Falstaff continued. "If she's feeling stressed by work, you can't pressure her into a relationship. Why do you think Manley waited until the end of the school year to ask her out?"

Satan's logic rattled in Dieter for a moment until it was finally settled. He finally turned toward his poster. "Promise you'll get her for me?"

"We can focus on her when Sanders and Manley and Gretel have been destroyed."

"But nothing is happening."

"Trust me. Have I let you down so far?"

Dieter's poster peered at his real self. Under his own gaze, Dieter returned to the Devil's question, one he'd reflected on before. It was true: he had succeeded in becoming a good teacher. He had moved the administration to a tipping point. And though things with Esther were now receding, he had gotten closer to her than he'd ever thought possible. Maybe this recent let-down was his own doing. After all, he'd been operating without the guidance of Satan for a few weeks now. And look at where it had landed him.

The picture of Dieter again implored him, "Can we just get back to the plan? Once you are Principal, everything will be under your control. But with Sanders still around, he'll keep getting in the way. Out of chaos, you can restore order, and with it, a relationship with Esther. It's that easy! What do you say?"

Dieter nodded weakly. "I guess."

"That's it!

The Devil was right. At the height of the commotion, at the moment when student engagement sizzled, Esther had opened herself to him.

"Let's get back to business! What do you say?"

"Okay," Dieter said, locking eyes with Satan.

"Good! Let's get that confidence up. Say it with me: Forget Esther."

"I'm not going to forget her," Dieter spat at the poster.

"Sorry. Let's try this a different way. Repeat after me: Down with Sanders."

"Down with Sanders," Dieter mumbled

"You are *so close*. One more time, with feeling: 'Down with Sanders.'"

"Down with Sanders," Dieter said, more clearly this time.

"Then, Esther..."

"Then, Esther."

After Dieter repeated the Devil's words, a rustling sound by his slightly open door distracted Dieter from his conversation. Worried that someone had heard him speaking to Satan, he pushed himself out of his chair and slowly walked to the door. He peaked out, but he saw no one and heard nothing except the annex door clanging from the air pressure. This was not an uncommon occurrence, especially on blustery days. Satisfied, he returned to his work.

As he settled into his seat, a lesson plan based on another heavily edited speech popped up on his screen. The Devil highlighted key quotations for students to analyze. One especially stood out: "*Let the world know the hypocrisy that's practiced over here. Let it be the ballot or the bullet. Let him know that it must be the ballot or the bullet.*"

After Dieter finished planning, he sent Esther an email, giving her observations for one of the students on her case-load. It was perfectly business-like: without feeling, without familiarity, without friendliness. He didn't feel great about the message, but as the Devil had said, it had to be done. Esther needed time and space, and Dieter obliged.

He had resolved himself to one singular goal, and Satan was the only companion on this journey. Everyone else was just a background character that he would return to when all this was over.

———

Every day since the pep rally, Manley had stood in the front his classes. And every day, the students' indignation burned at the sight of the Spanish teacher, who appeared to have been spared any discipline from the pep rally tackle. Every day, a parent sent an email asking what discipline the school was going to take for Manley's assault. By late February, Sanders was forced to give a response.

At the next PTA meeting, Sanders arrived with the union president, an imposing lady with tight hair and red-rimmed glasses. She sat defiant, scouring the audience while Sanders read a prepared statement that actually *commended* his Spanish teacher and basket-ball coach. He said that Manley's action was well warranted since he faced a clear case of sexual harassment...since the provocation had occurred at the hands of a male student who had a history of tormenting the teacher...since the student apparently had repressed same-sex attractions...since the student was close to disrobing in front of the teacher... What else could Coach Paul Manley have done to protect himself in the face of such lewd behavior?

It took Maria a couple of days to school Miguel on the implications of Sanders' words. Once Miguel understood, he spent the rest of the year blowing kisses and batting his eyes at Manley during lectures. And every two weeks, a heart-shaped box of chocolates was placed on Manley's desk with the words "*Galleta Salado*" written on the card. Though Manley knew it was Miguel leaving the notes, it was hard to prove since ninety percent of the students might call him a 'salty cracker.'

In addition to this lack of justice, resentment from the suppressed vote boiled dangerously close to abject hatred of the staff, and the teachers sensed it. Some teachers had quit giving homework assignments and projects. Others had stopped asking students to pay attention. Most refused to dole out detentions.

The members of the Mascot Selection Committee remained part of the handful of teachers persistent in their defiance. The secretary withheld work permits for students. Ms. Stewart assigned a fifty-page research paper on which a student's grade would depend. Mr. Cannon assigned a novel a week in his English classes.

The teachers who were not wrapped up in Sanders psychosis lobbied the union for support beyond merely saving Manley's job. The president, both a friend of Sanders and a politician in her own right, knew well the rumblings from the district about Reading High School. Seeing the mid-year scores, she viewed the school and its teachers as a lost cause. Besides, teachers at Hilltop needed a renovated teachers' lounge. What resources did she have to re-invigorate a failing school?

As the weeks progressed, so did the prospect of a larger, more explosive confrontation. Individual attacks on faculty, staff, and school continued throughout the month of March. The freshmen, inspired by *Animal Farm*, took to making barnyard noises at random intervals in class. Teachers who were outspoken against the Devil or were complacent in Sanders' tyranny found gum on their chairs and various classroom objects glued to the ceiling or desks. The cherished coffee makers were found filled with concrete one Monday morning. Unlocked desks were completely emptied during the night.

Dieter, Jose, and Esther were the three classroom teachers spared from the barbarism of the students. Father Manny met with students individually as guidance counselor, but even then word had spread that he spoke in their defense at faculty meetings. So, he was also granted immunity during the accumulating storm.

Mr. Wilson, who ran detention and coordinated with the security guard on campus, became regarded as a traitor since he carried out Sanders' punishments and initiatives faithfully. Even though he pleaded with students to change their behavior, they ridiculed him openly. Andre, who had previously regarded Mr. Wilson as a father-figure, started to call him Mr. Snitchin'.

The cold gloom of March only exacerbated tension within the building. Days were still short and frosty. It had been over two months since Christmas Break, with another three weeks until Spring Break. Teachers began to let apathy seep into their lessons. Their already frayed patience was beginning to unravel. Their words sharpened, and their reactions were dismissive. Student behavior became increasingly more threatening and violent.

Teachers' cars were keyed so frequently that Sanders assigned the security guard to the parking lot during those cold, late winter days, which left only Mr. Wilson to police the halls and classrooms. Manley's driver-side handle smelled like ammonium most days, so he spent his prep periods sitting in the front seat of his car. Bathroom stalls were plastered with wet-toilet paper. Doors were pulled off their hinges. The lunchroom was void of any adult presence because food was thrown with such frequency and such velocity that one unfortunate teacher had sustained bruises on his torso. Paper balls pelted teachers who turned their backs during lessons. Desks were barricaded against doors should a teacher arrive to class late. Upturned staples replaced gum on the teachers' rolling chairs. Gym classes were turned into study hall periods since dodge ball had devolved into teacher target practice.

Then, things turned demonic.

One day before basketball practice, a two-horned face was found spray-painted on the center circle of the basketball court. Sanders watched in frustration as the surveillance video revealed no culprit. In fact, it appeared that a student had edited the footage.

Needing answers, Sanders erroneously grilled the members of the Pokémon Club for two periods. He gained no new information. Instead, he opened himself to the wrath of those quiet, delicate teens. For the rest of the school year, the word "Colonel" replaced "Principal-Mayor" on the school website. The logo of a beloved chicken franchise appeared in place of his picture.

In the main office, a snake, or was it a series of snakes, tormented the secretary for three straight days.

The first day, she discovered the gray and black striped snake curled in the corner of her office. Sanders called animal control to remove the reptile. On the second day, the same snake slithered over her feet as she logged the day's detentions and suspensions. Again, animal control was called by Sanders, who berated the government employees for allowing the snake to return to the school. They insisted they had the previous day's snake contained in a terrarium. On the third day, she found the snake inside her desk drawer. This time, she called animal control after she called the school district office first. She had decided to take her vacation days earlier than expected, leaving a wounded Manley, a frequently absent Sanders, and the still resistant Ms. Stewart as the only outspoken Gretel supporters left at school.

When the secretary returned a week later, she resumed processing work permits and relinquished her role of inputting tardy infractions. Mr. Wilson had to assume that duty in addition to running detentions, meeting with parents, following up with teacher complaints, monitoring the hallways, patrolling the lunchroom, removing students from class, and writing up suspension notices. His attention was so consumed by dousing never-ending disciplinary fires that he could not even begin to address the renewed graffiti, which took an even darker hue.

An ominous sign repeatedly popped up around school, reminding the students of who they were and what they wanted to become. It started, as was the trend, in the bathroom stalls. It soon spread to lockers and classrooms. One morning, the hallways were coated with over thirty repetitions of a phrase written in red and black paint: *We are devils. We are devils. We are devils.*

The faces of the faculty were branded with panic. The words conjured images of far more malevolent acts that could be carried out if the wrath of the students increased. Teachers began walking the halls in pairs, only splitting from their partner when they neared each other's classrooms. Even the male teachers found pepper-spray keychains for added security during their walks to and from their cars. Scores of desperate emails filled Sanders' mailbox, beseeching him to just give the students what they wanted.

Knowing that he had a hand in the turmoil, though it was indirect in many regards, Dieter felt a fleeting sense of guilt. The teachers were good-enough people, simply trying to teach in a school battered by socio-economic disparities and systemic discrimination. But for years, they had carried apathy and disdain for him and his students. And while their biggest weakness was an age-created chasm with student culture, Dieter had vilified their whiteness through his propaganda, making it impossible for even the best teacher to establish a working rapport.

The misbehavior burdened even the highly regarded teachers like Esther and Father Manny because they felt the pain of their fellow staff members. They mourned the students' descent into violence.

But Dieter chose not to concern himself with the plight of the staff. They were pawns in the game he was playing, and his opponent was about to make another fatal move.

Chapter 14

MS. STEWART LEFT early on the Friday the basketball team won its first playoff game. It was the fourth straight day that she'd left before fifth period. The doctor had told her each of the previous three days that she was having an allergic episode, which was obvious to Ms. Stewart since she had a history of violent reactions to many allergens.

A few years ago a student had had remnants of a peanut butter and jelly sandwich on her fingers, and after shaking Ms. Stewart's hand for the semester award in Biology, Ms. Stewart's face began to break out in a rash that could only be treated with an injection from her Epi-pen. Fortunately, students learned about allergies from the experience, and the administration banned students from bringing food containing nuts to school. This saved Esther from facing a similar attack when she began working at Reading. It also provided Miguel an entire semester of testicle jokes.

Ms. Stewart's allergies were not just limited to nuts. Another time, a student had brought non-school issued lab gloves into class. When her gloved hand brushed Ms. Stewart, the latex set off a series of burning strips of skin that took two days to alleviate.

Recently, however, the reactions extended beyond skin aggravations. Her eyes became white desert patches with cracks of red snaking through them. Her throat swelled with an inflammation so violent it inhibited the flow of air to her lungs. It was similar to the reactions she had to chalk, mold, shellfish, purple carrots, and hairless cats. In a school setting, only the first two really seemed plausible, but as the school had upgraded to whiteboards four years ago (after she had threatened a lawsuit), she assumed mold to be the culprit.

She sent an email from home that Friday with threats of legal action if the school did not check for mold. Sanders called the Superintendent, who checked the fees for lawyers against a mold inspector, and that next Monday, the roof was examined, the walls checked, and the annoying leak in Dieter's room was fixed.

But when Ms. Stewart returned the next Tuesday, the allergic reaction flared up so suddenly and so seriously that she had to be rushed to the hospital in an ambulance. As she sat in the hospital, IV's running into her veins, the janitor swept a large pile of white dust from the room. Rumors circulated as to how the chalk had come into her classroom. Miguel's name was consistently proposed as the suspect.

The next day, Ms. Stewart tendered her resignation. When it was announced over the PA, Dieter had to turn to his board to hide the devilish grin creeping over his face. But if he would have turned around, that same sinister smile was playing across the faces of his junior class. In fact, the devious smirks floated about the school for the rest of the day as another Gretel supporter had been neutralized and another battle had been won by the students.

The weekend after Ms. Stewart's resignation, Miguel discovered, in a letter sent to his house, that he had been expelled. By Saturday morning, almost every student knew. Dieter found out Monday during his workout with Jose.

"Divo, I have bad news," Jose sighed. "Miguel was expelled. He is accused of poisoning Ms. Stewart."

Dieter hung limp on the pull-up bars and stared at his own reflection for a few seconds before putting his feet on the floor. "What evidence did they have?"

"They had nothing, but he apparently admitted to tracking in chalk on his pant legs. I don't know where he'd get that idea, and I don't know why he'd take the blame."

Dieter had shown *Shawshank Redemption* to the seniors, and in one scene, the main character, a prisoner, used his pant legs to dispose of debris from the tunnel he was carving. However, it didn't make sense that Miguel would be the one to introduce chalk. He wasn't in the film class. He didn't have Ms. Stewart as a teacher. And he didn't wear pants.

One of Miguel's strangest quirks was that he wore shorts the year round. Teachers would ask him why, and Miguel's stock answer was that his *huevos* needed to breath. The teacher would then drop the issue.

Even though Sanders had implemented a dress code, Miguel noted that Sanders never expressed whether 'khakis' meant pants or color or material. With ambiguity as a loophole, and with Maria's articulate advocacy, Miguel resolutely wore khaki shorts as a uniform, even through a series of polar vortexes. =

But Miguel's humorous exploitation of a gap in the uniform code wouldn't matter anymore. He was expelled. Most years, the teachers would have unofficially toasted this fortuitous development with an extra glass of wine at dinner. But this year they greeted the news with groans and heightened fear. They still poured extra wine.

"Divo, I'm sure you are upset about this. You've worked so closely with him this year. I mean, I was distraught when I heard about it."

"Really?" Dieter asked. Though he couldn't think of a student that Jose had animosity toward, he also couldn't think of a teacher that didn't have acrimony toward Miguel.

"I wept. But we can still bring him back."

Dieter had been staring at Jose in the mirror involuntarily while some obscure connection or question arose within him. A flicker in the gym lights deterred him from his thoughts.

"How?"

"Miguel has an IEP. They have to show that his behavior wasn't a result of his disability before they can expel him. Miguel can sue the school for his return if they didn't follow protocol."

That afternoon at the student council meeting Dieter shared with Maria what Jose had told him (leaving out that it was Jose who had made Dieter aware). By the next day the student body president had drafted a formal complaint that she intended to send to the superintendent, but first she needed to talk with Principal-Mayor Sanders, and she needed a teacher for support.

———————

"Maria, you know I would have helped."

"No offense, Mr. V, but Miss B knows a lot more about this kind of stuff. Besides, she already offered to help."

Dieter spent much of Friday chewing on Maria's rejection. She had convinced Miguel to fight the expulsion, and she and Esther were going to meet with Miguel's parents and a lawyer during spring break. Dieter gave a tight smile then looked away while Maria continued to gush.

"Miss B cares about us *so* much. She's kind of like you, Mr. V. She gets us, you know?"

Dieter nodded his head, but he betrayed his agitation when he asked her to sit down for the test in a harsher tone than he'd intended.

While the students scratched away at their Scantrons, Dieter chatted with the Devil on his computer screen.

"What's wrong, Dieter?"

"I don't know."

"You can tell me."

"Maria went to Esther for help getting Miguel back into school. She should have come to me instead."

"Why do you think she's so eager to help?"

Dieter stared blankly at his screen. He'd never questioned her motivations before.

"She's jealous of you. You're closer to her students then she is."

"She seems to really care for them."

"It almost most makes me wonder if that's why she got close to you. So she could get close to them."

If it weren't for Maria's comments and the recent disappointment, such a seedy suggestion might never have taken root. But Dieter now found himself examining every interaction, snipping loose words and actions until the Devil's design took shape.

"She didn't seem to care for Miguel at the beginning of the year, did she?"

Dieter shook his head.

"And now she's fighting for him? She might be a problem."

Dieter nodded weakly.

Esther had ignored him since their date, she had rejected his romantic gesture, and now she needled into the relationships that Dieter had cultivated all during the year. Rejection and loneliness began rebuilding the wall that Dieter had chiseled away at for the first seven months of the school year. He was the students' champion. He was the students' confidante and commander. Now, Esther threatened the only remaining relationship in which Dieter found certainty and comfort.

This train of thought circled the tracks in Dieter's mind all day until the final period when he got a phone call from his mom. He groaned and pushed aside his lesson plans as he answered the phone.

"What do you want?"

"So, this is how you talk to your mom? I'm practically dying and you can't even give me the respect that a woman who raised you deserves?"

His mom had been insufferable. Every night she called with an update on the cat. On weekends, she would guilt Dieter into spending the night in his old twin bed; the lumps in the old mattress formed a multi-layered pain in his back that complimented the rapidly growing pain in his ass. Most days, it took him half of first period to shed the cloak of agitation from his life outside of school.

"I'm busy. What do you want?"

"Maybe I should just die."

"I don't need this. I've got papers to grade."

"I need you to come over. Father Damien is going to examine Whiskers."

"You are getting an *exorcism* for the *cat*?" Dieter hissed.

"Yes, and I need you here to hold Whiskers."

"No. I'm not doing it."

"What's more important: your mom or your jo—"

"My job!"

Dieter slammed his phone on his desk and powered it off right as the door to his room closed. Esther stood by the door, solemn and staring.

"Sounds like I'm not the only one who's missed you."

She walked in front of Dieter and sat at Miguel's desk. Esther's words were soft and sorrowful, without a hint of accusation. But Dieter's conversation with his mom, coupled with his already conflicted feelings toward Esther, created a virulent response.

"I've been busy, but if you missed me, you should have responded to my texts."

Esther's lip twisted. Confusion gripped her words.

"I've been busy too, and I *have* responded to your texts," she said as she leaned on the desk. "You were the one who didn't respond to me. Besides, why not call?"

"You barely responded—" Dieter shot back.

Esther held up her hand, cutting Dieter off and sending an acidic trickle down his spine.

"Listen, I've got a lot on my mind right now with all this chaos going on and Miguel's expulsion hearing, which, by the way, thank you for. I didn't come to argue. I came to check on you."

"What are you talking about?"

"I've been worried about you. You've been so distant—"

"—No, what do you mean *thank you* for Miguel's expulsion hearing?"

Esther groaned, upset that Dieter had missed the main message in her words, and pushed herself from the seat. Dieter bound from his desk and ran in front of her.

"Esther, I would never accuse Miguel. I'm just teaching him how to fight—"

"You didn't accuse him!" Esther's face flashed in anger. "You made him think he needed to sacrifice himself for a *cause*. He talked about a conversation during chess—something about *needing* to get expelled. If you care more about a damn mascot than a student's life, then I had you all wrong. And if you are too busy for me, then I'm sorry we've wasted our time."

She veered around him, brushing against his shoulder as she stomped off. Dieter remained by the door for five minutes. His eyes moistened with warm, salty frustration.

Maria and Esther appealed Miguel's expulsion through a series of meetings and petitions. Maria invited Dieter to participate in the meetings. However, Satan pointed out that this would move Dieter into the category of 'agitator,' a distinction that would only draw scrutiny into his classroom, which would reveal the subversive lessons he'd been teaching, which would ruin Dieter's place as Sanders confidante, which would kill his chances of dethroning Sanders. Besides, the Devil added, Esther would be there, and it would only cause further harm to any future aspirations Dieter had to be with her. So, he didn't respond to Maria's requests during the week before break.

While Dieter remained complacent regarding Miguel's fight, the students used the week before Spring Break to carry on with Miguel's legacy. They altered all the picture frames containing previous graduating classes so that each one had the "cl" crossed out. As a result, there were eighty-two pictures that read "ass of" before the graduating years.

Then "#YouSalty" pins and "RIP Gretel" shirts reappeared. The students also wore "Free Miguel" t-shirts that had a large picture of the grinning class-clown. A handful of students even wore attire from college and professional sports teams that had the Devil as their mascot.

And they were unimpeded in their uniform disobedience. Mr. Wilson couldn't do anything about it: over half of the student body disregarded the rules. And having more than half the students in detention or on suspension was simply unthinkable, especially in a failing school.

The Devil face that had appeared at center court reappeared after each attempted cover-up by the janitor. The paint required for masking the graffiti became such a budget item that Sanders decided to quit fighting the vandalism altogether. The gym was indefinitely closed to all activities, including final practice sessions for the basketball team.

Not that it mattered. All week the team refused to practice, watch film, or strategize. They gave Manley an ultimatum to take to Sanders: Miguel or forfeit.

But Sanders did not want Miguel to return. Such was his disdain for the teen, the outcome of a promising basketball season meant nothing compared to the continued absence of the biggest nuisance in the school. When Sanders told Manley that he was not willing to relent, Manley only shrugged. After all, Miguel was supposedly behind the laced cupcakes, and it was Miguel who had provoked Manley to snap at the rally. There was also a faint hope in his mind that the basketball team was bluffing—that victory on the court meant more than this stupid fight over a stupid mascot and a stupid student.

That Saturday, Manley stood alone by the yellow bus, waiting for his student-athletes to show up for the game. Five minutes to tip-off, he received a message from Andre: *Miguel still out. So are we.*

When Dieter came back from break, two bits of good news greeted him. It started when the bus driver described how Manley had fallen to the ground and openly wept for ten minutes after being stood up by his team. Then, before first period, Jose told him that Esther had encouraged Miguel's parents to sue the district for not following protocol for expelling students with disabilities. Miguel was immediately reinstated and would be back in school that day.

In fact, it was under a direct order from Superintendent Ward that Sanders was forced to accept Miguel back. Starting after homeroom, the beloved urchin was chauffeured from class to class on the shoulders of his peers like a king. The students especially made sure to parade in front of Sanders office, though there was no sign of him on those first days of April.

Dieter reveled vicariously with the students until Esther walked past him on her way to the lunchroom. His joy left with the wind that trailed her body.

For the next three weeks, Dieter labored between happiness when he was teaching and abject emptiness when he was at home. The Devil only checked in to provide feedback. His mom only called to tell him that she was, in fact, still alive (for now). And the only messages he received were from Sanders to check on the school. In a moment of weakness, Dieter sent a simple "Hey" to Esther. That afternoon, there were times Dieter thought he saw a message from Esther light up his phone, but when he'd go to open it, there was nothing. Satan told him he was probably hallucinating from dehydration or stress. WebDr.com confirmed Satan's diagnosis, adding that it could also be brain cancer or mad-cow disease.

As April waned, Dieter's existence begged for human intimacy. He could feel himself sliding dangerously close to the antisocial isolation that defined most movie and comic book villains. Even his mom stopped calling. Apparently, the cat-exorcism had worked, and she no longer required Dieter's presence.

One night, after scrolling through movie selections on the Internet, he realized that those fantasy worlds he used to revel in were now vacant realms. The figurines, the movies, the books became hollow relics of his pathetic past. That night, he cleaned his shelf of all the domains in which he used to escape. He placed the box outside a comic book store, abandoning his childhood without remorse or reconsideration.

Whatever precipice Dieter was teetering on, he was anchored by the few genuinely positive forces in his life. The workouts with Jose and the interactions with his students tethered him from sliding down the slope of anti-social isolation. The decision to ride his bike to school also provided protection against the depression that was beginning to manifest.

Still, Dieter noticed a profound malicious urgency within himself—one that craved the conquest he'd set upon back in August—the promised ascent to principal and the control that would follow. For a few nights, Satan commandeered Dieter's computer to replay the vision from the beginning of the year—the one in which Dieter was principal. The one in which Manley got his just desserts and Esther came crawling to him. After a week, the Devil turned it into a video file so that Dieter could play it on demand whenever the Devil had other work to do.

The projection became Dieter's eyes, filtering light and dark.

Each week, his myopia became more pronounced. Each day, his schemes became more deliberate. Each hour, his mutiny became more daring. Each minute, his emotions became more and more calloused as he furiously fanned the coals of rebellion.

By May, he was a shell hardened from his own inferno.

Chapter 15

"THE PIG'S HEAD in *The Lord of the Flies* isn't just a part of an animal. It represents something greater. Something more powerful. Something that's been held back from you by your parents and teachers, but is rightfully yours!"

Dieter paused as he walked and gave a dramatic scan of the room. The freshmen's eyes glistened with his words.

"There's a secret that I'm going to tell you. It's the secret these boys figured out."

Dieter paused again.

"Turn the page."

Twenty-eight pages turned in unison.

Dieter read aloud: "Fancy thinking the Beast was something you could hunt and kill! 'You knew, didn't you?' said the head. For a moment or two the forest and all the other dimly appreciated places echoed with the parody of laughter. 'You knew, didn't you? I'm part of you?'" Upon reading, Dieter slapped the book shut and strode to the front of the class. "How many of you are forced to do things you don't want to do?"

Hands shot up.

"Antwon, who makes you do things?"

"My moms, man. She makes me clean up my room and go to bed by one."

A couple of murmurs rippled, and Dieter nodded his head in feigned empathy.

"And you, Maya, who makes you do things?"

A larger girl in the back shifted in her seat before responding. "My grams won't let me go out and she make me go to the store when she need milk."

Another peal of agreement, and suddenly more hands were up and waving back and forth. Dieter walked around again, slowly, before calling on Jaylen. He was sitting upright.

"If I'm being honest, the adults in this building are liars and hypocrites." His shrill voice pierced the class. A collective gasp sucked the air from the room, and in the resulting vacuum, Dieter had his moment.

"Why do you say that, Jaylen?"

"It's just that…" he began, hesitantly.

"It's okay. What we say in here stays in here. Right class?" Dieter looked around with a therapist's air of confidentiality.

The class nodded. Jaylen started talking again.

"It's just that teachers and parents are constantly making us do work and yelling and not listening to us."

The class murmured in agreement.

"And there are so many rules that they don't even follow."

The students continued to nod. Jaylen had moved from his desk and had begun to pace the front of the room. "Like, why do we have to wear khakis and a polo? No one else does. The teachers don't have to wear khakis! They wear jeans." The momentum was picking up and Dieter knew that if he stepped in, a torrent of disjointed gripes would ensue. He suspected that Jaylen's speech would summarize all the complaints that the students had about the staff, so he made the conscious decision to not say anything.

"We get suspensions for being late to class, but teachers show up late. We aren't allowed to eat in class, but teachers are always sneaking bites of food. Cellphones—who cares if we text? I see Coach Manley constantly on his phone. Teachers can insult us and yell at us, and we aren't allowed to respond. And worst of all, when we try to show them how unfair it is, they shut us down."

The class, the mob, the group of pubescent teens longing for an identity and a strong personality to mimic and follow, rustled and peppered Dieter with "yeah's" and "that's-not-fair."

"You are absolutely correct, Jaylen. We expect things from you that even we don't follow." Jaylen gave a nod of appreciation as he took his seat. "And you all must feel frustrated that you've been doing so many things to get the adults in the building to listen, you've been *so civil*, but still they won't let you choose the mascot or change some of the things you want changed," Dieter added.

The students nodded vigorously. Dieter had been having the same conversation with these teens for eight months, but now there seemed to be a fresh ascent. A final push, perhaps.

"So, now the secret…"

Every single ear was trained on Dieter. Likes puppies waiting for a t-r-e-a-t, the freshmen's tongues wagged in anticipation.

"You-are-the-beasts."

The students savored the word "beasts."

"Simon discovers that the beast cannot be killed because the beast isn't one thing!" Dieter's passion picked up. "The beast is inside of us. It is many people joined together. It is the Devil inside of us. Adults don't want you to know that if you wanted to, if you were hungry enough, you could do whatever you wanted."

Dieter's eyes touched each oily face.

"The secret is that we have these rules so that you don't have any power. We are like Piggy, trying to get you to follow us." Dieter knew that this was a stretch that could easily be refuted. But the students had a collective fifth grade reading level and had long since been entranced by his words.

"The secret to this book is that if anyone wants to have power, all they need is a beast inside and a leader outside." Dieter looked directly at Jaylen. "If there was something unfair, they wouldn't use words like Ralph and Piggy, and when other actions didn't change anything, the group would do whatever it took—"

Dieter stopped. He was treading on dangerous ground. Students could sense a delicious, forbidden subversion in the air. Ribcages pressed against desks. Mouths opened in suspended breathing. One student mouthed, "Do what?"

He needed to say something, but what could he say that would stoke rebellion without tying him to the treason? He had already ingrained Piggy's symbolic representation of the staff, but he couldn't suggest that the students resort to murder, even metaphorically. Dieter felt a surge of panic. He had them. He knew it. Now to seal the deal! His throat tightened as his moral reservation betrayed him. He was going too far.

A whisper inside him compelled him to say something about talking to their parents, but as he opened his mouth, the sweetest, most dramatic thing happened.

An unmistakable screech stabbed the air: "Warning: an emergency has been detected. Please exit the building. Whoop…Whoop… Whoop…Warning!"

Twenty-eight students slowly exited the room. Like one body, they moved toward the double-door exit that would lead them to the field in back of the school. A fondness for their teacher swirled in their hearts as they chewed the cud of injustice. Dieter followed behind with his class roster pinched in the clipboard. He was their shepherd now. They were his flock. And they would lead each other to greener pastures.

———————

Spring flourished around them as they stood on the lawn. The late April flowers were blooming, and Jose and his class of juniors were sitting underneath the shade of a large oak tree. Jose wore a baggy, off-white top that was buttoned only three fourths of the way up, revealing the top of his tan chest. His pants were of equally baggy brown linen that flowed to his sandal-clad feet. He waved enthusiastically at Dieter before walking the forty feet to where he was standing.

"Did you know about this fire drill?" Jose asked.

"No, I didn't hear anything," Dieter replied. "Normally, they do these during second period."

"Exactly," Jose said.

Dieter and Jose stood quietly as the students schemed in whispers out of ear shot of other adults. Some of Dieter's freshmen talked excitedly with Miguel and members of Jose's junior Art class. The phrase "by any means necessary" seemed to blow from group to group with the spring breeze. Dieter ignored the rule-breaking while delighting in the allusion.

To pretend preoccupation, he glanced toward the corner of the school, awaiting a teacher or administrator to come around the corner to give the all-clear. Jose, however, peered expectantly at Dieter, who could feel the warmth of his gaze.

After a few moments, Jose spoke again, quietly. "I heard that things are rocky between you and Esther."

Jose's persistent concern in his life suddenly irked him. "Well—"

Dieter stopped as he saw Manley burst around the corner of the building. His splotchy skin sagged underneath his eyes but seemed to be stretched tight everywhere else as his body had not adjusted well to the weight he had put on during the past few months. Though it was not part of the teachers' dress code, he'd had to resort to wearing athletic pants to accommodate his growing belly.

"This was planned," Manley began unconvincingly.

Jose's sagacious smile and Dieter's apathetic stare greeted his words.

"We needed to inspect some lockers. But Sanders wants us to keep an eye on the fire alarms throughout the building in case any kids copy-cat. When you go inside, stand by the alarms until the kids are inside the classrooms. No one goes to the bathroom, understand?"

They both nodded.

"Okay, well, go on inside, but like I said, eyes open."

Manley stomped off. Jose turned to Dieter and said, "That poor guy has been through hell."

Dieter shrugged.

Jose continued, "I hope he's okay. I hear he might quit teaching after this year."

Dieter shrugged again. "Maybe that's best for the students," he replied before waving his students to follow him.

As Dieter opened the annex doors to let his students inside, he turned to see Jose still standing on the grass, still smiling broadly. Smiling as the late-morning sun crowned his halo of wavy brown hair and wrapped itself around his face, illuminating the pearls in his mouth.

"Which is better? To be a tribe of painted Indians, or to be 'sensible'"—Dieter made air quotes—"like Piggy? To have rules decided by one person, or to rule by the majority? To sit around getting bullied, or to fight for what's right?"

Vigorous affirmations met the rhetorical questions. It was the second-to-last period of the day, but the freshmen's backs, like their peers the period before, were erect and their eyes were alert.

"We must choose whether to follow society's rules, illustrated by Piggy, or to pursue our own course and conquer those obstacles in front of us, like Jack and the boys." Dieter sat casually on the corner of his desk, slowly moving his eyes around the room for emphasis. "Sometimes rules need to be changed. And sometimes we have to be the ones to change them!"

He wanted his words to touch each student. He wanted his ideas to soak into their consciousness. He was close, so close. With twenty minutes left in the period, Dieter showed a clip of the movie rendition of the book.

"Warning…" The fire alarm's howl stopped the progress of the film. "An emergency has been detected…"

"Again?"

Dieter glared at the blinking light on the wall. The students dutifully filed toward the door. But the flow jammed to a halt—students ran into each other.

"Keep going!" Dieter barked.

A muffled voice shouted back. "The door is stuck!"

Dieter pushed his way past the throng to the double doors of the annex. Andre was holding down the metal bar and lowering his shoulder while another of Jose's students had her hands on his back. Dieter didn't think she was meaning to help, but rather seizing the moment to touch the basketball star's body. She wasn't even pushing him. As her hands stroked Andre's arms, Dieter gently pulled Andre to the side so that he could stand between him and the starry-eyed girl.

With students around him, Dieter shoved the door. A rattle of metal on the other side greeted his effort. He thrust his body into the door again. Jose's voice cut through the wailing siren.

"Dieter, there's no time. We need to walk quickly to the front. There's smoke!"

Dieter turned and noticed a light gray swirl in the left branch of the circle's split. Dieter turned toward Jose and instantly a transcendent calm enveloped him. "Lead the way, Jose."

Jose bound forward in front of the students and swiped his right hand towards him, beckoning them to follow. As the students moved in unison after their art teacher, Dieter again remarked to himself how much they looked like a herd of sheep, this time ambling doe-eyed after Jose, who seemed more like the sincere shepherd, unlike Dieter's wolf-like persona.

———————

When Dieter and Jose's classes neared the entrance, the janitor raced down the hallway in the opposite direction, a fire-extinguisher tucked underneath his arm like a football. A crowd had formed at the entrance, and it was immediately clear that there was a spectacle drawing concern. With the deafening alarm, flashing red lights, and sincere distress on the janitor's face, the students spun to Dieter and Jose.

"Let's keep moving toward the door," Dieter beckoned.

The large wooden doors were opened, but students clogged the aperture.

"Keep walking!" Dieter barked at the clusters jamming the exits. "Keep walking! What's going on?"

Dieter pushed through the students to find another crowd of bodies being guided back into the building. Teachers with clipboards at the end of their outstretched arms flapped at the teenagers. Straggling students stood on their toes, trying to see what was going on.

All they could see on the lawn across the driveway were members of the administration, who were looking toward the building. Sanders stroked his chin and shook his head. Manley ran his fingers over his scalp. Father Manny's head was tilted downward, eyes closed and lips moving softly.

Dieter finally squeezed past the students and was even with the teacher barricade. He looked for an answer but could not meet the eyes of any of his peers. Desperate for an explanation, he took a step toward Esther, who stood off to the side by a brick wall. She glanced at him. Her eyes were red, and when they met Dieter's eyes, he immediately turned away from her.

With an awkward pivot, he spun to make a solitary march toward the administrators on the field. After two steps, he sensed someone next to him. As if he'd come from the air itself, Jose matched his strides.

"That can't be good, Divo."

Dieter nodded in agreement but began to wonder whether Jose was referring to Esther or to the chaotic situation around them. They walked the remaining twenty yards in silence.

Manley acknowledged them first.

"Vogel… Cordero…"

"What's going on? Is there a fire?"

"Small trash can fire that the janitor is putting out. The exits were chained shut," Manley's voice cracked. "This was deliberate. They wanted to smoke us out."

"Who is 'they' and why would 'they' do that?" Dieter asked.

"Obviously, some of the students," Manley replied with a hint of his former condescension. "They wanted us to see *that*." Manley pointed toward the roof. Dieter and Jose rotated their bodies to face the scene.

At first it was hard to see what was fluttering on the roof, but then the wind diminished enough to reveal a crumbled pretzel costume impaled by a broom handle. The sharpened point, covered in fake blood, shot from one of the cloth cartoon eyes, which was also smeared with red paint. A shorn white bed sheet hung limp over the assassinated avatar. It fluttered for a few minutes until it finally caught the perfect breeze that stiffened it. Red words sliced through the air: "The Ballet or the Bullet." Under it, a demonic face smirked.

Dieter proudly knew what had inspired this act, and from the misspelled word, he had a suspect too.

"Is that…" Jose began.

"Yes, it is," Sanders sighed. His voice sounded shaky to Dieter, who was used to Sanders' more authoritative fullness.

"The dance team sure is getting aggressive," Jose said to no one in particular.

"They mean 'ballot'," Esther's voice cut through the masculine circle. Her words aimed right for Dieter, her eyes fastened to his face.

Dieter avoided looking at her, and, as a result, at his own complicity. He instead looked at the Principal-Mayor, who had moved his hand from his chin to the top of his head.

"Doesn't matter which group wrote it…"

Where Manley had put on stress-induced weight, the events of the past year had left Sanders bordering on emaciation. After a few anxious strokes, he pointed at the symbolically murdered mascot.

"…it's an act of terrorism!"

All extra-curricular activities had been cancelled, and after the final bell rang, students were pushed out of the building and the doors were locked. The janitor had used a ladder to get on the roof to extract Gretel's corpse, but in the chaos of dismissal, his means of getting down had vanished. Rather than face the humiliation of begging a student to help, he sat and waited, occasionally peeking his head out to flag down staff that were leaving the building. Since all the adults were in the cafeteria, he had to wait.

Sanders stormed into the lunch room.

"Okay. It's happening." He paused then smacked the table for emphasis, "It-is-hap-pen-ing!"

The staff looked at each other in confusion. Some began to talk, but Manley silenced them by slamming the doors to the lunchroom.

"Sit!" he growled. Even Sanders was taken aback by the ferocity of his voice, but when the two exchanged nods, Manley's fierceness transferred to Sanders, whose voice shook with maniacal energy.

"They have taken this too far. Too far!" He smacked the lunch table again with his palm. The tan tint of his bald head now flushed. He glared at everyone but fixated on no one particular.

Dieter stole a peek at Esther. Her curly hair created a translucent veil over her eyes. Rather than glaring at Dieter, though, she affixed her bloodshot eyes on Sanders and on her ex-boyfriend who stood next to him.

"Your jobs, starting tomorrow, will no longer be about teaching content. We'll be teaching obedience. We'll be teaching test skills. We'll be teaching these...these mongrels—"

Esther stood up, and Sanders saw her.

"no, not mongrels..."

Esther glared at him.

"Teaching these *students*," he softened his voice.

Esther bit her lip and slowly sat down.

"Things have gotten out of control." The soft-spoken politician now came out. "So, we need to tighten our discipline."

Some of the teachers nodded.

"I will borrow metal detectors from City Hall for the front entrance—"

Esther shot back up.

"Our kids aren't criminals!"

"—because of the use of a sharpened broom as a weapon. Furthermore, students with any of the 'pound-sign-you salty' buttons will still be given a detention *and* sent to in-school suspension unless they turn in the buttons. Anyone wearing a RIP Gretel shirt or a shirt with…" Sanders paused, "…*his* name on it will be forced to change or sent to in-school suspension as well."

Esther again protested. "But it's freedom of expression!"

"We have a uniform policy for a reason. In addition, security and Mr. Wilson will be conducting locker searches—"

"That's illegal and ridiculous," Esther shouted.

"—due to animals and poison being brought into school and used against the staff. Leadership will be popping into classes to ensure discipline is on par with our expectations."

Some of the teachers groaned. Esther, emboldened, continued. "Just let them have the vote! If you want to end this, give up Gretel."

Sanders didn't even look at her.

"We have two weeks until the end-of-year tests. Every lesson will be focused on the type of questions that will be on the assessment. Lesson plans will be emailed to leadership every day, and leadership will be observing classrooms throughout the day."

"This doesn't meet the needs of the students with disabilities," Esther said firmly.

More teachers stirred. Sanders continued averting his eyes from the woman glaring at him.

"Leadership will discipline anyone not aligning their curriculum with test-prep," he said, ignoring the waving hand of Jose, who merely wanted to know if art classes needed to teach test-prep too.

Teachers openly shook their heads. Esther continued to stand and stare. Dieter's cheeks tingled in frustration. Victory was only a step or two away. But if he had no control over his lessons, he might as well be a marathon runner crippled at mile twenty-five.

Dieter could hear a Science teacher whisper to another teacher, "*Should we contact the union?*"

"*What are they going to do?*"

Sanders gave a summative scan of the staff. "Have a good night," he said.

———————

Dieter sat in his room, eyes glazed and leg bouncing nervously. It was already four-thirty, and he'd have to start planning from scratch for tomorrow's lessons. Fortunately, his senior Film Studies class was exempt from the new test focus. Dieter decided he could assign a short, in-class paper on *Fight Club* since they had just finished the movie. Their amazing discussion today about how to dismantle oppressive systems should bleed into solid writing. That didn't, however, solve the issue of the other four classes.

A blank word-processing document opened on his screen. Dieter stared at the flashing vertical line before a familiar voice snuck from the top of his desk.

"Rough day?"

Dieter grabbed the copy of *Lord of the Flies* that was on his desk. The lone face of a boy wearing a crown of leaves stared back at him.

"What are we going to do?"

The face moved the leaves aside.

"What do you mean? We stay with the plan."

Dieter shook his head. "But we have to teach the test."

"Dieter, Dieter, Dieter!" The top drawer of his desk slid open. "Who do you think helped to write these tests?"

Dieter peered into the drawer. He could see a copy of a test.

"How did you—I mean—I could get in serious—"

"Relax," the boy on the book replied. "I just want you to see the questions on the reading section. It's last year's test anyway."

Dieter opened the booklet and began analyzing the questions.

"You've been asking these questions all year. Just have the students continue reading, put a timer on it, ask the questions on paper first. You're golden."

Dieter continued to inspect the book.

"I can see what you mean now."

Someone in the doorway cleared their voice. The test booklet fell back into the drawer.

"Who are you talking to?"

Dieter turned to see Esther standing with folded arms and tired eyes.

"Just thinking through this curriculum…" Dieter slammed his desk drawer shut. His nerves flared at the possibility that he'd been caught.

Esther sighed before taking a few steps into the room. "Dieter, do you know why our students like you?"

"Because I'm not Manley?"

Dieter instantly regretted the words. Esther shook her head, sending a tangle of hair into her face. She slowly brushed it to the side. Her eyes hung heavily over tight lips.

"Dieter, these kids are risking their futures to fight for a mascot. And the administration is too stupid and too insensitive to hear them out. There's a ticking time bomb that needs to be diffused. And you could diffuse it, but you don't." Her curls bobbled as she spoke. "It's almost like you want all this to happen."

Dieter scoffed in protest, but his defense was dammed by Esther's monologue.

"I thought you knew how it felt to be neglected, used, unappreciated, abandoned. Your students love you and look to up to you. But you take them for granted. Miguel bought into these lessons you've been teaching him, to the point he's willing to be expelled, and you didn't even show up to defend him."

Dieter's eyes dropped as he shifted in his seat. Guilt and defensiveness jostled for position in his mind as Esther continued.

"Maria told me all of the books you've taught them, and it's amazing that they are reading them, but they are antagonizing—"

Dieter's ego surged, pushing him to interrupt.

"Why is this situation my fault?" Dieter said, agitation thrusting his words like a spear toward some unseen assailant. "Besides, you were already there for Miguel."

"Look, with the letter over Thanksgiving, and the graffiti, the vandalism, Gretel on the stick, the message on the flag, snakes in the office, and what happened to Ms. Stewart—Dieter, the kids are misconstruing your words and turning them into violence. You need to tell them that there are better ways to—"

"I'm just teaching them classic literature. I didn't tell them to do any of that stuff, and I have no idea what that dumb letter that Sanders sent out has to do with anything. I didn't write it: those weren't my words."

Esther examined his face. Her lip was hooked by the grimace on her flushed cheeks. She crossed her arms before she spoke again.

"The kids don't need any more manipulation in their lives. They need someone to care about them instead of their own ambition." She brushed aside the hair that dangled over her eyes. "I need that, too." She took a half-step toward Dieter. "I really want something with you, but I'm not going to allow another person to ignore me because they are too focused on trivialities."

Dieter could feel his face radiate though his stomach had a frigid river coursing through it. His body pulsed restlessly, wanting to do something to assuage both sets of dueling emotions. The position he had craved since August, when the Devil had suggested that it could be obtained, sat just out of Dieter's reach. And then there was Esther, the girl he'd pined for ever since he was a teenager, the girl who seemed to be his, the girl who now stood in front of him after weeks of disregard saying she wanted to be with him!

A rush of thoughts burned into a single, colorful realization. He knew that she made him feel happier than any other person. He knew his loneliness could be solved if he stopped caring about his professional aspirations and started caring about her. Every inclination pulled at him to reach out to her. To take her hand and tell her...

Esther forced a smile as she stood up. She looked at him one more time, and then stepped into the hallway.

When the door clicked shut, Dieter found himself alone in the faint glow of his computer screen. The boy from his book cover spoke. "Glad that's over. Now we can get back to work."

Dieter's eyes blinked rivulets of water. He had missed his chance.

"Don't worry; I'll get her back."

Dieter ran his arm across his eyes.

"We have no other choice. We've spent eight months on this. Everything from now until Memorial Day should focus on our mission. The end is near. We just have to make sure that no one— especially Esther—gets in the way."

Dieter worked alongside Satan until eight o'clock. Not because his ambition pressed him, but because his labor detached him from the truth: he felt most alive when Esther was in his life. Now, he only had his work and a two-bit fallen angel and his convoluted promise, but like Satan had said, there was no other course now. Two weeks until the test. Three weeks until the end of the year. Esther would have to wait. After all, Dieter had waited his entire life to have control, to have power that he could wield, and to have respect and hope and justice in his hands. He watched the Devil's video of his future one more time before he left the school.

A springtime fog enveloped the landscape as Dieter stepped into the twilight. And as he pulled his bike from the rack, he saw three hooded figures moving along the tree-lined edge of the school grounds. Too apathetic to investigate, he pedaled away. Whatever was to come, he was resigned to let it happen. He'd come too far to care about anything else.

Chapter 16

WHEN HE ARRIVED at school the next morning, two local news vans blocked the drop-off lane in front of the building. Lights shone on two different faces painted with serious expressions as two jaws moved in synchronized force for thirty seconds without pause. When the two reporters finished, they each gave a curt nod toward the camera.

"Let's get out of here. This place brings up bad memories." The Channel 5 reporter was texting on his phone as he walked toward the van.

"Did you go here?" his portly cameraman asked.

"No, but I dated a girl who went here. This place has gone to shit. Nothing but ghetto trash now."

As the van doors slammed, Dieter felt a surge of anger. It was one thing to attack the school or the staff, but the kids didn't deserve such contempt, not to mention the bigotry implicit in the reporter's words. All Dieter could do was toss leftover coffee on the back doors as they pulled away.

The other reporter brushed aside her hair as she walked toward her crew's van. Dieter turned to her and asked, "What happened?"

"Do you work here? Hey, Gary, we might have another interview."

"Sorry, I'm already late."

"Never mind, Gary,"

"Did something happen?"

The woman from Channel 9 opened the van door. "Some kids tried to blow up the pretzel statue by the gym. Spooked the neighbors. Thought it was a terrorist attack or something. Bomb squad cleared the school. Homeland Security just left."

"Why would they think it was terror?"

The van's door slammed in response.

When Dieter turned toward the school, he saw Sanders gesturing madly at two solemn-faced police officers who raised their hands in an attempt to calm the furious Mayor-Principal.

Dieter had his answer.

And the school had its terrorist.

Dieter was sitting at his desk when Sanders barged in and sat on Miguel's designated seat. Sanders took a loud slurp from his industrial-size coffee mug. Dieter couldn't force a semblance of respect for this disheveled, supposed leader of the school and community. In truth, Sanders had no command of the staff. No connection to the students. No real understanding. And his manic decrees during the past months compromised the lessons that his students were learning; and, as a result, their future aspirations. Even in previous years when Sanders had successfully controlled the staff, Dieter had known that he lacked real leadership skills and a true understanding of adolescent education. But because Dieter was too frazzled by his own poor execution, and jaded by the very kids he had come to love, he had not felt the disgust he felt now.

"Miguel got away once, but we've got that sonofabitch this time," Sanders said, voice shaking from too much caffeine and frantic over-optimism.

Dieter knew that it probably had not been Miguel because yesterday was his birthday, and Maria had probably insisted on doing something special with him and his family last night. It was probably one of the students who had watched *Fight Club*. Therefore, it was probably one of the seniors. "How do you know it was Miguel?" he asked the principal.

"A little birdy told me..." Sanders glanced around the room as he spoke, "plus, it has all his markings. Remember when he set off the firecrackers in the lunchroom last year?"

Dieter did remember. The entire population of the room had fallen to the ground as if the Earth had suddenly come to a halt.

"And his freshman year when he set off a firecracker inside the frog?"

Dieter remembered that incident too, but only because it was now Reading legend.

"I don't think that there's much we can do without proof," Dieter began.

Sanders shook his head violently. "We've already got him for the fire alarm."

"Really?"

"Someone said he had ink on his hands."

Dieter shook his head this time. It was certainly not unlikely for a student to have ink on his hands. "The ink in the fire alarms is blue, shows up with washing, and stays on the hands for a few days. Miguel doesn't wash his hands. Besides, they were red from—" Dieter paused. Remembering the persistent gashes that had been spray painted on Gretel and the red face that repeatedly appeared on the basketball court, he improvised a quick excuse, "—helping me grade tests."

Sanders again shook his head. "Nope, his hands were blue. At least, that's what *I* saw. And I'm sure Manley saw it too." He winked as he spoke, not realizing that Dieter wasn't a true confidante. He also didn't realize that Dieter was taking a page out of Angie's book by recording the meeting on his laptop's camera. Dieter had stumbled upon a folder of recorded staff meetings on his computer a few months ago. He assumed that the Devil had been recording the meetings without Dieter's permission, but that was okay with Dieter since it was a treasure trove of damning material. Every racially inappropriate comment, every hair-brained idea advanced by Manley or Sanders, recorded and preserved in Dieter's computer for him to take to Superintendent Ward when the time was right. Deliberately expelling a student using fabricated evidence would be the nail in Sanders' coffin.

"It's our word against his. It's time we got rid of that rat."

"Sir, he's got an IEP. Remember, you have to do a manifestation hearing first, even if you think he did it."

Dieter made sure his knowledge of procedure was captured for when the superintendent would see the video. His impassioned defense of Miguel would have to wait until he was assured of Sanders' downfall.

"Mere formality. Manley will be the teacher witness. Our school psychologist is an old friend of mine. But Esther…"

Dieter felt his heart palpitate. Throughout his solitude during the past week, he'd noticed how badly he missed her and how badly he wished he would have told her so. He still didn't know what possessed him to sit idly by.

"*We'll* figure something out. That punk is as good as gone."

Dieter didn't respond. He had to look at the books on his desk to keep from betraying his true feelings. Sanders did not notice Dieter's affected silence. He had already made for the door and was calling the psychologist for a meeting. Before he left, he put his hand over the phone and looked back at Dieter. "And we're letting the students vote on the day before exams. We figure that that will be a morale booster to push up our test scores."

As Sanders' footsteps clopped away, Miguel's prejudged death sentence nudged Dieter to swear to an absent Miguel that this would be the end for the administration. Dieter's original quest for power was now colored by urgent, altruistic retribution. After a year of teaching students about discrimination and activism, he was fully committed to something beyond himself.

If Sanders hadn't joyfully cut out from school early that day, he would have seen Dieter's classroom alit by the faint glow of the computer screen until seven o'clock. After blowing through plans for *Hamlet*, Dieter began plotting the final act of the school year, which began with copying all the clips of Sanders' problematic diatribes onto a flash drive.

As Dieter began packing his things to leave the building, he heard his lone friend's voice. It took a second to find him in the dimness outside his computer's aura.

"So, *we just have to take care of Esther*, huh?" a talking peanut ruminated from the half-eaten package on Dieter's desk. His cane twirled as his other hand scratched under the mouth in an area that would be a chin if peanuts, cartoon renditions or real, had one.

"Not Miguel. I can't allow him to be expelled," Dieter's eyes began to feel heavy, "even if Esther did want to talk to me…"

The legume-Devil's voice softened. "Hey, champ, look at me."

Dieter rubbed his eyes as compassion condensed at the corners.

"You can always let Miguel back in next year…"

Dieter's face twisted in disbelief.

"Trust me. It will be a temporary suspension. He'll only have to take a few summer school courses. He could do them online, and then you let him return next year. Think about it: the resulting explosion from his expulsion would be huge!"

"You can't guarantee—" Dieter mumbled, but the peanut-person interrupted.

"Dieter, it's now been nine months that we've been working together. Have I ever failed you?"

Dieter shook his head.

"Look at the district website. There are plenty of opportunities for non-violent expulsions to be overturned, especially when there's a change in school leadership. It's temporary; but it would do so much. Miguel's second expulsion would be just the fuse to set off the bomb we've been waiting to detonate."

Dieter exhaled with the assurance that Miguel's future was still secure and the resolution that there was no other course. Since a second expulsion would seem permanent at the time, it would be the final provocation. If Sanders was dumb enough to expel Miguel, the vote wouldn't matter.

Miguel, not Gretel, now personified the student movement. Miguel represented the student body as well as all the staff's transgressions. He was the face of educational neglect; the exemplar of disciplinary abuse; the quintessentially misunderstood and mistreated teen. There could be no way the students and the community would let this action stand without severe consequence, especially if today's recording somehow leaked...

However, there was still a roadblock to Miguel's martyrdom.

"Esther won't be on board."

"She doesn't have to be."

"She has to sign off on it. He's on her roster."

"Well, there's another Learning Specialist on staff, right?"

Dieter nodded, not sure how that information fit into this puzzle. The monocle-wearing peanut held up his hand in assurance.

"Don't worry; I've got it."

"Okay, what do I—"

"*I've* got it. Just get some sleep."

It was seven-thirty. Too tired, too emotionally drained, too entangled to probe any further, Dieter packed his belongings and tossed the can of peanuts into the garbage can.

Chapter 17

"THAT DUDE LET his uncle kill his dad and sleep with his mom, and now he wants to put on a play? Hamlet's weak, yo!"

The student had a point. Dieter nodded in concession.

"Poison is a bitch move, too," Andre chimed.

Dieter shook his head.

"It's effective. Sure, it's sinister. But it works. You've seen how—" Dieter stopped there, not wanting to explicitly point out that Ms. Stewart had been poisoned by someone at the school, maybe even in the class. "—it works in the story."

Students nodded as the bell rang. When they stretched from their seats, they removed their pins and t-shirts as they moved toward the hallway. Mr. Wilson and the rest of the staff had unified to clamp-down on uniform infractions. After students were sent home for being out of dress code, and after one student was arrested for refusing to leave the premises, the students acquiesced. After all, clothing seemed so petty when real injustice existed inside and outside of those walls.

Dieter followed his students out of the annex. He wanted to swing by the office to make copies of an article about the French Revolution, which he could loosely connect to *Hamlet*, and another about coup d'état that he would just have to pray would eventually pay off.

As he rounded the circle, he immediately realized something upsetting had occurred near the front office. A line of adults, lips pulled tight in authoritative expressions, steered students away from the entrance and into classes. Their eyes, however, conveyed anxiety. Students craned their necks around the human barricade, and those who could witness the scene covered their mouths with their hands and shook their heads. Angie looked on through a veil of tears as Andre held her in an embrace.

The flashing lights of an ambulance played through the open doors of the entrance. Dieter hoped a binge coffee-drinking episode had somehow incapacitated Sanders, but from the students' reactions, it seemed unlikely. Hesitant, Dieter slid past the teachers and into a scene that instantly paralyzed him.

Esther lay strapped to the gurney, an oxygen mask laid over her swollen lips. A burn covered her face and arms, and her hands twitched sickly on her chest. Dieter fell to one knee and watched one of the EMTs coerce an IV into her arm before rushing her out with the school's secretary in tow, past a shockingly complacent Sanders, who weakly asked the secretary to update him on her status before walking toward the line of teachers and students.

Noticing something on the ground, he moved quickly toward the steps and pounced on the object, which appeared to be a broken coffee mug. With the pieces clutched in his hands, he turned sharply toward his office. Before he marched into his dimly-lit room, he turned toward the lingering throng of gawking, worried eyes.

"Get to class!" he growled. "You have only one more day to prepare for your tests."

"These tests are stupid," Val mumbled. Dieter, though mildly shocked to hear Val speak ill of a means to promote herself, was too consumed with his own trauma to give a rebuttal. Esther fluttered into his thoughts. Her labored breathing wheezed on repeat, suffocating any intentions Dieter had of teaching. The sound of each tortured inhalation became a reminder of the vacuum that Dieter had left with his empty response. And each exhalation echoed her exhortations: *You have to stop this craziness.*

On the day before testing, all madness dissolved into lethargy or traumatized silence. Students that worked with Esther or were in her dance class shuffled the halls with grief and confusion evident on their faces. The remaining students, who had voted again in homeroom for the Devil, withdrew inside themselves. Though they were cynical that the vote would be counted correctly, the end of the year was in sight, and the passion that had consumed them slowly abated as the year crept toward completion.

Thus, every teacher in the building was able to give frantic test-inspired, multiple-choice questions, uninterrupted. They barraged students with test-taking tips and content specific strategies while Sanders and Manley watched on in misguided satisfaction.

Dieter gave the students a study-hall loosely presented as 'meditation time.' The administration didn't bother peeking into his class. Sanders and Mr. Canon hadn't observed Dieter once this entire school year since their once decided indifference had now transformed into an unquestioned assurance of Dieter's ability.

"Yes," Dieter responded while slouching at his desk, "the tests are stupid. But you, as juniors, need them to get into college."

"But Mr. V, if we try, then they win."

Dieter sighed and stood up slowly. The students flinched, concerned that they had upset him, and fearful that he would abandon them as so many other adults had abandoned them in the past.

"Look, forget about the school," Dieter said with a wave of his hand. "Forget about this year. Forget about the movement for one day." He ran his fingers through his hair. A message popped up on his screen: *What the hell are you doing?*

Dieter closed his computer.

"Tomorrow is about you. It's about your abilities, your knowledge, your future."

"But, Mr. V, if we do good, then the school looks good," Miguel responded.

Miguel had grown so much over the year. His silly immaturity had been replaced by resolve and a hunger for knowledge. Dieter was thankful that he had not been expelled, even if it would have accelerated Dieter's ascent to the position of principal.

Dieter smiled. "I can't take the test for you—it is your decision. But I will say this..." He took a step toward Miguel "...you are too smart to not take it seriously."

Miguel returned Dieter's gaze. His eyes widened for more direction, more affirmation.

"All of you are too smart. You've been told your entire life that you aren't capable. You've been treated like...like *circus animals*. And now? Now you know: you are so much more than that."

The students' eyes either dropped to their desks or welled in tears. Andre nodded.

"The test tomorrow isn't about showing what the school can do. It's about showing what you can do. The school has tried to take your freedom, but it can't take away your future. You are battling inequality every day, but you can change that! Fight the good fight, finish the race."

Dieter stepped back to his desk. He breathed deeply before he finished speaking.

"Our world needs you to share your voice. Our community needs you to be engaged. Your family needs you to be successful. Tomorrow is the first step toward doing that."

———

Every teacher proctored the three-hour exam. Per testing regulations, they stood in their testing rooms sans phone, book, and computer while the students worked. Instead of losing themselves and the time in the blur of technology, they had to stare at the faces of those students who had terrorized them all year.

Dieter examined his roster. His room housed juniors with

learning disabilities since they all got extended time for the test, and, Dieter suspected, because they were the biggest behavior concerns.

Angie, Andre, and Miguel were supposed to be in his room, but as the clock started on the test, Miguel still hadn't arrived. Dieter was initially concerned, but he convinced himself that Miguel was probably in a different testing room. Maybe he had the test read out loud as an accommodation. Soon, the task of administering the test replaced his concern for Miguel's whereabouts. He started reading verbatim the pages of unnecessary directions.

"There is to be no looking back at other sections, no use of unapproved calculating devices, no smoking or use of tobacco products, no alcohol, no fighting..." Sensing the anxious fidgeting of the students, many of whom had diagnosed ADHD, Dieter stopped. "Look, you guys will do great. Just fill in as many bubbles as you can, don't work on other sections, and don't cheat. You ready?"

Ten heads nodded.

"Alright, you have sixty-seven minutes for test one. Turn the page and begin."

A flurry of turned pages precipitated an accumulation of scratching pencils. Dieter turned to write the time on the board. When he turned back, every student's eyes were glued to their test booklets in earnest investment.

The students plodded through the first two sections. Every few minutes they had to brush hair from their tests due to how often they ran their hands across their scalps. Andre let his head drop onto his desk during the math portion.

After a twenty-minute break, they began the Reading portion of the test, the section tied to Dieter's performance (as if that mattered to him anymore). For such a high stakes assessment, Dieter felt remarkably calm. His students bit their lips in concentration, and fastidiously flipped the pages back and forth to check their answers. He was pleased to see, as he walked around the room, that all the students finished the Reading section by the call of time. Most of the other sections had blank ovals or long stretches of concurrent

'C' answers. Angie even gave a confident thumbs-up before they transitioned to the final test.

When the final section was finished, the students collectively exhaled. Exhausted and mentally comatose, they gave Dieter high-fives as they left his room to go home. The time had come for them to turn off their minds on padded sofas in front of glowing television screens.

The students walked only a few feet from Dieter's door when a fierce yell echoed down the hallway. The howl was followed by a single series of patters that raced toward them with a stampede of heavier footsteps close behind.

Maria flew from around the right-branch of the circle down to the entrance of the annex. Her red, gritted eyes shot down the length of the hall. From quivering lips, she screamed: "They expelled him! They expelled Miguel!"

Sanders, Mr. Wilson, and the security guard soon appeared behind Maria, who continued shrieking. Tears stained her cheeks with black lines. Under the dark streams, her face glowed red in rage.

"Get your hands off me, *cabrón*!"

The security guard had one arm, and Mr. Wilson had the other. They lifted her hundred-pound body easily, but her legs kicked violently and her body writhed. She turned toward Sanders, showering him with expletives and saliva.

"You're going to pay for this, *pendejo*!" She spat at his feet before twisting toward Mr. Wilson. "*Hijo de puta*, let me go." She gave one last glance at Dieter's students. "We can't let them do this!"

The school's leadership transported the class president down the hallway like an unruly prisoner, and though the spectacle disappeared, Maria's voice hovered in the hall. The words "we can't let them do this" swirled around the annex. Andre's breaths fumed from his nostrils. Angie's eyes pinched her nose in loathing.

Jose had stepped into the hallway to witness the commotion. For the first time, Dieter saw a hint of deep sorrow in his normally joyful neighbor. Jose closed his eyes, titled his face up to the ceiling, and mumbled a stream of incoherent words.

At the end, Jose sighed and whispered, "They know not what they do."

As was custom, students had the day off after state tests, though teachers were still expected to arrive at school for end-of-year meetings. Sanders, however, cancelled them. Instead, he sent out a five-paragraph email that outlined procedures for closing out the year—items detailing when grades were due, how to fill out evaluations for other teachers, where to store materials, when and how to turn in keys, the timeline for when teachers would find out if they had a job next year.

Dieter got another email from Sanders. In this one, also addressed to Manley, Mr. Wilson, and the school secretary, he thanked the staff for continuing to fight for Gretel and for the school. He confided that Miguel was indeed expelled (thanks to the staff members' "diligent pursuit of justice"). He even quipped in the email (which would be used against him later) that expelling Miguel had saved the school from a low test score that would hurt their average.

At nine o'clock that night, Dieter received one last email. It was the most surprising one since it was from Jose, who almost always saved his correspondence for morning workouts and happenchance meetings in the hallway. However, since Dieter hadn't shown up to the gym during the previous two weeks, and since Dieter had secluded himself in his room, Jose hadn't had the chance to connect with him.

Hey Divo,

I just wanted to reach out after yesterday's incident. I know it's easy to be angry, but I ask that you show patience before you rush to judgment. After all, you would want grace if you were in a similar situation.

Divo, there's a lot of darkness being spread to our students and our staff. And with the loss of Esther, we need our people of influence to fight for peace, to broker understanding. Divo, we need you to let your light shine. You have the respect and adoration of many people. I hope you recognize the responsibility that comes with this. Your students and your community need you.

Humbly yours,
Jose

Conviction trickled through his body. Dieter's fingers coursed through his hair, coaxing his brain to make a decision. He thought he had made one until another message popped up on his screen from "Beelzebub." It contained a link to a video. Dieter clicked it.

Immediately, he knew what it was.

The video began with Dieter standing across from a braying Manley, who was sitting on a bench over a tank of water. Manley threw insults and animal noises at Dieter. The video panned the crowd. Dieter saw Mr. Canon pointing and laughing in his direction. Mr. Lee and another teacher licked their ice cream in malicious bliss. A few other teachers smirked.

Before he could think further, the video cut to snippets of clandestine class recordings of various teachers. The ten-to-twenty-second films showed them either berating their students or sitting at their desks, neglecting their jobs. Other clips showed them openly gossiping about Esther and the students. The final video came from the security camera outside Sanders' office. The five-second clip replayed Maria's physical removal from school. How the security guard had dumped her onto the ground and then pulled her out by the arm.

Dieter watched the video three more times. After the final playing, he deleted Jose's email. For the next three hours, he furiously alternated between typing on his phone and posting on the Internet.

In Hilltop and other surrounding communities, Reading High School's teachers dusted off margarita pitchers and travel brochures. They commiserated with friends and family, who politely listened while they withheld their condescending disbelief that teaching could be *so hard*.

Meanwhile, Angie's long-forgotten recording of Sanders, which was presumed to have been deleted, floated through the sea of social media. On a "Mr. Vogel 4 principle" webpage, wild accusations were made about staff members changing grades, planting drugs, and calling immigration on the families of disruptive students. Video of Manley tackling Miguel had thousands of views and an addendum on the video's description that read: "guess which of these two is still at the school? Yep, the teacher!"

At the district office, a mysterious package appeared on Superintendent Ward's desk. Enclosed was a USB drive with recordings of Sanders conspiring to frame Miguel for various activities around the school. It also contained Sanders' various terrible initiatives and other unethical actions implemented throughout the year

Ignorant to the tape's release and the USB's existence, Sanders and Manley decompressed after a long year, starting with lunch and early afternoon drinks that culminated in a midnight toast at Peg's Pub. In Reading's residential neighborhoods a mile away, the students connived on social media and convened in vacant playgrounds. Due to the symbolic execution of Miguel, the students' standard-bearer, the somnambulant student body reawakened. All the lessons, all the literature, all the statistics and theories and anecdotes and experiences buzzed forth in clarity. Gretel could move the students to adolescent indignation. But Miguel inspired a righteous outrage—an existential crisis that could no longer go unaddressed.

The staff had been weighed and found wanting. The year's

injustices would be reconciled—by any means necessary. That night, Maria made the only impactful decree in the history of Reading student government: the final battle would take place Thursday morning.

Chapter 18

NEXT MORNING THE students sat statuesque with tight mouths and frosted eyes. At other schools, such expressions might have been interpreted as the focused dispositions of students preparing for final exams. At still others, the fatigue of burnt-out teenagers. But at Reading, this collective expression was at the very least an oddity, and possibly an ominous one. In past years, students, feeling the promise of summer freedom, were so fidgety that most teachers simply showed movies and gave take home exams. This year carried on the cinematic tradition, but this year the students were not interested in the movies. They sat erect and stared at the teachers instead of the flickering screens. The teachers moved to the backs of their classrooms, but the students responded by turning in their seats with eyes following every movement. Their haunting gazes spooked the already fragile teachers, leading some of the adults to panic.

The first period Spanish class goaded Manley, who was hampered by a pounding hangover, into a manic outburst. His students only watched, emotionless and without reaction. After a ten-minute tirade, he reached for his water-bottle and slumped onto his seat, where he spent the remaining thirty minutes of the period sipping from his animosity towards the students.

During the transition between first period and second period, a few of the teachers noticed that many of the students were assembling in hurried, hushed groups in the hallways. After a few whispers, the students would break away like summer clouds. A behavior that portended a fight.

Concerned emails flooded Mr. Wilson and Principal Sanders' mailboxes, but they did not offer any response. Mr. Wilson called in sick that day, and Sanders slouched underneath his desk with the lights in his office turned off. Nausea over Superintendent Ward's email churned along with the remnants of alcohol in his stomach.

In her message, she revealed that she had personally expedited the scoring of the test results for the school and had them in her possession, and she wanted to talk about matters related to Reading High School's future existence. She would visit the school that afternoon.

With leadership absent and incapacitated, the teachers faced the students' menacing conduct without support or explanation. For the first three periods, the strain of an expectant action harbingered by the students' shifty behavior became insufferable. Some teachers positioned themselves against the lockers, eyes and attention spasmodically darting from one cluster of students to another. Other teachers fastened themselves to their desks, refusing to move from their corners where they were relatively safe from whatever chaos might ensue.

When the third period bell clanged, the teachers' concerns were realized, though not in the way they were expecting.

The doors to the classrooms immediately popped open, and a gush of soundless, stone-faced students flooded into the hallways. But the flow wasn't like a two-way street; en masse, the students crept silently toward the entrance. When teachers became aware of the one-directional momentum, they moved themselves into the flow of the dark river, but they could not impede its current. Their words carried no power anymore. The teachers were but white boulders redirecting the ebb as the stream slid past them. They could do nothing.

The swell surged down stairwells, past walls of lockers until it squeezed into the vestibule and out the exits. The secretary, uncertain of what was happening, rushed to the office door and locked herself inside. Her breath fogged the glass as she stared out at the spectacle, mouth agape.

By the time the bell for fourth period rang, the hallways and classrooms were empty. Thirty stunned teachers stared down the vacant hallways, longing for an explanation.

After a few minutes, Sanders' shaky voice stammered from the intercom: "Meeting in Vogel's room…now!"

The mesmerized staff walked around the loop, converging on the annex, far away from the front lawn where the students had assembled.

———

Manley paced in front of the window, an aluminum bat resting on his right shoulder. Members of the Math department huddled below the windows like a family of mice. Science teachers were assessing 'social' experiments, while the history teachers cited prior events. The English teachers circled around Dieter and whispered magnificent but empty connections to famous stories, grasping for clues to foreshadow whatever was to come next.

Like magistrates pouring into a court room, members of the administration filed in from the hallway. Dieter seemed unruffled as he methodically erased the board and filed papers into his desk drawer, checking his phone occasionally as he sat casually on the edge of his desk, one foot planted and the other dangling. Sanders placed himself next to Dieter and scanned the room before debriefing the staff on the seriousness of the situation that was unfolding.

"I need everybody's full attention."

Dieter continued looking at his phone. A smirk played across his face.

"We are in crisis mode. The students have assembled out front, and we don't know—"

"Ah! Sorry, all. Have to start the furnace. The clay won't blast itself." Jose skipped out the door, hands raised like a referee. Gray mud was caked on his cheeks and fingers.

Sanders chest deflated as he let out a sigh. He picked up his chin, gave a quick look at the ceiling and began again, but softer: "The students are out front. I don't know what they want, but we sure as hell are not going to give in to the demands of these—" he paused and let out a growl, "—savages."

The staff only whined and moaned. Various forms of "Please" and "Make it stop" filled the air. Sanders shook his head in defiance.

"We can't let this behavior go unpunished! We can't let them think they have power—"

As if on a timer, the power suddenly cut off. Every eye in the room stared dumbly at the ceiling as if the teachers could spot the source of the outage in the lights themselves—as if they could will the lights back on through their gaze, as if they could incite electricity with a surgical glare, as if they could control the energy the same way they controlled student behavior, at least before this year...

While the staff examined the ceiling, the air pressure in the hallway temporarily shifted. The annex doors clanged and a metallic rattle echoed from the hallway as something clattered toward the classroom door. The security guard rushed to the frame of the door and peered out. Seeing nothing, he peeked back inside with a shrug. But as he did, a hiss exploded around the door. Wide-eyed, the guard jumped three feet backward as waves of smoke slithered into the room.

"The bastards are gassing us!"

The overweight guard flopped onto the floor and attempted a military crawl as smoke poured in behind him. His lack of fitness and a pronounced belly anchored any desired forward movement. Teachers gazed on in alarm, yet relieved that the security guard seemed to be the only person affected.

The annex doors reopened, and a masked blur kicked the canister into the center of the room. It rolled to a stop three seats behind Miguel's desk. Another can scuttled on the ground in the hallway, and the door to the room slammed shut. Gas fully enveloped the prone security guard. In a fit of gagging and coughing, he begged for help.

The teachers, however, were already sprinting toward the windows. Desks flipped. Chairs crashed. Smoke slithered unimpeded into and throughout the room, bringing with it an unmistakable sulfuric, rotten-egg odor. When the smell intensified, one history teacher heaved. Hearing the retch, five other teachers gagged, with one more actually vomiting on Manley's shoes.

"Open the goddamn windows!"

Teachers twisted the latches, pushing them open to the maximum six inches. Instantly, a *thunk-thunk-thunk* smacked the glass with a splatter of red and yellow. Through the paint, the teachers could see a line of ten camouflage-clad teens spraying paintballs at the building. Red and black painted masks hid their faces.

For two minutes, blue, red, green and yellow bursts peppered the windows, and smoke choked the lungs of the teachers. Panic twisted the faces of all the staff except Dieter, who sat under his desk with a smile on his lips and an old shirt over his mouth and nose.

One of the teachers pulled out his phone and dialed 9-1-1. A sly-voiced male, more reminiscent of a car salesman than an emergency operator, answered.

"Nine, one, one, what's your emergency?"

"We are at Reading High School. The students have thrown gas into our room and they are shooting at us."

"So...there's gas in your room, you say?"

"Yes!"

"And do you know the attackers?"

"Yes!"

"And you said you were a teacher?"

"Yes!"

"And you said they are shooting at you with guns?"

"Yes! Well...paintball guns."

"What kind of paintball guns?"

"Why does it matter?!"

"Calm down. Law enforcement is on the way, but I need you to listen to my directions."

"Okay!"

"You need to get to the front of the building."

"But *they* are out there!"

"By the time you get outside, police will arrive. If you stay inside, you are sitting dicks. Do you understand me?"

The teacher nodded with the phone pressed to his ear. Teachers around him asked what the operator said. He clicked off his phone as a fresh barrage of paint smacked the windows above him.

"Police are coming and we need to get out of the building as soon as we can. We're sitting *dicks* in here?"

"Sitting *ducks*," Manley snapped from the desk next to him.

The stained glass emanated a multitude of colors in the smoky room. Darkness spread between the multicolored rays. The paint spatters, the hissing smoke, the creeping claustrophobia, the dizziness, the puking, all became too much.

Father Manny yelled out first: "We need to get the hell out of here!"

Teachers coughed in agreement.

"Make a break for the hallway!" Manley shouted as he propped himself up with his metal bat. "We're sitting dicks in here!" Manley shook his head violently as he ran. "Ducks, goddamnit. Ducks!" he shouted to himself.

The staff took a collective gulp of air and then sprinted around desks and right over the hacking security guard, and into the hallway. Manley took out his phone and shined the light toward the teachers.

"Follow me!" he shouted, pulling his shirt over his nose and mouth as he walked to the back entrance. Dieter remained under his desk. The faint glow of his cellphone filled the nook. He could hear the commotion, but did not follow his peers.

Manley threw his shoulder into the doors.

For a moment, the sunlight burst into the smoky hallway, and the staff coughed at the promise of fresh air. Manley stepped out the door, propping it with his shoulder.

"It's okay, everybody."

Through the chaos, Manley didn't realize how easy it would be for the students to merely walk ten feet from Dieter's class to the annex doors. He quickly discovered his error as a burst of air-propelled pellets thwacked against building and body. Screams erupted from the hallway. A new noise joined the smacking of paint.

Moaning in disgust and pain, Manley leapt back inside. The last glimmer of light from the sun shone on a cracked egg that oozed from his forehead. Noticeable red and yellow dents dotted his stomach and chest.

"To the office!" he yelled as he ran past the cowering herd.

The teachers turned and followed him down the dim hallway, hands bracing the wall to keep their bearings. They shuffled along for twenty yards coughing and crying, shirts pulled over their mouths and noses until they neared the junction to the main building, where the smoke dissipated. Manley dropped his shirt.

"Let's go!" he shouted as he bound toward the left fork of the hallway.

But as he began to run down the curved corridor, and as he went to plant his left foot, his weight slipped out from under him. His arms raised in desperation, bat flying out of his grip while he grasped for an invisible rope. With a thud and a groan, his back smacked the oily ground.

Mr. Canon had bound down the right branch of the fork only to meet the same fate as Manley. Triumphant teenage yells came from the smoke around Dieter's room. Teachers' faces went from fear to utter terror. A scream went up from the trembling mob. "What do we do?"

Manley wheeled on his back like a turned turtle. His head seeped droplets of red around the orange yolk. From his back, excess vegetable oil drizzled to the tile.

"Crawl," he muttered. His voice, though still decisive, could not cloak his pained whimper. The staff looked at each other and then slowly crouched onto all fours. Most followed Manley, but others took the right fork. A chorus of disgust went up as the adults felt the oil on their hands and knees.

The urgency from approaching footsteps propelled them down the hallway, where, like a herd of baby deer, they wobbled on the slicked linoleum. Some of their arms slid in opposite directions, and they tumbled head first onto the tile. Others were trapped in frantic motion with little progress to repay the effort.

The soft squeak of sneakers on laminate announced the approach of their attackers. The teachers turned to face their assailants. Remnants of smoke poured in from behind the teens, who hovered behind the teachers. The students pointed and laughed maniacally. With their assault temporarily halted by the comedy playing out before them, they gave the teachers time to find their footing.

One science teacher discovered that if they pivoted their hands like ski poles, they could slide their knees forward. Soon the rest of the teachers took the example. Coughing, the teachers cursed through the muck, drunk with fatigue and fear, hoping to find rest in the distant offices.

Seeing their targets slide off, the students straightened up, reloaded their paint ball guns, pulled out more eggs, and resumed their onslaught. Cheers and eggs and pellets and revenge rained upon the staff. Sanders moved in the middle of the pack as eggs started smacking walls, floors, and buttocks.

"I swear to God I will find those responsible and...and...I'll fry them like...jimmychangas...These little shitheads will not get away with this!"

Father Manny, who moved steadily on Sanders' left, whispered "shut up" as an egg exploded squarely against his left butt-cheek. One teacher tried to open the door to the stairwell, thinking the second floor could bring reprieve. Instead, he became a prime target. He yanked on the handle while paint and eggs blasted his body, but the door would not budge. The only thing he successfully accomplished was diverting the splatter for a few moments while the rest of the staff continued down the hallway.

When he fell to the ground, the hail of paint and eggs resumed for everyone else until after four minutes of struggle through slick floors and protein-bombardment, the herd finally made it around the curve, safe from projectiles.

Most teachers had egg leaking down the seats of their pants or the backs of their heads. Some had tears trickling from their cheeks. The front of the pack, led by the still-bleeding Manley, silently crept across the final thirty yards of floor until he and his group neared the vestibule, where five yards from the stairwell the floor became dry. Manley pulled his feet around his body so that he was facing the teachers. Slowly, he pushed onto his feet until he was upright. The rest of the staff, still on all fours, lifted their heads to Manley like a groveling group of peasants looking upon their leader. The teachers on the right branch could see their compatriots across the entrance and exchanged pathetic waves of acknowledgement.

Manley sighed and arched his back. "It's okay. Almost there." He cracked a small smile of assurance as tiny rivulets of drying blood lined his neck from behind his right ear. He nodded at the opposing group and ambled forward from the hallway into the larger entrance. Teachers chuckled in delirious relief as Manley surveyed his body. His knees and back and chest were stained with the oil that had mixed with various paint splotches and eggshell remnants.

But just as Manley picked an eggshell from his shoulder, a thunder of footsteps came from the second floor, down the steps near where he was standing. He turned to the noise and was greeted by the all-too-familiar gust of air-powered guns.

Teachers watched as tiny bursts of red popped from Manley's chest, stomach, and crotch. As if in a dream, he floundered and stumbled on the tiles, hands groping the air as if he were drowning. Each shot of paint that slammed into his body jolted him backward until he tripped, landing squarely on his tailbone. Renewed cries of terror came from the staff. The shooting paused.

"Punk bastards!" Manley sputtered as he held his chest and

spun onto his knees to get up. Three more bursts hit him squarely on the exposed seat of his pants. In a fit of rage, he turned and hobbled toward the steps.

"I'm going to kill you," he growled. Like an enraged grizzly, he trudged against the barrage of paint smacking his body. His eyes locked on the four mask-wearing teens in a firing position on the platform above the first flight of stairs. Manley's foot slammed the first step, sliding away from his body, so that he had to grab the railing at the last second. He tried to lift his other foot onto the second step, but a paintball hit him squarely in the forehead. He slipped again and was left hugging the railing while the brutal paint-filled flurry continued.

The staff shrieked. Sores already had formed on Manley's forearms and forehead. Howling like a wounded beast, he jumped from the steps and bounded toward the front doors. Thick spots of red and orange covered his face and body. Yellow patches dotted the seat of pants.

"Run!" he gasped, digging at the paint and blood and egg mixture covering his eyes. "Run!"

The staff shuffled forward frantically and pulled themselves up. In their loafers and flats, they took off in a sprint toward the double doors that could provide a barrier to the barrage of paint flying around them. Screams of pain and shock rippled the air as the flying pellets hit back, butt, shoulder, arm, and head.

"Run in a zig-zag motion," Sanders barked. "Run-in-a-zig-zag-motion!"

Manley ran face-first into the office doors in his blindness. After realizing where he was, he frantically jostled the locked doors. Father Manny grabbed Manley across the chest and pulled him from the door. Manley's eyes were clenched shut, and his arm draped over Father Manny's shoulder as they stumbled away from the building.

The other adults ran with their heads crouched under their hands, yelling until they burst through the large wooden doors, where they wheezed and sobbed and collapsed onto the heated concrete under a luminous late May sun.

In front of them, laughter and applause pealed in the distance. The battle was not yet over.

Teachers lay scattered, dazed and in pain. Those that could stand were bent over with their hands on their thighs. Big splotches of oil covered various sides of their bodies and stained their knees. Hair was tussled. Shirts were untucked. Faces were gray from the smoke. Red and yellow paint speckled their clothes and skins. Hidden welts and bruises swelled and nagged for relief. The male teachers that were not incapacitated lay against the wooden doors to bar another assault from their rear.

Sanders stumbled in front of the disorganized pack. When he appeared from the human rubble, a roar burst from about two hundred yards in front of him, where the students amassed in a large semi-circle. In the front of the swarm, rows of shirtless boys flexed with red and black and white paint on their bodies and faces. Stripes, hand-prints, tribal patterns, and various other designs adorned their skins. They tied shirts around their heads like guerrillas. Some of them gripped paintball rifles. Some held basketballs, soccer balls, volleyballs, or dodgeballs inside the crook of their arms. Others clenched rulers and meter sticks, smacking them against their free hands menacingly.

Defeat squealed from the teachers' deflated lungs. Manley, crippled by an egg-paint combination in his eyes, disengaged from Father Manny's support and collapsed onto the ground.

"Does anybody have a phone?"

The staff looked around. A few teachers produced broken phones that had been crushed in the mayhem or corrupted by oil. Manley fumbled his phone from his pocket. His shaking hand extended to Father Manny. Calmly, Father Manny punched the three numbers.

"No signal."

"What do we do?"

An English teacher mumbled that they could have run into one of the many classrooms and barricaded themselves, but this did not help the present situation. In the fight against rebellion and high stakes testing, Sanders had scrapped the tornado drills and active shooter training required by the district. He replaced the necessary emergency preparations with a two-part meeting on how to write multiple choice answers that mimicked the end-of-year test and how to assert dominance in the classroom through heavy-handed discipline. His neglect for district requirements had led to this moment, where he knelt wounded and cornered outside the very building he was supposed to control. And there was no guarantee his selected focus for the meetings even paid off. Judging by the superintendent's call that morning, it hadn't.

Sanders stared into the abyss and spoke.

"I don't know what they want, but I don't intend—"

Manley grabbed at the air near his mentor's arm. "Just give them what they want."

Sanders smacked Manley's hand away. "I won't!"

Manley dropped his head and sighed. Tears welled in his eyes, flushing out some of the paint. Sanders' incarnadine face shook violently. His eyes darted wildly between the teachers and the building as if searching for someone or something. His lips appeared to mouth "where are you?" in his desperate hunt for relief. After a fruitless search, he turned toward the students, pointed his finger at them, and stammered, "We will not negotiate with *terrorists*! It's—"

An air horn rose from the distance, cutting off Sanders and triggering the mob to slowly unzip from the back down to the front. Four heavily painted students appeared on white, black, amber, and gray horses. They galloped forward in pairs as the students filed in behind them until the horsemen reached the front of the throng.

"What the hell? *Horses*?" Sanders muttered in disbelief. Father Manny reclined to his back. His right hand caressed the rosary beads he held in his left.

The four riders, a junior, two seniors, and a sophomore, broke in opposite directions along the line of students. With guttural roars, they raised large wooden meter sticks in salutation. The minions responded with a magnificent boom. Hollering with savage zeal, the students brandished their weapons of choice, as the four riders returned to the middle to be joined by Andre and Maria, who had manifested from the mob also clad in war paint.

Maria had red eyebrows, while a circle of black surrounded her eyes. Her lips extended with black paint that mimicked stitching. Andre had three red lines streaking from his cheek bones down to his jaw. Two horns were painted above his eyebrows on his expansive forehead. The presidential pair stepped in unison behind their cavalry, who escorted Maria and Andre through the lawn while the rest of the students maintained their position.

Meanwhile, the staff murmured in confusion and angst.

"Walt, what's happening?" asked Manley, his eyes still shut.

Sanders turned to survey his staff. Mr. Canon was wildly attempting to spark his lighter for an invisible cigarette dangling from his parted lips. The Social Studies department was sitting and rocking with their heads in their hands, tears streaming down their faces. Science formed a prayer circle around Father Manny. The gym teacher lay frozen in the fetal position, gazing at the concrete in front of him. Again, Sanders' eyes darted wildly, combing objects for some apparition. He pulled out his school ID, and after a minute of silent reflection, his resilient eyes softened, and his lips unclenched. With a drop of his chin, he pushed himself from the pavement and took a step in the direction of the two students, who had taken a position near Gretel's mangled remains.

His body moved rigidly, breaths vacant like a man walking to the gallows. The horsemen trotted back to the students' battle line upon seeing their principal's approach. When Sanders stepped onto the driveway, his head lifted toward the sky in resignation.

Suddenly, a whirl from a golf cart came around the corner. Behind Sanders, the staff flinched, fearing another assault. But Mr. Canon yelped in surprise. "It's Vogel!"

Dieter turned the cart down the driveway and angled toward Sanders. The teachers, not comprehending what was going on, let out a small cheer, as if Dieter were leading a legion of angels against the demon horde in the field across from them. When Dieter reached Sanders, he leaned out and confidently extended his hand in a gesture meant to aid Sanders ascent into the cart. "I'll help, sir, if you'll let me."

Sanders looked at the formerly worthless teacher. A small tear of gratitude formed in the corner of his left eye. "Yes. They'll listen to you. Yes, please!"

His body awkwardly flopped onto the padded seat while the cart lurched forward. With a loud click of the gas, they drove onto the grass, the fate of Reading rattling within the golf cart.

———

They stopped six feet from the teens. Sanders leaned forward, but Dieter lightly restrained him with his arm. "Stay here, sir. Rest."

"Maria, Andre," Dieter began, as he climbed from the golf-cart.

"Punk-bastards," Sanders barked from his seat. The temporary reprieve from the assault had given him time to shake off fear-formed adrenaline. Fresh outrage took its place.

Maria shot a condescending glance at the Principal-Mayor, but it was Dieter's scowl that subdued Sanders. Turning back to his favorite students, Dieter continued: "Listen, we want to end this peacefully. What can we do to fix this?"

Sanders gurgled in agitation, but Dieter again turned quickly and raised his hand in a plea for confidence. Maria unfolded a sheet of paper. Firm and measured, Maria's words addressed the two adults.

"We the People of Reading High School, in Order to form a more perfect School, establish Justice, insure racial Equality, provide for the common experience, promote the general Safety, and secure the Blessings of Education to ourselves and our Siblings, do proclaim—"

"Terrorists! Traitors!" Sanders shouted.

"Go on," Dieter responded with a smile that was hidden from Sanders.

"We have four demands, and if they are not met, we will continue our siege of the school. In addition, we will release the tape of

Principal Sanders' racist remarks to the press, as well as testimonies of a multitude of other abuses and injustices."

Dieter puffed his chest and winked at Maria. They both knew the tape had already circulated social media, but threatening to leak it to the news was a nice touch by Maria to appeal to Sanders' disdain and fear of the press.

"I will have to check with the principal, but what are your demands?"

Andre stepped forward, stone-faced. "One: an election given for the students and by the students to decide our mascot."

Sanders shifted in his seat and grumbled. "We will not negotiate such un-American—"

But Dieter cut him off with a glare. "Go on, Andre."

"Two: Reading High School will hire more high-quality teachers of color in at least two of the five job openings that have been posted."

Dieter nodded, though he was taken aback at this provision. In fact, he felt vaguely threatened, albeit impressed by the students' perceptiveness and maturity. He and the students hadn't talked about this type of measure before. Andre's voice became more impassioned.

"Three: immediate reinstatement of Miguel Saguaro."

Again, Sanders gurgled his agitation: "This is preposterous. Reading doesn't need rabble-rousers like him—"

"Four?" Dieter asked calmly.

"Four: effective immediately, Principal Sanders will resign."

At this statement, Sanders jumped from the golf cart and hobbled angrily toward the meeting, finger wagging at the adolescents. "Now you listen to me, you little pieces of—"

Andre's hands rose into two tightly formed fists. Maria also met Sanders' words by raising her hand, where her phone, ready to record any other regrettable words, was brandished like a shield. Seeing the device, Sanders slunk toward Dieter's side and seethed into his ears.

"This is outrageous. They're bluffing. We deleted the tape recording. Right, Vogel?"

But Dieter did not match Sanders fury, nor did he give affirmation to Sanders question. Instead, Dieter turned with derision. "You shouldn't have let it get to this point, Walter."

Sanders' eyes bulged and his mouth moved without producing a sound.

"I'm taking charge now. As the tape shows, among other things, you are not fit for leading this school."

The collusion seeped from Dieter's words. Sanders' bottom lip quaked. Never had Vogel had the gall to call him by his first name. Never had Vogel, the formerly corpulent laughingstock, spoken to him with such airs. Never had Sanders been so betrayed.

"You...are doing *what*?"

Dieter continued to stare as he took a step backward toward his two star students. Both Maria and Andre folded their arms and smirked at Sanders.

"Walter, I've sat for three years and watched you run this school into the ground. It's time you focus on your mayoral duties and leave education to people who actually care."

Sanders continued to stare at his insubordinate. The magma under his skin grew alarmingly red. Each breath wheezed from his nostrils, tickling his protruding jaw.

A single luxury sedan disrupted the silent stand-off. It pulled up the driveway behind the students and circled the lawn toward the entrance of the school. The four of them watched the car creep along with a gawking black woman in the driver's seat. Her jaw hung so low it could have pressed the button to open the windows. The ire in Sanders' eyes melted into fear.

The black car twitched as the brakes were slammed down, and the tall, baffled woman jumped from the driver's side. After a brief scan, she stormed toward the meeting, high heels disappearing into the soft grass as each step slammed into the earth. Her leather satchel swung violently from her shoulder.

She scoured the mob of students and the wreckage of adults. "What in the world is going on here?" the woman cried out.

"Superintendent Ward, I—" Sanders sputtered, arms open in surrender.

The superintendent raised her hands to silence him, just as Dieter had moments prior. She turned to Maria and Andre. "Explain!"

Andre's mouth was vacuous and still, lips frozen an inch apart. Maria shrugged and stepped forward.

"We are *protesting…*"

"Protesting what?" the superintendent cut in calmly.

"We are protesting the continued injustices that this administration has carried out against the student body."

The superintendent looked quickly to Sanders, then back to Maria.

"Such as…?"

"Such as the wrongful expulsion of a student with special needs. Racially insensitive rhetoric and policies. And—" Maria shifted, looking for the right words to summarize the struggle over a mascot, which she now held as so insignificant, though it was the cause that catalyzed the entire year.

"And?" the Superintendent questioned.

Maria's eyes fixed on the ground before shooting up in sudden assuredness: "The silencing of the student body and the tyrannical suppression of democracy."

The superintendent gave a nod of acknowledgement. Maria's poise had impressed her. She reminded her of the woman she was in high school.

"Thank you, Miss—"

"Lopez, ma'am."

"Miss Lopez… Finally a face behind all the emails I've received from you." The superintendent smiled genuinely for the first time, briefly, before her face pulled back to the serious situation in front of her. "Thank you for filling me in. We've been made aware of some of the things you've stated. I would like to meet with you and Mr. Williams—in the building, of course—after I speak to these two."

Maria nodded

"Now, I need you to help me out. I need whatever *this* is," the superintendent motioned toward the students, "to disperse."

"What do I tell them?" Maria asked. "They want justice."

The superintendent smiled again. "Tell them *all* sides will get justice. And they can have the rest of the day off. Tomorrow, as well. We have a board meeting tonight about the school's future. They do need to show up for finals next week, though. Your grades still matter. Understand?"

Maria nodded. The two student presidents turned and walked back to the mass of adolescents, where they were absorbed by their constituents thirsting to hear what had been said.

Superintendent Ward turned to Sanders and Dieter and pulled an envelope from her purse.

"Now I can see why your test scores were so low," she said sternly before striding toward the school. She spun suddenly. "Except in ninth and eleventh grade reading—those scores were quite impressive."

On the lawn, the students hoisted Maria and Andre onto their shoulders and cheered. At the entrance, the teachers gave a deep, collective sigh before picking each other up from the pavement.

Chapter 19

THE FINAL DAY of school seemed like a hangover after the debauchery of the past week. In the hallway, a janitor thrust his mop from tile to tile. At times, he would pause, lean the wooden handle against the wall, pull out a chisel, then bend over to scratch a stubborn, sticky spot of paint from the floor. "Damned animals!" he cursed.

"No need for profanity on this lovely day, Gus," Jose chirped as he glided from the stairwell to the first floor. He wore a sky blue blazer, fitted pants, and a bright pink tie that glowed in the dim hallway. His smile stretched onto his rosy cheeks. His chestnut-brown shoes glided on the clean tiles, giving the illusion that Jose hovered over the sea-green linoleum.

"Yes sir, Mister—pardon me—um, Principal—"

"Jose is fine! I know it's unorthodox, but I'm an unorthodox guy."

With that, Jose floated off to the main office, stopping to polish the new copper-plated sign by the door: *Principal Josué Cordero-De la Cruz.*

The janitor shook his head, pulled the mop off the wall, and resumed pushing red shavings around the floor. The shells of paintballs tumbled around the red and yellow puddles. Forward and backward, circular and side to side, the strings from the mop meandered. When the familiar pain in his knees flared up, he hobbled to the steps and sat down. He had already worked for thirty-six hours cleaning the oily hallways and the remnants of gas canisters that were strewn throughout the annex.

Massaging his knees, he chanted repeatedly that this definitely was his last year. He had cleaned enough graffiti, enough wet toilet paper, enough gum caked to desks and tables, enough sticky piles of food, enough oil-slicked floors, and enough rooms where garbage filled the floors. This year's janitorial duties and random repairs had exceeded the amount of work he'd done over the past thirty years. At least it seemed so. There was an RV somewhere out there for him—a nice, compact area that wouldn't need much cleaning and could move from space to space. He'd had enough of Reading's filth.

Down the east hallway, he could hear commotion: an elevated, irritated voice, uncompassionate rumbles in response, and the squeaky sound of futile resistance.

"But I'm giving an exam! What's the meaning of this?"

Around the corner, the stern-faced, pudgy security guard appeared, gripping Dieter's elbow. Dieter jerked his arm away only to have it grabbed again when it fell to his side. Like a petulant child being led to his room, Dieter looked more like he was being pushed than walking of his own accord.

"Principal needs to see you," the guard responded with a blank forward stare.

"About what? This is crazy!"

The guard shoved Dieter, causing him to stumble past the janitor and slip on the wet floor. With a smack of his palms, he fell to his knees and jerked his head to glare at the guard, who returned Dieter's daggers by pointing to the main office.

Dieter twisted his head towards Sanders' former cave, where Jose had just stepped out with two large, uniformed police officers. Dieter's jaw dropped as he remained on his knees in the middle of the soapy floor.

"You're in trouble now…"

———————

The Principal's office had lost its hyper-masculinity. The trophies and motivational posters had disappeared. The German flag was removed from behind Sanders' massive oak desk. Instead, paintings of flowery meadows, serene purple mountains cast against an orange sunset, and a man who looked vaguely like Jose with a beard decorated the office.

The installation of a skylight above Jose's desk was another noticeable change. When asked about it, since it had appeared the day after Jose was officially made principal, Jose told those who asked that he had it installed by his father. The work order itself was signed by a man named "Elroi," who had charged no fee for the work.

Jose further defended the decision, saying, "Any student who ends up here definitely needs to see the light!" So, it stayed, along with the perpetually luminous Jose. As a result, a bar of sunlight beamed directly on the lone seat in front of Jose's desk—a fitting omen for what was to come.

"Take a seat, Mr. Vogel," Jose said with a calm politeness. His tone was a friendly salve to the sting of his command.

Dieter looked apprehensively at the two officers standing with arms crossed by the door. His escape was impeded by those two menacing figures. He lowered his eyes and slid onto a chair in front of the desk. The scratchy cloth padding immediately aggravated his skin, even against his clothing. Equally uncomfortable was the sunlight pouring directly onto his face. Embarrassment and defiance glued him to his circumstance.

Jose moved to the counter where the coffee-maker had been replaced by a large water cooler and a stack of cups.

"If you could give us a few minutes, gentlemen," Jose said to the guards as he filled a plastic cup with water, "I'd greatly appreciate a moment to discuss this matter with Mr. Vogel."

He had gone from "Divo" to "Mr. Vogel" over the span of a week. This formality could not portend mercy.

"We'll be right here," the largest guard responded as he glanced at Dieter before forcing the door shut.

"You look warm," Jose said as he handed Dieter a glass of water. "I hope you are comfortable."

"Of course," Dieter replied, wiping a sheet of perspiration from his forehead, "but I'd like to know why I was taken from the exam in such an unprofessional manner."

He tried to sound offended, but his voice was shaky from what he could only guess was a preliminary trial to ascertain his level of guilt over the year's debauchery. Dieter lifted his glass to take a sip. As he lowered the glass, he noticed a large smiley face on the outside of the cup with the words "Have a blessed day!" printed underneath it. Dieter was thrown into a coughing fit.

Jose moved behind his desk as Dieter hacked. After all the changes to the office, one final one drew Dieter's attention. A simple wooden chair, stained in a burnt umber hue, replaced Sanders' large purple throne. Jose pulled it from the desk.

"We have much to talk about," Jose said. He slid onto the seat with a coy smile. "Please, drink some water so we can continue."

Dieter took two big gulps, and while there was a tickle in his throat, his coughing was temporarily suppressed. He looked at Jose, who sat perfectly erect with his right leg tossed over the left, his hands resting on his knees.

"No doubt you've heard, Mr. Vogel, my name was cleared on Sunday from any connection to the year's more *extreme* behaviors. There was an email you sent last Friday that had accused me of instigating the riots and violence. I'm not sure why I became your scapegoat, but Superintendent Ward and I had a great conversation, which of course led to me becoming interim principal."

Dieter shook in frustration. He'd never accused Jose, although he suspected how an email with his name on it might be sent without his knowledge. As he opened his lungs to defend himself, he was stifled with a violent hacking. For ten seconds, he struggled to suppress the cough.

Dieter took another gulp of water and opened his mouth to again insist that his email had been hacked, but the cough again rose up unexpectedly, forcing him to again return to chugging water to quell the persistent itch. In seconds, the cup was empty. Jose leapt up, walked around the desk, and grabbed Dieter's cup.

"All is forgiven, Mr. Vogel. I can understand why you might have thought that I was complicit. I was spared the barbarism of last week's assault, after all." Dieter's brow was still clenched in defiant innocence. "But that's not why you are here."

Dieter shifted uncomfortably in the heat of Jose's stated forgiveness and swift transition. He still wondered where Jose had been during the assault on the school.

"I've been meeting with some of the instigators of this year's series of demonstrations. While we were investigating the events, I was rather fortunate to have been granted access to cell phone conversations, social media accounts, and your class blog."

Jose returned with another full cup of water and handed it to Dieter before dropping onto his seat.

"I noticed in the blog, which I understand was yours for Film Studies, that there were two users who seemed to be outspoken proponents of a coup-de-tat. Their names," Jose opened a manila folder on his desk and looked at the top paper, "were sexiechica5 and Balla4lyfe. Balla4lyfe, in fact, wrote, and I quote, 'We going to eviscerate that bitch just like in the movie, yo, LaughOL.' He or she was, of course, referring to the statue of Gretel and the attempted dismantling."

Dieter responded by silently staring at his cup, praying that the words would shift to form some *divine* guidance.

"Beyond your nonexistent monitoring and censoring of such rhetoric," Jose said with a condescending glance, "I was struck by 'going to' and 'eviscerate', which seemed out of place with the slang and vulgarity of our youth. The 'Laugh O-L' was also quite suspicious. I asked myself, 'What kind of student talks like this?' I suspected a non-student may have been involved."

More like a *non-human*. Dieter took more nervous gulps of water.

"I hired a friend of mine to trace the source of the comments. I won't bore you with how he did it, but it turns out the IP address was 616 Tartarus Dr. And upon further research, I found that you live in this apartment complex."

As Jose laid out his case, Dieter stared at the wood grain in the desk and the pictures on the wall. Dieter had not typed that blog post, but he knew who had. Hoping its author would manifest and give him advice, he nervously took another drink of water. Besides the email he'd received, Dieter had not seen the Devil since before testing when he shut his computer on Satan.

Dieter's cough seemed to erupt whenever he opened his mouth, as if oxygen irritated his vocal cords. Again raising his cup, he found no water to greet his lips; and again, Jose refilled the cup.

"So why would you write such things or allow these things to be written in your presence? I did more searching, and stumbled upon a post by sexiechica5 that had a link to 'Mr. Vogel 4 principle,' a social media group started by a Miss—"

Jose gave Dieter the full glass and went to his desk. He reopened the folder and shuffled through some papers. As he was doing so, Dieter looked around desperately. His eyes skimmed each painting until he focused on the oceanic scene behind the desk. A large red crab scuttled out from a hole in the reef and gave its right claw a wave at Dieter.

Relieved, Dieter looked at Jose, who had snatched a print-out of the page.

"Ah, Miss Sandy Ramirez... The notoriously truant Ramirez, who moved to Mexico in the middle of the year. However, she never had a social media account. You see, I called her relatives who still live in Reading. They told me she never had a profile, nor would she ever want you to be principal. So again, my friend traced the IP address, and it again led to your residence."

Dieter finished the fourth glass of water.

"One more?" Jose chirped, changing his serious tone to peachy hospitality.

"Well, I—"

"I insist..."

With that, Jose snatched Dieter's glass and marched to the cooler. Dieter looked up at the painting where the Devil-possessed crab had somehow found a white sign on the ocean floor and had scribbled a message on it: "Legal?"

Dieter felt a swell in his chest in addition to the sudden, rapid expansion of his bladder.

"It surely can't be legal for you to trace IP addresses?" Dieter said.

Jose finished filling Dieter's glass and smiled. "Mr. Vogel, the blog was an extension of the school's website. I have full right as Principal to investigate such posts."

The crab froze.

"Now," Jose continued as he handed the glass back to Dieter, "I was amazed as to how a teacher who struggled to establish rapport and classroom management could gain power over students who struggled to learn or even stay conscious in class. I marveled at how students who could not comprehend simple texts could suddenly identify perfect parallels to Nazi propaganda in our *anonymously* crafted letter to the parents—"

Jose gave a coy smile before he returned to seriousness.

"—and how students that were stuck at a grade school reading level could almost magically spout canonical literature and speak of complex psychological theories while growing their reading scores at historic rates by the year-end test. How a group of lethargic and apathetic teenagers found passion, purpose and terrorist zeal in the mundane world of mascot selection. I must applaud you, Mr. Vogel; you became a masterful teacher. The most effective I've ever seen in my many, *many* years."

Dieter filled with pride, forgetting that there were two chiseled officers of the law standing outside, presumably waiting for him. His bladder also continued to swell. The crab held up another sign: "Crime to be a good teacher?"

Dieter nodded at the picture, and though Jose noticed the peculiar gesture at a seemingly invisible person, he continued to stare at Dieter.

"Jose, I was merely trying to teach the kids civic responsibility—democracy, if you will—and the resilience to pursue their dreams."

A smug self-assurance grew with each word. Where he had temporarily felt the hopelessness of past years creeping back, he rediscovered the devious power he had established with the Devil as his accomplice.

"They were the ones who took my lessons and made them violent. The two screen names were merely personas used to show the power of suggestion and peer influence. Perhaps I explained this to my students and they failed to tell you. Regardless, you have only conjecture. I've done nothing criminal. I didn't blow up Gretel. Some crazy student took my lessons on *Fight Club* to the extreme. So, you've really got no reason to keep me in this office under the possibility of arrest. And you have no grounds to fire—"

Jose held up his hand. Dieter leaned back, satisfied with his defense. He took a confident swig of water for dramatic effect. The crab in the picture began pumping his claws and scuttling in victory. Lowering onto his seat calmly, Jose pulled back his cheeks in a gracious smile before he responded.

"You are quite correct, Mr. Vogel. None of those things are criminal. However, that brings us back to the text messages." He pulled a stapled set of sheets from the folder. "*Esther won't agree. Need another way.* This message was sent from your phone to Sanders the day before she ingested peanut butter-laced coffee."

Dieter shot up to protest. He didn't mean he was going to attack her. He meant she was not going to help Miguel get expelled. Dieter sent that to Sanders after pretending to have had a conversation with Esther. It was a pathetic attempt to keep Miguel in school, but Dieter couldn't bring himself to talk to Esther.

"I never meant—"

But another raised hand met him, compelling him to lower himself back to the seat. He had to cross his legs to try and keep his robust bladder in check. A buzzing in his head intensified.

"She's recovering, by the way. Poor girl asked about you when I visited her. I have some messages from her *and* from you that I think you'll want to see."

Dieter spied the crab creeping back towards the hole. He could feel his cheeks sag in guilt. He hadn't even checked on Esther, and though his heart fluttered that she had asked about him, a stubborn thirst for truth dulled his emotions.

"I didn't do anything to her."

"Perhaps you didn't, though we could also tie Ms. Stewart's allergic reaction to your class as well. And I have a box with your name and a residue of laced cupcakes on it."

"Circumstantial. And I sent him an email warning him…"

"Your email never arrived. Perhaps you meant to send it, or maybe it was intercepted?"

Dieter's jaw clenched. Intercepted? There was only one way it could be…

"All of this is circumstantial, of course. But I can solidly prove your part in the attack on the school, which I found from texts you sent to Miguel's phone. This, at minimum, is in line with contributing to the delinquency of a minor."

"Hard to prove," Dieter mumbled.

"My evidence would be sufficient. As for motives, you were bullied ceaselessly by Manley. You had a falling out with Esther. And, of course, you were under probation, which seems like another good motive for attacks on the school itself. There was a video sent to you that chronicled the various torments you suffered at the hands of staff. Certain teachers also heard you talking about taking down Sanders…"

"Hearsay! Insanity," Dieter shouted, hand clamped on his crotch.

Jose chuckled and looked at Dieter with a grin. "It seemed as if you were *possessed* this year."

As he scrutinized the seascape on the wall behind Jose, Dieter's eyes clenched in desperation. This had not been their plan. Dieter was supposed to supplant Sanders, not Jose. And Dieter certainly was supposed to be free from punishment. Nausea began to rock him as his eyes implored the crab for salvation.

Jose turned to Dieter, then to the picture, then back to Dieter. Staring intently, Jose snapped his fingers. In response, the crab gave Dieter a tight wave, and then disappeared into the reef. As suddenly as he'd appeared in Dieter's life, the Devil scampered out of it. Hopelessness and betrayal, Dieter's familiar friends, were now his only accomplices. He would never see Satan again.

"Dieter, I know everything. I know you were not alone. And I know," Jose turned to the painting of the sea, "you have been led astray."

Dieter continued staring at the ocean painting, which now rendered an overwhelming emptiness.

"You never showed such ambitions before. Nor had you shown any inkling of callousness or vengefulness."

Dieter's legs began to shake.

"So," Jose concluded with a bow toward the door, "this person pushed you and pulled you, dangling illusions of grandeur so you would follow him."

Dieter scoffed, "Look, my friend just told me I could do better. Okay? And I still haven't done anything wrong."

Jose smiled.

"Criminally? Of course, you haven't, Dieter. But you've threatened your standing at this school. You've taken a wonderful talent and used it—"

"I can find a new job, if you are going to fire me. I have the best test scores of this school and an impeccable letter of recommendation from Sanders…" Dieter rocked forward to get up.

"Please, Dieter. I don't want you to leave. But if you do, I just want you to stop following Satan."

Jose's words slammed Dieter back onto his chair.

"Satan? Are you crazy? Does the Devil even exist? This is nuts!" Dieter replied as he rocked forward, glancing back at the painting.

"Dieter, your vision has blurred. You've drunk in the Devil's plans while he devoured the rest of your life."

When Dieter stood up to leave in feigned indignation, he instantly felt his lips numb, his eyes grow droopy, and his legs buckle. The wooziness circling his brain exploded into thousands of tiny needle pricks.

"What? How? I only—"

Dieter searched his empty cup for answers. Jose smiled and glided back to his seat. Dieter saw the ceiling light follow Jose toward his desk, stopping right on the folder of evidence, but Dieter was feeling drunk, so he couldn't trust what he was seeing.

"Dieter, there is something that most people don't grasp. You like to think your actions are cloaked in a shroud of secrecy—"

Dieter wobbled, hand grabbing his crotch to dam his bladder.

"—that your transgressions are unseen and without consequence. People use violence and exploitation to build their kingdom of influence on this Earth but they don't—"

Dieter dropped to his knees. "Please, get to the point," Dieter moaned as he tried to stem the tide.

"Dieter, when someone gives in to the Devil, he becomes so hooked on false promises that he dulls his heart to the truth. Drastic measures are needed to bring them back. Truly, truly, I say to you, there's only one way that a person can become right again."

"What are you talking about?" Dieter whined, bent over at his waist.

Jose pointed to the previously transparent water jug, which now sat in a perfect deep-purple hue.

"*No!*" Dieter gasped.

With a snap of Jose's fingers, it turned clear. Dieter's dilated eyes returned to Jose as the beam from the skylight moved slowly like a spotlight until it fully encapsulated Jose's cedar throne, cloaking Jose in a white light that surrounded his omniscient smile.

Dieter's drunkenness swirled until Jose snapped his fingers once more. All the symptoms of alcohol disappeared. In renewed clarity, a hollow vision of guilt painted the walls of Dieter's thoughts.

Sobered and alone in his culpability, Dieter fell to his knees. Looking again at the seascape and finding nothing, Dieter's defense slipped from his heart and poured down his leg in a hot clear stream. Betrayal trickled from his eyes. Even if he didn't pee himself, Dieter sensed an incredible smallness within himself. He'd gone into teaching to escape further into fantasy worlds. Then, he discovered that he could live in the present, in community with people hungry for his knowledge and guidance. And he'd jeopardized everything by following a cause and a being that required indifference and corruption.

For the next minute, his tears were as uncontrolled as the urine spurting down his leg. Heat from his flood of poor choices clung to his skin. Jose lifted from his chair and crouched beside Dieter. A wave of defiant anger crashed into his body, sending a torrent of thoughts coursing through his mind.

He was supposed to be in charge. He was supposed to save the school. He was supposed to finally get all those things his life was devoid of: power, control, respect. Now, in the presence of He who deserved those things, the pettiness of his quest, the obviousness of the Devil's deception, the emptiness of revenge, all lashed at Dieter as he knelt on the floor covered in regret: for how he'd treated his students and how, at the counsel of Satan, he'd distanced himself from one of his true friends. The other one remained silent until Dieter's breathing became less labored.

"You've found your influence, Divo. The students followed you to great and terrible places."

Dieter's lips trembled. His students: his brilliant, wonderful students.

"That's power, and it feels good for a while, but it will not satisfy you. I can show you how to find the love, respect, and acceptance that you had, and that you will want again."

Dieter sniffled. Could he really get those things back?

"It's not too late to fix things."

Dieter's eyes wandered up to Jose's, whose eyes were moist in tender concern.

"What do you say? Are you ready to start over?"

Another surge of resentment bolted through him. His eyes pulsated and his lips pursed. Like his dad, Satan had commandeered Dieter's life to satisfy his own agenda. Like his dad, Satan had used Dieter to wound the ones he loved. Like his dad, the Devil had left him broken in a messy world. Cream filling plagued Dieter's life in many ways.

Jose's hand fell softly on Dieter's shoulder, instantly relaxing the muscles in his face. His thoughts cooled. Was Jose really going to pardon everything?

"I messed up. The students shouldn't have been—and the things that happened because of me..." Jose kept his smile as he nodded in understanding. Dieter wiped his nose before speaking again. "And you don't want to fire me?"

"All is forgiven."

Jose's eyes embraced Dieter's concern while his other hand fell on Dieter's shoulder. Instantly, the vitriol left him. There was no residue on his pants either. Dieter's eyes searched Jose's face.

"I needed to get you to listen, Dieter. All the hurt that's been untreated left you hungry for power."

Dieter sniffled and nodded in agreement. Satan had spoken for him, censored him, manipulated him, pushed him away from everything good, everything pure, everything that gave him life. And Esther! Had the Devil convinced a student to poison her?

"Dieter, Esther and I know who set off her allergic reaction and how she got the tainted coffee. While we can't impeach him, his firing is enough punishment…for now."

So, Sanders did it. And Esther knew it wasn't Dieter. A rush of relief caused Dieter's eyes to soar to the skylight. Jose helped him to his feet.

"Now that you are in a proper state of mind, I need to ask: are you willing to stay on as a teacher? Are you sure you want to follow me and fix the school? It won't be easy, so I'll let you quit if you change your mind."

Dieter's jaw and cheeks relaxed as he looked Jose in the eyes. Here was a chance to start over. Here was a chance for the life he wanted. A crisp clarity filled him. Dieter made a promise to himself and to the one who was willing to give him a second chance.

"I'm ready to make things right."

"Good, let's go to work. I'll fill in for your classes today before the assembly: I have a folder of deleted and altered messages that I think you'll want to read."

Chapter 20

BANNERS DANGLED FROM the gym's rafters. Mustard stitching proclaimed past league, sectional, and district titles. The one state championship in bowling had the year 1958 boldly printed at the top in unfulfilled optimism.

The basketball court lay before students perched on the bleachers. A microphone stand was set on the hastily painted brown dot that partially hid the spray-painted devil face. Most of the teachers sat on the team benches that were against the wall on the opposing side of the gym. After the year's events, they wanted to have the students in front of them at all times. The only teacher standing near the students was Father Manny, who had his status as a minority and a man of God to save him from harassment, even though the frenzy of the previous year still caused an irrationality among some students.

The crowd sizzled with excitement. Sanders had been fired. Manley was suspended. Gretel was as good as dead. They were driven beyond the boundaries of punishment or logic but had realized the power they held as a collective.

At the back of the bleachers a chant arose. Starting as unified noise, it soon picked up dominion.

"We are Devils—*clap, clap, clap clap clap*—We are Devils—*clap, clap, clap clap clap.*"

The seniors picked up the chant with fervor, adding a resonant baritone to the chorus .

"We are Devils!—*clap, clap, clap clap clap*—We are Devils!—*clap, clap, clap clap clap*."

Once assured that it was indeed cool to participate in the cheer, the freshmen and sophomores joined in.

"We are Devils!—*clap, clap, clap clap clap*—We are Devils!—*clap, clap, clap clap clap*."

Father Manny's eyes lifted to the rafters as his lips moved in prayer.

"We are Devils!—*clap, clap, clap clap clap* —We are Dev—!"

"Hello, students!"

The frenzy shuddered in surprise. Even Father Manny was taken aback by the sudden intervention. No one had seen Jose walk to center court. Some students would later swear that he had materialized from the dusty wood planks. Others claimed he'd floated down from the aluminum ceiling. As the crowd hushed in confusion, Jose spoke.

"Welcome to the last day of school!" His teeth shone and his eyes sparkled. After the year of terror, his words still carried sincere compassion and a sense of pride that even diluted Andre's anger.

"We have had quite the *eventful* year," Jose continued, eliciting a few chuckles from the savvier students who understood the understatement. "And while there have been unfortunate words and actions by both students *and staff*—"

There was a mixture of angry growls and chirps of surprise. Here was a principal that admitted error on behalf of the adults. How he would reconcile the previous year's transgressions remained to be seen.

"—a year that is now over, and we must prepare for the future of this school. I would like to offer a chance for you all to vote on the new school mascot—"

The gym burst in a savage roar.

Disjointed yells of "Devil" and "Yeah, right" were thrust at Jose. He permitted the raging dissent to go unchecked for ten seconds before he smiled and raised his hand.

The students silenced. The power of his presence compelled obedience.

"You certainly *will* have a chance to vote, and whatever you decide *will* be final. I know there have been promises made and broken, but that is behind us now. First, I want to lay out changes for the year. Can we agree to listen so that we might get to the vote at the end of this assembly?"

The students looked at each other. Here was an adult who didn't raise his voice or lecture them. Of course they would listen if it meant that they'd finally get what they wanted. Sensing their tolerance, Jose resumed.

"Your student government will be more important in the coming years. Students elected will meet with me personally twice a month to discuss issues that you face."

A murmur of approval met the remarks.

"Student discipline will be transparent and fair. Expulsion and suspension hearings will be communicated to the student government, and students will be given an opportunity to defend themselves."

A larger rustle cascaded from the back of the bleachers.

"We will hold workshops for the staff on cultural sensitivity—"

Maria's head and arms popped out above the sea of brown and black around her as she yelped loudly in approval. The teachers stared at the ground.

"And we will change the dress code to be more accommodating for students."

More students cheered.

"Now, before the mascot change, there is, in fact, a different name change. As some of you know, the school was in desperate need of money to continue operating. The end-of-year tests essentially decided the future of the school. Since there were such disruptions throughout the year, and since some students deliberately performed poorly on the state tests, the results were not what was required for this school to receive necessary funding."

The students who grasped what was being said dropped their eyes in guilt.

"Furthermore, the money we did have as a school was depleted, used by repairs for broken toilets, paint for graffiti-removal, replacements for stolen equipment, and medical expenses for teachers who were hurt during the course of the year."

This time, more students' heads dropped.

"So, when many of you failed your state achievement tests, you made it impossible for us to continue to operate."

Even Miguel felt shame.

"As a result, our school was forced to pursue a different identity. There was an emergency meeting with the school board. We drafted a charter and submitted it to the city for approval. Because of the reputation of our school, partly due to this year's events," Jose paused momentarily and scanned the crowd for emphasis, "the city decided to approve our charter rather than try to turn the school around. As a result, the Archdiocese will be taking over Reading High School next year."

In rapture, Father Manny's eyes flew back up the rafters at this revelation. He let out a quick yelp of unadulterated approval while a rustle of confusion raced through the students. Jose again raised his hand.

"This changes nothing for you. It just gives the school leadership more control over what we teach, among other things. If anything, it will be a great benefit."

The students, still standing, said nothing.

"The only change you need to be concerned about is that the school will no longer be called Reading High School. Instead—"

A collective inhale was held in as all eyes stared expectantly at the microphone. Reading had become synonymous with white heritage and oppression. The name choice would surely be an indication of the school's new direction. Jose scanned each pocket of students and then faced the faculty.

"—we will now be called San Miguel High School."

The students turned toward each other. That the new name was partially in Spanish came as a pleasant surprise. But there was also the glaring issue of the name including the word "saint," which seemed to wrench the *Devil* movement to a temporary halt.

Next to Maria, a voice climbed above all the others.

"Wait! San Miguel? *My* name is Miguel!"

Some students laughed at the childish epiphany.

"To explain this change, Mr. Vogel will now speak to you."

A gasp went up from the staff and the students as Dieter emerged from underneath the bleachers. As he approached the microphone, whispers circulated throughout the congregation.

Wasn't he just taken to the office by the security guard? What is he still doing here?

The staff was concerned.

Wait, he approves of this? What about identity and stuff?

The students were in crisis.

Jose stepped back with a reassuring smile as Dieter stepped up to the podium. His hands tilted the mic upward. A large, electronic shriek pierced the gym and the crowd groaned.

Dieter coughed. His hands trembled. Embarrassment painted his face a deep red. Jose whispered to him. "Go on. It'll be fine. Speak from the heart."

To this day, some students and staff claim it was as if a ghost had pulled Dieter's shoulders upright. Some swear a breeze swept through the gym just before he spoke. Others gossip that Dieter's eyes flickered like a flame.

Regardless, Dieter presented an impassioned fifteen-minute speech about how this was an opportunity to build a new identity: a chance for the students to change the community by making the school a shining example of what a new beginning can do for people. He ended by imploring the students to think hard about what they had learned, about justice and unity and strength. He asked them to use the power they possessed to work toward a better future for the school, and equally important, for themselves.

"One more thing: when you choose a mascot, think about what you want to represent us. Our school is now *San* Miguel, the archangel who fought Satan."

Dieter exhaled and shuffled off the brown mark. He looked

around the gym for a place to stand, but found himself surrounded by students who couldn't figure out if they felt betrayed and faculty who suspected that Dieter was behind much of the year's torment. So, Dieter stood outside the circle at mid-court while Jose resumed control of the assembly.

By the double doors that led to the parking lot, Dieter spied the familiar curly hair and tan face he had come to miss. And surprisingly, she smiled broadly at Dieter and waved before sliding out of the gym. Dieter wanted to dart out those doors right then, but he knew he had to wait. Jose trusted him to be present, to finish the day. Hopefully, Esther would be willing to wait.

"Thank you, Mr. Vogel, for the inspiring words. Now, students, the moment you've been waiting for. As a community, we have the unique opportunity to choose a representation of our history and our fight."

Jose held up his right fist before letting it return to the podium. From the crowd, Andre lifted a fist in salutation, acknowledging Jose's homage to Civil Rights history.

"We will also need to decide the school colors, which will be a separate category on which to vote. At this time, any nominations for school mascot will be brought forward by students and staff. Simply come forward to the microphone and say the mascot you wish to nominate, and/or a color combination for the school. From there, we will record all the options, and you will vote."

What student would be first to come forward in front of all his peers and speak into a microphone? A minute went by and no student emerged to offer a choice—or rather, *the* choice.

A sly smile slid over Jose's face. He stepped back up to the microphone.

"If no one wants to put up a nomination, I will."

The students turned to him.

"The San Miguel Angels... And I personally enjoy sky-blue and white!"

Some students nodded their heads. Others shook their heads in concern, though the nomination was not met with immediate protest. The staff discussed the changes among themselves, but Father Manny enthusiastically gave a thumbs-up to Jose.

The security guard, who had spent most of the assembly hidden behind the bleachers, strode forth. His teeth covered his bottom lip, and his large belly lifted higher as he walked to the microphone. Jose stepped back. With his right hand on the mic, the security guard leaned forward: "I nominate Gretel the Pretzel. Brown and Yellow: the colors of tradition, pride, and—"

"Pee and poop!" students shouted as they hurled a wave of boos. The guard's face tightened. His left hand raised with his index finger stabbing the air as he shouted: "She's a part of this community's—"

Jose stepped forward and put a hand on the guard's shoulder. Instantly, he quieted and re-integrated among the faculty, who gave him nods of commiseration. But the security guard's audacity had re-ignited the students' passion. Bedeviled by the adult's obstinate proclamation, a scrawny freshman with ears too big for his face strode to the microphone. With a raised fist, he screeched: "I nominate the Devil!"

While trying to be emphatic, his voice cracked. The teen raced off to the bleachers, where he could melt back into anonymity. Jose interjected, cutting off the boy's retreat.

"Colors?"

The student twitched back to the microphone in embarrassment. He paused until a sudden thought jumped to his consciousness. "Red and black. The red and black Devils!"

Dieter's face tingled with guilt, though to his surprise there was not a clear outpouring of support. While many students nodded in agreement, some others shook their heads and seemed to be saying "Angels."

"You see, Dieter, you truly make an impact," Jose whispered after patting the freshman's shoulder.

"Do we have any other nominations?" Jose asked as the freshman was absorbed by a sea of hi-fives. Jose waited ten seconds before he continued.

"So, we have three nominations for mascots: The Angels, The

Devils, and The Pretzels. Three nominations for colors: Blue and White, Red and Black, Brown and Yellow. The teachers will be dismissed to their rooms. Students, you will then go to your homerooms and take out a sheet of paper. Write one choice for mascot and one choice for the color combination. Your student government will tally the votes. Again, your options are The Angels, The Devils, or—"

The students cut off Jose with a large rumble of collective voices debating the first two options. Jose sighed and quietly said, "Pretzels," before turning to the teachers. He approached them with resolute eyes and a reassuring voice: "Last day. On Monday, we'll have a meeting to discuss the changes. Then we'll start summer early. Go to your homerooms now and let's be done with this."

Twenty minutes later, Dieter pushed into the library to find Angie, Maria, Miguel, and Andre, the students whom Jose had called upon to be witnesses to democracy in action. Angie and Maria both gave genuine smiles. Miguel pumped his head. Andre gave a short, "Sup, Mr. V." And Jose greeted Dieter with his familiar beam, as if none of the many transgressions had transpired.

Dieter sat down on the last open chair at the circular table. Jose, in turn, stood up.

"Okay, now that we are all here, I'm going to step into the hallway so that there's no influence from me. Tell me what has been decided."

He galloped out of the room, leaving the five in awkward silence. Viewing the faces of his students, who looked at him with love and confidence, Dieter noticed a significant feeling of degradation, one that had been festering since his talk with Jose. Remorse commanded him to break the silence.

"Look, guys, I'm sorry for this year."

The students' eyebrows shot up in confusion. Still, Dieter continued.

"I feel like I manipulated you and pushed you all to do bad

things. I left the school in a mess. I took it and ran it through hell and now...now we aren't even Reading anymore." Dieter could feel tears begin to form. Each word thumped from his heart. "I wanted to be in control, but I shouldn't have influenced you to rebel for my personal gain. You are all too special—"

When he lost the strength to finish, he stared at the stack of papers in front of him. To Dieter's surprise, Andre cut in first.

"Not gonna lie; you did play us."

Dieter nodded.

"I mean I been pushed around and treated like an animal all my life. But I ain't gonna let people use me like that no more."

Miguel's head nodded effusively.

"Even if you was trying to be principal, I still felt like you cared about us, you know? And those books were dope. Yo, I grew a ton on the test. My AAU coach thinks it'll help me go D1 after next year."

Dieter was proud of Andre. His reading score on the ACT had risen 10 points, an almost unthinkable jump for most students.

"And even if I don't play ball, I can still go to college and study Politics. Be the first Obama, you know? I guess I should thank you for that."

Angie nodded before standing up, an unnecessary step, but it was custom in Dieter's class for students to do so when sharing their work. "Mr. V, I would have been lost this year. Your class was fun. We read some great things. And I learned a lot about myself. That's something no other teacher has done for me."

When Angie sat down, Maria spoke up: "Mr. V, the stories and our discussions...I think they helped us care. I mean, Mayor Sanders would still be in charge, I'd still be a fake president, things would just be the way they were. Sure, we aren't Reading anymore, but isn't that a good—"

Miguel, feeling some unspeakable urgency, interrupted: "Mr. V. I know I be goofy and all—"

The joke caused the group to chuckle. Maria laughed and shook her head before sitting.

"—but I needed someone to take me seriously, 'cause I want to be somethin' too, you know? All the world's a stage, and I was playing a fart. You and, um, someone else really helped me realize that."

Miguel sat back down solemnly, but not before glancing at Maria, who had joined Dieter's sniffling. Miguel reached out and grabbed her hand.

"And look, the students have never gotten along this well. We couldn't agree on anything," Maria added cheerfully through sobs.

Dieter smiled and nodded in gratitude. He tried to think of something meaningful, but all he could say was, "Thank you."

The students smiled back. After a minute, Maria gave a deep breath, dabbed her eyes, and refocused the group.

"Well, I guess we better count the votes."

Miguel nodded profusely.

"Yeah," he said, "we aren't an Olive Garden after all."

The teens laughed.

"Boy, it's oligarchy. Ol-i-gar-chy," Andre said as he clapped out the syllables.

With that, Dieter stepped out to a grinning Jose. The two leaned against the wall and watched the four adolescent leaders through the door's window. Inside the library, Maria took command of the voting process and the future identity of the school.

———————

When the final bell rang, a stream of jubilant teens poured into buses and minivans. The new name, the new mascot, and the new colors bounced around conversations. Teachers remained in their rooms, fossilized in silent meditation. The exception was Dieter. On his bike he raced out of the parking lot, down Reading Road, past the shuddered windows of Perkolate, past City Hall where Sanders was hiding for the rest of his two-year term, past the large fairground, and onto the residential streets. His pedals pumped quickly as the bike swerved back and forth under his force. Right, right, left, down the hill, until he ramped onto the long black driveway that wound through trees and led to a tall, two story red-brick house. On the deep green lawn, he dropped his bike and ran to the front door.

Sweat had caked his navy polo to his body and left his forehead covered in a slick sheen. With one final attempt to control his breathing, and with a quick wipe from his shirt, he jammed the doorbell.

A small, gray-haired black woman opened the door.

"Yes?"

"Ms. Bishop, is Esther home?"

"She is, but I don't know if she's feeling well enough for visitors. May I take a message?"

Dieter could see a familiar face looking at him from the kitchen.

"Um, I'll try to call her later."

The woman nodded politely and turned to close the door.

"Ma, wait. It's okay."

Dieter watched the shadow in the kitchen emerge into the afternoon light.

"Hey, Dieter," Esther said softly.

Dieter exhaled his entire year. "Esther, there's so much...I just..."

She looked up at him in forgiveness. Her smile and the sparkle in her eyes calmed Dieter's urgency. He inhaled and held his breath before speaking again.

"Esther, can we start over?"

Epilogue

THE FIRST DAY of school arrived quickly that summer.

Dieter had the same nervous knots in his stomach that he had felt every year since kindergarten. This year, though, he didn't have the dread that bubbled caustically in his chest, because this year, Dieter knew, was going to be different.

He had many of the same lesson plans from last year, tweaked to be less manipulated by his own agenda and, in some cases, exorcised of half-truths. In addition, he had spent his summer working with Jose and taking classes on curriculum design and methods of learning. In twenty years of education, Dieter had never felt this confident in August.

It was also the first time he wasn't dropped off in front of school by his mom. His new car, a modest yet sleek hybrid, hummed softly to a halt in the faculty parking lot.

Dieter slid out of the driver's side and grabbed his computer case and lunch from the back seat. In the distance the new janitor, a husky, middle-aged white man, unfurled the welcome banner. The man's slicked back hair and broad shoulders were a sight Dieter hadn't seen in the three months since his firing as Spanish teacher. He had apparently lost much of the stress-induced fat he'd added last year.

"You think it will be awkward with him?" a female voice said as Dieter's passenger door clicked shut.

"I hope not. I think it'll be okay."

Dieter gave Esther an encouraging grin. He had grown to love the way loose strands of hair rebelled from her thick tangle; the way her pointy nose wrinkled when she was in thought; the way her eyes sparkled when she looked lovingly at him—the way she was looking now. His eyes widened with the force of his smile.

With a lack of students around them, they interlocked hands as they walked the pavement. Esther hugged her left shoulder into Dieter's when their hands met.

"Your mom asked me if we were going to come over for Founder's Day," Esther began.

"I think we're out of town that weekend," Dieter responded.

Esther turned her head. "We are?"

"I got us a room at a bed and breakfast by Lake Norris. Close enough to make it there after work; far enough that my mom won't bother us."

Esther cooed and hugged Dieter's shoulder again.

"I don't think she'd intrude," Esther chuckled

"I'm afraid that if my mom were around, we'd end up drinking more."

"Oh, that'd be terrible!" Esther gasped. "I wouldn't be able to keep my hands off you. And then what would happen?"

Dieter laughed. "Grandchildren, I suppose. And she'd be okay with that."

From the top of his ladder, Manley gave a nod of acknowledgment as Dieter and Esther walked near. Esther looked at the ground, but Dieter met Manley's eyes.

"Morning, Coach. I hear you've got some talent coming in this year."

Manley smiled. "Yeah, I think I got a center to compliment Andre."

Dieter still didn't quite know what a center did on court, so his words were dammed inside his throat. For a moment, the three stood in awkward silence. Manley broke the tension.

"Good luck today, you two. Please keep the rooms clean."

"Thanks, Paul," Dieter said. Esther forced a half-smile in response.

At that, they turned to the large wooden doors of the entrance, where the school's new name hung in bold white letters: *San Miguel High School: Home of the Reading Blue Devils.*

Acknowledgments

MY SINCERE GRATITUDE goes out...

To God for giving me the wonderful people below, in addition to his son Jesus. I would also like to take issue with Him for not blessing me with rhythm or an ability to grow six-pack abs. But I'll just write Him a strongly worded letter about that.

To my parents, who did not rescind their support, even after I switched majors from Finance to Creative Writing. Thank you for being patient with me when I was a terribly selfish person during adolescence and young adulthood.

To my siblings, who are the goofiest and most wonderful family I could have asked for. Please don't tell mom and dad about the time my friends and I snuck alcohol from the liquor cabinet.

To my students—past, present, and future—who have inspired, grown, and challenged me beyond what I could have ever done for them.

To my former colleagues at DRW and Urban Prep. Simply, you guys are saints (except during Happy Hour...then ya'll a bunch a heathens). I especially want to thank Matt Kelley for his mentorship. And Josh Rhoad: you took me under your wing when I first started: I owe my sanity to you.

To the real Mr. Lee and Mr. Cannon: Jamyle and Cornelius, you broke my walls down in the best ways and are my inspiration still.

To my current colleagues: thank you for walking alongside me in faith and pedagogy. You've made me and my family feel welcome in this crazy place called California.

To David and Kelly: thank you for giving me a chance.